Their Angel Reach

Livi Michael was born in 1960. Her first novel, *Under a Thin Moon*, was published in 1992. She lives near Manchester with the poet Ian Pople and her two sons.

Livi Michael
Their Angel Reach

First published in Great Britain in 1994
by Martin Secker & Warburg Limited,
an imprint of Reed Consumer Books Limited,
Michelin House, 81 Fulham Road, London SW3 6RB
and Auckland, Melbourne, Singapore and Toronto

A CIP catalogue record for this book
is available from the British Library

ISBN 0 436 27882 0

Typeset by Deltatype Limited, Ellesmere Port, Cheshire
Printed and bound in Great Britain by
Clays Ltd, St Ives plc

To Ian

This thing of darkness I
Acknowledge mine

Shakespeare, *The Tempest*

Contents

1
Not Even the Rain

You have to remember that Steve hated queers.

Fucking brownhatters, he called them.

Once Steve and the lads had waited for this old queen outside his local, the Grapes. They had stamped on him in their big boots until blood streamed from every hole in his body.

Steve told Karen this triumphantly, but with a kind of defiance, like he expected her to tell him off.

Karen felt sick.

God Steven, she said, that's awful. Why don't you leave them alone? I mean, I don't like them either – it's not natural – but I wouldn't do owt like that –

They enjoy it, Steve interrupted her, and he went on to tell her about the other things they enjoyed until she nearly was sick – fist fucking with big metallic gloves being about the least of it. Afterwards Karen couldn't get rid of the pictures in her mind, but she still didn't think it was right.

Friday nights when Karen was fifteen, Steve used to whistle at her as she walked along the street to her best friend's house. The other lads joined in too, but Karen could tell it was really Steve. Sometimes he would follow her a bit down the street while his mates called out after them, but she was nearly sixteen before he asked her out. He was seventeen. In those days going out with Steve meant hanging round street corners with him and the lads, trying out the bikes which they all, eventually, got.

It's a bit different now, Karen thought, sitting in the pub. Nearly twenty years later Friday night was still their regular night out, but now there was only Steve and Gazzer (Gareth these days) left of the original gang, with herself and Shar, of course. They sat facing one another in an alcove going over the same old topics: kids, bills, work.

Gazzer used to be the leader, the toughest of any gang for miles around. Now he worked for the Post Office, delivering mail.

So I told him, he was saying, either you get a proper letter box fixed or it's no more mail. I shouldn't have to bend to floor and struggle with one that won't open, state of my back. They should be made to get proper ones.

Sometimes Karen wanted to laugh. The urge came over her at times like these when it wasn't really appropriate, and she would have to turn a giggle into a kind of snort.

Went down the wrong way, she explained.

Shar stared back at her vacantly.

The main thing Karen hid from Steve was the housework. This had started right back when they first married and they lived in a tiny bedsit in a council house that had been made into four separate bedsits. It was a large estate. From her window Karen could see kids in the playground, which was made up of some sawn-off tree stumps and a steel climbing frame. Beyond this and leading away from it were the shops which served the whole estate: Kumar Bros. Off-Licence and General Groceries, the chippy, newsagent, butcher's, post office and laundry. The estate was a bus ride away from the cheaper shops, so Karen mainly used these. To get to them you went up a ramp, beneath which were the garages where the older kids played football, smoked and pissed.

There was no real reason ever to leave the estate. By the time they finally moved there was nothing about it Karen didn't know, especially in the view from her window, the single window they had. She used to sit at the table beneath it, smoking, watching the kids play and the old people shop. In those days Steve did odd jobs, anything he could get, there was plenty of temporary work. But wherever he worked he had to get off the bus on the main road behind the shops and walk across the playground. Karen used to watch him getting nearer and nearer. She used to leave it until the very last minute before jumping up to tidy the scattered clothes and pots, put the kettle on, sweep the bits under the rug, making it look like she had been doing housework all day. By the time Steve came in her palms would be sweaty and her throat a bit tight. She would greet him with an armful of laundry saying, Hiya, do you want a cup of tea, conscious all the time of steering his attention away from the areas where the dirt was worst. It was crusted on the floor round the cooker and behind the table, but the rug hid that. There were big clumps of fluff beneath the bed settee, but he never looked there, and the washing-up bowl hid the grease in the sink. Dirt was Karen's province, she guarded it jealously, not wanting Steve to see it at all.

Later, when he got the job at the dental floss factory on the other side of the estate, it became a real art, because she couldn't see him coming home. Her timing became uncanny. As she heard the tread on the stair she would wipe the last pot and slam the ironing-board back into position, folding a few items on to the back of a chair as if she had ironed them already. All this meant that Steve could come in without comment, sit down heavily at the table and wait for his dinner or tea. Each time Karen felt the pressure at the back of her neck building up, but her timing never failed.

It got harder again when Steve lost his job. By that time they had Dawn and the one room in which they all lived became unbearably cramped. Steve's temper got worse, she could do nothing right. He took to staying out for most of the day and when he returned he often smelled of beer. Karen's sixth sense held, supernaturally, but now she had to work harder at it, washing nappies all morning and preparing bottles, clearing away toys and pots at the very last minute as she heard his key in the door. Then, when the worst of his temper was over, she would set about restoring his good humour, telling him the news she had heard in the day, who else had lost his job, and the bargains she had managed to spot.

Don't worry love, she always said. You'll get another job.

It took three years. By that time they had Karl as well, and had finally managed to move out of the bedsit into a two-bedroomed maisonette. It was better than the bedsit, but hardly perfect. Karen had to bump the kids up two flights of stairs; the neighbours were noisy but complained whenever the kids moved. Karen never stopped worrying about the balcony, that Dawn, now two and a half, would climb over it and fall, or that the whole structure would collapse.

Whilst he was out of work Steve went to the job centre every day, and sometimes he was summoned by the dole for an interrogation. This always put him in the worst mood of all. Though she didn't dare to be out of the house when he got back, Karen would take the kids and stay with them in the bedroom, trying to stop them from making a noise. When she finally got up the nerve to tell him she was pregnant again he went out without saying a word. Karen didn't know if he would come back at all, but he did, carrying several cans of beer. He sat up most of the night by himself, drinking them. Karen sat in the bedroom and cried, wanting to hit him, wanting to talk, wanting to scream at him, where had he got all this money from for beer, wanting to walk out of the house and never set foot in it again. She thought often and often of leaving him. Every day there was something

6

else wrong with the way she kept house, some new excuse for him to get out and stay out, but where could Karen go, with no money and the kids?

In those days her routine got seriously messed up. But her instinct for knowing when Steve would return became so good Karen almost thought she must be psychic. She let the maisonette get as messy as it could with small kids, nappies, toys, crayons, food, but by the time Steve got back it was always brought under some kind of control. Karen put it down to some instinct for self-preservation, not that Steve ever hit her, even in his worst moods. But she wouldn't grant him that one small further power over her, of seeing the house at its worst so he would have another excuse for carrying on. She felt triumphant each time she pulled it off. It was her own way of beating him, the only way she had.

The main thing Vi hid from Tony was sex.

What, you never have? said Karen curiously. Vi shook her head.

Not even once? said Karen, and again Vi shook her head. Karen was astonished. She herself was always required to come and usually did. She had only ever faked it once or twice for the sake of peace.

So do you fake it then, or what? she said.

Vi began to pull clothes carefully out of the laundry basket, not looking at Karen.

Sometimes, she said.

The man on the radio said that another body had been found, another young girl, in a derelict house.

Karen watched Vi's back as she loaded clothes into the washer, resting one hand on the top of it for support. Then she sat down thankfully in the chair on the other side of the table from Karen, still not looking at her. She held her stick in her hands and twisted it, gazing steadily at the handle.

Of course, she said, still staring at the stick, we don't really do it at all these days. And she smiled directly at Karen. Karen looked away. She had thought of saying, that must be a relief, but she could see quite plainly in Vi's eyes that it was nothing of the kind.

Well, she said instead, men are all bastards, and she went on to tell Vi about Steve not fixing her washing-machine, he knew how to but he hadn't got round to it yet. But every time she talked about getting a man in he said it would cost too much and he would fix it. And there it was, still broken, and Karen still had to use the laundry. And Vi laughed and talked about how Tony and the kids got out of ironing, a different excuse each time. The last time Kate had said Mam, my hair's wet, and sounded really shocked. Then they talked about how terrible it was about these murdered girls and how they worried about their own daughters, and soon Karen finished her cup of tea and it was time to go.

She didn't stop thinking about it though.

Steve, she said that night. Would you still love me if I was ill?

Mmm, Steve said behind his paper. Karen repeated the question.

'Course I would, said Steve, without even twitching the page he was reading.

No, but I mean, would you still fancy me, like?

Silence. Karen flicked the newspaper and Steve moved it slightly.

What? he said.

I said, would you still fancy me –

O for Christ's sake, said Steve. You're not ill are you?

He retreated once again behind the *Evening News*. Karen stopped asking questions. She looked round the kitchen, which was half done up with sage green tiles and the occasional crimson one placed at intervals for contrast. It was an idea she'd got from a *Homes and Furnishings* magazine she'd seen at the dentist's and something else Steve hadn't got round to finishing. She tried to imagine what it would be like to have a progressive disease, to wake up each morning a stranger to your own body, not knowing how it would work for you that day, and to watch the people around you growing away, but she soon gave up. She got up to make a cup of tea, hugging Steve's unresponsive shoulders lightly on the way and dropping a kiss on the top of his head.

Later that night, though, Karen felt very angry. Steve moved his fingers conscientiously between her legs and kissed her neck. Karen lay stiff and furious.

Have you come yet, whispered Steve.

Fuck off, Karen wanted to shout. She shook her head. Steve rolled on top of her.

Little willy wants to come in, he said. He pressed himself into her groin. Great big willy now, he said. Karen wanted to rage and scream as he pressed himself inside.

O that's better, he kept saying. O yes.

Karen hated him but she didn't know why. She didn't know why she didn't just push him off. She was damned if she was going to fake it this time, so why didn't she just push him away? She lay as if paralysed in the dark room.

What's up, Steve said.

Karen shook her head. She felt close to tears but she wouldn't cry. She was damming it all up inside, choking back the tears until they froze. Steve couldn't come like this. His erection dwindled and he rolled off her. Karen turned away from him. He put an arm round her.

Come on love, he said.

Karen snapped. Leave me alone can't you, she hissed. Just let me get to sleep.

Steve was absolutely quiet. Then he turned away from her. Karen rolled herself up tightly in the bedclothes and lay alternating between rage and despair. She felt guilty about not doing it for Steve. But why should she have to? Yet he hadn't done anything to make her angry. Karen was powerfully awake, wide-eyed. She wanted Steve to turn back to her and felt she could not bear it if he did. She didn't want to have to explain herself. But soon Steve's silence became a deep, regular breathing with an occasional gentle snore. Karen was enraged again.

Bloody typical, she could hear herself saying to Vi. Whatever happens a man can always get to sleep.

All eyes were on Karen in the pub that night. She was aware of it and so was Steve. She was so much better looking now, at thirty-four, than she had been at sixteen. And now that they had more money Steve liked her to dress up. Karen looked good in the latest fashions, wide baggy trousers and waistcoats or short, clinging skirts. Steve liked her to dress like a young man; she had her fair hair cropped in a boyish style, but tonight she was wearing a tight, flame-coloured dress made of stretchy material with two soft wings over her shoulders which left most of her shoulders bare. Steve liked this dress too; it emphasised her slim hips and flat chest. In her red sling-back high heels she was taller than Steve who was broad and squat by comparison.

Getting dressed in front of the mirror Karen had thought she should have been a model. God, all those years she had been gawky and angular, well into her twenties, and now she had blossomed when it was too late to do anything about it. There was no one to see the beautiful swan she had turned into except for the regular punters at the local pub. The pub had become a kind of theatre in Karen's mind. She made the most of her entry now on Steve's arm, stepping delicately past chairs and tables. She was conscious of her own reflection, without looking directly at it, in the mirrors behind the bar and on the tall columns down the centre of the room. She was conscious too of not appearing to react to the gaze of men which followed her as she walked towards Gazzer and Shar. She was most conscious of Gazzer's eyes, half-lidded but intent at her approach.

Unlike Karen, Shar had not improved with age. They had both had three children, but Shar had become distended and cow-like in the process. Must be the Italian blood, Karen thought, noticing with a vague pleasure the way Shar's black dress was too tight across the bust so that she had had to pin a brooch there to stop it gaping. The lace ruffle made her look like she had no neck. Although there was only a month between them Shar looked ten years older than Karen that night.

Karen slid gracefully on to the bench behind the table. I like your dress Shar, she said.

Gazzer lifted his glass appreciatively towards Karen.

What's yours love, he said, and stood up ready to order a round. Steve said, no, no, I'll get these, and ambled off awkwardly to the bar, shuffling his hand in his pocket. Karen crossed one long leg over the other.

Well, she said, how's things? As if she didn't know, having seen Shar two days ago in the butcher's. Shar was sullen. Had they been rowing? It was hard to tell with these two, they never did speak much. Gazzer leaned forwards and flicked a cigarette from a packet.

Take one Kas, he urged. He had always called her Kas, ever since the days when she used to stack shelves in the supermarket and then get changed at work so she could ride off with the gang when they drove up for her, leaping on the back of Steve's bike, and all the bikes roaring off in formation, into the night. Those Friday nights made the whole week bearable. She only worked so she could save up for the leather gear she needed.

Ta, she said as Steve handed her a drink. She leaned back, reminded irresistibly of clinging to his broad back on dark, rainy nights. She could almost smell the leather and the rain.

These nights were not the same. After he sat down Steve started talking about his boss Jim, whom he hated, and Gazzer

11

talked about the enormous bill they had had for the central heating. Shar rarely had anything to say, but occasionally put in a story about one of the kids. The men had nothing to say either really, but they kept on saying it as if they hadn't realised. Sometimes Karen would break in and take centre stage, mimicking Steve's boss, or the kids, or the woman at the bank, making them all laugh, but tonight she wasn't in the mood.

Gazzer drained his pint.

You're quiet tonight Kas, he said. Karen smiled a pale smile. All this effort, she was thinking, remembering the hour or more of preparation for this evening, showering and washing her hair, applying nail polish and make-up, wearing her best underwear, for what?

I'm just a bit tired, she said. She sat back, noticing the signs of age in Gazzer's greying hair, Steve's sagging chin. She felt remote, detached from everything around her as though she were enclosed in a light, clean bubble of air.

She was remembering, without wanting to, the bikers' clubs where in order to join, to get into the building, you had to be initiated. At theirs this involved being stripped naked and wrapped in clingfilm, then you lay in the muddy earth while everyone stood round and pissed on you. Steve, Shar and Debbie had got very drunk and had submitted to this more or less meekly, but while the other bikers stood round them Karen had reached over and taken the keys to the front door from Gazzer's belt. By the time they turned round she was standing in the open doorway, framed in light.

I'm in, she said. I'm over the threshold.

O no, someone said, that's not fair.

Karen didn't care. She felt entirely self-possessed, standing in the doorway, holding the keys.

Either I'm in, she said or you're all out, and she made a move to lock the door.

Gazzer held up his hand.

She's right, he said. You have to let her in. Karen smiled. She had won by their law, which she knew they would never break. She felt tall and powerful as the others left Steve and Shar and Debbie trying to unwrap themselves from the soaking clingfilm and surrounded her, propelling her inside for the celebration drink.

Bored, Karen looked round the pub. It had just been done up in pink and blue, with mirrors everywhere, but some of the old brasses had been left on the wall, as if the pub had failed to fully make the transition from the old-fashioned dive it was, where old men played darts and pool, to the new, trendy establishment intended to appeal to the young.

Karen felt powerfully in the grip of the past. She looked at Steve and Shar and Gazzer as if they were not quite real, as if at any moment now their new selves would fall away like husks and things could go back to the way they used to be.

It didn't happen. They were all too respectable now for that kind of thing. They had all grown up and gone respectable. Dave now worked as a long-distance lorry driver, they hardly ever saw him these days. Debbie had been his girl, but she had gone on a hairdressing course and then off up north to work in a salon. The last Karen had heard she was living with a bloke who worked in insurance. The other Steve, called Cess, had got tired of being unemployed and had gone off down south to work on a building site. When work on that site ended he had drifted on to another and then another, eventually losing contact. He had also lost touch with his wife Diane, one-time member of the gang, now a full-time cleaner, bringing up their two kids on a different estate. Mick was dead. He had gone out with Marie first and then Lou, but Karen didn't know where either of those two was now.

Steve was still talking about his boss in the timber-yard, about how he had put him in his place that morning. He had worked there nearly six years now and had been promoted to under-manager of logging and distribution, whatever that meant. They had never had enough money, even so, for a deposit on a house of their own. Each time they had almost got the money together house prices seemed to shoot up. But they managed to get a move, from the two-bedroomed maisonette to a three-bedroomed semi, well, the end one of four, on the better side of Marley's big estate. Then they had had the chance of buying it cheap. Last year they had applied for a mortgage and a few months ago it all went through. Now they were doing the house over slowly from the IKEA catalogues and *House and Home* magazines Karen collected. It was no use leaving it to Steve, who had no taste at all and would have done everything up in chrome. It was at a half-way stage at the moment, the kitchen half tiled, a new carpet in the lounge but an old suite, but Karen felt that things were finally moving their way. After Darren she had been sterilised, so they didn't have to worry about more kids. They were set up at last. There was nothing left to worry about at all.

Karen sighed and wriggled on the uncomfortable bench. She watched Gazzer through the smoke with half-closed eyes. Though he looked older he still had 'it', that quality Karen and Shar and Lou used to giggle about; it rested somehow in the heavy-lidded eyes, the swaggering walk. It seemed ridiculous to think of him in his little hat and uniform like Postman Pat. No one could fancy Postman Pat. But watching him in the pub that night through the smoke as he sat in his open-necked shirt, resting one foot on the rung of a chair, and him watching her also when he thought she wouldn't notice, Karen fancied him then.

Three years ago he had been a hero, in all the newspapers. He had chased after armed robbers who had taken a mail van and had clung on to the side of the van as they drove away. Then he had attracted the attention of a police car as the van drove past and had saved the Post Office thousands. They had given him a little silver trophy. Karen and Steve couldn't help laughing about it when they read it in the papers. At one time if Gazzer had been in the papers it wouldn't have been for helping the police.

Someone changed the record on the juke box.

When a man loves a woman . . .

It was Karen's favourite song.

Gazzer leaned forwards.

Eh Kas, he said, let's dance.

It was strange, as though he had sensed that she had been willing him to make something happen. She looked around. No one's dancing, she said.

So, said Gazzer.

A sour look from Shar decided Karen. All right, she said, and got up lightly. Gazzer took her hand and drew her to him. Karen was aware of herself moving beautifully, slowly, and everyone watching. She was aware of Gazzer's rough cheek, the smell of aftershave and smoke, his hand resting in the small of her back. She was aware of Shar and Steve not speaking to one another, watching them, and of the look on Steve's face, a kind of wary hunger, which reminded her painfully of something she did not want to remember.

It was the night of her engagement to Steve. There was a big do at the bike club, everyone was well out of it. Gazzer must have followed her when she went to the toilet, she walked straight into him in the cloakroom, he held on to her and did not let go.

Karen was hardly even surprised. All evening she had been aware of his eyes following her, even when she had looked directly at him he had not looked away. It was almost like she had gone out expecting him to follow. And here he was, pinning her arms to her side, pulling her closer to him and looking at her like he knew she would not try to get away.

How about a kiss, he said, to celebrate.

Karen was very sober. All night she had felt the peculiar

experience of drinking a lot and feeling more and more sober; laughing, playing a part, the things around her becoming more and more clear, though she was tired. Now however, as she felt Gazzer's breath on her cheek, she was wide awake.

Unresisting she turned up her face. He kissed her, a soft, long kiss, still holding her arms to her side. Karen did not want the kiss to end, but after several moments she became aware that his hands had moved on to other things.

No, she said, pulling her skirt down.

Why not, Gazzer said, pressing even closer so that she was pinned between him and the coat rail. He caught her wrists and held them up, pressing with his thumbs just hard enough to hurt, and gazed very steadily into her eyes.

Karen, he said. He called her Karen when he had always called her Kas. Karen wanted to give in. She wanted to do what he wanted, right there in the cloakroom; she wanted to break away, to prove to herself that she was not at the mercy of his, or her own desire; she wanted him to force her into it, to get it over and done with, once and for all. He kissed her again as she stood paralysed, and murmured Karen into her ear.

Eh Karen, Steve called, and the lights went on. There was Steve with Mick a shadowy figure behind him. They were brought up short by the sight of Karen and Gazzer.

With a deliberate slowness Gazzer released Karen's wrists and moved away.

Just getting a kiss from the bride-to-be, he said.

Karen felt a sick tightness in her stomach, she didn't know why, she wasn't afraid of Steve. But she couldn't read the look on his face, not anger, it was a painful, hungry look. For a moment she wondered if her legs would work, then she moved unsteadily away, past Steve, who was watching Gazzer, and Mick, who handed her her jacket with a strange look in his eyes like pity. And it was funny, she could hardly remember Mick's face now after all this time, it kept shifting out of focus, but she never forgot that look. She found her way back to the table where Debbie and Lou were getting ready to leave and downed her drink quickly, all at once, ignoring them. She wanted to stop the feeling in her stomach, she didn't know what was the matter with her. She felt like she was suspended between powerful opposing forces and might at any moment be torn apart. She felt like she would be trapped there for ever, between fear and desire, like there was no other way for her to be.

Karen didn't want Dawn to go out with bikers. There was a biker on their part of the estate who slowed down as Dawn approached, keeping her company as she walked home from school. Karen had asked around. He was known as Scud and he was eighteen years old. Fortunately Dawn didn't seem to fancy him. She could have her pick, Dawn, though she wasn't blonde and leggy like her mum, more short and squat like Steve. But she was outgoing and racy and the boys semed to like that. One morning she came into Karen's room after Steve had gone.

Mum, she said, there's a gorgeous boy delivers papers round here. He's coming now.

They waited near the window, Karen with her arm draped loosely around Dawn's neck.

There he is, said Dawn. Isn't he gorgeous.

The lad was about fifteen with longish brown hair and the beginning of a moustache.

Dead average I'd say, said Karen. Then as he walked beneath the window she wolf whistled shrilly. Dawn elbowed her hard and they ran giggling out of the room.

Later that day Karen saw him again. He was helping someone across the road. At first sight Karen thought it was an old lady, but a second glance told her that the woman was quite young. He was carrying her shopping and she was leaning on his arm. When they had crossed the road they went up the garden path of one of the old council semis and the woman let them both in. Must be his mother, Karen thought.

That was how she had come to know Vi, although, as it turned out, they had known one another most of their lives. They had gone to the same schools, primary and secondary, though Vi was two years older so they hadn't mixed. One day, not long after seeing her with the paper-boy, Karen saw Vi at the supermarket, trying to push open the door and walk through with her stick which seemed to be caught in the mat. She tottered and it looked like the door would swing back in her face, but just in time Karen caught it.

Thank you, said Vi, detaching her stick. She had a beautiful smile.

Ever since infants Karen had had a weakness for the prettiest girls in her class. She would pick different ones out as her favourites at different times, and while they were her favourites she would do anything for them at all. Karen was tall and gawky herself, with a big nose. She worshipped an ideal of prettiness which would change from one term to the next. Her tastes ranged wide. Amanda Baxter had wiry red-brown hair, big hazel eyes and a lisp which Karen tried hard to imitate. Christine Langdon had fair hair in curly bunches and dimples. Karen spent hours pressing the point of her pencil into her cheek to try to make a dimple, and begged her mother to curl her hair, but her mother always said she didn't have time. Then there was Julie Bagnall, the smallest in the class. She had short black hair and freckles and could skip for longer than anyone else. Karen used to make up stories in which she looked just like Julie Bagnall and was a heroine. She served her favourites faithfully, sharpening their pencils, doing their classroom duties for them and spending her pocket money on them. Most of all she liked to play with their hair, brushing it, plaiting it and winding it into ringlets round her fingers. Her own hair was fair but scrappy, there wasn't much you could do with it at all.

The situation didn't really change at secondary school, though Karen got the idea that it wasn't acceptable. By second year you were supposed to have changed all your affections over to boys, or at least to a pop group. Karen managed this eventually. By the time she was fourteen she was going out with Michael Henshaw and fantasising about Michael Jackson, but it didn't stop her secretly worshipping the prettiest girls in her class.

Vi's hair was straight and thick, silky-brown. It fell in a smooth curving line to her chin. You couldn't imagine a hair of it ever being out of place. Under the fluorescent lights of the supermarket it shone red-gold and auburn. It was the kind of hair Karen wanted to touch. She followed Vi cautiously along the supermarket aisles, observing her smallness and neatness and her clothes which were immaculate if a bit old-fashioned. Vi walked stiffly, as if she thought that if she bent her knees at all her legs might give way. Once or twice she lost her balance and veered off in the wrong direction, colliding into people, then apologising and smiling the beautiful smile. It couldn't be easy managing a trolley when you walked that badly, Karen thought. You must get tired of smiling. Vi reached out a hand for a tin of beans. It was thin and wasted and the whole arm trembled as she stretched.

Karen got to the check-out before Vi but she waited in the area beyond for her to finish packing her bags. Then she walked in front of her to the door and held it open. Vi smiled again and thanked her and Karen said, I think we're going to the same way, and told Vi where she lived.

Vi hesitated a bit then said, I might hold you up.

O no bother, Karen said. I'm in no rush.

So they walked together and by the time they reached Vi's Karen had found out that the paper-boy was Vi's son, that he was called Philip, and was fifteen years old and was not going out with anyone at the moment. Karen told Vi that Dawn was crazy about him and Vi laughed and said maybe she should come round and clean his room a few times – wash his socks . . .

O no fear, Karen said.

Vi also had a daughter, Kate, aged twelve. Neither Philip nor Kate went to Dawn's school because Vi had heard it was a bit rough. Karen felt a bit affronted by this.

O no, she said. It's a good school. Dawn and Karl like it a lot.

The worked out where they had met before. At school Vi was known as Vivienne.

Vivienne Lee, she said and they laughed.

Don't tell me you married Clark Gable, Karen said.

No, Anthony Hopkins, Vi said, and they laughed again.

They laughed and talked easily all the way back to Vi's. Karen thought the outside of Vi's house looked nice. She had always liked the older type of council semis. They seemed more roomy, and better built, but they hardly ever came free. Karen and Steve had been lucky to get one of the smaller, newer ones on the other side of the playing fields. Vi's house overlooked the playing fields at the back. It looked a nice view. Karen hovered foolishly on the doorstep as Vi opened the door.

Well it's been nice meeting you, Vi said. Maybe I'll bump into you again one day.

Karen passed Vi her bag and stood watching the door as it clicked shut in her face. She felt her cheeks burning as she hurried away. She should have asked Vi round to her own house, but she felt a bit delicate about this, as if she sensed that Vi wouldn't come. It was clear that, for whatever reason, she hadn't wanted to ask Karen in at all.

Of course she did see Vi again. One day, when the rain was falling in a persistent kind of way and Darren was off school with a sore throat, Karen decided she couldn't stand being in any longer. Despite Darren's protests she wrapped him up warmly and dragged him out to the shops.

It was a mistake. Darren wanted chocolate in one shop, a model aeroplane in another and a computerised games system in another.

Mum, can I have an ice-cream, he said as the van pulled up outside the co-op.

I thought you were supposed to be ill, Karen said.

Ice-cream's good for sore throats, said Darren.

Karen's head was beginning to ache by this time so she gave in and whilst he ran over to the van she stood, staring moodily at the adverts in the job centre.

Machinists, cleaners, waitresses. Sometimes Karen felt desperate at home, like the walls were closing in on her, but the only jobs she ever saw involved her being at everyone's beck and call and doing the same things all day as she did at home, making food, shifting muck. She was damn sure she didn't need any more of that, yet she didn't know what else she could do. Maybe she was scared after so many years at home. While Darren was still at junior school she felt like she had an excuse. They had so many days off for one reason or another and someone had to be with him. But Darren was nearly nine, he wouldn't always need her, and soon she would have no excuse for sitting in and staring at four walls. But she had no experience, no qualifications. Karen stared at the notices without seeing them, wondering exactly when her horizons had started to shrink. She was startled when a voice said,

Looking for a top-notch career?

When she turned round Vi was there, smiling brightly.

O aye, Karen said. I thought Director of the BBC'd do, something like that, only they haven't advertised it this week.

Vi scanned the job cards briefly and smiled, but all she said was, Fancy coming back for a cup of tea?

Karen was suprised. I've got Darren, she said as he reappeared carrying the biggest ice-cream he could hold. He's off school ill.

He looks ill, Vi said. Bring him along.

So off they went, Karen feeling suddenly that the day had taken a definite turn for the better.

After that Karen was always calling on Vi though Vi never came to see her. Dawn and Phil got together for a while and then broke up, but Karen and Vi went on seeing one another throughout that spring and summer, laughing and talking in Vi's kitchen for hours at a time. Karen always felt welcome there. At first Vi seemed very conscious of the house which looked so respectable on the outside, but inside was in a sad state of disrepair, yellowing wallpaper hanging off the kitchen walls, threadbare carpet and all the window frames leaking at once. Karen had been a bit surprised, because she had somehow imagined that Vi was quite well-to-do, but after a while she found the air of neglect quite homey. It was the kind of house you could relax in without feeling you should be cleaning and tidying all the time. Tony, Vi's husband, was a plumber and should have been handy round the house, but Vi said it was all the same with plumbers, joiners or builders, they were always too busy to work on their own homes.

Tell me about it, Karen said.

Vi's house became like a second home to Karen. She liked it best as the summer afternoons began to shorten into autumn, when the light in the kitchen was yellow and you could watch the light outside slowly extinguishing itself. She would sit at the table and watch the birds scatter and gather themselves like dark confetti across the sky, or the tree outside the window which had no limbs – they had all been sawn off by the council – but thin delicate shoots sprouted from the amputated branches and birds clung on to these tightly as they were whipped about by the wind.

Vi never talked about her illness and Karen never asked. She didn't know if this was tact, or because she knew she wouldn't want to know Vi if it meant taking on her illness as well. Mainly Karen talked and Vi listened, from time to time asking Karen the kind of prompting questions that made her talk some more. It was good to be listened to for a change. It made Karen realise how rarely anyone at home really listened to her. With Vi she was always interesting, fluent and witty. They laughed a lot together. When Vi did talk it was mainly to make jokes against herself. After a while Karen realised that Vi didn't like herself much. It was as though the illness was seeping inwards, destroying her on the inside as well.

Sometimes she talked about death. Once she told Karen about this programme she had seen on reincarnation. Apparently, if you committed suicide, you reincarnated straight away with the same set of problems to face. So there goes another option, she said. Then another time Karen was walking home with Vi from the shops and just as they were crossing the road a car came speeding round the corner. Vi seemed to be rooted to the spot as the car swerved and Karen began to haul her across the road.

He could have killed us, she said in a rage.

Vi stooped to pick up her stick. O well, she said. He'd have saved me a job.

And once, when Karen had been complaining even more than usual about men and kids and the unfinished state of her house, Vi listened with a peculiar little smile and when Karen paused for breath said, Well, life's a bitch and then you die.

Karen never knew how to take these remarks. Most of the time she changed the subject. She talked a lot about men; there was always some man Karen fancied, Mel Gibson, or the milkman. Vi laughed and said she would end up like a character in a Benny Hill song, fancying milkmen.

O I know, but he's gorgeous. Have you ever seen *Drop the Dead Donkey*? He looks like —

The dead donkey?

No, no no, the randy reporter, you know the one . . .

Or they would talk about how men never listen. Karen mimicked Steve.

He picks up his paper and says 'what have you been doing love', and after that, whatever you say, all he can say is 'mmm'. I say 'O you know, I went down to Wharf Mill, picked up a bus-load of men, shagged them all senseless, I thought it'd help with the mortgage,' and Steve says, 'Mmm, that's nice love, what's for tea?.'

So it went on, Karen talking, Vi listening. If she ever fancied any men herself she never mentioned it, and she never talked about herself and Tony.

One day in late autumn Karen came running in breathless with the cold.

Shit, she gasped, I told her, I told her, but she wouldn't have it. I *knew* she was going out with him . . .

Steady on, said Vi, what's up?

Dawn, said Karen. She's going out with that flaming biker. He's nineteen years old, *nineteen*, and she's not even sixteen yet . . .

She had to stop, out of breath, clutching the chair back.

Well hang on a minute, said Vi, not all bikers are bad news you know.

Karen snorted. Don't talk to me about bikers, she said. You can't tell me anything about them I don't know.

I'll make a cup of tea, said Vi.

Karen sat down, feeling suddenly limp and empty. She gazed out of the window. Outside there was a thick frost and mist, it looked like the ground was smoking, like dry ice, like a freezer smokes with cold. It reminded Karen of something that tugged at her with a vague, nostalgic pull, but she ignored it, pushing it to the back of her mind.

He's too old for her, she said. He's up to no good.

Vi sat down with the steaming mugs of tea.

Wasn't Steve a biker? she said. Karen mumbled something.

The voice on the radio said, Police today are widening their search for the killer of three young girls, after the discovery of a third body in the basement of a derelict house. A nationwide search is being launched . . .

He wants hanging, him, Karen said. Vi said nothing.

Well he does, said Karen. He's a sick bastard. They're not going to cure him are they?

O well, said Vi. They're not going to cure me either, if it comes to that.

Karen said nothing to this.

– Tell me about that gang you were in, said Vi, after a pause.

Vi had a way of saying something that triggered off feelings and memories. So many of these flooded Karen now that she hardly knew what to say.

Vi said, How many of you were there?

So Karen began, reluctantly at first, but once she started she couldn't seem to stop. She felt like she wasn't making much sense, but Vi didn't seem to lose interest. She kept asking questions and bit by bit it all came tumbling out. The time when Karen used to stack shelves at the supermarket, and the whole week was only made bearable by Friday nights when she finished at eight and got changed at the back of the store. Then she would run out to meet them as they waited on their big machines, Gazzer with Shar on his bike, Cess with Diane, Dave with Debbie, Mick with Lou and Steve with no one, waiting for her. She would leap on to the back of his bike, clutching his jacket and they would roar off, leaving the other shop assistants behind, watching.

There was more to it than this though, more than Karen could ever put into words, the smell of rain and leather, the flash of street lights, the long, long roads. She trailed off into silence.

Vi said, What did you say the leader was called?

Gazzer.

What was he like?

Karen couldn't think of anything to say, then she said, We all fancied Gazzer.

What, all of you? said Vi.

O aye, Karen said. He were top dog. He could have any girl he liked and usually did.

I thought you said Shar was his girlfriend.

She was, but that never stopped him. At any of the dos he was always with someone – one of the girls from another gang. Sometimes he ran into trouble, but the lads always backed him up. Had to, if they wanted to be in the gang. Besides, no one ever beat Gazzer in a fight.

Didn't Shar mind?

Karen shrugged. I expect she did mind, but she turned a blind eye. There wasn't much else she could do. As far as I know he's still at it now. She gave Vi a brief update on Gazzer and Shar.

Did he ever try it on with any of you?

Karen hesitated, then she said, No, that would have been like breaking the gang up.

Vi had run out of questions. Karen had run out of words. She had forgotten about Dawn, about everything except this powerful sense of loss. She tried to think about everything she had now, compared to what she had then, a nice house, kids, and a wardrobe full of clothes, but she knew, suddenly and unmistakably, that none of it added up to what she'd lost. Draining the dregs of her tea she stood up, pushing the chair back and said dully, I'll have to go.

Vi looked at her curiously but said nothing. She began to clear away the pots. At the door Karen paused and said, I'll see you soon, and Vi smiled. Then she closed the door and set off through the smoking frost.

Her chest hurt, just as if she had never stopped running. And she knew, as she tramped over the frozen playing fields, what the light reminded her of – the time they had driven off to Whitby, staying out all night. They had hit the beach at night, lighting bonfires just off Robin Hood's Bay, drinking and smoking joints beneath far-away pin pricks of light in the sky. Then they slept in sleeping bags and Karen woke cramped and colder than she would have believed, sand in places she didn't know she had. She had thought she would mind and hate it, but there was something hypnotic about waking in the peculiar light of the frosted beach. The light and the water, gleaming like a metallic plate, affected them all. They took their bikes and rode through the water and it rose up behind them like great shining wings. They screamed and cried like the gulls overhead, but beyond this, beyond them all was the vast silence of the milky sky. Then, getting tired, they had ridden back cross-country, over the stiff white grass, with the sun a pale disc like the moon through the mist, and a feeling of absolute quiet inside.

Karen let herself in. She felt remote, untouched by the familiar objects. The house was a mess, Steve wasn't due home yet. There was Dawn's laundry on the floor in front of the washer, Karl's football boots, caked in mud, crumbs and pots on the table. Karen sat down ignoring it all, hands in pockets, legs spread out.

Maybe it all went wrong when she got married, but at the time it didn't seem like there was anything else she could do. She remembered Steve saying her name over and over again when he made love to her until it sounded like crying. You couldn't turn down love like that, not unless you had a real alternative in mind. And you didn't. You couldn't see any other way of living your life. Karen remembered the day of her wedding; how, in the field behind the registry office all the bikers for miles around had assembled, forming a great circle, and when the wedding party came out one of them came riding up to Karen and swung her on to the back of his bike. He had driven off with her riding pillin, her short white skirts flying up in the wind, round and round the field, then he had passed her on to someone else's bike, round the field and off into the streets of the town, Shar and Debbie and Diane, the bridesmaids, following closely behind. They rode round all afternoon, out of the town and up on to the moors. When she looked back it felt like the last time though of course it wasn't. There was no real reason why they should ever have stopped. Bikers took their kids along with them everywhere – once they had taken Dawn to a rally – and there was Jed, who was retired and had been to a hundred rallies all over Europe. There was no reason to give it all up once you got married. But after getting married it all seemed like one long slide into unemployment, debts and kids. In the middle of the long spell of unemployment Steve had sold his bike. He had loved it and he never mentioned it again.

Karen looked round at the darkening kitchen, the pots and crumbs and dirt. This isn't me, she wanted to shout. This isn't how it was going to be. For a moment she sat still, staring at a crack in the wall and feeling her heart thud loudly in the tightness of her chest. How had they ever got this scared?

Maybe they had always been this scared.

Karen remembered watching Mick grab hold of Lou's arm at a party. They had been going out for nearly a year then, but Mick said Lou had been avoiding him. He thought she was seeing someone else. Gazzer said they would sort it out. So they had gatecrashed this party in a squat, with another gang for numbers.

Get out Mick, Lou said in a low, furious voice. Leave me alone.

She had been dancing with this thin guy. Dave and Cess had him up against the wall, Mick had hold of Lou.

It's all right, Gazzer said, addressing everyone. She's his girlfriend. We just want a quiet word.

There's a room free up here, said Shar from the landing.

Take her upstairs Mick, Gazzer said. For a quiet word.

Lou screamed No, piss off, stop them, but Gazzer talked right over her.

Now no one need concern themselves with this, he said. We don't want to break up the party, let's have the music back on. Al and Pete are going to stay down here, just to make sure the party gets going again.

Al and Pete moved forwards silently from the shadows of the room. Mick was already hauling Lou out. She sobbed and twisted and suddenly broke free, running straight into Steve. Steve looked as if he didn't quite know what he was doing, but between them they bundled her out of the room. Half-way up the stairs she turned round in their arms and saw Karen.

Karen – Kas, she said. Don't let them do it. Stop them Kas, please.

Her face was twisted with fear.

Karen was conscious of wanting to say the right thing, the thing that would make her seem right in the eyes of both Lou and the gang.

Don't worry Lou, she said. Mick only wants a word. As she said it she believed it was true.

Lou was hauled, sobbing, into the bedroom. Then they were all in the bedroom, Mick, Lou and Steve in the middle, near an old mattress that stank of piss, Shar and Debbie near the door, Diane by the window. Gazzer crossed to the window where a curtain hung half off its rod and pulled it across, though it didn't fully cover the pane.

Lou had pulled away from both Mick and Steve, she was quiet now. She stared at Mick, breathing hard, her crinkly, brownish-yellow hair falling all over her face. Karen couldn't help noticing how pretty she was. She had always liked Lou, who was pretty and funny. But she understood how Gazzer felt. If Lou betrayed Mick, she was betraying the whole gang.

Lou was speaking under her breath to Mick, looking at no one else.

Don't be like this Mick, she said, don't be daft. I wasn't doing owt, honest, it were only a dance. Just let me go Mick, eh? We can go somewhere else and talk.

Next to Shar the door clicked open and Lou shot a wild look towards it. Dave and Cess came in.

Keep the door shut Shar, said Gazzer, and Steve screamed,

Shut the fucking door, can't you?

Karen didn't know why he screamed like that, he looked almost as worked up as Lou. Shar shot a sidelong glance at Debbie then stepped in front of the door, shutting it with her backside.

Lou put a hand on Mick's arm.

Mick, she said, you don't always have to listen to him you know, you don't always have to do what he says.

A look flickered across Mick's face like he was thinking of giving in, then Gazzer said,

You going to let her talk to you like that, Mick? What does she think you are, some kind of puppy dog?

Mick shot a look of pure hatred at Gazzer, but he screamed at Lou,

Shut up, just fucking shut it.

Lou took a half step forwards then seized the front of Mick's shirt.

Don't let him tell you what to do, she said.

Gazzer snorted and clicked his fingers.

Here boy, he said.

Mick hit out at Lou.

He must have hit her on the side of her head, she fell to the mattress without a sound. Immediately she tried to scramble up but this time Steve caught her and twisted her arm violently so that she fell back down again. This time she did make a sound, a little whimpering gasp.

Why doesn't she scream, Karen thought, then felt in her own throat the kind of constriction Lou must be feeling.

Afterwards Karen always told herself that at the time she hadn't known what they were going to do. This was only partly true; it would be truer to say that she felt like it was all inevitable, like a scene that had to be played out, that at some level she wanted to be played out. When Mick climbed on top of Lou holding her arms down she heard someone giggling, a stupid, out of place noise. It was herself. All the rest were watching silently. Karen felt her own attention grow to a point of absorbed concentration nothing could shake. Here in this room, now, they were making their own rules, nothing could stop them. Karen wanted to see. She felt the lure of what you were not supposed to see more powerfully than she had ever felt anything in her life.

In fact she didn't get to see much at all in the bald yellow light of the bulb. Mick didn't take his trousers off, there was only the jerky movement of his backside covering Lou. When he rolled off Karen saw his prick, shrivelled and wet, and a flash of Lou's pubic hair, which was darker than the hair on her head.

Lou dragged her skirt down and leapt up from the bed.

Bastards, she screamed, bastards all of you.

Steve and Dave moved forwards. As she watched them Karen knew what they were going to do.

Eh, said Steve, taking hold of Lou. Karen could see the desire on his face, but then Mick caught hold of Steve, driving him back into the wall.

Leave her alone, he shouted.

Steve opened his mouth to say something but the look on Mick's face stopped him. Dave and Cess fell back uncertainly and Shar moved away from the door as Lou ran at it. Mick stood glaring savagely at them all as they heard her clattering down the stairs. No one moved.

Gazzer was the first to recover.

31

Steady on Mick, he said. No harm done.

Karen could hear Mick breathing as he stared at Gazzer, but then slowly he seemed to relax, or collapse, all the tension sagged out of him. Karen had to admire Gazzer. Of them all he had remained calm throughout, in control. Now he laid a hand on Mick's shoulder. Karen half expected Mick to hit him, but the new, crumpled Mick didn't move or say a word.

Gazzer patted his shoulder.

The night's young yet, he said, addressing them all. Shall we move on.

One by one they left the room and went downstairs, Debbie laughing loudly at a joke Cess made. They went past the door of the room where the party was still going on and left the house. They rode to a bikers' club where the drink went on after hours. They drank a lot. Dave and Diane danced a wild, freakish dance that had everyone standing round stamping their feet. Karen stood a little way from Steve. When he put out a hand to touch her she moved slightly. She knew he was hot for her, yet a few minutes ago he would have done it to Lou. She felt disturbed, stirring with desire herself, but she didn't want to give in to Steve, to feel him lying on top of her while they were both thinking of Lou, to imagine them all doing it to her, one after another, and seeing, even as she came beneath Steve, Lou's face all pulled back in an agony of fear.

Gazzer and Shar were dancing now, clinched together in a slow embrace, and a few other couples had moved on to the floor. Steve touched Karen's arm. What's up, he whispered. Karen wouldn't look at him. Nowt, she whispered back. She allowed herself to be steered on to the dance floor and she began to dance, still not touching Steve, her face assuming a careful, blank expression as she looked over his shoulder. Out of the corners of her eyes she viewed the dancers and Gazzer and Shar, the painted portraits of Jimi Hendrix and Jimmy Page on the black walls, and behind the dance floor, in the corner of the room, Mick drinking slowly, steadily, alone.

It was as if all the light were being absorbed from the kitchen. Karen could hardly see the clutter any more, but she still sat feeling the coldness of tears on her face. It was daft, she told herself, crying for something that happened all those years back. Mick was dead and gone, he had overdosed a week later, just before his twentieth birthday, she never knew what had happened to Lou. Was she crying about that or because after the funeral no one ever mentioned either of them again? Maybe they were always that scared, she thought, shifting finally, stiffly, in order to start tidying up the kitchen in preparation for Steve's return.

Hello stranger, Vi said.

Karen was forced to look up from her supermarket trolley and smile weakly.

I haven't seen you for a while, said Vi.

Karen had been avoiding Vi, ever since the day she had spilled out her past in Vi's kitchen. Now she felt guilty.

I've been a bit busy, she said. Kids've all had colds, then there's the Christmas shopping. Time runs on before you know it . . . She stopped, aware that she too was running on.

Well, said Vi. Why don't you come round now and have a cup of tea?

A number of excuses ran through Karen's head but they all seemed weak. She looked at Vi's smiling face and saw how much she wanted Karen to go.

All right then, she said, a little ungraciously, and went back to packing things into her bag.

On the way back Karen noticed that Vi was walking less well than usual. Karen slowed down without commenting on this to give Vi a chance to catch her breath. If anything Vi seemed brighter than ever, more talkative, anxious to talk in the face of Karen's silence.

I've missed seeing you, she said. How's Dawn? Did she go out with that biker?

Karen didn't know. She couldn't get anything out of Dawn these days. Short of following her she didn't know what she could do. Vi changed the subject.

How's the decorating coming on? she said.

Unfortunately there were no developments there either. So they went on, the conversation limping and flagging, until they reached Vi's house. When they were almost on the doorstep Vi's legs buckled and she collapsed without a sound. Karen's hand shot out, gripping Vi's arm and hauling her up. She felt curiously like dead weight.

Thank you, said Vi, not looking at Karen. She fumbled for her keys and opened the door.

With a spasm of irritation Karen noticed that the radio was still on. Vi always seemed to leave it on whether she was in or not. As Karen sat down the announcer's voice went on about identifying a fourth body. Karen didn't want to know.

The kitchen was bright in the fluorescent light, the winter daylight outside seemed dark. Vi put the kettle on and began wiping pots in the rhythmical, functional way Karen had realised was a response to extreme tiredness. Karen stretched her legs.

So, she said. How's things?

Vi clutched momentarily at the sink to steady herself.

O, she said, so-so, you know. She went on wiping the pots, reaching for tea. Karen waited. It seemed like now Vi had got her back she didn't have anything to say. After a while Karen said,

How's Tony?

O, Vi said quickly, he's fine. He's got a lot of work on at the moment, I hardly see him. Seems like everyone's central heating's breaking down at once. So he's tired. But he's all right, you know. And the money's coming in.

Vi sat down suddenly opposite Karen at the table and was silent for a moment. Then she said, He's started sleeping downstairs now, you know.

Then she was crying. Not quietly and with dignity like people do on films, but with great harsh sobs, she was also grunting. Karen stared at her. She didn't know what to do. Her first thought was that she didn't need all this. She wanted to leave quietly without disturbing Vi. Then she had an impulse to take Vi in her arms and rock her like a child. She moved her chair round the table and put an arm awkwardly round Vi. Vi leaned towards Karen, her shiny brown hair fell across Karen's cheek. For a moment Karen didn't know what she was doing, then she did know. She was pressing her lips into Vi's hair, then turning Vi's face to hers and blotting the tears away clumsily with her lips. Hardly knowing how far she dared to go she undid two buttons of Vi's shirt and slipped her hand inside. She felt the nipple through the cup of Vi's bra.

Vi didn't resist any of this, or draw away, but her eyes were open. Karen gazed directly into Vi's eyes, noticing for the first time the small circle of gold around the pupil. She wondered if she looked now like the men looked who had wanted to sleep with Karen, very intent, searching.

Shall we go somewhere else, she said.

cunt
snatch
twat

So many hard words for something so soft. When Steve was mad at people at work he always called them cunts, or twats. Karen never thought about it, but now, spreading it open finger by finger she thought *this* is what he meant. Karen wanted to look, she felt the lure of what you were supposed to see, but she felt also that she didn't know how to look. She closed her eyes and tried to see it through her fingers, soft and dry at the top, then a kind of spongy wetness, her fingers made a sucking noise. Karen hesitated, not knowing what to do next, feeling a rapid movement between tenderness, lust and a kind of frustration in which she was able to feel nothing at all. Then remembering what Steve did to her she lowered her face to it gingerly, expecting it to smell. It smelt sour, but Karen did not find it dirty. She had always thought before that that was what they were. Dirty cunts.

Experimentally she touched it with the tip of her tongue, then explored further with the flat of it, like a cat giving itself a good wash. Vi spread her legs further apart and arched her back. Soon she began to shudder and moan. It wasn't like the noise Karen made when she was coming, she didn't know quite what to do. But then Vi rolled to one side into a foetal position.

She did not stop moaning.

Karen clambered up the bed and held her tightly, stroking her hair and arms, but she couldn't stop the terrible shuddering moans. She became frightened. It was like they were breaking Vi apart.

Come on love, she said. Hush.

Vi clasped Karen's arm and said nothing, but gradually the moaning died away, leaving only the shuddering breathing.

That's better, Karen said, as though she was talking to Dawn. I'll make us a cup of tea. She tucked Vi up in the blankets and went downstairs.

Karen hunted for the tea and milk and sugar. She felt unexpectedly vivid and powerful. She hummed as she carried tea up on a tray. Vi was out of bed already, half dressed. The blue shirt fell open, showing the small pink points of her breasts. Karen felt a wave of lust again. She wanted to slip the shirt off Vi's shoulders and kiss her breasts, as if she hadn't really got to the heart of her desire before and wanted to try again, but something told her not to push it. She put the tray down on the dressing table and passed Vi her bra. Looking for this, she said.

Vi still seemed shy, somehow, pulling on her clothes without looking at Karen. Karen didn't mind. She sat in the wicker chair and looked out of the window, thinking happily about the time and about getting home for Darren. Part of the sky was deepening into a cherry red.

There's the gas van, she said as it pulled into the drive of the house next door. Gas bill's due next. One bill after another, I don't know.

She talked on. Vi was silent but it wasn't an unhappy silence. Karen gave her time by talking about nothing in particular. They finished the tea and Karen carried the tray downstairs. She washed the pots, making jokes about hands that wash dishes, and Vi laughed a little. Then when it was time to go Karen felt suddenly shy.

I'll call round sometime soon, she said, if that's all right, I mean.

Vi leaned against the door-post and smiled.

O, I think that'll be all right, she said.

For some reason Karen found this funny. She laughed aloud as she went down the path, then turned to wave, but Vi had already gone.

When she was almost home Karen laughed again, ignoring passers-by. I've heard about women like you, she told herself. Was this what it meant to be a dyke? An image of huge, muscular tattooed women crossed her mind and she couldn't stop laughing. It all seemed unbelievable and funny, especially when she thought of Steve's reaction. Of course she wouldn't tell him. She wasn't that daft yet.

Karen opened the door of her house on to the mess inside. For once it didn't get her down. She hummed her way around the house, flicking a duster here and there, clearing things away and wiping the pots.

She knew that she wanted to do it again, that once was not enough. She wanted to get inside what she felt, to make it real to herself, to get at the heart of her desire. And she wanted Vi to make love to her as well. She pushed out of her mind the thought of what might happen, where it all might lead to. The beauty of it was, she didn't have to think like that, just like she didn't all those years ago when she was a biker. For the first time in years she felt a sense of things opening out.

When the kids got home Karen was still buzzing with energy. Karl had a copy of the play his class were doing for Christmas, a kind of spoof western. Karl was a tough kid. He had a slight stammer, which meant that he had learned how to fight. This was the first time he had been in anything sociable like a play. Karen was usually too busy, but tonight she turned the pans off and wiped her hands on her apron.

Let's hear you then, she said.

I can't on my own, said Karl. Karen took the apron off.

I'll be the saloon owner, she said, taking the script, Dawn can be the bar-girl and Darren's the baddie. Now go.

Go Mam go, said Dawn, running upstairs to get changed.

When Steve came home they were all hard at it. Dawn was wonderful as the whore-with-the-heart-of-gold, Karen hammed it up as the saloon owner and Karl got better as the Indian chief. He strutted up and down looking immensely proud. Steve watched from the doorway with a half smile. Karen didn't care. For once she was not performing for him, not seeing herself through his eyes. It was a long time since she had been like this and she could sense Steve sensing it. He was watching her, not the kids, and at the end of the performance he clapped. Karen bowed.

Right, she said, taking charge. You can all pitch in with the tea.

For a wonder everyone did. They made spaghetti bolognese the way Karen liked it, with vegetables stirred into the meat sauce and grated cheese on top. Steve and Darren set the table and Steve washed the used pans. Dawn chopped vegetables, talking all the time about her best friend Kirsty who was going out with two boys at once and couldn't choose. Karl grated cheese and Karen made the sauce. She was aware of Steve wanting to be near her, to be included somehow in her mood. She was aware that she and Dawn were talking like good friends again for the first time in weeks, and she was aware also, newly aware, of Dawn's body, its broad back and low, heavy breasts so unlike Karen's own. She was like Steve's sister, Angela, even in the swaying way she walked. Karen felt a new tenderness for Dawn and Dawn's body, but she didn't want to do anything to interfere with this momentary closeness.

Later that night all the kids seemed to disappear early. Even Dawn went upstairs without being told to do her homework. By half-ten there was just Karen and Steve left in the lounge and Steve was reading the paper; reading the print off the sports page as usual. Karen was bored. She flicked at the paper.

Ask me a question, she said.

How many feet make a yard, said Steve.

Karen wasn't amused. Men never asked questions.

No, I mean a real question, she said. I bet you can't think of one, can you, eh?

There was a silence. Karen could almost hear Steve thinking, then getting bored, behind the newspaper.

At last he said, What have you been up to today then?, but he didn't put the paper down or even look over it.

All the times Steve hadn't listened to her in the past seemed to rise simultaneously to the surface of Karen's mind. She didn't answer him now, just to see if he'd notice. When he didn't, she said, A fat lot you care, and marched into the kitchen with the mugs.

When she returned Steve lowered the paper slowly. Well, go on then, he said. What?

Karen wasn't going to tell him, of course she wasn't, but maybe it was the expression on his face, or the fact that she couldn't bear to hear herself saying the same old thing in reply. Whatever it was, she opened her mouth, fully intending to say something like, O, I went for a walk in the park, and then heard herself, without a reason in the world, as if it were someone else speaking, telling him exactly what she had been doing that day.

At first he didn't believe her.

You what? he said, laughing a bit.

So, though she was more scared than she could ever remember being, Karen said it all over again. When she finished he sat staring at her. She watched the changing expressions on his face and knew that he believed her now. Suddenly he got up and strode across the room. Karen flinched as he walked past but he ignored her. He stood facing the wall, then all at once he hit it hard with his fist and turned around.

You, he said. You, and her –

Why, why did she tell him, Karen thought. She remembered the old queen at the Grapes. Steve's face was white like a fist, like he wanted to stamp all over Karen with his big, dirty boots. He stood staring at her as if he was about to speak, then he made a strange noise like gagging and pushed himself away from the wall, out of the room. Karen jumped violently as the back door slammed.

She stayed where she was, opening her fists slowly and spreading out her fingers against her knees. She'd done it now, but she couldn't take in the implications of what she had done. She had thought there would have been a row, that she would have to try to explain herself, though she didn't know how, but now there was nothing, only silence and the shut door. Karen stared at the faded pink suite and the new grey-flecked carpet. All she could think of was Christmas, Christmas coming up in less than four weeks' time and the kids' presents still to get. She rubbed her hands against the fabric of her jeans. There was nothing to do, she could do nothing. Outside the night was black, like tar on the road. There were fine tracks of rain on the window but it wasn't a heavy downpour. Karen felt the walls around her closing in. She hurried into the hall for her sheepskin jacket.

It was crazy to go out alone at this time, pub closing time, leaving the kids in by themselves. There might be a fire, or burglars. Karen knew all this, but she couldn't stay in. She gathered her bag and keys and clicked the door shut behind her.

Wednesday evenings the pubs weren't too rowdy. Even so she attracted some attention as she walked as inconspicuously as possible in the shadows with her collar turned up against the rain.

I'll see you home love, someone shouted. On the next corner there were catcalls and whistles. Karen felt the invisibility of women as never before, their absence from the streets. She should be invisible too, locked inside her home.

Without realising it she had walked nearly all the way to Vi's. But there was nothing for her to do there, she could hardly go visiting at this time of night. There was nowhere else for her to go, however, so she kept on walking. And soon she stood beneath the tree with no branches, looking at the back of Vi's house. There was a light in the kitchen and one shining through the bathroom window from the hall. They weren't all asleep then. Maybe Vi was up. But then Karen caught a glimpse of Tony in his shirt sleeves, moving about the kitchen, filling up a kettle. Maybe he was brewing up for both of them; they would sit together in front of the fire in the living-room, a married couple, having a last drink before bed. Karen shivered a little. Don't be daft, she told herself. Vi would be in bed by now, she tired early.

Still Karen stood in the fine rain. She knew there was no way on earth she could knock on the door and intrude herself into the

41

family home. Late at night the family homes around her seemed like fortresses, keeping some people in and others out. In the lamplight the fine shoots of the tree with no branches were spindly and drooping. Sometimes they sprouted leaves, but not at this time of year. As Karen moved from one foot to the other in the cold she watched first the kitchen light and then the landing light flicker out, leaving the entire house in darkness.

Karen sat at the kitchen table, smoking one cigarette after another. She was not dressed. Steve had not come home. Normally by now she would have dressed and taken Darren to school, but this morning at about a quarter-past eight Dawn had poked her head around the kitchen door and said,

Mam, what about Darren? Then she said, Are you all right?

It was strange, but Karen felt no need at all to respond.

Dawn came in and touched Karen's shoulder.

What's the matter, Mam, she said. Karen looked at Dawn and saw Dawn looking back at her in fear. She saw herself through Dawn's eyes, straggly, old. That was why Dawn was afraid, Karen thought. She was seeing the straggly old bitch she herself would be in twenty years' time.

Where's Dad? Dawn said.

Karen moved her lips almost soundlessly, Dawn had to move forwards to hear.

Will you take Darren to school, she said.

Normally Dawn would say, No way, then there would be a screaming match. Dawn would say she'd be late and Karen would say that she could never get anyone in this house to do anything for her, she'd have to be dead before anyone even did the washing-up, aware all the time of how her voice carped on like the voice of all housewives. But today she just looked at Dawn and Dawn looked at her a bit and then said, All right. Karen heard her clattering up the stairs shouting Darren, get your shoes on. A few minutes later she heard her shepherding the other two out of the front door, explaining that Mum wasn't well. Darren said, Where is she, but he too was bustled out. Dawn called, see you later Mam, for the three of them and the door clicked shut. Dawn always was bossy, Karen thought, thanking God for her bossiness now.

Karen was alone.

All over the kitchen were the remains of breakfast. Upstairs she knew bedclothes, socks and underwear would be lying in tangled heaps on the floor. She felt no urge to do anything about any of this. She stared at a scratch mark on the new pine table, wondering in a disinterested kind of way how long she could stay here like this, doing nothing, caring about nothing.

She felt old. She was thirty-five now. She had no education, no training, no experience. Seventeen years keeping house and bringing up kids didn't count. She could maybe get a job at the corner shop, or in a pub, or both; Dawn would have to babysit. She would be able to keep the house, at least until Darren was sixteen. Steve would have to pay what maintenance he could. Dawn wanted to leave school at the end of the year and get a job, not that there were any. There was the family allowance. Karen traced the mark on the table with her finger. None of that would even pay the mortgage. She tried to imagine herself on one of the new courses for women at the local college – typing, word processing – but she couldn't do that and run two jobs at the same time. She remembered, without wanting to, days she had spent on the road, brief flickering memories of long hot roads, camps and bonfires at night. Her memories couldn't help her now.

Just before nine Steve came in. Karen looked up but he ignored her. He walked over to the table deliberately brushing past her and dropped his newspaper on it without once looking her way.

Nervously Karen picked up the newspaper and began twisting

it from one hand to the other. At the back of her head and down her neck small prickles of tension registered Steve's movements around the house: clumping footsteps up the stairs into the bedroom, then the bathroom. Karen heard the whirr of the electric razor the kids had bought him last Christmas. Every muscle in her body tensed as she waited for him to come back down. She wanted him to speak and dreaded it. She wanted to find something to say that would make everything all right again, but knew there was nothing. Without her permission her stomach clamped up and began to churn.

She expected violence. He would seize the hair on the back of her head and smash her face into the new pine table. Even so she didn't turn as he entered the room behind her and walked right up to the back of her chair. Reaching over her with one arm he wrenched the newspaper out of her hands. Then he was gone, without saying a word. Karen laughed a little, it was all so funny. Then she was crying, though he hadn't hurt her, because of the violence of the contact. She rubbed the tears away with the heel of her palm, but more came, spilling hot and fast down her cheeks. Then suddenly she was angry. Bastard, she thought, and stood up, almost knocking the chair over. She hugged her blue robe tightly around her, suddenly knowing what she was going to do. She was going to wash and dress and then go round to Vi's.

Vi said, What did you want to go and tell him for! She walked unsteadily towards the sink, keeping her back towards Karen. Karen didn't know what to say, she could no longer remember what she had come to say. That what they had was special? That she wanted people to know? It all seemed stupid now. She had just talked, getting less and less sure of herself as Vi's face froze over. When she had finished she seemed crazy, even to herself.

Jesus, Vi was saying. He might tell Tony.

Karen felt wholly miserable. He won't, she said, searching

around for something more convincing to say. I'll tell him it was all a mistake, she said. A joke. She laughed in disbelief. The words sounded ridiculous to her even as she said them. But hope leapt into Vi's frightened face. She half turned towards Karen and with a twist of her stomach Karen recognised the look on her face as the look on Lou's face all those years ago.

Yes, Vi said quickly, tell him that. Tell him you were angry and you wanted to upset him, to make him listen. Tell him – Karen could see her searching for something to say – tell him you don't know what came over you but it'll never happen again . . . she trailed off as she saw Karen's face.

In Vi's face Karen read all the desperation and fear of her own life, so she couldn't look. She looked instead at the blue-painted drawers, the brass clock. Rules, she was thinking, all the rules you have to live by just to be allowed to live, all the people you have to please. When you're little you think there'll be fewer and fewer rules as you grow up until one day there aren't any left, but it just gets worse . . .

When she spoke her voice was shaking a little.

Well, she said. I thought it was a bit more than that, what we did – then she said nothing.

Vi said nothing either, her silence seeming to harden into stubbornness. Then Karen spoke again though she didn't know why. It seemed like she was speaking from the bottom of a great lonely pit.

It seems like we've always been scared, you and me, she said, not looking at Vi, looking at the peeling wallpaper. Seems like we've forgotten how to be any other way. If we're not picking things up off floor, or shifting dirt, we don't feel like we're owt. But we don't have to live like that, do we? There must be some other way to live.

She was not really talking to Vi but to herself, and the air around.

Anyway, she said. Maybe that's why I told Steve. Maybe I got sick of being scared. As she said it it seemed true. She kicked the toe of her boot against the leg of the table.

You know I even thought once, she said, that you and me might get it together, the two of us, you know, without men, or even kids. Just imagine, not having to think about men for once. She laughed shortly. What a bloody laugh.

She had meant it as a criticism of the general situation rather than Vi, but Vi turned suddenly.

You thought! I'm sick of hearing what you thought. I never get to hear anything else.

Karen stared at her, astonished.

When did you ever ask me what I think, eh? You never have. What did you think? I'd throw over an eighteen-year marriage for the sake of an afternoon fling? That I'd be flattered? Or just grateful –

I never meant – Karen started, but Vi carried on,

Why should I throw up everything for you? You're just the bloody same as him!

Vi's voice rose shrilly, her face was white as a knuckle. Karen stared at her. She had never imagined all this rage in Vi. She tried to speak but her voice choked up. She stood absolutely still for a moment, unable to breathe, yet taking in everything about the room with a peculiar clarity, then she turned and ran, knocking a chair over on the way.

Run Karen, run Karen, run, run, run.

Tears streaming back from her face in the wind she fled, bumping into people on the street and ignoring them. Back home she let herself into a house she no longer thought of as hers. She sat down unsteadily at the kitchen table and wiped her face with the back of her hand, remembering as she did so that she always told the kids not to do that. They ended up with dirty streaks all over their faces. Karen didn't care about her face, she didn't care about anything at all. Yet she was still crying, and as she cried it was as though she was crying for everyone, herself and Vi, the kids, Mick and Lou and Shar, even Gazzer, even Steve. There were no words for her grief, it flowed out of her like it would never stop. Then it did stop and Karen wiped her eyes. She felt absolutely quiet inside. All around her was the morning's debris, cups and dishes, crumbs, knives smeared with butter and jam, a packet of skimmed milk, leaking. It was nearly lunch-time. Time for Steve to come home. Time for Karen to run round wiping surfaces, clearing away pots, making beds, preparing all the time the kind of home Steve could just walk into and ignore. She didn't know, today, if Steve was coming back or not, and she didn't care. For the first time in her married life she didn't care. It felt like she had lost something fundamental, and she didn't know if she had anything to take its place. She sat staring at the half-tiled walls, the smooth green tiles and the rough wall above them. When she heard the sound of the lock and Steve's heavy footsteps approaching she didn't move. She heard the kitchen door sliding over the carpet, but all she could see were the sage green tiles running smoothly to the window and the bright, blank square of sky.

2
A Song for Carol Fisher

Whenever Helen raised the lid of her desk she could see the pictures of Ashley. Her favourite was the one of him in the white cat-suit, then there was a smaller one of him singing in a purple leotard that her mother said didn't leave a lot to the imagination, and then a close-up of his face, a picture that her brothers said made him look like a big girl, with the pale hair hanging round. These were pinned to the inside of her desk lid and under all the books in her desk she had an Ashley Waters scrap book and fact file, with newspaper clippings and interviews carefully pasted in. When they had lessons in the form room like this she often managed to lift her desk lid a bit and look at the pictures. When the lesson dragged it made her feel better just to see his face.

This particular lesson, on sheep farming in Wales, seemed to have been going on for ever. Helen glanced round the room, to where Lisa lay slumped across her desk, then back to where Sian was whispering with Emma. Sian had pale silky hair like Ashley's. It was the colour Helen admired most in the world, especially since she had found out it was also the colour Ashley liked best. Helen's hair was a dull brown, though it was thick and long. She had decided to have streaks in it as soon as she could, at the best hairdresser's she could afford, the one the others used, in the next town.

Helen no longer sat next to Sian, not since they had had the row about Ashley's favourite hair colour. Sian had told Helen in a fit of spite, combing out her own flaxen hair. They had just played a fortune-telling game which said that Helen would get the man of her dreams, but Sian would always have to put up with second-best. Sian had got spiteful then, looking at herself in the mirror with pale eyes. She had told Helen that Ashley only liked blondes like himself.

I don't believe you, Helen said, and Sian showed her the clipping. She hadn't showed her before, and they always showed one another every scrap of information about Ashley. Helen felt the injustice of it tightening in her chest.

But he went out with that black model last year, she said.

He didn't go out with her, Sian said. He was only seen with her. At the Awards. She was so cool, not looking at Helen, smiling a bit. Helen felt her face burning. Well it's not likely to do you much good is it, she said, and Sian tossed back her hair. She was angry now.

At least if I did meet him, she said, I wouldn't be too big.

That was unforgivable. Helen left Sian's house without another word. Of course they had fallen out before but this time they never got a chance to patch things up. Sian's father had been promoted a while back and over the summer they moved off the estate where Helen lived into a smaller house (now they weren't renting any more) further up the hill. Worse, she got more pocket money than Helen these days, and went out more, and had drifted into Lynne Baker's set. She went out with Lynne, Emma, Gayle, Kerry and Marie, and had paired off with Emma now there were six of them, though in that set it didn't matter whether you were part of a pair or not. Nothing mattered when you went out five nights a week and didn't have to be in before eleven, and had an endless supply of clothes to go out in. But now Sian went everywhere with Emma Kirby, and Helen sat alone. She felt this badly because she had been best friends with Sian since junior school. Sometimes she hung around on the edge of the group and managed to join in from time to time when they talked about Ashley, since they were all fans as well, but mostly she felt left out. And Sian's pale gold hair had made her an instant success in the group. Emma and Marie had had their hair dyed the same colour. Helen had decided against the dye – it cost too much to keep going back to have your roots done, whereas with streaks it didn't matter too much when they were growing out. In any case she knew she would never be part of the set. She couldn't afford to go out more than once a week, and didn't have the clothes for it if she could. Her parents weren't made of money as they were always telling her. And besides all of these things, she would never be slim like the rest. So now she was on her own.

Of course there were other girls in the class, but four of them were born-again Christians who went to the same church in Upper Marley, and out with boys from that church. That left Lisa. Lisa Jackson had only been in school two terms and didn't seem to belong to any group, or to care. And no one liked her because she came from the wrong side of the estate Helen lived on and never wore the right uniform. Lynne's set didn't wear the right uniform either, but theirs was a fashionable version, with short tight skirts and high heels. Lynne said Lisa's looked as if it had been found in a jumble sale, or at a few different jumble sales – a shirt just the wrong shade of grey, a navy skirt that was too long and hung off her, and greyish-white pumps, the kind you were only supposed to wear in gym, but Lisa wore them all the time. And the teachers had given up telling her about it because she didn't respond. She didn't get rude or angry, she just didn't respond.

Helen didn't really want to be friends with Lisa, and Lisa didn't seem to need a special friend, but they went home the same way, which meant that they sometimes walked together, and in some lessons like science, where you had to be in pairs to use the equipment, they always seemed to end up together. That was all. They would never have moved desks to sit together in the form room like Helen and Sian. They never had anything to talk about, because Lisa didn't even like Ashley, but the lead singer of an American hard rock group called Mean Dream. But increasingly she was the only friend Helen had, because there were no other girls in the class. Now that Carol Fisher had gone.

Officially the school was still investigating the death of Carol Fisher, trying to find out who the boys were she had mentioned in her note. She had written down everything in her note, it was more like a letter, but apparently you could hardly read it, and when you could it didn't make sense. But her family were after blood, and so everyone in the school had been questioned and would be questioned again until the headmaster, Mr Hill, had got to the bottom of it. Helen was sick of hearing about it. She had been questioned, of course, like everyone else; the thought of it made her feel hot and cold and sick. Because she could act big, and put on a hard face, but she couldn't stop her face going red. Because of course she knew. Everyone knew except for the born-again Christians, who might have felt it their duty to tell. Even Lisa knew, though she would never tell, it wouldn't enter her head. But Helen knew Lisa knew, because it had almost happened to her. Helen had seen it, the group of boys dragging her over towards the garages behind the side gates to the school. She had fought them. Helen had never seen anyone fight so hard, with her whole body, teeth and fingernails and feet, until one of them, Gary Mitchell, had dropped her leg with a cry of pain and said, Come on, leave her, she hasn't got anything worth looking at anyway, and they had dropped her on the floor, Kieran picking up the camera she had kicked out of his hands, and left her with a few well-aimed kicks. Helen had stood by in breathless indecision, but when they were gone she ran over and asked Lisa if she was all right. Lisa said nothing, just glared at her with fierce, almost white eyes as if it were Helen's fault, and then set off running very fast. Helen hurried off as well, in case any of them came back. She was a lot more well-developed than Lisa, probably exactly what they were looking for for their stupid magazine, so she needed to get away. But that was how she knew that Lisa knew what was going on, though she didn't know that Lisa cared, so long as it wasn't happening to her. And maybe that was true of all of them.

So most of the girls knew, and all of the boys she was sure, but they wouldn't tell, not even though they were under the most suspicion. And none of them had been directly involved, though one or two might have tagged along. But it was the boys from the year above, Gary Mitchell, Kieran Connor, Karl Wallace, Mick Bain, and others, but mainly those four who had had the idea for an 'alternative school magazine'. Kieran had said they would photograph the tits of every girl in the school, run off copies and charge, and split the profits.

Helen scrolled her name and Ashley's together on to the back of her rough book, in one of the few spaces she had left. The front of it was already covered with new and unusual ways of combining their two names in different kinds of writing. On the back she had been writing all the names she would rather have been called than Helen: Tiffany, Madeleine, Genevieve, Jade, even Ashley. She had written the two Ashleys together in mirror image in letters like fat worms, then in italic print. Though she was no good at art she was pleased at the overall effect. Now she had written her own name in as well there was only a small space left and she had to decide between the other names she liked. Eleanor had to go in; she always used to pretend she was called Eleanor rather than just plain Helen. She liked almost any name better than Helen, including quite plain ones like Julie, though Julia was better. And as for Sowerby almost nothing could be worse. It was particularly bad because of her size. At five foot nine she was the tallest girl in her class, and bigger than most of the boys, and her size made her name a standing joke. She was Fat Sow, or Pig's Arse; at primary school she had been Nellie with the big fat belly. There were only three boys in her class who were the same size or taller; Peter Sykes, who was very tall but dead ugly and covered in zits, David Morris, who was quite good-looking she supposed, but a real creep and anyway he was going out with his sister's friend in the year below, and Rick Adams, who she did quite fancy – he had brown hair and grey eyes and a fairly clear skin – but all the girls fancied him, and she was sure he would ask Sian out soon. None of them would ask her out, she was too big. Last year she had thought that a fifth former, Chris Ward, might have been going to ask her out after kissing her at the Christmas party, but he never did. Anyway, her parents wouldn't have liked it, but at least he was taller than her. The worst thing of all was that Helen thought she was probably bigger than Ashley. She wasn't sure about this since none of the mags ever seemed to get it right. She had read in one that he was five foot nine, but another said only five foot seven, and Helen had felt despair. She supposed it was because he wore high heels that no one was sure. But he did seem to be very slim, unlike Helen who would never be slim, even though some days she starved herself, throwing away the sandwiches her mother made for her lunch. But then by evening she was always starving and needed double helpings for tea. Even if she starved off all the weight though, she would still be left with the big build she hated, that people who wanted to be kind called 'bonny' or 'strapping'. She would always look big beside Ashley, and this made her feel worse than anything.

When the bell went Mrs Jordan's voice was still talking about sheep farming but there was the usual scramble of chairs and banging of desk lids. Mrs Jordan rapped loudly on the table. The following people are to see Mr Hill this break, she said, and everyone groaned. Lindsay Carson, Graham Holt. And Lindsay, one of the born-again Christians, left the room looking important, and Graham followed, pulling hideous faces at Mrs Jordan behind her back.

Helen saw Sian and the others form a cluster at the back of the room. She raised the lid of her desk and with one finger traced round Ashley's lips, listening all the time to what they were saying.

Stupid cow, said Lynne. What did she want to go and do that for.

It were only topless, Emma said, and Helen lowered the lid of her desk. She looked over towards Lisa who was still slumped over hers, looking, as she always did, not a part of anything that was going on. Helen wandered casually towards Lisa, as if not caring much whether she spoke to her or not. Lisa didn't raise her head, but as Helen came nearer she spoke.

I got tickets, she said. For Mean Dream.

Helen was surprised. She knew the tickets cost a lot and had thought they were all sold out. How? she said.

Two tickets, Lisa said. Do you want to come?

Helen hesitated. She felt a bit flattered, since Lisa never seemed to need company. And the concert was going to be a big one, in the football stadium on the other side of the city, it had been in all the papers. But she didn't like Mean Dream and she didn't think her parents would let her go. If it had been Ashley she would have killed to go and she knew she would have a hard enough time with her parents then; she should probably save her strength. Also she didn't know how Lisa got the tickets; she suspected Lisa stole things, but she didn't know. On the other hand it would be her first gig, and the ticket was free.

When is it? she said, though she already knew.

Two weeks Saturday, Lisa said. Helen thought hard. Now might be a good time for her to practise for when Ashley came around. If she won the battle it would be easier next time and if she lost they might feel bad enough about it to let her go the next time she asked.

How were you thinking of getting back? she said, and Lisa shrugged. Helen knew Lisa wouldn't bother about it, she had slept out before, but Helen had to think of a way back home.

Do you think we could get up enough money for a taxi, she said.

Cost a fortune, Lisa said, and Helen nodded.

I'll see what my mam and dad say, she said.

Behind Helen David Morris twanged her bra strap. She turned sharply but he dodged. Fuck off, she said.

It's your turn next, he said, backing away towards the door and wagging his finger at her. Your turn next Sowers, and several of the other boys laughed. Helen swung her satchel off the desk.

Get stuffed Morris, she said, walking towards the door. The bell was ringing for the end of break.

It was hot for September, hotter than it had been in July or August. Typical now they were back at school, Helen thought, shrugging her satchel further up on her shoulder. She had taken her blazer off and could feel a burning patch of sunlight through the thin shirt, sweat gathering between her shoulder blades. She had looked for Lisa before leaving school, but Lisa had disappeared. Knowing that she didn't always go home after school, or even at all some nights, Helen had set off alone. As she walked along the avenue which led away from the school, one of the boys from her class, Nick Robson, caught up with her.

Nick Robson was another of the boys Helen quite fancied. He spoke in a posher voice than the other lads and was quite nice-looking, but he was much smaller than her, maybe five foot three or four. As he drew close to her she immediately became conscious of her size.

Hey Sowers, he said, slapping her arm. Helen felt a bit nervous. He had never singled her out before, she didn't know why he was doing it now. Perhaps he liked her, but if so he had kept it to himself.

Yeah, what? she said. Now he had caught up with her he didn't seem to have anything to say. He grinned his slightly lop-sided grin.

Going home? he said.

What's it look like, Helen said.

Looks like you're going home. He grinned at her again and Helen grinned back.

Christ physics eh! he said. What a drag.

Uh-uh, said Helen, wondering what he was leading up to. Did he want help with his homework? But physics was hardly her subject either.

Physic-al Education now, that's different, he said. All you girls in short skirts, showing your knickers, and he made a sucking noise.

You'll have to be careful Robson, Helen said. You'll be turning into a dirty old man.

I hope so, said Nick, and he went on to tell her about Melanie Pierce in 4C who had jumped up and down so much in netball that all the padding had fallen out of her bra.

You wouldn't have that problem though would you? he said, and Helen swung her bag at him.

Don't be cheeky Robson, she said, but he caught her bag and began pulling her along.

What're you doing, she said, laughing a bit.

Then suddenly, out of nowhere, David Morris was pushing her from behind, and in a rush she remembered what he'd said at break. But she hadn't believed him, not with all the fuss about Carol Fisher. She still didn't believe it, and struggled only half-heartedly, half laughing as they pushed her towards a gap in the school fence.

But Robson said, We thought we'd take a closer look, make sure it's not all padding, and through the gap in the fence Helen saw the older boys, Mick Bain, Gary Mitchell, and behind them Kieran Connor with the camera.

Helen dug her heels in and threw her back against Morris. She was bigger than both of them, heavier anyway. Both of them put together weren't going to get her through that fence. She swung her bag at Robson in earnest this time and hit him in the chest. Then the others were coming at her through the fence and her books were flying out all over the road. She was being tugged and pulled and hauled towards the gap.

Helen wasn't laughing any more. She screamed at them to stop. Her hair was in her eyes and mouth, she couldn't see. It flashed into her mind how Lisa had fought, wildly, with all her body, she knew she couldn't fight like that. Already she felt the animal urge to give in to the overpowering odds. One foot was through the gap in the fence, Morris was prising her hand off the railing, then, impossibly, as she made one final lunge towards the road, she saw her brother Matt with his mates. For a moment she didn't believe it, it was just one of the images flashing through her mind, then she screamed with all the breath in her lungs, Mat-thew . . . Miraculously he heard. He came running, him and all his mates. Helen had never been so pleased to see him. He came running, shouting, What the fuck's going on, and first Morris let go of her then Robson, and ran.

Her brother was a big lad, almost eighteen years old. He caught hold of Mick Bain and swung him right off his feet, he landed sprawling on the road. Helen saw one of Matt's friends batter Wallace, the blood spurting from Wallace's nose. She grabbed at her scattered books, feeling her face flaming red, just wanting to get away. But at the bottom of the avenue her brother caught up with her.

What were going on, he said.

Nowt, said Helen, crosser than ever. She didn't want to talk about it to Matt. They were just messing around.

Suit yourself, Matt said, but they won't be bothering you again. I told them I'd break their legs. Helen knew she was being ungrateful and managed a wobbly smile.

Thanks, she said. She walked with Matt and his mates to the edge of their estate. Then she was alone again, walking past the semis on the better part of the estate, this side of the river. A lot of tenants there were buying their own council houses, like Helen's family, whereas on the other side hardly anyone was. In the holidays Lisa had called for her twice, but Helen wouldn't have dreamed of going over to the other side to call for Lisa.

The sky shone a deep burning blue. Small kids played all over the roads, it was a wonder more of them weren't run over. The kids made a lot of noise and there was noise from the main road. Down the street someone was revving an engine and playing the car radio very loud. But beyond and above all these noises there was silence. It was as if none of the noises mattered because everything was wrapped in silence. Helen felt that she was slipping out of time, that here and now on this street, with its squares of lawn and quiet windows, nothing would ever change. She had had these feelings before, like seeing another world, or the same world a different way. Usually when she felt nothing would ever change it was on a wet Sunday, or when her parents were rowing, or when she was trying not to eat, but this was different. Even as she felt the timelessness around her she knew it wouldn't last. She wanted to hold on to it but it would slip away. These moments came and went and she couldn't make them come. Already as she turned into Cedar Drive, the next but one to her own, she was thinking not about timelessness and silence, but about Carol Fisher, and suddenly she was hot and cold again, remembering the things she had said the day they got back to school, when it was announced in assembly that Carol had killed herself and there was going to be an investigation. That break everyone had clustered round talking about it; for once Helen was not on the outside of any group. Lynne was in the centre of course, but Helen was standing near Sian, she wasn't left out. And Helen knew more about it than the others, she had known first, because a cousin of Carol Fisher's mum worked in the bakery where Helen's mum worked part-time. So Helen could give them all the details. It had happened Sunday morning, two days before school started. In her note she had said that she couldn't face going back. All her family, her mother, grandmother and brother, had gone to church, but Carol had said she had a headache. When they had all gone she had written the note and then searched the house for tablets. She had eaten what there were, but there weren't enough and it was Sunday so the chemist's was shut. Then she'd turned the gas on, but of course it wasn't poisonous, so that didn't get her anywhere either. She went through the house looking for stuff, then finally in the garage she'd found the petrol. She had taken it out of the house, down to the waste ground at the bottom of the garden, where she had poured it all over herself and lit the match.

It wasn't funny, of course it wasn't funny, but Helen managed to make it sound as though it was, Carol hunting through the house looking for different things to kill herself with, an egg whisk, a home perm.

I might just try perming myself to death, she said.

Why didn't she hang herself, said Gayle.

Or cut her wrists, Kerry said.

O they're very house-proud, Helen said. Not on the carpets.

She could have hanged herself, said Emma. Then they were all off, planning other, unusual ways for Carol to have killed herself: by videotaping Dawson, the biology teacher, so she could bore herself to death, or by sucking her insides out with a vacuum cleaner.

They were all funny, but Helen was funniest, whipping up the laughter when it looked as if it might be going to die down, conscious all the time of Ashley watching her. She made up details as if they were true. Carol had to stop writing the note, she said, her pen ran out, and they all screamed with laughter, it was hysterical. The four Christians, Emma Bowden, Lindsay, Martha

62

and Shelley, separated themselves off and then left the classroom altogether, and this too was funny. Emma Bowden had been crying all morning for Carol, but everyone knew it was put on, she had hardly known her. Helen hadn't laughed so much for months, not since she had fallen out with Sian, the glow of it stayed with her all day. And always at the back of her mind she could sense Ashley watching her as she stood centre stage, laughing with the rest when she was funny, getting some of the jokes they didn't.

Now however the scene came back to her in a rush of heat, then a long slow chill, the awful, clenched sensation in her stomach. She wondered if she would ever be free of the guilt of it, she wanted to press herself into the shadows at the side of the road and never be seen again. But other memories kept coming back to punish her. She remembered David Morris showing the first photos, one of them enlarged with a rough heading, Fisher's Boobs, tacked to the top. He passed the photo to Lynne first. She raised an eyebrow and said, That the best you could do? then she passed them round. Most of Carol's face was cut out of the picture, what you could see of it looked as if it was being pushed into the dirt. And her arms were splayed wide, someone must have been holding them down, but you couldn't see that either. Carol's bust was at the centre of the photo, pale and floppy, angular. To the left her bra struggled out of the picture. Helen couldn't help thinking that hers were nicer than Carol's and wondering why they had picked her, she wasn't pretty, though she did have a big bust, and nobody liked her. Unless it was because she went a different way home from everyone else so she was easy to get. When the photos came to Helen she said loudly, They're not even the right shape. One of them's longer than the other, and Gayle had nudged her violently, and said Sssh, then Carol Fisher had left the room.

You're cruel, you, Gayle had said, in a voice that meant it was a kind of compliment, and Helen had laughed with the others, but the truth was she hadn't known Carol was there. And now she felt bad about it, just terrible, but who could have known Carol would take it all so badly? Most of the girls just thought it was a big joke. Gayle had said, You'll have to do better than that, you need some real women in your mag, and she had pulled up her shirt and bra and shaken her tits vigorously at Morris. Everyone fell about laughing as he backed off. Helen couldn't help admiring Gayle, she wished she had the nerve. But Gayle's bust was the right size and shape, small and high and pointy, whereas Helen's was nearly as floppy as Carol's, only a bit more round. Anyway, everyone had forgotten about Carol in the general uproar that followed, Gayle stuffing her bust hastily back into her bra as Mr Winter came in and everyone giggling silently, helplessly. But Helen remembered now, and it was just as though all the sunlight had been suddenly snuffed out. She made herself move away from the shade at the corner of the road, walking slowly, holding her satchel to her as a cushion. She remembered the first time she had heard of the magazine. Karl Wallace had come into their classroom. It was dead unusual for someone in a higher year to walk in like that and Gayle had nearly choked because she fancied him. Helen thought he was good-looking too. He stretched himself over two desks in front of Lynne's group and lit a cigarette.

We're going to photograph the tits of every girl in the school, he had said, and Helen had felt a thrill of horror. For once in that group no one knew what to say. At least, he had added, those of you with something worth showing, and he had grinned directly at Gayle, who seemed to lose her cool entirely and coloured up.

You dirty bastard, Kerry said, and Lynne said, Sure you are.

You wait and see, Wallace said.

Helen had felt a thrill of shock and something else, a dirty thrill she didn't want. She found herself wondering if it was only a topless mag or if they would go further, like the really mucky pictures they sometimes found scattered around the school field, or left in the girls' changing rooms. She didn't want to think like this but she couldn't stop. Then weeks had passed and she had forgotten about it. And then it had happened to Carol Fisher, a few weeks before the end of term, and again, apparently, on the last day, though no one had known about that. But Carol had mentioned it in her note.

Almost without knowing it Helen was home. She wiped the sweat from her upper lip and pushed the gate. She would be good from now on, she thought, she would be good. But she could feel her whole life stretching in front of her, bleak as ash.

Helen's mother was called Barbara; she was a tiny Irish woman with fiery hair. Barbara's grandfather had thought that red-haired women were unlucky – if he saw one on the way to work he would go straight home – but all four of his granddaughters had bright red hair. Helen had always wished she looked like her mother, but the four of them looked just like their father, big and burly with red faces and thick brown hair. Helen's father was a Yorkshireman, that was where the name Sowerby came from. Helen loved her father, but she wished she hadn't inherited everything from him, including the name. Her mother's name used to be Doyle, which Helen thought much nicer, but she was stuck with her father's name, and build. It was all right for the lads, she always thought. They were both over six foot tall, but it was bad news for her. And it had been bad news for her mother when they were all young. Neighbours used to feel sorry for the little woman with the four huge children, especially when she was pregnant, and pushing one in the big pram, with another one balanced on top, or carrying Stuart with all the shopping whilst pushing the pram because he wouldn't walk uphill. And it was a peculiarity of Marley that whichever way you walked seemed to be uphill. In each pregnancy Barbara had nearly doubled in size. She was barely five foot tall and none of the babies had weighed less than nine pounds six; Matthew had been eleven pounds. The oldest, Nicola, was also the smallest. Helen used to pray that she would stop growing and be like her mother, then, when that looked less and less likely, that she would stop at Nicola's size, five foot six and a size fourteen, but she had passed Nicky's build at twelve. Anyway, somehow her mother had brought them all up, though the neighbours who remembered said they didn't know how she coped. But Helen's father always said that her mother had guts, real guts and stamina, and he thought the world of her.

Helen let herself in at the back door, called out Hiya, and slipped upstairs to change. She washed her hands slowly, thinking about the best way to raise the subject of the concert. Downstairs her mother was peeling potatoes. She looked up and smiled as Helen came in. Chop us some carrots will you love, she said, without a trace of Irish in her voice. She had lived too long with a Yorkshireman in Lancashire. Without her usual protest Helen lifted a huge bag of carrots from the vegetable rack.

What's for tea, she said.

Chops, mashed potatoes, carrots, peas, her mother said. But it won't be ready yet.

Helen wondered if it might be better to tackle her father first.

Where's Dad? she said. Her father worked shifts and was on earlies that week.

On the allotment, her mother said. Where else?

Helen began topping and tailing the carrots. Her father had been spending more and more time on the allotment. He had taken it on to relax him, her mother said, because he had been so upset about the poll tax. Helen had never seen him so upset. He had resigned from the Labour Party to avoid being thrown out when he kept disrupting the meetings. He was furious with them for doing nothing, and with the council for sticking extra charges on the bills of those who paid to make up for those who didn't. They're just dividing people, he said. Making it easy for *them* (meaning the government). Whichever meeting he was at people said it wasn't their fault, it wasn't up to them, they had to go off what the government said. And that got John mad until he was banging on tables and shouting. What was the use of having a bloody opposition party if it had to go off what the government said? Twice he had been thrown out of meetings. All his life John Sowerby had considered himself a staunch member of the Labour Party, but he had never had to get radical before, because in Marley Labour were voted in routinely, they hardly had to campaign. But this poll tax thing had changed him, he wasn't the same man. He used to come in from work and grab Helen's mother and sweep her off her feet saying, I must have done summat right in my last life, because I won the lottery in this one. And Barbara would swipe at her big husband with the tea towel and say he was more Irish than any Irishman she ever knew. Then at tea he would always be laughing and making jokes, but all that changed. Each night he had some new tale of injustice to tell. He drove them all daft, bringing up facts and statistics.

You know your old headmistress, he said to Helen, that Miss Woods. She lives on her own doesn't she?

Helen said she didn't know, but her father went on anyway.

She lives on her own in a detached house – a big detached house left her by her parents, so she's no mortgage to pay – and she's on a good wage. You know how much poll tax she pays? And he looked round at them all. Of course they knew, since it was a standard amount, but no one said anything.

I'll tell you how much, he said. A third of what we have to pay, that's how much. A quarter when Matt comes of age, and that's for this little dump. And what do we get for it eh? They don't come round for our bins more often do they? We've not got half the street lighting they've got up top, and you never see the police round our way, they're too busy doing up the station. So her bill's halved and ours has trebled. That's fair isn't it, he said looking round the table. Don't bother looking for work, he said to Matt. Just don't even try, we're in enough of a mess as it is. And he always finished up with, What this country needs is a General Strike. O it could happen, never fear, he said, seeing their faces. It happened once, not that many years before I was born, and it can happen again.

For a long time he talked about not paying the bill, of joining the group of people who were being sent down, but Barbara begged and pleaded with him. That kind of thing was for them that were self-employed, like builders and handymen, or them that wouldn't lose their jobs if they did get sent down, but there'd be no job waiting for John if he went to jail. He'd been unemployed on and off all through the eighties, and Barbara had had enough.

I don't care, John said. Something'll have to be done.

You're a fool then, said Barbara. You'll never change anything that way. Only a fool'd think they could make the system fair, when it never has been.

John followed her into the kitchen.

So what am I supposed to do then, he said, Just lie down and put up with it all? Say 'Come and take more money off me please, I don't think you've had enough'? If you don't do something nothing'll ever change.

Nothing'll ever change anyway, Barbara said. It's no use thinking you can change things. That way lies madness.

And it did seem for a while as if John had gone mad, especially after the government were voted back in, and John was summonsed to court, but paid his bill at the last minute. He took it very personally and stopped talking to anyone, and sat in his room brooding over books about the time when the Labour Party had got things done. Sometimes he went on about this at meal times, then seeing the blank faces of his four children he would push back his chair and say, This country's politically dead, and leave the table, sometimes without eating. There was no comforting him at all, even when the poll tax system was finally changed. Barbara went about with a queer, buttoned-up look on her face and the atmosphere got really bad. Whatever else the poll tax had done, she said, it had ruined their home life. Helen sometimes wondered if Nicola had married Mark so fast just to get out of the house. Things only started to improve when John got the allotment, because he was out most of the time and seemed to feel a bit better when he got back, though nothing much got grown. If he was there now he was either in a bad mood because things were getting him down, or he might have worked it off. But Helen thought she might as well try her mother first.

Mam, she said, Have you heard of that big American group, Mean Dream.

I can't say as I have, her mother said.

Well, they're coming to Manchester.

Yes, her mother said, in the tone of voice that meant she knew something else was coming.

Only Lisa's got tickets, two of them. She's crazy about the lead singer as I am about Ashley, only her dad says she can't go on her own and she's got no one else to ask. Helen was making this up. She laid it on a bit thick, knowing her mother felt sorry for Lisa. Can I go Mam, I know how I'd feel if Ashley came round and I couldn't go because I'd got no one to go with. And she hardly ever gets to go anywhere.

Helen's mother looked at her sharply.

From what I've seen of her dad, she said, he wouldn't care either way. He couldn't give two hoots about that poor child so don't tell me he wouldn't let her go on her own, I doubt he'd notice.

Helen felt her face redden.

Well, that's what she told me, she said. Anyway Mam, it's a big concert, the tickets'd cost a fortune if I had to pay, but I don't, so –

Where's Lisa got the money from then?

I don't know, Helen said, beginning to feel as if she wasn't getting anywhere. I think she's been saving up. She's known they were coming for months. And she bought one of the tickets for me. I can't say no, Mam.

Helen's mother was silent, then she said, Where are they on? and when Helen told her she said, How were you thinking of getting back?

Helen knew this was the weak point of her argument.

She said, Well, I thought, since I haven't had to buy a ticket, I could get us a taxi.

O no, her mother said right away. All the way from the other side of Manchester –

I know Mam, but I've got some money saved, Helen said.

And you could find a better use for that, her mother said. You could try saving it, for one thing.

Hearing the Irish note in her mother's voice Helen began to feel defeated. Maybe she should try her father after all, her mother was far harder to deal with in a temper.

It's not fair, she said. I bet any of the other girls'd be able to go.

You're not any of the other girls, her mother said at once. I don't care what they do. I know what these concerts are, people drinking, smoking dope or worse –

Mam –

And what about these killings, eh? Five young girls your age, more missing. There's a maniac on the streets, and you want to wander around at night by yourselves, two young girls?

That's not here, Helen began.

Near enough. It's not safe, and you know it. You're not even fifteen yet.

Helen sighed. They were on familiar ground now. Her mother was about to tell her what she had been allowed to do at fifteen, which was practically nothing. But Helen kept her peace for the time being, knowing a stalemate when she saw one. She didn't want all-out war just yet, she wanted to ask her father first, before he came in. She knew that if they got together her father would take her mother's side. She sucked her upper lip and finished slicing the last carrot, then carried the pan over to the stove.

Can I go and tell Dad tea's nearly ready, she said.

Aye go on, her mother said. But don't think you'll get him on your side, she called after Helen, because you won't.

The sun was still hot as Helen made her way to the allotment patch where her father spent his time walking round thoughtfully, removing every weed he saw by hand, digging in, walking round some more then digging in again. His was the neatest of all the allotments. Some of the others were neglected, and tall purple onion puffs rose out of a tangle of peas and beans and shattered greenhouse glass. As she picked her way through the paths Helen felt troubled, not by any one thing in particular but by a mass of things, not understanding her physics homework, losing Sian, having to face the boys in her class again on Monday and the row there was most likely to be at home about the Mean Dream gig. And behind and beyond everything else Carol Fisher lay like a dull ache. She wanted to shake off these thoughts but she couldn't, and soon they all resolved into one big grief about her size. She used to worry that she would end up a giant, but she did seem to have stopped growing upwards now at least, though other bits of her body were still expanding. At primary school she had been as big as her teachers and nearly twice the size of her best friend. Now she was more than twice the size of Lisa who was less than five foot tall and weighed a little under six stone. Helen hadn't looked so bad next to Sian, who was slim and tall, but next to Lisa she felt grotesque. In all her fantasies Ashley somehow miraculously made her feel small, kissing her as men kissed women on the telly, bearing down on them. But now, in her troubled state, she couldn't even imagine this.

Helen's father's plot was the furthest away, nearest the canal. She could see him as she approached, walking round the plot one way then another, digging over the same old ground. She had intended to start right away on her arguments for going to the concert, but as she came up to him and he turned and said, Hello princess, she said nothing, but sank into a crouching position and pulled half-heartedly at a clump of grass.

What's up princess, her father said, and all the things she'd been thinking flooded into her mind and she couldn't sort out which one of them she had to say. Finally she said,

Dad, do you think I'm – nice, which wasn't what she had meant to say at all. Her father looked surprised.

Of course I think you're nice, he said, turning back to his shovel. Fathers had to say that, Helen thought. She tried again.

No, but I mean – attractive, like.

Of course you're attractive, her father said. Who said you're not? Helen sighed.

I'm too big, she began, but her father cut in.

Now see here Helen, he said. You're a bonny lass, I'm not just saying that. You've got bonny pink cheeks, and beautiful eyes, you're like a big bonny peach and don't let anyone tell you different, and he struck the earth hard with his shovel.

Helen felt better. She knew she had nice eyes, large and hazel and thickly lashed, but her father hadn't finished.

All this fashion and dieting and having to be a size twelve, he said, it's all my eye. Don't you fall for it Helen. You ought to be proud of the way you look, not trying to look like everyone else, and he stopped as if his mind was jammed with things he wanted to say, then he sighed and started digging again.

Helen was pleased. She hadn't know her father felt so strongly about it before. At the same time she felt that she had hurt him somehow, or that he was hurt. It hurt him that he thought his daughter was beautiful, but he couldn't make her see it. She could only see herself through other people's eyes.

Helen didn't want to hurt her father, but she could tell he was vexed, from the way his forehead was all rumpled up, and the way he was digging hard into the same bit of earth. She could see she had triggered something bigger than she had meant, as though everything you said these days aggravated the same sore place in his mind. Helen was sorry she had started him off on the old track and she took his arm.

Mam says tea's ready, she said, and they walked back from the allotment together. She didn't even remember about the concert until they were almost home.

Later that night Helen lay in her bed in the room she used to share with Nicola, gazing at the pictures of Ashley she had pinned all over her walls. If you looked long enough in the dim light the faces seemed to come alive and change expression. Helen was glad she had this room to herself now, though at first she had missed Nicky. She had been Nicky's bridesmaid nearly two years ago, soon she would be an aunt. When she was younger and scared of the dark, Nicky used to hold her hand across the divide between the twin beds. But the room had been very crowded with the two beds in it, and Nicky wouldn't have let Helen cover the walls with pictures of Ashley, she would have had her own pictures up.

Helen hugged the blankets round her and thought about the concert, wishing it was Ashley she was going to see, for she had won her battle to go. It had led to the expected row over tea and things had been going badly. In the end her father had said she could go, but she would have to be back by midnight, he would drive her home himself. Then her mother had said he was soft, and Helen had said not to bother, there was no point, the band probably wouldn't even be on till about eleven, she'd have to leave as soon as they got on, and she was sick of being treated as a child. Then her father said if that was her attitude she could stay at home, and Helen said it was typical, when Matt was her age they used to let him out all hours, but Helen couldn't go because she was a girl, and her father said, Well go then, stay as long as you like, I don't care. Then things had taken a bad turn, because her mother had said that that was him all over, he didn't care about anything any more, not even his own family, he wasn't the man he used to be, and her father had collapsed backwards in his chair. Helen had been sorry about the way things were going. At the same time she felt mad enough to burst into tears, though she never would. She had forgotten that she didn't even like the band, and that earlier she had felt so bad about Carol Fisher she had known she didn't deserve to go, all that mattered to her now was to win.

Finally it was Stuart who saved the day. He arrived home late from work, listened to the row for a while, then said he would be going to a party that night, not far from the concert. He could drop Helen and Lisa off and bring them home. Helen was over the moon. There wasn't much her parents could say to that, though she could tell they still didn't like it. But with the ticket paid for and a lift both ways, what else could they say?

Lisa'll be made up, she said, hugging them both when they finally said she could go, and ignoring the defeated looks on their faces.

So she was finally going to her first big gig, though she didn't like the band and she wished it was Ashley. But he would surely come round some time soon, and it wouldn't be so hard to convince her parents then that she had to go. So she only had two problems left. She wanted to have streaks put in her hair before the concert and it would cost a fortune with her hair being so long and thick, and she had nothing to wear. Even though she didn't have to pay for a taxi now she still couldn't afford both streaks and a new outfit. And there weren't many fashionable clothes around for girls her size. She had a loose dark green T-shirt with long sleeves and buttons up to the neck, and baggy black trousers in the same kind of material, but she was tired of wearing them. And the only shoes she had were her school shoes, which were black, but shabby and worn down, or some blue shoes with a low heel that didn't go. She had only bought them because she'd been so surprised to find anything her size in the sale. She really needed something new, she'd have to see if she could do some baby-sitting for Stephanie and Russell, because even though it wasn't Ashley she wanted to look her best on the night. She intended to starve herself – in two weeks she might lose half a stone. She could imagine herself slimmer, in a new outfit with streaks in her hair, she would have to get the money somehow. It was no use asking her parents, that was for sure. Helen buried herself further in the bedclothes and imagined the new Helen, slimmer and trendy, going to Ashley's concert. She could see herself taking a wrong turning in the concert hall afterwards and walking right into him, his look of interest. She could hear his voice inviting her back to the party at the hotel afterwards. She imagined this for a long time, unable to sleep, trapped somewhere in the half-lands between sleeping and waking.

So it were you I heard last night, Helen said. Scrabbling round my window. I wondered what the hell it was.

I knew your window'd be open, Lisa said. But it weren't open far enough. Helen stared at her. I just wanted to kip on your floor, Lisa said.

Helen did and did not want to know why Lisa couldn't sleep in her own bed. She knew she didn't want her climbing in through her bedroom window in the middle of the night.

Why couldn't – she began, then Mr Hill walked in and the class fell silent.

Mr Hill was very serious. He hadn't had anywhere near enough co-operation, and the police would be coming in soon. He wanted the names of the boys involved and he would interview them all again and again until he got them. Anyone suspected of withholding information would be immediately suspended.

Helen's thoughts drifted back to the previous night, she tried to remember exactly what had happened. She had only partly woken up, sure she'd heard a noise, then when she heard nothing more she had drifted back to sleep. But even in her sleep she felt she was hearing noises, and all her old night fears had flickered back. Ever since she was small she'd been frightened of people breaking in. It was a bit of a problem that she had to sleep with the window open but she was also scared of small, enclosed spaces. In the end she'd got her father to fix a window lock that could lock the window when it was partly open. Then she only had to worry about the insects that flew in at night.

Christ, Nicola used to say. Is there anything you aren't scared of?

Now conflicting thoughts were running through her mind. Part of her felt that she should open the window further so Lisa could get in if she needed to. The rest of her wanted to shut it altogether, it was her room. She felt almost sick at the thought of Lisa crawling in whenever she liked. Besides, what would her parents think?

All these thoughts chased each other round her brain while Mr Hill was talking. Helen had started off in a good mood that morning, full of the news that she was going to the concert. She didn't even feel worried about the boys in her class since Matt had sorted them out. And she was right. When she walked into the classroom that morning Morris and Robson ignored her and she them. Even so she was careful where she sat in class so that no one could mess with her bra fastening as they sometimes did. And the whole morning had gone smoothly until Lisa had told her she had tried to get into her bedroom last night. That and the promise of further investigations hanging over them all. They would never be allowed to forget Carol Fisher. Helen wished someone would crack and get it over with; she hoped it wouldn't be her. She didn't know any more why they were all being so damn loyal, except that Karl and Gary had put it round that whoever split would have their legs broken. Helen almost felt that even that couldn't be worse than endless interviews with the head.

After Mr Hill had read out the names of the two people who were to see him that break and everyone else breathed a sigh of relief, Mr Winter went on with the history lesson. Helen tore a sheet of paper from her rough book and passed a scribbled note to Lisa – Why couldn't you sleep in your own room? – and without turning towards her Lisa shrugged. Then she wrote on the back of the note in her cramped, difficult way – They wouldn't let me in. Who? Helen wrote. Your mam and dad? Lisa nodded. Why not? Helen wrote. Lisa paused. She seemed to have to think about this one. Then she wrote, Sometimes if I come back late they won't let me in.

Helen felt as if she was getting nowhere. She was still staring at the note when she realised Mr Winter was asking her a question. He repeated it loudly,

What date marked the beginning of the French Revolution?

Helen could feel herself going red.

1812? she said.

Nowhere near, said Mr Winter. You haven't been listening at all, have you?

Helen was forced to admit she must have missed that bit.

You'd better wash your ears out then, hadn't you? he said, and passed on. Anyone else? he said. Helen breathed out deeply. It could've been a lot worse. He might have seen the notes.

When break came Helen wanted to get back to questioning Lisa but Lisa pulled something from her bag and held it towards her. It was a full-size colour pin-up of Ashley. Helen squeaked in excitement.

Where did you get it, she said. It wasn't from any of the magazines she knew.

I found it, Lisa said, and for once Helen didn't ask questions. She was too busy reading the information down the side of the poster. There were two facts she didn't know before, age first kissed a girl (eleven) and favourite eye colour (hazel). Helen whooped. She turned round flapping the poster at the class.

Hey everybody, look at this! she shouted. Favourite eye colour, hazel. She pointed to her own eyes. Hazel, look, and flapped the poster again and in no time she was surrounded, at the centre of Lynne's group who were all talking at once, and even the born-again Christians were pushing forwards in excitement. In no time at all break was over and Mrs Jordan was walking in – sheep farming time again. Helen hugged the poster as everyone returned to their seats. Then in a burst of generosity she whispered to Lisa that she could kip in her bedroom whenever she liked, she would leave the window further open from now on. So long as she went before Helen's parents found out. And Lisa pulled the peculiar quick face that passed with her for a smile.

Right, she said.

Later they walked part of the way home together. Helen was going to the library for books for her science project, but Lisa said she had to do some shopping for her mother. They walked without talking and Helen couldn't help remembering what it had been like to walk home with Sian, screaming with laughter most of the way. They used to call one another their favourite names, Tiffany and Charlene, and whistle at lads who walked by on their own. Sometimes on Saturdays they would catch a bus to town and go through the big department stores spraying themselves with testers of the most expensive perfumes or trying on the make-up, and then heading towards the butcher's stall in the market where there was a lad Helen liked, and they would lurk around the next stall and dare one another to walk past. Helen couldn't imagine doing anything like that with Lisa. Lisa's mind seemed to be blanked out to anything other than Mean Dream. She didn't even talk about them, but Helen knew that while she herself might take a passing fancy to someone other than Ashley, without betraying him in her heart of hearts, Lisa never even thought about anyone else. She certainly wasn't interested in any of the boys they knew, she wasn't interested in anything. It was a real strain on Helen, who liked to talk, and given half the chance would have talked about Ashley all day, but there was no point with Lisa. It was like talking to a wall.

As they finished the long upward haul to the library Helen could see the valley sloping away before them to the town, and all around them on every side were the hills, partly covered by the houses, shops and streets of Marley. When you walked past them they were just houses and shops and streets, but from this point you could see how Marley was just a thin, lumpy skin over the surface of the hill, the main thing was the hill below giving it shape. It hadn't struck Helen before how Marley was wild and bare below the surface, like the moorland surrounding the village where you weren't supposed to go, or the more distant hills blunting the horizon. On the next hill there was a white house half way up.

Isn't that where Carol Fisher lived, Helen said.

Yeah, said Lisa, adding after a moment, Daft cow.

Helen stared thoughtfully up at the house.

They must have had some money, she said, and Lisa shrugged.

Helen remembered her mother saying they weren't without money, though they never seemed to spend it. They kept themselves to themselves and led quiet, regular lives, always in church on Sundays, and the elder Mrs Fisher used to shop in Marley on Thursdays, though recently she had been taken bad. Helen's mother said that the most unexpected thing Mr Fisher did was to die suddenly, but he'd left them well provided for. But having money hadn't done anything for Carol Fisher. She was just quiet and plain, not popular. Helen had never even seen her wearing any decent clothes, and this seemed strange to Helen, who always thought that more money would solve most of her problems. She would buy more clothes and go out every night with Lynne's set, she and Sian would be friends again. She would invite people back to her house if she had a nicer home. But now she looked up at the lonely white house and thought how cut off they all were, miles from the school or the shops.

She had a long way to go home hadn't she? Helen said.

Umm, said Lisa, not interested. Helen looked at the library.

I'd best go in, she said. Lisa looked in too.

Fat Bag's in, she said by way of warning. Fat Bag was one of the librarians, famous for shouting at school kids.

Helen had come to realise that Lisa had her own name for everyone. Carol Fisher was Daft Cow, the librarian Fat Bag, she called her mother Fat Slag and the man her mother lived with Fat Bastard. Fat was the word she used for anyone she particularly hated, it didn't have much to do with their size, some of them were smaller than Helen. Helen sometimes wondered what Lisa called her behind her back, she felt sure she would have a name for her as she did for everyone else. She had been shocked at the names Lisa used for her parents. Helen herself fell out regularly with one or both parents but she wouldn't dream of calling them names like that.

Lisa said See you to Helen, which reminded Helen about the bedroom window and made her feel bad, then she went off and Helen went into the library. She wandered over to the science section wondering again about Lisa being shut out at night.

Didn't she have a key? And what was her mother doing, locking her out, or letting the man she lived with lock her out? Helen had stopped asking questions about Lisa's family, realising that there were endless complications and that Lisa wasn't going to talk. She did know that the man Lisa's mother called Lisa's father wasn't her father at all but a man called Alan Proctor. He wasn't Lisa's brother's father either, though Jack's father wasn't Lisa's. She had found this out in one of the brief frustrating conversations they sometimes had. Helen had said it was funny that Jack was called Jack Jackson, and Lisa had said that he wasn't.

Wasn't what, said Helen.

Jack Jackson. He's just Jack.

He must have a surname, Helen said.

His surname's Riley, said Lisa.

Jack Riley? said Helen.

No, Peter Riley, Lisa said.

His name's Peter Riley but you call him Jack, Helen said.

Right, said Lisa.

Helen gave up. As usual in their conversations she was left feeling that there was more to find out than she would ever know. She got bits of information from her mother, who picked up a lot of gossip at the baker's, and Lisa herself had eventually told her what had happened about Jack's name. When Lisa had started taking Jack to school the teachers had assumed he was called Jackson like his sister, and there were never any parents around to register him properly. By the time they'd sorted out the mistake the name had stuck and for a while he was known as Jackson Riley, then just Jack. Helen's mother had told her that Lisa's mother was called Christine Mercer and was only thirty-two, though when you saw her waddling up the main street from the council estate to the shops you would have thought she was at least forty-five So they all had different names at Lisa's house. Once Helen had tried to talk about Lisa's real dad.

It must be funny not knowing who your father is, she said.

No answer.

Wouldn't you like to know who he is?

Who?

Your father.

Lisa shrugged. She thought about it for a bit then said, without a trace of humour, I know her type.

Lisa told Helen that Jack's father had been a bookie called Ted Riley. She could just remember him coming round Fridays after shutting up shop. Then one day his wife had come round instead and given Lisa's mum a good going over, as Lisa had said with some satisfaction. After that there had been a spate of men coming and going, and then Fat Bastard, who had moved in right away and stayed around so long now Lisa had almost given up hope of him going. Fat Bastard worked from time to time in the lumber yard where Dawn Langdon's father worked. He didn't like Lisa much but he hated Jack.

That was all Helen knew about Lisa, apart from her being mad on Mean Dream, and Helen couldn't see what she saw in them at all. They were all dead ugly. The lead singer was called Kevin Sebastian, though he was mainly known as Rookie, or the Rook, because of the big black bird he had tattooed on his chest. He was at least twenty-eight, with a thin, hook-nosed face and greasy black hair. He was given to doing the kind of things on stage that Helen hoped her parents wouldn't hear about before the concert. He screamed out his songs, spraying everyone with spit, and was generally gross; nothing like Ashley, who was usually pictured in white, with a kind of mist about his face.

Helen chose three books and took them to the counter, thinking now about baby-sitting for Stephanie and Russell. They had a three-year-old son called Jarvis who never slept, so it would be hard work for the money, but she had set her heart on new clothes and a new hair-do. Stephanie always had wonderful clothes, Helen thought she was the last word in cool. She used to be a dancer and had the kind of figure Helen could only dream about. Russell was handsome as well in a heavy kind of way. They lived near Helen's sister. Helen decided she would go to see Nicky that night.

Then, as the librarian stamped her books, Helen saw Dawn Langdon waving and pulling faces at her outside the window. Helen liked Dawn, who was a laugh, but in the year above her at school so they couldn't be better friends.

What are you doing here? she said to Dawn.

Staying out, said Dawn, unlike some. What've you got? Helen showed her the books.

Dead brill, Dawn said. What do you do when you're not having fun?

They walked back to the estate together. Helen was pleased to be walking with Dawn who was going out with a biker. Helen thought this made Dawn cool, though Lynne said it made her a slag. Helen's parents would never have let her go out with a biker. She told Dawn about going to see Mean Dream.

Yeah? Dawn said. Scud'll be dead jealous. Wait till I tell him. He'll be after those tickets – you don't want to sell them do you? Helen had missed out the fact that the tickets were actually Lisa's.

O no, she said, wondering what she might have made on them. I had a hard time getting my mam and dad to let me go. They think it's all drugs and gang-bangs.

That's what mine think about bikers, Dawn said. And I wouldn't care but they used to be bikers themselves. All I can say is they must have had a better time than us.

Dawn turned off at her street and Helen finished the walk home alone. She went upstairs as usual to change before helping with the tea. Then after tea Nicola called round unexpectedly. She manoeuvred herself through the narrow vestibule and sagged into the nearest chair.

This heat'll be the death of me, she said. She was seven months' pregnant and her fingers and ankles were already swollen.

I want five kids, Helen said.

Wait till you've had your first, said Nicky.

Helen knew Nicky wasn't thrilled about being pregnant, though Mark was over the moon. Lately when she talked about the joys of pregnancy, constipation, and having to get up in the night to wee then listening to your husband snore when you couldn't get back to sleep, there was a sour note in her voice that hadn't been there before.

Eh Nicky, Helen said as soon as they were on their own. I'm going to see Mean Dream. Nicky rolled her eyes.

What do you want to see them for, she said.

I don't, said Helen, but Lisa's got tickets, so I'm going free. And Stuart's running us there and back.

Very good, said Nicky, and Helen nodded.

Only, she said, I've got nothing to wear.

Nicky snorted. I don't suppose you'll need owt special, she said. Borrow some of Dad's allotment clothes and roll about a bit in the mud, you'll look well.

Ha ha, said Helen.

I mean it, Nicky said. It'll be pitch dark, people swilling beer all over you and throwing up – you don't want to dress up for that.

Helen rocked restlessly on her chair. I know, she said. But I wanted it to be special.

Nicky looked at her consideringly. Well I've got a blue dress that might fit you, she said. But I don't want it back soaked in lager.

But you're about six sizes smaller than me, Helen said.

No I'm not, said Nicky. Anyway, it's a bit big on me. I wore it till I was five months' gone. You can come back if you like and try it.

Later that night Helen was almost perfectly happy. She had

managed to get into the blue dress though it was tight and very short, and her bust spilled over the top whenever she leaned forward. But it went perfectly with the blue shoes she hadn't worn yet, and she had a denim jacket, nearly as long as the dress, which Nicky had advised her to keep on. For one thing it hid her stomach. Then she had rung Stephanie and Russell from Nicky's and was fixed up for baby-sitting that Friday. If it were only Ashley she was going to see she would have been entirely happy. Most of the time in her mind it was Ashley; he had replaced Kevin Sebastian on stage in her dreams. She thought about seeing him repeatedly and how, when she met him, she would say all the right things and make him laugh. Wrapped in the moment when she would go with him backstage, she fell asleep.

Later that night, however, she woke up with her heart knocking. She had dreamed there was someone clawing at her window. Lisa, she thought, and ran to open it, remembering that she had forgotten to open it wide enough the night before. But when she got to the window it wasn't Lisa at all but Carol Fisher, her face peculiarly flattened against the pane.

When Lisa got in that night the first thing she did was to check on Jack. She always did this and felt bad when he wasn't there. Sometimes she took him with her, more often she didn't get to see him in time. He would skip school, or run off straight afterwards, sometimes she didn't see him for days at a time.

Tonight he was in though, already asleep in the top bunk, still dressed, apart from his shoes, with a single blanket pulled over him and one bare foot stuck out. Lisa thought Jack was pretty. He was nearly as tall as her though he wasn't ten yet, and he was very thin. He had dark hair and light eyes like Lisa, but a brown skin and full lips, whereas Lisa's face was pale and shrivelled, older than the rest of her. Now she looked at the dirty crooked toes poking out from the blanket and wished, as she often did, that someone would take better care of him. But it was past eleven, she had been walking the empty streets and long blank canal for hours; she was too tired to think about it now. She switched off the light Jack always left on when he was alone and fell down on the lower bunk without undressing. At least she had managed to stay out until her mother and the Fat Bastard had gone. They always went out late to the pub.

Even in the darkness Lisa could see the pictures of Kevin Sebastian she had pinned to the frame of the bunk. There were luminous bits on the pictures: lettering, or strips on his costume, white rings round his eyes. She focused on them until the darkness gathered in her eyes and she could only see the luminous strips and circles, burning in the centre of her vision.

The door banged open, rocking the wooden bunks. Lisa leapt awake in the glare of light to the bump and drag of Jack, swung from the top bunk to the floor where he lay sprawling, almost blinded. Fat Bastard kicked out, there was a noise like air being driven from a ball. Then he was dragging Jack out by the hair, roaring all the time about money, someone had taken his money. Down the stairs Jack went, backwards. He wasn't making any noise but his mouth hung open and saliva ran from a corner of it.

Fat Slag stood slobbering at the top of the stairs, I only said he might have took it, Alan –

Lisa was on her feet now, leaping down the stairs after her brother, screaming at Fat Bastard to leave him alone.

I'll give him might have, Fat Bastard shouted, and he hauled Jack up to the stove. Lisa knew it was hot from the high thin shrieks pulled out of Jack as Fat Bastard pressed him down.

Did you take it, did you? he shouted.

Lisa screamed at her mother, Fucking do something you stupid cow, but all her mother could do was to make a loud bawling noise. Lisa saw Fat Bastard go for the burner. She grabbed the mug of hot tea on the table and dashed it at him. The next thing she knew she was on the floor. Fat Bastard was roaring in pain and Jack slid off the cooker. She could just see him getting himself out of the door, then her mother was blocking the doorway shouting No Alan no, and being dragged aside.

It's all right, Lisa heard herself muttering as she got herself on to her knees and elbows, it's all right. Jack would have got himself away. Her mother was in the back-yard now, crying Alan, Alan, like a sick cow. Lisa made for the front door. Her head was still ringing from the blow so she hung on to the walls as she went. Soon she was on the street again, no one around, a fine soaking rain in the air. She didn't know where she was going until she'd put a big enough distance between herself and the house, then the thought of Helen's house grew in her mind. As she gathered speed she had the feeling of running down a long dark tunnel towards the changing-rooms behind the stadium where Mean Dream were playing.

Helen was sleeping badly. The night before last she had dreamed of Carol Fisher; last night she had woken with the same sick fear to the scuffling noise at the window and the dark shape that was Lisa wriggling in.

Who is it? she cried in a whisper.

Me, Lisa said, let us in. And without a word Helen struggled with the window and hauled Lisa in. But after that she couldn't sleep. Lisa had said she was all right on the floor, Helen had given her the duvet that used to go on Nicky's bed. Then she had turned this way and that and finally offered her the bed again. Lisa said again that she was all right. Then Helen lay awake listening to Lisa's rough shallow breathing. She seemed to fall asleep right away, but it was nearly morning before Helen got to sleep. She woke dully to the sound of her mother shouting up the stairs that she'd be late. The window was wide open again, Lisa was gone.

All day things just seemed to get worse. The fine weather had gone and the drizzle fell so mournfully it made you tired. Helen's head ached, she couldn't concentrate, and she was told off four times that morning for not listening. Lisa didn't show up in school so no one spoke to her at all. At break she watched Sian with the others and Sian seemed to deliberately avoid looking her way. Helen began to feel nothing would ever go right again. Probably Lisa would disappear altogether and Helen wouldn't even get to the concert. She wasn't worried about Lisa, who was always skiving off, she was just pissed off that Lisa had spent the night in her room and then sloped off without a word. When in the afternoon it was announced that she was one of the pupils to be interviewed by the head the next day she could feel actual tears welling in her eyes. And as she packed her bag to go home Sian passed by, giggling with Emma. Helen said, Bye Sian, but Sian barely glanced her way.

Bye, she said, and disappeared.

All the way home Helen imagined Ashley watching her. She was the star of his own private screen, popular, the centre of attention, making everyone laugh. While he was watching she was always at her best, witty and cool. It was as though he had become a part of her, the bit that could only see her the way she most wanted to be.

The next day she tried to get out of going to school. She had a headache, she said, she was sick. But her mother was in a bad mood. She said Helen had eaten too much the night before and a bit of fresh air would do her good. Helen pulled her uniform on and considered walking out of the house but not going to school, coming home later just as if she had been, but she couldn't think how she would spend her day. What did Lisa do all the times she missed school? Helen had no idea. Wearily she hauled herself out of the house.

That morning started just as badly as the day before. Helen got her physics homework back with 'Do again', and 'See me', scrawled all over it in red. She was told off in biology because she hadn't done the science project she should have done in the holidays, and once again Lisa didn't show up. She hadn't turned up last night either, though Helen still didn't sleep properly in case she did. She began to think seriously that Lisa might have disappeared and for the first time wondered if she should tell the police. In French she sat on her own, tracing the graffiti on her desk lid with a pencil. When at the end of the lesson the reminder was given that she had to see the headmaster that afternoon she raised the lid of her desk and traced the outline of Ashley's lips with her finger.

Then, during the dinner hour, the miracle happened. The news spread round the school like fire. Danny Murray, a younger cousin of Kieran Connor, had cracked and told the headmaster everything. The older boys were in the headmaster's office that very moment and Helen was off the hook. She flushed in excitement, as much because Sian was telling her the news as anything else. Sian was speaking to Helen, even though Emma Kirby was right behind her, like a bodyguard, Helen thought.

What about Danny Murray though? she said.

O he's in a right state, said Sian. Mr Hill had to say he'd take him home himself. And he told Danny if anyone touched him they'd have him to deal with personally.

That'll be a comfort, Helen said, when his legs are broke, and Sian looked as if she was about to agree with her, but the bell was ringing for them to change classrooms and Emma was already pushing Sian towards the door. Before she left Helen raised the lid of her desk again, kissed her finger and pressed it briefly to Ashley's lips. Things were looking up.

Then the next day Lisa was back.

Where've you been? Helen said.

Just about, said Lisa.

Things were back to normal.

That night Helen got ready to go baby-sitting. Because she always felt shown up next to Stephanie she put her best clothes on, the black trousers and baggy green top. She lined her eyes with blue kohl and swept her hair back from her forehead with a curved comb. She had to wear the flat black shoes she wore for school, but the trousers hid them a bit, and before she left she unbuttoned the neck of the green T-shirt a bit further than usual. Then, slipping on the denim jacket, she set off.

Although it was getting dark when Helen got to Stephanie's and Russell's, Jarvis was still out in the front garden, swinging on the gate and asking everyone who passed where they were going.

Why? he said when they told him. Helen took his hand and led him back to the house.

Hiya gorgeous, Russell said as she went in. He winked at her and to her annoyance Helen blushed.

Hello, she said coolly. She didn't know if Russell really fancied her or if it was just the way he was with everyone. She knew older men had fancied her before but she never knew how to react. She was glad when Stephanie came in.

Stephanie looked amazing. She had on a black leather cat-suit, skin tight – Helen knew they cost hundreds – a short black leather jacket and calf-length boots. She had dark bobbed hair and vivid lips. Helen sighed in envy. If she looked like Steph she thought, even Ashley might forget about blondes.

You look great Steph, she said.

Ta, said Steph, bending down to kiss Jarvis.

Possums be dud for Mumsums den? she said. Mumsums back soon and possums have a wuverly time. Jarvis let out a penetrating wail.

Don't want to, he said. Don't go, and he threw his toy car across the room.

Baby baby, Russell said, and they picked him up and petted him as he sobbed. Helen picked up the toy car and held it out to Jarvis.

Don't worry about him, she said a bit awkwardly to Russell. He'll be fine. And she took Jarvis off Russell and cuddled him. Jarvis stopped crying.

You've got big busties, he said. Stephanie and Russell fell about laughing and Helen blushed scarlet again, she couldn't help it, though she laughed with them.

Bye bye sweetheart, Stephanie said, and Russell slipped on his jacket.

See you later, he said. We'll be back around twelve.

By ten-thirty Helen had played police cars with Jarvis, read him a story and watched six videos of Postman Pat. While the last one was playing she managed to tug his pyjamas on as he watched, and as soon as it was over she carried him upstairs. Jarvis protested loudly all the way. She could still hear his distant wail as she sat on the settee, ploughing her way through the chocolate biscuits Stephanie and Russell had left out. She ate most of the packet and then felt bad. It wasn't fair, she'd been trying to cut down all week. But she needed something to get her through the evening.

Jarvis's wail turned into a high-pitched shriek. Helen leaned forwards and turned the telly up. By eleven he had quietened down into a kind of monotonous, discontented sing-song, and soon Helen fell asleep. She woke up the sound of the key in the lock and sat up rubbing her eyes, remembering too late about her mascara. The clock on the wall said ten to one. At least there was no noise from Jarvis.

Stephanie and Russell breezed in as bright as when they left, offering Helen a drink which she refused.

Just a cup of tea, Steph said, picking up the kettle. Has he been all right for you?

Helen said no thanks, and, yes fine thanks, and that she should really be getting home.

No problem, said Russell picking up his jacket again. I'll drive you.

Helen wondered how much he'd had to drink, but didn't like to ask. She said goodnight to Steph, picked up her jacket and followed him out to the car.

They were quiet on the way home. Helen almost fell asleep again, but woke up when Russell pulled into a dirt track a little way from her home and touched her hair.

Has anyone ever told you what a pretty girl you are, he said.

Even to Helen this seemed like a corny line, and part of her wanted to laugh, but another part didn't want to offend him.

All the time, she said, batting her eyelashes, and Russell grinned. He always looked to Helen as if he should have gold teeth, but in fact he didn't. He stroked her cheek with one finger and then ran the finger down her throat and round the neckline of the green top. He pulled it away a bit and looked down.

Jarvis is right, he said. You do have big busties.

Helen felt the same queer thrill she had felt when she first heard about the girlie mag at school. She wanted to get out of the car and run home, at the same time she wanted to know what would happen next. She wondered if he would kiss her, and what she would do if he did. It would be the first time she'd been kissed since necking with Christopher Ward at the last Christmas party. But he didn't kiss her, he just went on looking at her and running his finger over her cheek and throat.

In her mind's eye Helen could see Ashley; she was with him in his white limo, he was stroking her cheek and hair, telling her how pretty she was. As if sensing that he was being left out, Russell leaned forwards.

I could do anything now you know, he said. I could rape you if I liked. Again Helen felt the same sick thrill. Just for a moment she saw not Ashley, but a madman with Ashley's face, that man the police were all looking for, who was doing the killings. But they were saying he must have medical knowledge. Russell wasn't like that, nor was Ashley. She heard Ashley saying, I could rape you if I liked, and watched her own reaction, the startled look turning to fear. She saw Ashley becoming compassionate, then tender, she could hardly see Russell at all. She couldn't wait to get out of his car so she could be alone with her fantasy.

Russell leaned back.

I were only joking, like, he said, but Helen hardly heard him. She released her seat belt and opened the door.

Ta for the lift, she said, and Russell nodded. He watched as she hurried down the lane, head held high, hair swinging, locked into her opaque dream.

It was the night of the concert. Lisa was calling for Helen. It was raining and the sole of her right pump was loose so that it flapped in and out of puddles.

Jack was home, but for once Lisa didn't have to worry about him, since Fat Bastard had disappeared shortly after the night when he had held Jack on the stove. Lisa had stayed off school to look for Jack, only calling home briefly for his shoes. It had taken her a day and a half to find him. They had stayed the night in a derelict shop they had slept in before, eating the chocolate and crisps Lisa had lifted from a newsagent's, then she had insisted on taking him home.

I don't want to go, Jack said.

I know, said Lisa.

I want to stay here Lee, he said as she pulled him by the hand. I don't want to go home, I want to stay here, I don't want to go home.

Shut up, Lisa said savagely, pulling him along. We have to go home.

But I don't want to.

Lisa turned suddenly on Jack, grabbing the front of his shirt.

Look, she said, we have to go home. And she glared at him as if the force of her glare could make him understand that there was nothing else she could say. She couldn't say that she would take care of it, it wouldn't happen again, everything would be all right. There was just nothing else to say. And Jack did seem to understand, at any rate he stopped pulling against her and went limp. But he cried all the way home, a hopeless, quiet crying that made Lisa feel bad. And by the time they got home his face was a mess because he kept wiping it with the back of his grubby hands.

Once they got home, though, things looked up. For one thing no one was in, and then they found some spread cheese and crackers in the pantry. And things got even better, because when their mother did come in she was on her own, drunk, but alone. And in the morning Fat Bastard still wasn't there. Lisa wasn't getting her hopes up, he had disappeared before for a few days at a time, but it was over a week now and he still wasn't back. And now she was finally on her way to the concert, the tickets stuffed down the waistband of her jeans. She had kept them on her since getting them, it was the only way of keeping them safe. And now she was finally going. The one cloud on her horizon was that Fat Bastard might return while she was out, but she wasn't going to ruin her night thinking about it. She wasn't going to let anything distract her from what she had in mind.

All the hours she had spent trudging the streets looking for Jack she had thought only about the concert and about Kevin Sebastian, the Rook. She thought about going to the concert and not coming back, hiding in one of the vans they kept the equipment in, going wherever the equipment went, across the Atlantic maybe. At any rate, by the time they found her she would be a long way from home. Maybe they would even let her stay. And while she was thinking this her thoughts changed to an absolute conviction. It would happen. She didn't try to question it, reason it out or wonder what would happen to Jack, she just knew it was going to be. All the time she hunted through the dark streets it burned in her mind like the luminous strips and circles in the pictures pinned to her bunk.

Helen's mother let Lisa in, smiling the uneasy smile she always gave Lisa, the one that meant she felt she should do something about her but she didn't know what.

Go on up, she said, Helen's upstairs.

Helen was standing in front of the full-length mirror, lifting her hair up, spreading it in a fan then letting it fall about her shoulders. She had just had the streaks put in that day and she loved it. She had swept it up and back from her forehead with the curved comb in her favourite style. She had set it in big rollers and now it tumbled down her back in a brown and gold fall. And she was wearing the blue dress and shoes with new tights she had bought specially. For two weeks she had been trying to lose weight, giving half her sandwiches to Lisa and eating less tea. Then by ten or eleven o'clock she'd been starving and had eaten biscuits or made toast, but she had managed to lose two pounds. She had put make-up on, green and grey eye-shadow, the blue kohl liner and mascara and a shiny lipstick. Her face was so pink that that was all the make-up she could risk, but it looked good. She had even painted her toe nails though there was no chance at all that anyone would see them, and she felt great. She turned as Lisa came into the room.

What do you think? she said.

Lisa looked and a different kind of silence came over her. She said nothing and went to sit on the bed. At first Helen didn't understand this, then she took in the way Lisa looked, grubby and wet from the rain. She hadn't noticed before because Lisa always looked like that, but now she said, Haven't you got anything else to wear?

No, Lisa said, not looking up. Helen thought about her own clothes. Of course she was twice Lisa's size, but she did have a T-shirt that was too small for her that she hadn't thrown away because she liked the colour, a pale sage green. It might be too big for Lisa, but it was in to wear them baggy. She began rummaging through drawers.

I've got a T-shirt you can wear, she said.

It's all right, said Lisa.

No really, Helen said. I don't wear it any more, it's too small. Here it is.

Lisa felt annoyed.

It doesn't matter, she said, but Helen held it out to her.

Look, she said. How often are you going to get to see Mean Dream?

So Lisa took off the black, faded-to-grey T-shirt she was wearing and tried it on. Helen hadn't known before that Lisa didn't wear a bra, just a grubby vest with holes, but then she didn't have any bust. Not that that stopped other girls in her class. They wore the Miss Teens double A size fitting, for the newly-developing girl.

Tucked in, the T-shirt looked good on Lisa. It was baggy the way you were supposed to wear them and the colour suited her.

That's great, Helen said. You can keep it if you like, it looks much better on you, and Lisa said Right. Then she let Helen put some of the blue kohl liner round her eyes, and back comb her hair into a different style. She found some blusher she never used because her face was already too pink, and smudged it on to Lisa's face. Lisa didn't resist at all but was quite limp in Helen's hands. It was like playing with a doll. When she'd finished they both looked at Lisa in the mirror.

You look great, Helen said again, and Lisa seemed pleased, but to herself Helen wondered if she'd actually made her look like a doll as well. Perhaps it was the two bright spots of colour on her cheeks. Even with the make-up she didn't look much more than twelve, whereas Helen looked at least eighteen. You would never guess that there were only three weeks between them. Helen wondered if it was being brought up the way Lisa had been, real poor, her mother called it, not just badly off, that had robbed her of everything, not just money. She felt a bit guilty thinking this and wondered if she should wipe off the blusher and try again, but Lisa seemed to like it and anyway there wasn't time. Stuart was waiting in the car. It was time to go.

All evening Helen had been crushed in the press and heave of the crowd, deafened by their noise and by the roar of the amplifiers. She had watched Kevin the Rook hack his way through six dolls as the crowd moaned in a kind of joy, and in 'Peace Between Nations', wring the necks of four doves. Everyone on stage was dripping fake blood and spraying the crowd with spit as they screamed out songs she couldn't hear. She'd been shoved and elbowed and jostled all night, the new tights were spattered with mud, but by a miracle she'd kept Nicky's dress intact. Now she was very tired. The band hadn't come on until even later than she'd thought. There had been long intervals of heavy rock music when no one was on stage but the roadies, and much earlier on an unknown group she hadn't liked either. Of course the crowd had been hysterical when Mean Dream finally arrived; for a few moments Helen had been caught up in the surge and swell of it, she even screamed once or twice. Only Lisa didn't scream. She stood stock still clenching the seat in front of her, shivering like a dog. Most of the time though, Helen felt apart from it all and alone, especially when the crowd kept calling the band back. She had a banging headache from the noise and flashing lights and was desperate to leave. They were already late for Stuart and it was a long walk to the car. As the last chords died away Helen took her hands from her ears and turned to tell Lisa they would have to get going. Everyone was surging forwards out of their seats, the bouncers were working overtime. In the darkness and confusion it took Helen a few moments to realise that Lisa had gone.

From the time of the first encore, when the crowd first began to push forwards, Lisa began to push with them, scrambling over seats to the pitch. The crush was suffocating, she was kicked and shoved and almost trampled on, but she felt nothing. By the time she got to the front there was a cut on the side of her head where someone's metal stud had scratched her, and her nose was bleeding, but she struggled on towards the side of the stage where the equipment was being moved. Lisa was good at not being seen. The bouncers were busy with the more rowdy fans at the front and Lisa crept and crouched amongst the equipment. When big speakers were stacked on a trolley she clung to the front. Then she was being pushed through a doorway into a dark corridor leading down. Before the speakers overbalanced she leapt off and began to run. The roadie pushing the trolley shouted and ran after her but Lisa only went faster, down and down the winding corridors towards the changing-rooms, the thought of Kevin Sebastian burning as white fire in her brain.

At first Helen thought Lisa must have been carried along by the crowd. She made her way to the nearest exit, where bouncers were busy evicting whole groups of fans with big black birds tattooed on their faces, arms and chests. Others left peacefully enough, singing, One Kev the Rook, there's only one Kev the Ro-ok, to a football tune. A great number didn't seem to be leaving at all, die-hard fans milling around in the rain and mud. It took ages for the ground to clear just a little bit and still there was no sign of Lisa. Stuart would be furious, and Helen herself had been in better moods. She had begun to attract attention standing where she was, she stood out because of the way she was dressed, and because she was alone. She had been shouted at and whistled at and someone had groped her bum.

When one of the bouncers noticed her hanging round and said

with a kind of smirk, It's no use love, the band aren't here any more, she felt even worse. She felt like saying, It's a good job I don't give a shit where they are then, but didn't. She thought about going, but felt as if she couldn't, though she knew Lisa had looked after herself often enough before. There were too many rough types hanging round. Helen looked round at them thinking thoughts that might have come straight from her own mother.

When the bouncer came back she said, very politely, I've lost my friend. I don't know where she is and I can't just leave her, she can't get home on her own.

The bouncer shrugged. She's probably waiting round one of the other exits, he said. Fancying her chances.

Even in the mood she was in the thought of Lisa as some kind of groupie almost made Helen laugh, but she stopped herself and said, But she's just disappeared and I'm really worried. What do you think I should do?

The bouncer thought for a moment, rolling a cigarette.

What's her name love, he said.

Lisa, Lisa Jackson.

Well I could announce it, he said, over the tannoy. Then he turned and called over to another man, Hey Phil you haven't seen a young girl hanging round have you.

You kidding, said Phil. Only about four thousand of them out back.

Helen looked at him coldly. I've lost my friend, she said. She's only small and she's wearing jeans and a light green T-shirt. I've got to find her.

Phil looked her up and down, then he glanced at his friend who was standing by and back to her. He smiled a big smile and sauntered over.

Sure you do honey, he said, and I'll help. He put one arm up on the gate post near her head. Stevie'll help too, won't you Stevie?

Sure, Stevie said.

You could come backstage with us, said Phil, and we'll talk about it there. If you're a good girl, he said, we might even arrange an introduction.

Helen couldn't believe it was happening, the kind of thing she had dreamed about so often whenever she thought of going to one of Ashley's concerts. But now she didn't like it, she didn't like their atttitude. Phil slipped an arm round her.

What do you say, he said. Helen pushed him away.

No thanks, she said, and walked off.

Suit yourself, he called after her. I was only doing you a favour. It's be kind to dogs week, and behind her they made yelping noises.

Helen was furious now, with them, with herself, but most of all with Lisa. She would find Stuart on her own, she thought, and leave Lisa there. She slipped and skidded on the muddy ground, imagining all the things she would say to Lisa if she did find her; she could never share Helen's room again, Helen would shut the window every night from now on. She didn't even want Lisa calling round for her any more. She imagined Lisa's white, shut face as she said these things and could hear herself telling her that she had walked straight into Kevin Sebastian whilst looking for Lisa, he'd been dead interested and had invited her backstage, but she hadn't wanted to know. Then as her foot slipped on wet paper and she wrenched her ankle, she thought maybe she'd say that she had wanted to know. They'd gone back to his hotel room together and made out. Then she turned a corner and almost fell over a small crumpled figure on the steps of one of the side entrances to the grounds.

Lisa, Helen said. Where the hell have you been?

Lisa said nothing. Her face was a mess and the things Helen wanted to say were stopped by the absolute bleakness in her eyes.

What's the matter Lee, she said, sitting down. What happened?

Lisa raised the lightless eyes to Helen's face, but still didn't seem to be looking at her.

He didn't see me, she said. I was there, but he didn't see me.

She had run down endless corridors, slamming doors on the roadies behind her, running faster than she had ever run in her life. Then, turning a corner she had run straight into Kevin Sebastian, rebounded off him in fact, and hit the wall. He had looked at her and looked away. He had walked off, talking to his manager. Lisa clung to the wall, staring at his retreating back, then the roadies chasing her had prised her away and hauled her back up the corridors to the pitch. She hadn't resisted so they hadn't been too rough. They had thrown her out at the nearest exit where she had sat on the steps ever since.

I didn't say anything to him, she said. He were right there and I didn't say owt. She paused a moment and her eyes seemed to focus more specifically on Helen. I didn't have owt to say, she said.

Helen didn't know what to say either. She could imagine how she'd feel if she'd just blown a chance like that with Ashley. She slipped an arm awkwardly round Lisa's shoulders. She'd never done anything like that before, but Lisa neither responded or resisted.

Well, she said. What were you supposed to say – Hi, I'm Lisa, marry me? Anyway, she said, half joking, he's probably sick of fans trying to talk to him. He'll probably remember you for saying nowt. Then she said, I wouldn't have known what to say either, knowing as she said it that it was true.

Lisa looked at her earnestly. Wouldn't you? she said.

'Course not, said Helen. What can you say to someone like that? He wouldn't listen anyway, she said, and as she spoke some of her old fantasies seemed to drift away like smoke.

Lisa didn't say anything, but she seemed to be listening. Helen pulled her arm.

Come on, she said. Stuart'll be doing his nut, but Lisa stayed where she was, a dead weight on Helen's arm.

I saw her, she said.

Who? said Helen.

Carol. I saw her there with him. Helen shook her head.

Carol who?

Carol Fisher. She was there.

Helen laughed a bit.

She couldn't have been.

She were. She was hanging on to his arm and he was looking down at her and smiling.

Helen felt a bit chilled by this, and by the look on Lisa's face. She thought it must all have been too much for her.

Come on Lisa, she said gently. Let's go home. You can sleep in my room tonight, you can have the bed. But we'll have to find Stuart, he'll have been waiting hours. She pulled Lisa up from the steps.

For a minute she thought that Lisa still wasn't going to move, she looked dazed, as if the rain had got into her eyes. Then she took Helen's arm, she could feel the tentative fingers on her sleeve.

3
As If the Marks There Were Made by Him

Rachel read her husband's newspaper. TRAIL OF BLOOD, she read.

FEAR of the Sandman has haunted Britain for three years. His reign of terror included five murders and three attacks.

SHEONA Weston – only 14 years old – was the first victim to be found – brutally mutilated – in the basement of an empty house.

ALL his victims were young girls. Sheona was the oldest, and the youngest – little Naomi Shore – was only 9. Greater Manchester's Assistant Chief Constable William Carson said: 'Although the girls were all different ages they were all at about the same stage of physical development – just entering puberty'.

Police have always refused to give details of the horrific injuries to the young victims. But dread of them has struck deep into the hearts of thousands of families.

The official silence has led to grotesque speculation by the public: Rumours were that the Sandman drugged and crucified his victims; he plied them with chloroform while performing his gory surgery.

Most of the bodies were naked and had been sexually assaulted. One – 13 year old Kerry Holt – was raped. All of them suffered multiple stab wounds and were slashed with surgical tools.

On more than one occasion the kinky killer went back to the scene of the crime . . .

Rachel heaved a sigh that was half a yawn and went on rubbing her baby's back. Half-way through his bottle and he had brought up no wind yet. The doctor had told her to wind him very carefully, so here she was at five to three in the morning; it had taken him nearly an hour so far and he had only managed two ounces of feed.

Some babies are slow feeders, the health visitor said.

It could be wind, her mother said.

Maybe he's having trouble swallowing, said Marion. It might be thrush.

He'll grow out of it, they all said.

Rachel stood up, holding Roy against her shoulder, and wandered over to the window. It would soon be light, it was almost the longest day. It wasn't so bad being up at night when the nights were short. She gazed out at the dimly lit yard, the wheelie bin and the sloping roof of the shed, wishing they lived somewhere nice. She sat down again, yawning hugely. Soon the nights would get longer again and Roy was showing no signs of growing out of anything. He was over five months old.

Rachel tried him again with the bottle. Roy's lips closed and he turned his head away. But the health visitor had told her to keep trying, he needed more than two ounces at a feed.

He'll take what he needs, said the district nurse.

It must be wind, said her mother.

Rachel's head began to bob forwards, she couldn't help it. Roy was quiet now, but she knew that the moment she put him down he would start straining and whimpering again as if in pain. And he wasn't gaining weight.

It's probably a bit of colic, the health visitor said.

Wind, said her mother.

Poor little sod, said Marion. Is he always like that?

Rachel had met Marion at Marley Mums and Tots, she'd met Julie there too. Julie was a single parent, Rachel didn't know how she coped. Not that Pete was a lot of use, but she could usually get him to give Roy an evening feed while she got the tea. He had to be fed at strict hours round the clock. If that didn't work they were going to take him into hospital for observation. At first the idea had frightened Rachel, but now she could only think about having a break.

They'll expect you to stay in, Julie said. They always do.

Julie had stayed in with Dermot when he had a hernia and was crying all the time. It was a fucking nightmare, she said. Dermot was a funny name for a black baby, Rachel thought, but Julie said his father had been Irish and he was called after him. Later that day, in only a few hours' time, Rachel was going to meet Julie and Marion at Marion's house. They had started going back to Marion's two or three times a week, after Mums and Tots. Rachel sometimes wondered if she should invite them back to her place, but Marion's was much bigger. Sometimes she thought it was only her meetings with Julie and Marion that kept her going.

Unexpectedly Roy opened his mouth and began to suck again in his feeble way. His eyelids drooped. Rachel held him and the bottle in one hand and chucked him under the chin and tickled his feet to keep him going, shifting his position whenever he really looked like giving up, but she could feel her own eyelids drooping. She flicked over a page of the newspaper. An article on witchcraft in Barrowdale, the satanic abuse of children. Further down there was a paragraph on a man who had rolled on to his baby son while they were both sleeping and suffocated him. I just can't believe it, said the grief-stricken lorry driver (37).

Well it was all good news, Rachel thought, for a change. She chucked Roy under the chin again and jiggled his bottle but she couldn't get him to suck. Yawning again she glanced at the clock and tilted the bottle to see how much he'd taken. Two and a half ounces. She pushed the feed into Roy's mouth again but his mouth hung slack. As she waited her head sagged forwards and her eyes closed. She forced them open and they closed again, she'd had enough. She took the bottle from his mouth and very gently sat him up. She felt the familiar nervousness: sometimes it took two hours to give him a feed, then when she sat him up he brought it all back again. This time however he was all right. He sat slumped over her hand with his eyes closed, making the little noises he always made when she rubbed his back. He couldn't sit up properly, not even with support.

Some babies do take a long time to sit up, the health visitor said, but the doctor said his spine might be a bit weak.

We might have to think about physiotherapy for him later on, he said. And maybe some tests.

When he talked like this Rachel felt a well of dread opening inside her. No one really knew what was wrong with her baby, but despite what they said to comfort her they all seemed to think something was. It made her want to scream at them, to make them tell her what was going on. More than that, it made her want to run.

Carefully Rachel lowered Roy into his cot. Immediately he tensed, screwing up his face and straining, whining his usual tetchy whine. Rachel tucked him in then retreated to her own room next door. She could still hear him. Though the noise he made rarely rose above a whine, the house was too small and the walls too thin for peace. It made sleeping difficult, though as the months had passed she'd got better at it. It just took her a while, and she only had two hours until his next feed.

Rachel kicked her slippers off and crawled into bed next to Pete. She curled up, trying not to hear the broken little cries next door. Night-time is the loneliest time in the world, Marion said. Rachel moved closer to Pete, trying to get some warmth from his sleeping body.

Once Rachel nearly did run away. She had just been to the clinic, Roy wasn't breathing properly, he was having real trouble sucking. He didn't stop straining and whimpering when she picked him up, nothing she did gave him rest. And he was bringing his feeds back all the time. She weighed him, he had lost four ounces.

The health visitor said she would have to try harder to get the food down him.

But I already feed him for two hours at a time, Rachel said, and then he throws up.

The health visitor said that she would have to try him again with the bottle immediately afterwards. Rachel stared at her. She felt like shouting, but she said,

What's the use of that?

There's no point getting worked up, the health visitor said. That wouldn't solve anything. They knew there was a problem, but all they could do for now was to monitor his development.

Rachel didn't want to hear any more. She snatched Roy up, bundled him into his pram and left. She almost ran all the way to Marion's, though she didn't know her very well at the time.

What's up? Marion said when she opened the door. Come on in.

Rachel could hardly talk. She sobbed as she tried to explain. Marion took Roy off her and jiggled him gently.

They don't help, do they, she said. No one helps. In the end there's just you and the shit. And Rachel stood in Marion's kitchen and cried.

Look, Marion said. Why don't you let me take Roy for a while. Just go for a walk round the block – you look like you could do with a break.

Rachel stared at her, unable to believe that she meant it, no one else had ever offered.

Go on, Marion said. Get going.

Rachel went. Down the main road, turning off into a little network of terraced streets, then down a ginnel and some steps on to another main street. Faster and faster she went until she was really running, like she used to as a kid at school, without purpose or direction. It didn't seem that long ago. When she finally slowed down she thought, Marion didn't know what she was doing, she could run away now, just leave and never come back. At the end of the street she paused to think about where she was going, then took a sharp upwards turn and headed towards the little park.

All the blossom was gone, but Rachel sat on a bench overlooking the valley. She could just see the roof of the house where she lived. She looked the other way.

It wasn't easy to get help with Roy, he wore you out, not because he screamed, but because he whined and strained all the time and didn't seem to respond. Rachel's mother had taken him for the odd afternoon, but she worked full time in a supermarket, and anyway her arthritis was bad. Rachel's older sister, Joanne, lived two bus rides away and was busy with her own three kids. Then there was Pete. Roy didn't seem to like Pete. He squirmed and strained even harder when Pete held him. Though Pete gave Roy his evening feed Rachel could tell he didn't like doing it, especially after a long day at work. It hurt Pete that Roy didn't seem to like him, it made him angry. Rachel had sometimes noticed him being rough when he handled Roy, rubbing his back for wind or strapping him into his trolley. Even so at weekends she made him take Roy out for a walk so she could sleep. Housework was a thing of the past.

The light filtering through the bushes was a dappled green and yellow. Rachel leaned back on the bench and closed her eyes. She could hear clearly what the social worker had said, there were people who would look after children like Roy, and love him like their own. Rachel hadn't been able to bring herself to say yes, but the social worker had said to think about it. Pete would do it, Rachel thought. Pete would do it tomorrow, especially if Rachel left. But that wasn't likely to happen, she had nowhere to go.

A small wind stirred the massed bushes. Rachel sat still, thinking that sometimes having a break made it worse going back. But she had better not stay any longer. She should just go without thinking about it, just get up from the bench and go.

Feeling better? Marion said. Rachel followed her inside. Roy was in a baby bouncer, Marion's baby, Kylie, in the play-pen. Whilst not exactly still Roy seemed better than before, still squirming but only whimpering occasionally. He was kicking so that the bouncer moved up and down and sucking his hands. Marion had the telly on. She was the only person Rachel knew who had a telly in the kitchen.

It's the best place, she said. I'm always in here.

There was a feature about changing your hair style to suit the shape of your face. One woman was having her hair coiled into a kind of knot.

Do you think that'd suit me? Marion said, piling her hair up to nothing like the same effect. Marion got all her ideas from the telly, she'd even called her three children after people on *Neighbours*. She had tried all the recipes on breakfast television and the *Good Food* programme. She had made quail in oyster sauce and potato and apple crumble. The kids hated it and demanded fish fingers, of which there was an apparently endless supply, but Jim bore it all with patience.

Rachel crouched down over Roy and stroked his hair.

How's he been, she said.

Fine, said Marion. Look at that perm.

Rachel felt an impulse to pick Roy up, and she held him but there was no response. Are you stopping for a coffee, Marion said and Rachel glanced at the clock. It was nearly time for Roy's feed, but she didn't want to face it just yet.

All right, she said, and Kylie gave a terrific squawk. Marion rolled her eyes.

She keeps doing that, she said. It's a right pain.

Kylie threw her plastic brick at the side of the play-pen and squawked again. Rachel looked round Marion's kitchen, thinking how much bigger it was than her own. Marion's had a dining area and there was a dining-room as well though it was still only a terraced, but it went back a long way from the road.

Sugar, Marion said, and Rachel told her two.

I'm trying to lose weight, Marion said. I do all the exercises with that Rosemary Conley woman but they don't seem to be working.

Marion looked slim enough to Rachel and she said so.

O I'm not, she said, pinching a minuscule roll of fat around her waist. It's all flab. Anyway, she said. How do you think you'll cope?

It was one of Marion's sudden changes of subject. Rachel didn't know her well enough yet.

O I'll manage, she said, then she found herself telling Marion what the social worker had said, about taking Roy away. He'd be well looked after, she'd said.

O no, Marion said, and her cheerful, sometimes empty-looking face became quite hard. No. You don't want to do that.

That was all she said, but Rachel was surprised by the way she said it. She took a gulp of her coffee.

I'd best be going, she said. I have to feed Roy.

He seems all right, Marion said, and Rachel explained that Roy never seemed to mind one way or the other, but she had to feed

112

him at certain times. And it takes hours, she said. She began to pull on his outdoor suit.

Well look, Marion said. If you ever want to give him a bottle here to pass time on, feel free.

Rachel thanked her, but didn't commit herself one way or the other, feeling suddenly shy.

After that Rachel went round to Marion's at least twice a week, and she always took a feed for Roy. Sometimes they watched a video. Marion always wanted to watch *Gone with the Wind*. Scarlett was her favourite heroine of all, she said, because she lost everything but still came back fighting. She had wanted to call Kylie Scarlett, but Jim put his foot down. She still watched the video though, nearly every week, and always cried at the end when Scarlett said, Tomorrow is another day. She talked about the sequel they were planning in Hollywood.

They'll never find another Vivien Leigh, she said. Rachel couldn't imagine a sequel. Scarlett and Rhett would get back together again, she supposed, they might have a couple of kids to replace the ones they'd lost, then what? Middle age, the menopause, how could you make a film about that? She said as much to Julie, but Julie hated *Gone with the Wind*, she said it was racist crap, so they never watched it when Julie was there. They watched Anne and Nick instead, or *Home and Away*. They ate crackers and flicked through the many magazines permanently scattered round the front room. Currently Marion was having a phase on slimming magazines. There were pictures of very thin women next to pictures of very fat ones. Even the biggest T-shirt couldn't hide all Lorna's unsightly bulges, it said beneath one picture. Marion was still on a diet, and thought Julie should be too, but Julie wasn't interested.

None of them work, she said. If dieting ever worked why are there so many fat people around? Nobody wants to be starving and miserable the whole time, that's why.

Yes, but on this diet they say you'll never be hungry.

They're lying.

Yes but listen. It tells you here what you can have in a day. Breakfast, one cup of hot water –

Wow, said Julie.

No listen, Marion said. Half a grapefruit –

Rachel fed Roy and let them get on with it. She didn't need to diet. She was tiny and at twenty-two still sometimes had trouble getting served in pubs. Julie was a bit broad around the hips, but not really fat. Anyway she didn't want to know.

Marion always read their horoscopes in the different magazines, to see how different they were. Rachel was a Virgo, Julie was on the cusp between Capricorn and Aquarius and, I'm a Leo, me, Marion told them every time. Often Marion would roll a couple of joints. Rachel never used to smoke, though Pete sometimes had draw, but Marion said you couldn't do motherhood without drugs.

You could just stop having kids, Julie said and they all laughed.

Well I have now, said Marion.

Both Julie and Rachel were determined to have no more kids.

It's a mug's game this, Julie said, retrieving Dermot's teething ring from the floor for the fourth time. She'd had a lot of trouble with Dermot, first with the hernia and then with eczema, which had kept them both awake at nights. Dermot used to scratch himself until he bled, then the sores infected and life was just hell, Julie said.

It sounded bad, and Rachel inspected Roy's skin every day for signs of dry patches, but his skin at least was fine. She took two or three bottles of feed with her to Marion's so that when he threw one up he could start another one. Marion didn't seem to be bothered about the carpet, she just helped Rachel mop up, then Rachel began again with the feed. It wasn't so bad when she had company, and in the evenings she still made Pete feed Roy, though she could tell it made him feel ill, watching Roy vomit so often. He looked sick himself, white and sick, and they had no words of comfort for each other. They barely spoke at all, except to say who would get the nappies and who should give the next feed. In bed sometimes Rachel cried, but Pete didn't put his arms around her any more.

Marion wore her hair in a short pony-tail from the top of her head. She had a floppy fringe with strands of it dyed different colours, turquoise and pink, and a longer strand at each side. No matter how cold the weather was she wore jeans with a sleeveless vest. In winter she wore one of the quilted patchwork jackets she made herself, but in summer she just wore the vest and jeans with jewellery and sunglasses, even when the day was dull. Julie wore the brightly coloured trouser-suits in thin cotton you could buy on the market for under a tenner, or a sweatshirt with a long, flowered skirt. She took her black fizzy hair up in combs. Both Marion and Julie had more style than Rachel, who wore her dark hair in a simple bob, and jeans with Pete's old cagoule, whatever the weather. There never seemed to be money for anything else, she didn't know how Julie managed. She knew where Marion got her money from, Jim was the boss at the lumber yard, and the house was full of gadgets for peeling or chopping things, or getting cat hairs off furniture. There was a cordless phone in every room as well as a telly, but still Marion didn't always seem happy. One time when they went round she looked really fed up. The house was getting her down, she said. Rachel couldn't see why, and Julie said as much.

What've you got to worry about, living here? she said.

What's here? Marion said. You should see my friend's house.

Marion's friend, Cynthia, lived in an enormous house at the top of the hill, Marley Crest; it had spectacular views and three bathrooms. The house itself was always immaculate, even though Cynthia worked – she was a dance instructor.

I was there the other week, Marion said, and we got talking, you know, and suddenly she said, Marion, what do you use to keep the grout between your tiles clean.

Julie couldn't stop laughing. And I thought life was too short, she said. Maybe she's planning to live a long time.

It's not just the cleaning, Marion said. She stencils her own wallpaper as well.

Julie and Rachel fell about and Marion began to laugh too.

And whenever she sends cards, she said, they're all written in her own personal calligraphy.

They were helpless laughing. Dermot didn't like it and began to punch Julie's knees for attention. She fended him off, still laughing, and Rachel said,

You need different friends.

Why do you think I bother with you two, Marion said.

Still, Rachel thought, Marion's place was nice enough, much nicer than her own. She tried not to feel bad about this, but she couldn't feel good. And she felt worse when Julie and Marion had talked about the things they'd done. Both of them had travelled. Julie had been to Africa on VSO work, she'd met Dermot's father there and later had gone back to live with him in Ireland. She still went there sometimes to visit his family; Rachel didn't know how she could afford the fare. In Ireland they'd got mixed up with political groups and had moved back to England because Dermot was in trouble. In England they joined a communist group and went to Cuba on a cheap trip. But when they came back they got in trouble with the police again. They joined in with a group who were refusing to pay the poll tax and organised a protest against the bad housing on the estate where they lived. Dermot even went to prison for that. Then in the middle of a big campaign against racial attacks on the same estate, Dermot died of a heart attack. He was only twenty-one. He hadn't been beaten up by the police or anything. Julie was twenty-three, homeless, because the flat where they lived was in Dermot's name, and seven months' pregnant. She went into labour early, just like they do on the films. At least the council rehoused her when she came out of hospital, though they had picked the world's arsehole out of spite, she said. And that was how she had ended up in Marley.

Marion had left home when she was fifteen, and had joined up with a group of travellers. Together they had toured all the festivals, it was before the police had started banning all the best ones. She had lived as a traveller for nearly three years and had got quite good at making things to sell at the festivals: corn dollies, painted pots and pipes.

Rachel could see it all, camping by starlight, fires and roasted food and songs, moving on when you felt like it, never being alone. It must have been great, she said, but Marion said it wasn't always. There was the rain and the dirt and the leaking roofs, and the constantly being moved on. And some festivals were sad affairs, she said.

Rachel's roof leaked though, and she never got to go anywhere, they just sat under it. It seemed to Rachel that both Julie and Marion had a past and she hadn't, she had nothing to tell.

All their talk was limited because of the kids, who fell over and screamed, demanded attention and cried, or fought and were sick. Kylie was a big, bald baby, nearly as big as Dermot though she was only ten months old and he was seventeen months. Kylie didn't move around much though, whereas Dermot was into everything. Julie was constantly running after him and pulling him down from the tops of cupboards, kitchen units and shelves. Only Roy lay still, watching nothing. Both Dermot and Kylie were hungry all the time. Rachel watched Kylie taking a bottle, grasping it with both hands and sucking until she gasped. She watched the powerful focus between her eyes and Marion's and felt great pangs of loss. Roy wasn't interested in food or the things around him, he still couldn't meet her gaze or sit up. Rachel sometimes felt sick with dread at the thought of what might be wrong with him. Once she started crying in front of Julie and Marion and felt really shown up. He wasn't doing any of the things they said he should be doing at the clinic, she said.

Marion told her to stop listening to other people.

That child doesn't know he's not perfect, she said. You should stop comparing.

Rachel hadn't thought of it that way before.

It's the clinic, she began.

Then stop going, Marion said.

So Rachel stopped going, because it seemed to her that Marion was right. And she did feel better, though the fear was still lurking at the back of her mind, waiting for its moment to come.

One day both Kylie and Dermot fell asleep. There was an unusual silence, no one knew what to do. Marion rolled joints and got into the pensive mood she always got into with draw. She told them why she felt the way she did about clinics and doctors and social workers.

I left home when I was fifteen, she said.

You told us that, said Julie.

Yes, Marion said. But what I didn't tell you was that by the time I was seventeen I had a baby.

Rachel's mind was a little clouded from the draw. Todd's not that old, she thought.

A little girl, Marion said. I called her Saffron because of the colour of her hair, we were all into flowery names then. Her father were no one, just someone I met at a festival, I never saw him again. Anyway I had her and it was hard going. But I was lucky. I was sharing a van at the time with a family, Sean and Nessa and their two kids. There was always someone around when I needed them, and I did need them. Saffron had three months of screaming colic, she screamed every night from about five till ten or eleven, and she went straight from colic to teething. It would've driven me daft on my own.

Where is she now, Julie said. Draw seemed to make Julie more talkative and impatient as it made Marion pensive and Rachel almost totally silent.

I'm getting to that, Marion said. Our group of travellers broke up. There was a row between two families, I can't even remember what about. Anyway, some joined up with another group, others went to try to get housed. Sean got to hear that his mother was ill. I always thought Sean was poor, travellers never have owt, but his mother lived in a big house near Preston and they went off to stay with her. I could hardly go with them, but Nessa gave me a load of things for Saffie before they left. I think she felt sorry like. Marion took a draw of the smoke she was holding.

I suppose if she died they'd have got the house, she said, gazing through the window.

So what did you do then, Julie said, and Marion exhaled deeply.

It was a bad time for me, she said. I tried to tag on with another group but they didn't want me with Saffron. So one day I left and declared myself homeless, but the council said they didn't have anywhere going. I had to sit all day in a waiting room and at night they put me in a hostel.

How old was Saffron then? said Julie.

Just over a year, Marion said. About thirteen months. Anyway, we were in this hostel and it was godawful. But one day I ran into a cousin of mine who was passing through. It was a real coincidence, I hadn't seen him for years. My dad and his dad fell out when we were kids. But the real coincidence was he was a traveller as well, only he travelled on his own.

Marion paused and passed the smoke to Rachel.

He was squatting with some other people in an empty council house. Col said there were all these families waiting for houses while empty ones stood boarded up and he was right. Anyway, I couldn't leave the hostel or I'd've never got housed, but Col said in the day instead of wandering around I could stay in the squat. It was winter, so I needed somewhere to go, and somehow he talked the other squatters into it. So I were better off than some of the other poor buggers in the hostel. I felt like taking them with me, but Col had a hard enough time getting me in. He always got a heater going for us and if Saffie wouldn't sleep he used to push her out while I kipped in his sleeping bag.

Marion took the smoke back from Julie.

But didn't the council throw you out? said Julie.

O aye, said Marion. Eventually. When I got there one morning there was a big crowd of people round the front door with Col in the middle spouting off – saying things like, they'll keep good houses boarded up and throw young mothers out on the streets, and, who thinks Marion here should have the house, and some people started clapping. I felt a real fool. Of course I didn't get the house. The council had Col driven off by the police and I didn't see him after that. But about a week later I was offered a flat on the Mossbrook estate, like the one where Julie lives now.

Dermot shifted in his trolley, spreading his fingers like a fan, and Julie pushed him back and forwards.

I was happy at first, Marion said. I even got given a grant for furniture. I used to push Saffie round the estate and up the road to the shop and the park, some days we walked as far as Marley. Of course she slept when I pushed her but the minute I stopped she was wide awake. I never got much sleep. But the real thing was this, she said, leaning forwards: no one ever spoke to us, no one at all. Well, except at the clinic, to tell me she wasn't gaining enough weight, and why wasn't she walking yet. I used to see other mothers at the clinic or in the park, but they always seemed to be talking to someone else. In the end it got me down. I used to think every day things'd get better, but they never did. There wasn't a

Mums and Tots then. And you know what it's like with kids, you love them and that, but they're no company. You're never alone, but you've no company either.

Julie shook her head, agreeing.

In the end I stopped going out, Marion said. I didn't want to be out with all the people that didn't speak to me. I don't know how I stood it now, all day on my own with a baby in that flat. She was bored too. I just used to pick her up, put her dummy in and walk round from one window to another. I don't know what I was thinking. Maybe I thought it'd all change one day if I just stayed where I was and waited, and she smiled a pale smile.

The smoke finished and Marion stubbed it out.

Of course one day it would have, she said. But you know what it's like when you're on your own with a baby. Time never ends. So there I was, stuck in.

On the couch next to Marion Kylie woke up and began to fret. Marion picked her up and rocked her.

Sssh-sssh, she said.

What about shopping? said Julie.

O I did that, Marion said. Shops were only across the road. I just had to cash my giro at the post office and buy stuff at the other shops and get back as soon as I could. I just couldn't stand being out.

Didn't it get you down? Julie said. I can't stand being in.

Dermot woke up and right away began to scramble out of the trolley. Julie scooped him up and held him on her knee.

Of course it did, Marion said. There were days when I felt like I was climbing the walls. It got so bad I even went to see the doctor. I wanted him to give me something, you know, to make me sleep.

Marion was quiet for a while, staring at her coffee. Julie and Rachel waited. Eventually she said.

I thought I'd just gone in for some pills, but when I was in I started screaming. Screaming and butting my head into the wall.

121

When the doctor tried to stop me I bit right through his finger – so I were told anyhow.

She stopped and smiled a bit defensively as if they might find this funny, but no one laughed, so she went on,

That's what they told me anyway. I bit the doctor and started shouting that I was going to do myself in and take Saffron with me. All I remember is waking up on the loony ward – ward sixteen. All hanging baskets and macramé.

Kylie wriggled and Marion set her down.

I was in six weeks and at first I didn't even know my own name. They let me out when I asked about Saffron. They reckoned that meant I was normal.

What happened to Saffron? Rachel said. Her head was clearing a bit now the smoke had gone.

She were fostered out, Marion said. And when I got out they said I couldn't have her back right away. I don't think I even cared at the time, I was too doped up.

Couldn't you get her back? Julie said.

After a time, Marion said. They asked me if I'd like to have her back for a weekend just to see how things went. I said yes, I was desperate to see her. I was worried that she might not remember me but she did. She gave me her beautiful big smile when she saw me and held her arms out – I was so glad I cried. But after that I don't know what happened.

Marion caught Dermot neatly as he tripped over Kylie, then paced up and down with Kylie who had started to cry.

I was looking forward to seeing her all week, but when the time came I couldn't cope. I just couldn't cope on my own again, even for one weekend.

She shook her head and looked as if even now she couldn't understand it. I ended up, Saturday night, locking myself into the bathroom with her skriking on one side of the door and me on the other.

She sighed and put Kylie down again.

Of course I didn't tell them that. I really wanted her back, I just wanted to be able to cope. When they asked if I wanted her the next weekend I said yes. But the next weekend were no better. I were crying when they came for her this time and they asked if I wanted more time before her next visit. I said yes and I waited a month, and all the time I was thinking about her, I couldn't think about anything else, but when the time came again I just felt like I was suffocating. And Saffron changed too, she wasn't used to me and my way of doing things. She started throwing tantrums when things weren't the way she wanted.

So what happened? Julie said, pulling Dermot away from the cupboard door. Dermot shouted and kicked and Marion waited a bit before going on.

Well, she said. It went on like this for a while, maybe four months. Then the social worker said that the couple who fostered Saffron wanted to adopt. Of course they would do, she was such a beautiful baby.

Marion looked as if she was getting quite emotional but she carried on.

They were a nice couple, very well-to-do. They could give her everything, the social worker said. She kept saying that. I cried at first, I said I wanted to give it another go, so they did and it was still just as bad as ever. It was no use. And it wasn't fair on Saffie or the people she was with. So in the end I signed the papers.

Marion got down on her knees and shook toys out of the toy box for Kylie and Dermot.

The last time I saw her, she said, I bought her a big doll, it took all my dole. I don't know if they let her keep it. She showed Dermot the big pieces of a wooden jigsaw, then she looked up. The thing is, she said, no one ever asked me if I wanted any help, just could I manage on my own or did I want to give her up. That's what it came down to in the end.

Dermot began to fling pieces of jigsaw across the room. Julie said, Cut it out Dermot, and went to fetch them back.

Rachel jiggled the bottle in Roy's mouth and watched Marion's face.

Marion was silent a while then she said, They changed her name you know, I think they called her Sophie in the end.

There was a silence.

Rachel felt awful, really depressed, but Julie said,

And then you met Jim?

Eh? Marion said, as if coming round slowly. O aye, but not at first. He was a council workman then, sent round to check all the flats for woodworm and dry rot and stuff. I didn't care who he was, me, I just stayed in bed. One time he made me a cup of tea and I thought then that he was coming round more than he should, but I didn't care. Then one day he came right into the bedroom – he could've been anyone but I still wasn't bothered, and he said, Are you getting up or what? And I opened my mouth to say something but I just burst into tears. And then, well, he got into bed with me.

The dirty pig! said Julie, but Marion shook her head, laughing.

He didn't try anything on, she said. He just got right into bed and held me. I must've been too far gone to even think about it. But it was a long time since anyone had just held me, I don't even remember my mam doing it. I told him what had happened and he didn't say anything about it, he just rocked me like a baby. But after that he came round every day and we just sort of ended up together. He was desperate for kids was Jim. I couldn't help thinking if I'd just met him a year or so earlier things'd've been different, but there you go.

It was getting harder to talk now. Dermot snatched a plastic cup off Kylie and she squawked and hit him with her rattle. Julie and Marion pulled them apart.

It was Jim who wanted these three really, she said, picking

Kylie up and standing to collect the cups. I said I wouldn't have any more, I couldn't, but he mithered on and now look at me. When I had the two lads I said right, that's me finished. I got really down when I got caught with Kylie, but I was glad when it was a girl. And now we really are finished. I've had Jim done. And she laughed, but her hand as she gathered up the cups was shaky.

She'll be seventeen now, she said. Just my age when I had her. I think about her and I think, I hope you haven't done anything daft like your mam, ruining your life at seventeen.

But you're all right now, Julie said, and Marion flicked some ash from her jeans.

O yes, she said. We're fine. All set up.

She took the cups into the kitchen.

So don't you go listening to clinics and social workers, she said to Rachel when she came back. They won't do you any good. You stick by your baby, that's what's important. And Rachel smiled and said she would, but she wouldn't have another drink, she said she'd have to go. And all the way home she thought about Marion's story and about what had happened to Julie. It was terrible, really bad, but as she walked home, pushing Roy, increasingly the feeling grew in her that both Julie and Marion had a past, tragic and dramatic as a past should be, while she, Rachel, had no past at all, just an unchanging procession of days making up her life.

It was a bad summer. One day of persistent rain followed dully after another, you only had to be out five minutes to be soaked. When she wasn't at Marion's Rachel stayed in, wiping pots, sweeping the kitchen floor, ironing. She didn't feel that she could call on Marion more often than she already did. Sometimes in spite of the rain and wind she went out, trudging doggedly round the shops or the park, and struggling with the trolley cover which kept collapsing and coming off, flapping in the wind and tangling itself in the trolley wheels. One time, pushing her way slowly round the edge of the park, she met Julie coming the other way.

Get a buggy and see the world, eh? Julie said, grinning in a resigned kind of way. They walked together for a while, in single file because the paths were narrow. Rachel didn't know if they were really walking together or just going the same way. Progress was slow with Roy's trolley cover and the tray full of shopping beneath Dermot's trolley, which fell off whenever Julie pushed it up or down a kerb. They were a bit like a travelling circus, Rachel thought. They toiled on grimly, then Julie motioned Rachel over to a bench in the stone bus shelter.

So what are you doing out in this? Julie said.

I just couldn't stand being in any more, said Rachel.

Same here, said Julie.

There was a silence because Rachel didn't like asking questions, but then she said,

What do you usually do, days like this?

Well usually, Julie said, I park myself on people who don't want to see me and stay as long as I can.

Rachel laughed. She didn't know who Julie's other friends were, and she didn't feel as if she could ask. Julie bent forwards to let the struggling Dermot out of his trolley harness.

He goes mad if I don't let him run about, she said.

Rachel thought about Julie, how her life used to be. She said, Don't you ever miss the kind of things you used to do, the politics and that?

Sometimes, Julie said.

Free of his harness Dermot clambered out of his trolley and ran. Julie ran after him.

Just in the shelter, she told him. Not outside.

But don't you ever think about getting involved again? Rachel said.

No, said Julie, catching Dermot again as he ran outside. You'll go back in your trolley, she said. Dermot shouted then went back to running the length of the shelter, making brmmm-brmmm noises. It seemed like the end of the conversation, but Rachel still wanted to know.

She said, Why not?

Eh? said Julie, watching Dermot. O well, she said, I just lost interest. I couldn't go back, it wouldn't be the same. She caught hold of Dermot again and turned him away from the road. I keep meaning to get some reins, she said. Next time I'm feeling rich.

Rachel thought it was true, once the time had passed you couldn't go back however much you wanted to, it was never the same.

Then Julie said, Besides, once you're a mother you know there's no such thing as power.

Rachel didn't know what she meant at first, then she thought maybe it was true, maybe all the politicians and leaders were kidding themselves about power, maybe they couldn't control things any more than mothers controlled their children. The thought made her laugh, you were always brought up to think someone was in control.

It's true though, innit? Julie said. You can't control the way things turn out, you just have to put up with them when they do. And she waved on a puzzled bus driver who was pulling up at the stop. Dermot made another determined run at the road and Julie leapt up again and caught him.

I'll have to be going, she said, thrusting the protesting Dermot back into his trolley. Sorry, she said, either to Rachel or Dermot, who was howling. The last time I had a good conversation was just before he was born.

Rachel got up with her and began once again the uphill struggle in the rain. She was glad she'd come out now though. She said, Don't you ever get a break?

No chance, Julie said. There's no such thing as a break from motherhood.

Rachel had meant to ask if Julie had any family around helping her out, but Julie didn't seem to want to talk any more.

At the top of the hill she said, I have to go this way now, and it occurred to Rachel that she didn't even know where Julie lived. Dermot was still kicking the sides of the trolley and crying. Julie looked at him, then she looked at Roy and said,

He's really good, him, isn't he?

Roy was squirming as usual, chewing his hands and whining in the way Rachel hardly noticed any more. Sometimes she forgot to look at him altogether, but now she looked and said,

I suppose he is, in a surprised kind of way. In his own way Roy was a good baby.

See you at Mums and Tots, Julie said, grinning as she turned around.

Rachel said, If you ever want to park yourself on someone who does want to see you, you can come to my place any time.

Julie smiled and waved.

Cheers, she said. But she never came. And she never invited Rachel to her place either.

Rachel turned back the way she'd come, still holding the flapping trolley cover down with one hand and steering with the other. Six more hours till Pete came home, she thought. He was out nine and a half hours each day, sometimes she counted the minutes. Not that she was desperate to see him, but it did mean she could hand Roy over. She was weaning him now. The health visitor had turned up at the house now she no longer went to the clinic and said she had to, he was six months old. This meant that she spent a good hour or so spooning in food and watching him let it trickle out again. Still, Julie was right, compared to some he was a good baby, he demanded nothing. And she had stopped worrying that he would starve to death, he was still here though he ate practically nothing. It could be a lot worse, she told herself, and for the hundredth time she reminded herself that Roy was getting older every day, one day he would go to playgroup. The nursery in Marley had been closed down but there was a playgroup where you could leave them for a couple of hours three mornings a week when they were dry. Then, before he was five, there was school. Rachel told herself all this regularly in a kind of litany. Time passed, it just didn't seem to. It was a kind of defence against the fear, always pressing at the back of her mind, that in fact Roy would do none of these things at all.

Rachel let herself in. She lifted Roy from his trolley and took him out of his outdoor suit before hanging up her own wet cagoule. Then, putting off the moment when she would have to feed him, she put him in front of the telly in his bouncer and made herself a coffee.

On telly a man dressed up as a postman sang a song about Florence-Fly-By-Night who kept moving house. On the table was the magazine Marion had lent her, Rachel never bought them herself. There was an article on Mystic Madge, who'd had a string of successes with the Tarot and a crystal ball. And next to it there was an article on New Age witches who met regularly in places like Alderley Edge, taking their clothes off and performing pagan rituals. We do it to celebrate the mystery of life, a spokesperson said.

Marion read all the articles like this, she'd met people just like them at festivals, she said, and they were always interesting to talk to. Rachel thought they were daft, but she did think it must be nice to have a sense of the mystery of life to celebrate. All that stuff was on the telly: mystery, romance, excitement. Rachel cupped her hands round her coffee and gazed out of the window at the terraces opposite. Lots of people in Marley had a view, it was so hilly, but they didn't. She watched the rain drumming against the pane. All over Marley the rain was drumming against the roofs and pavements, there were mothers like Rachel and Julie stuck in their houses, somehow passing the time by until it stopped. It helped Rachel to know that, but she couldn't help thinking that not everyone's life was the same. For a lot of people life was flat and grey, but in some people's lives there was colour.

One day at Marion's house a youngish man opened the door.

Hi, he said.

Just for a moment Rachel thought she'd come to the wrong house, then she heard Kylie's wail from upstairs and Marion herself appeared from the kitchen.

Come on in, she said, waving to Rachel and disappearing again. The man bent down to lift Roy's trolley over the doorstep.

You don't have to, Rachel began, but he did it anyway. He was nice looking, Rachel thought as she pushed the trolley through. He was slightly rough-looking, unshaven, but with very light blue eyes.

Upstairs Kylie gave several loud squawks and then wailed again. Marion reappeared from the kitchen with two men behind her. There was the sound of drilling.

It's a madhouse, Marion said. I can't get anything done.

Shall I go? Rachel said.

No, no. Just come in and enjoy it all. Col'll make you a cup of tea, won't you love? This is my cousin Col, she added. The one I told you about.

Rachel glanced back at him over her shoulder and he smiled and inclined his head.

Kylie gave a terrific squawk which petered out into a bad-tempered cry. Marion rolled her eyes.

She's been like this all morning, she said. I've just put her down.

Rachel pushed Roy into the back room, there was someone in the front.

Just sit yourself down, Marion said. I'll be with you in a minute. Shut it Kylie! she thundered, running upstairs.

Rachel waited but no one came in. She was relieved, really, that she didn't have to talk to Col, she wouldn't know what to say. She propped Roy up on cushions and jiggled his rattle for him. Then she picked up one of the magazines on the table. SERIAL KILLERS AND THE WOMEN WHO LOVE THEM she read.

It was about women writing love letters to murderers in prison. Rachel had never heard of that before, but there were extracts from letters written to 'the Surgeon'.

Hi there Jacko, one began.

So, who's been a naughty boy then? Messing with little girls? And now he's locked up for a long time without any pussy at all to mess with. Well what naughty boys need is naughty girls to visit them. And here I am. Your fairy godmother.

So what can I tell you about little old me? I'm a bit older than your usual type, but beggars can't be choosers, eh Jacko? I've got long brown hair and little tits, as you'll no doubt notice when I come to visit. I can make my nipples go hard for you when we're talking Jacko, I won't wear a bra. I can make my body look like any thirteen-year-old's. I can shave my pussy so it looks like the hair's just growing and forget to wear my knickers when I come, if you'll pardon the pun. Then when the pigs aren't watching I'll move forwards on the chair so my skirt rides up a little bit each time. You won't know just how much I'll let you see, if anything. But if you're a good boy I might just open my legs all the way before I go. If you're extra specially good I might send some piccies by way of a taster . . .

The next one started:

Dear John,

It seems strange writing to you though I don't know why

131

when I think about you all the time. I talk to you all the time in my head and I can always feel you there watching me.

I know this is hard to explain but I know there will never be anyone else for me. Even though we can't be together and we might never even meet I want to live my life as if you are always there. I have always lived on my own but from now on I want you to know that it will be just like you are living here with me. There are two chairs in my front room and I always think of one of them as yours. I bought slippers for you though I don't know your size so I just got slip-ons and I keep them under your chair. I've been buying shaving things for the bathroom and a toothbrush. I know it sounds daft but it makes the house feel more like home and I want you to know you will always have a home with me.

I want to visit you but I don't know what you will think. I am nothing special to look at and I know you like younger women. Sometimes I look in the mirror and see another wrinkle and a bit more grey in my hair and I know I don't stand a chance. But I can wait and be patient and a long time after the younger ones have lost interest I will still be here. I am saving up for a double bed instead of my old single one and some new bedding. And I thought I could get some pyjamas for your side of the bed. If you write back you can tell me what your size is and your favourite colour. I want you to know about the things I do for you and then when it's all done I can walk through the rooms of my house every day and feel as if you are here with me. Even in an empty house I will never feel alone . . .

There was a bit from a social worker, saying that you couldn't generalise about these women, they came from all walks of life, but a lot of them had been abused when young . . . Then a third extract, which began:

When I was a little girl, scared of the dark, I used to dream that the sandman would come and send me to sleep. Now I feel that you have come, just as you came for those little girls . . .

I feel as though I know you in a very intimate way . . .

Rachel had read enough. She felt sick, and angry. She sat tight with anger on the settee, wishing she could just go home.

Everything all right? Col said, appearing suddenly in the doorway and making her jump.

Yes thanks, Rachel said, wishing Marion would come. She didn't want to talk to Col at all.

Is it a boy? Col said, and he walked across the room to Roy and crouched down. Roy ignored him as he ignored everyone. Then Col put his hands out to Roy and lifted him. Rachel expected Roy to start his straining, whimpering protest, but he didn't. He lay almost still in Col's arms the way he never did, even for Rachel. Rachel stared up at Col.

He never usually likes that, she said, but Col didn't reply. He seemed to be examining Roy closely, Rachel didn't know what to make of it and she didn't know what to say. Eventually Col said,

He seems as if he's in a world of his own.

The way he said it made it sound as if it was a nice way to be.

Then he said, He'll need a lot of love, this one, and handed him back to Rachel.

Rachel wanted to say Why? What did he know about Roy that she didn't? But at that moment Marion came in holding a tearful Kylie.

Every time I get her settled they start flaming drilling again, she said. She looked distracted, her pony-tail askew.

Col, be a love and put the kettle on, will you? she said, and Col went out. Marion rolled her eyes.

I don't know, she said. It's like Piccadilly Circus in here!

A man poked his head round the door.

Can I just fill this bucket with water? he said.

Yes go on, Marion said crossly. Do what you like.

She had been on at Jim for months about the extension, they already had a kitchen extension but she wanted a fourth bedroom over it. All these months he'd been putting it off Marion had got fed up and decided if he wasn't going to get it done she'd at least have the front room decorated, something else Jim was always putting off. Now both lots of people had turned up on the same day and to cap it all Col had arrived on her doorstep last night out of the blue, looking for somewhere to stay.

I could hardly turn him away, she said, when he was so good to me. And I haven't seen him for years.

Col reappeared, carrying a tray of tea with a bowl of sugar and a small jug of milk.

Well aren't you organised, Marion said. You know it's great having your own personal waiter.

Col smiled his enigmatic smile.

Have you read that article, Marion said. About women writing to psychos?

Yes, Rachel said. She didn't want to discuss it in front of Col.

Mad, I call it, Marion said. These women, she said to Col, write letters to psychos in prison – love letters and that, not hate mail. They even send dirty pictures of themselves.

Rachel felt ashamed, but Col didn't seem particularly moved.

What do you think about that? Marion said.

Col said he didn't know, some people did seem to get into a head-state. Rachel was glad he didn't say anything about women in general, but Marion went on,

Yes but what do you think makes them do it?

Well I don't know, said Col. What makes people chase after anything that's not real?

Search me, said Marion. Let's have some draw.

Col didn't say much while they smoked and neither did Rachel. Marion went on about the price of paint, but Col didn't even seem to be listening. He had a vague, dreamy look. His gaze wandered about the room, eventually settling on the view outside the window, sky and the tips of trees.

Probably stoned out of his head, Rachel thought, but she couldn't help watching him, the light clear tan of his skin, the brownish-yellow hair. He wasn't very tall, Rachel noticed. He wore his shirt unbuttoned and he had two pendants round his neck, one was an amethyst and the other an ankh – Rachel recognised it from Marion's *Prediction* magazine.

Let's have a look at your pendants, Col, Marion said as if reading Rachel's mind. Col held them up. They were both to do with healing, he said, and the amethyst was also used for something he called dowsing. Neither of them had anything to do with his birth-sign, which was Libra.

Are you some kind of healer, then? Rachel said, a bit scornfully, but Col only smiled.

Not yet, he said. I might be one day, but first I have to heal myself.

Rachel wasn't going to ask him what he meant by that. She was about to say something even more scornful when there was a terrific clatter in the kitchen. Even Roy jumped, and Marion ran out of the room. Col smiled at Rachel and she looked quickly away. She wondered if Julie was going to turn up. Marion didn't come back and Rachel had nothing to say to Col. He said nothing back, but seemed unfazed by the silence, which was growing monstrous, Rachel felt. She looked down at the floor and then at Roy, taking hold of his hands and clapping them together. She thought of going to the toilet and rehearsed saying this in her mind, it sounded ridiculous. Then just as she was going to speak Col said,

So how did you get to know Marion then?

We met at Mums and Tots, Rachel said. As she said it she felt as if it was the most boring thing in the world to say. She felt keenly the contrast between herself and Col, though she didn't know him and was inclined to think him a fool.

Col said nothing, as though what she had said was too boring to deserve a reply, and Rachel said in a kind of defence,

So what brings you to sunny Marley, then?

Friends, Col said. I'm meeting up with a few friends in Barrowdale at the end of next month. I just thought I'd call in on my lovely cousin on the way, and he smiled at Marion as she reappeared.

They've only gone and knocked my shelves down, Marion said. I've told them, they either get them put back or pay for new ones.

Col laughed at her.

Marion the dragon-lady, he said, and Marion smiled in a pleased kind of way.

He always calls me that, she said.

After that there wasn't much to say. Col stayed in the room and Marion and Rachel just couldn't talk in the way they usually did. Marion talked a bit about her new diet, and about Todd being in trouble at school, then Rachel said she would have to be going. Marion saw her to the door.

What do you think, she said, about Col?

Rachel didn't know what to say.

He seems all right, she said. Marion said,

He's a Libran, you know. Very attractive to women, and she winked.

Rachel didn't know why she said that. She pulled a face, implying Marion was off her head, and lowered Roy's trolley down the step.

You know you like him really, Marion called after her, laughing, as she pushed Roy out of the front gate.

After that whenever Rachel went to Marion's Col was there. The builders were there too, it wasn't easy to talk even when Julie turned up. Julie didn't think much of Col.

What a wanker, she said to Rachel when Col called them all manifestations of the goddess in her motherhood aspect. Rachel kind of agreed, but she did think Col was interesting. And it had to be said he was a great help to Marion. He took Todd and Josh out now they were on their summer holidays and played cricket and football with them in the park. He went shopping and even changed Kylie's nappy.

He's a little treasure, Marion said all the time. It didn't seem to Rachel that she wanted him to leave, which was just as well, because he showed no signs of going. He had come for the big festival, he said, at Lammas, the time when the goddess went underground with the coming of winter. Barrowdale was one of three ancient centres in the north west, along with Pendle and Alderley Edge, where the goddess had been worshipped for thousands of years. Marley was an important ancient site too, you could tell from the number of stone circles and earthworks on the hills. It used to be on a direct line of communication between Pendle and Alderley, called a ley line; druids would have lit beacons on the hills to guide the ancient Celts around the country, from one centre of power to another. Rachel had never thought of Marley that way before and she liked hearing Col talk about it. He made the past seem magical, as if a long time ago the earth was a more magical place to live in; now they had lost touch with it all and everything had lost meaning.

Col talked a lot about stone circles and lines of power, and about how men and women today were trying to save the power in the land by keeping the ancient festivals at all the significant sites.

It's just a bunch of weirdos dancing round with no clothes on, Julie said. You make it sound like it's important.

It is, Col said, turning his light eyes towards her. It's the most important thing there is. The earth was being ruined, people were being conned into thinking if they bought the right kind of product and recycled a few newspapers they could save it, that was crap. The only way to save the earth was by a massive change, a widespread return to the Old Religion.

137

Rachel couldn't quite go along with that, but she could tell Col really believed what he was saying. His face lit up with earnestness as he spoke. She almost envied him, she didn't feel about anything the way he felt about his beliefs.

Marion, Julie and Rachel didn't get to talk any more about the things they used to discuss; TV programmes and kids. It wasn't that Col interrupted them or seemed bored, but he didn't join in and he didn't leave the room either, so after a while they always ran out of things to say. Then Marion would start a conversation about something Col was interested in, like astrology, and he would open up right away. There seemed to be nothing he didn't know about that kind of thing: how to cast a chart, the difference between black and white witches, the right- and the left-hand paths. He answered all their questions and never got riled when they laughed at him. But that was all they could talk about and it irritated Julie no end. Rachel thought Julie might stop coming, but there was one of the builders, a young black lad called Luke, who seemed keen on her.

Hi there Ju, he said each time he saw her.

Hi there Lu, she always said in return, and each time he fell about laughing, he seemed to think she was really funny.

He's keen, Marion said, nudging Julie. Julie pretended not to care.

He's just a kid, she said. But in spite of Col she didn't stop coming to Marion's. Rachel knew Julie hadn't been out with anyone since Dermot's father died, maybe she was more interested than she let on, even though Luke was only nineteen or twenty and he acted even younger.

Marion and Col got on really well, Rachel wondered sometimes whether Jim minded. She bossed Col about and made fun of him all the time. When Col was telling them about the Egyptian gods she kept pretending to misunderstand him so he had to explain again.

So Osiris Had-it and Horus Nu-it, she said, but Col only laughed. He had visited the Great Pyramid on the astral plane, he said, he only had to concentrate on it in his meditations and he could see every detail.

Well concentrate a bit bloody harder and see Tesco's, Marion said. We need two packs of sausages and some lard.

Once Col hit her with a cushion and she hit him back and then they had a cushion fight. They ran around the lounge shrieking with laughter while the children and Jim watched. Jim shook his head.

Just like two kids, he said. He didn't seem to care, though he did sometimes say Col should get a proper job.

Pete had a proper job, but it didn't make him happy like Col seemed to be. He stacked wooden crates in Wharf Mill. Rachel knew he would leave in a minute if it wasn't for Rachel and Roy. As it was he just drank more when he wasn't at work, and even sometimes when he was. He went drinking at lunch-times with two of the blokes he worked with when he could easily have come home to see Rachel. And there wasn't enough money for him to drink, they were hardly managing to pay the mortgage as it was. Rachel got at him so much she managed to stop him going out at nights except for weekends, but she still hated it when he came home from work smelling of beer. They rowed about this a lot. Rachel hated the way she sounded at these times, whining and peevish. Sometimes she wondered how she had got to be the kind of person she was, always suspicious, always on Pete's back. It wasn't the way they'd started.

One day they got a letter about the mortgage. Pete hadn't paid it that month though he'd told Rachel he had. Rachel waited for Pete to get in. As soon as he opened the door she went for him, punching and kicking and tearing his hair until he dragged her to the settee and threw her down. Then he stormed off to the pub. Rachel punched the old settee so hard it nearly collapsed. Then she sat down on it, letting her head fall into her hands. She felt an aching trembling in all her limbs. Sometimes she just didn't feel young any more.

That night Roy had a convulsion. When she was feeding him his eyes rolled back and his face turned blue. Rachel ran out into the street holding him and crying. She looked one way and then another, then set off running in the only direction she could think of, to Marion's to use the phone.

Col answered the door. Marion and Jim were out for the night, he said. He was baby-sitting. Rachel clutched Roy tightly.

I need to use the phone, she said.

What's up, said Col. Rachel told him and he looked at Roy.

He seems all right now, he said. Roy's colour had come back and he was breathing properly. Rachel stared down at him, not knowing what to do.

Come in, Col said, and she followed him inside.

It was quiet, the kids seemed to be already in bed. Col led her into the front room.

A lot of babies have fits, he said. His sister's baby used to have them all the time, but she'd grown out of them and now she was fine. Rachel sat down.

I was going to call the doctor, she said.

Sure, said Col. Can I have a look at him first?

He took Roy off her and laid him across his knees. Then he suspended the amethyst pendant over him. It revolved slowly then began to swing in a definite direction. Col held it over different parts of Roy's body, but the direction of swing remained the same.

He's fine, Col said. It's probably just a one-off, and he explained to her about dowsing.

While he was talking Rachel began to feel better, more calm. Maybe she wouldn't call the doctor after all, she thought. She'd become wary of anyone medical, they always seemed to worry her about something. Maybe Col was right and she didn't need to phone them at all.

Col made Rachel a cup of tea and they talked about the way he lived, travelling from one festival to another, selling the little pipes he made for smoking draw, never settling or needing to settle.

But what do you do when the festivals aren't on? Rachel said.

O I've got friends here and there, said Col. I visit them. I do odd jobs for them while I stay. Sometimes I sleep rough, but not a lot.

You must have a lot of friends, Rachel said, shifting Roy from one knee to the other. It occurred to her that if she had to rely on people she knew for travelling she would get just five miles down the road. Col had connections on all the islands round Britain, from Orkney to Guernsey and the Isle of Wight. He visited them a lot. He was hoping to make friends with someone on the Faroes, and from there to strike out to Iceland, even Greenland.

It's a different kind of magic there, he said.

What do you mean? said Rachel.

Apparently the islands around England and Ireland, which Col called Avon and Erin, were dominated by a Celtic stream of witchcraft and the worship of Druidic goddesses and gods. The further north you went the rituals and gods became Nordic, Odin, and older than Odin, the sky god Tiw. All these gods and goddesses went back thousands of years, at one time there had only been one religion which celebrated the forces of nature, then a race called Aryans had spread the world over. They were warlike and had made boundaries between one place and another, so the Old Religion had been divided, the goddesses married off to gods in the myths and in the end the gods became more important. They were given different names in different places, though essentially the myths and rituals were the same. Col was studying the similarities and variations.

141

What do you mean, studying, Rachel said. Vague thoughts of the Open University went through her mind.

Col was studying under the High Priest of his coven, in order to become a High Priest himself. It took years of studying rituals and comparative religion and folklore, the thesis was only one part of the work he had to do. His friend Rupert was doing his thesis on the Qabalah, but last year when they went to Egypt together they both nearly changed their subjects of study.

Egypt was something else, Col said.

How did you get there, said Rachel. She wasn't really interested in mythology. Col told her they had travelled in Rupert's van, where he lived even when he wasn't travelling. They had sold the draw Rupert grew to get to Morocco, then they went buying and selling all kinds of junk in the markets to raise cash. He would like to go to South America sometime, to look into old mythologies there, but the place he really wanted to get to was Iceland.

It's a way of life there, he said. A modern civilisation had developed, but they hadn't forgotten their old, magical roots.

As he talked Rachel felt the narrowness of her life as a kind of pain. She wondered how it was that some people got lumbered with kids and a mortgage and others travelled the world, following old, magical paths. From the way Col was talking thousands of people did it all the time, her way of life would be as alien to them as theirs was to her. She fell silent and eventually Col noticed this and stopped talking. Roy was asleep, still twitching, his breathing loud in the silence. It was ten to ten.

I'd better go, Rachel said, and Col didn't say O must you? or, Stay a bit longer, he got up to open the door.

I wouldn't worry about the fit though, he said as she went down the path to the gate. He'll be fine.

In the end she didn't even mention it to Pete. Pete came in late and fell into bed as usual, she didn't even tell him she'd been out.

When Monday came she went back to Marion's and didn't mention it there either. She knew Col hadn't said anything or Marion would have pounced on it, making more of it than there was to make.

It was a fine day for a change and though there was only a small square of garden at the back they all sat in it, sunning themselves. There was no sign of Col. Rachel felt a bit embarrassed about asking, but eventually she said,

Where's Col?

O he's off to Barrowdale, Marion said, for that meeting, Lammas-whatever-it-is.

Calling up the goddess, Julie said. If she's any sense she'll stay where she is.

Isn't it funny, Marion said, how the back of your neck always gets burnt no matter how white the rest of you is, and Julie said she didn't have that problem.

Rachel didn't say anything, but she felt disappointed somehow, that Col hadn't said anything when she had seen him. But why should he, she told herself, and tried to concentrate on the conversation Julie and Marion were having about health resorts.

That night Pete didn't come home from work. Rachel made tea, feeling more and more furious inside. It wasn't that she needed him to feed Roy any more, these days she just poked the odd spoonful of baby rice or yoghurt down him from time to time rather than labouring her way through full meals, but she was used to having tea-time as her time to be alone, to chop vegetables and make gravy and turn the radio on so she didn't even have to hear Roy. She was furious at Pete for not taking his turn. She walked Roy out then left him in his trolley in the hall and finished making the casserole, turning the radio up loud. By seven o'clock Pete still hadn't turned up and she had to turn the casserole off.

Too angry to eat herself she got Roy ready for bed, pulling and tugging his nightclothes on, not giving him his usual bath. It was funny, when you didn't have a partner you just got on with it, Marion said, but when you did you were watching all the time to make sure they did their share. It held you up in the end and made you angry because they never did.

By midnight Rachel was still waiting, sitting up in bed, staring into the darkness. She heard Pete's stumbling tread in the kitchen, the creak of stairs. Then he was in the bedroom, falling about in the dark because he thought he could get away with it, she was asleep. As he reached the bed she switched the light on full.

What do you think you're doing, she said.

Pete stood, blinking stupidly.

O hiya, he said. I thought you were asleep.

Rachel was so angry she could hardly speak.

Get out, she said. You're not sleeping here.

I am, Pete said. He bent over to pull off his trousers, staggering a little. Rachel pushed him and he fell, swearing loudly, Fuck me. Then just as if she hadn't pushed him he went back to tugging his trousers off where he lay. Then he tried to climb into bed.

She went for him with the hair brush this time.

I said get out, she said. Pete tried to dodge the hair brush and fell heavily across her. Rachel clambered out and dragged him off the bed. She didn't know how she managed it, he wasn't very big but he was a dead weight. For a moment he lay where she left him, then patiently he began to pull himself on to the bed again, clutching at the duvet and pulling it off. Rachel stared at him in despair. She thought of sleeping on the couch but didn't see why she should suffer. Eventually she lay as far away from him as possible, occupying the minimum space in the bed and listening to him snore. She heard the clock strike two before getting to sleep herself. Then she had a dream. She dreamed she was at some kind of meeting with Col, wearing a loose gown. Col stood in front of her and there were people standing all round them in a circle. Col slipped the gown from her shoulders, then anointed her breasts with oil.

Rachel woke with a powerful feeling like an ache between her legs. She clutched the duvet and stared at the dim light coming through the curtains. Pete was still unconscious beside her but Rachel had never felt more awake. After a while she got up and went to the window, pulling the curtain a little to one side. There was the row of terraces facing, beyond them the tips of trees quivering in the dawn breeze. Rachel looked but she didn't see any of this. All she could see was Col's face as he rubbed the oil gently into her breasts.

Rachel stayed where she was, one hand resting on the curtain, only able to think about Col. When did that happen, she asked herself. When did that happen.

CHILD SEX HORROR: WITCHCRAFT ORGY IN BARROW-DALE. The headline was printed huge on the cover of the local paper. When Rachel saw it her heart thudded once then fell and seemed to go on falling. She decided to take the paper to Marion's.

Marion was teasing Julie because she was going out with Luke. He was a bit of a fool, Julie said, but he made her laugh. And he didn't mind taking Dermot with them when they went out, and once he'd even paid for a baby-sitter.

Yes, but what's he like in bed, Marion said.

How should I know, Julie said, and Marion laughed.

How should she know, she said.

Rachel felt bad. She eased herself on to the settee amongst a litter of toys and began to unbuckle Roy's trolley straps. She almost didn't produce the paper, then before she could change her mind she said.

Have you seen this? and took it from her bag.

Marion read it, making shocked noises, and held it so that Julie could see. She didn't seem to make any immediate connection to Col, but Julie said,

Where's that daft bastard who stays here then?

Col? Marion said, looking even more shocked. You don't think Col's mixed up in this do you?

Well where's he been then, Julie said patiently.

Yes I know but – it's not Col, that's just daft. She searched for a reason to show them why it was daft, then said, You've all seen what he's like with kids, he loves them and they love him. I'm telling you he wouldn't be mixed up in owt like this.

Marion looked upset. Julie looked at Rachel and neither of them pressed it any further. There was a silence then Marion said,

Anyway, he came back last night, as if that proved his innocence. She picked up a few toys from the settee. When he gets up I'll ask him, she said.

Yes, he's likely to confess, said Julie.

Rachel said nothing. She was confused by the thought that Col was there, that at any moment he might walk into the room. She hated herself for feeling like that, how could she be bothered with a man who might be mixed up in something terrible, and for a moment she thought of those daft women who wrote love letters to murderers. She shook her head as if trying to dislodge the thought. They were mad. She wasn't like that.

Marion finished picking up the toys and dropped them into the box.

I'll make some coffee, she said, and disappeared. Rachel could tell that really Julie wanted to leave, but neither of them wanted to offend Marion again. Julie looked at the paper.

A bad do, eh? she said.

What do you think, Rachel said, meaning what did she think about Col.

I don't know, Julie said. I never thought he was a bad bloke, just daft. She broke off as Marion re-entered the room carrying mugs.

Eh, she said, did you hear that Linda Brooke's having triplets? and the subject seemed to be closed.

But later Col got up.

Morning everyone, he said, stretching. Then he said, What's up?

Rachel couldn't look at him. Marion said,

Nothing's up, we were just looking through the papers, and she handed Col the newspaper Rachel had brought.

Col looked at it and laughed.

O shit, he said. Then he looked at them all with an odd expression on his face. Got you worried, did it?

No, Marion said. Of course it didn't. We just wanted to ask you what you thought, that's all.

Col sat down. He read a bit more of the paper then he said, Look.

He was talking to Marion.

You know what it's like. You get a group of people who don't live like anyone else and no one trusts them. No one wants them around. You know what it's like for travellers, as soon as they park somewhere the rumours start, things've been stolen, or vandalised –

That's hardly the same, Julie said, but Col said, Yes it is, it's exactly the same. They just like us even less than travellers.

No one said anything and Col looked at them all. He looked as if his mind were full of things to say, then he got up and walked to the window.

How can you believe anything it says in the papers? he said, turning round. They're all full of shit. He was still speaking to Marion but she didn't look at him. He walked back again and as he passed Julie she caught the paper off him.

Two children were found naked, tied together and smeared with chicken blood, she read. Who's going to make up something like that?

147

So what are you saying? Col said. He seemed angry now, then suddenly he sat down again.

Look, he said. This has all happened before, all of it. Five hundred years ago they'd be telling you witches had sex with the devil and you'd be sitting there, believing them. Now it's kids. It's just the worst thing they can think of, that's all. Because they're scared. Scared shitless of anything that threatens their precious society, their Christian society. He said it as if there was a bad taste in his mouth. Where are these kids, eh? he said, flapping the paper at them. Where's the proof? They can write anything they like in the paper and people think it's true. It's just like Hitler and the Jews. They can make you believe anything in the end, because no one knows what's real.

Col stopped and no one else spoke. Then he said,

I'm wasting my time. Rachel looked at Marion. Marion got up, wiping her hands on a tea-towel.

Don't be daft, Col, she said, but she still wasn't looking at him. I'll get you some breakfast.

I'll help, Julie said, hurrying after her.

Col looked at Rachel.

So what do you think? he said. Rachel didn't know what she thought, but she did feel sorry for Col in a way. He had no way of making people believe what he said. For the first time she saw there were disadvantages to being free, you never got close enough for anyone to trust you.

It's all lies in the papers, Col said, and Rachel half believed him. She said, Will the police be looking for you?

Col shrugged. They don't know what they're looking for, he said. They probably think we're all on broomsticks.

Rachel said they'd probably be looking for people who were passing through the area, but Col didn't seem worried. He said he was clearing out anyway. He had some business down south, in Cornwall.

I'll be coming back though, he said, turning his mild, light eyes towards her. And Rachel whose heart had sunk when Col said he was leaving felt it leap again.

Daft, she told herself. Just bloody stupid.

Marion and Julie came back carrying tea and toast and talking about dreadlocks. Julie was thinking about having some put in and Marion said she fancied them too.

We could have them done together, she said.

Yes, and then we'd look like twins, said Julie, and they laughed. They talked about Marion's knitting and the new extension, and the injections Dermot had just had, months late. Rachel said she was still waiting for Roy's six-month assessment, he was getting on for eight months now. As usual when the conversation had nothing to do with the things he was interested in, Col was silent. Rachel fell silent too, waiting for an opportunity to leave. As soon as she could she said she would have to be going. Col stood up to open the door for her as she pushed the trolley through, but she didn't look at him at all.

How could it happen? she thought. How could it happen to her?

She thought about Col all day and most of the night. She planned what she would say when she saw him again, how she would act. She got depressed because she didn't know if she would see him again. Then she got angry because she was getting into a state over someone she hardly knew; when he came back she wouldn't go round at all. Then she got depressed again, because no matter what she said or did, whether she went round to Marion's or not, it would make no difference. Col wouldn't notice, he had never given her any reason to think he might be interested. Then the next minute she felt the look he gave her when he told her he was coming back and was chilled by a feeling that was most like fear. But it was daft to feel like that, nothing could happen between them, he lived his life, she lived hers. And apart from anything else, there was Pete.

149

They were making love again, when he wanted to. She didn't want sex with Pete but it didn't matter. It was like the way she was living the rest of her life, washing, changing and feeding Roy, Hoovering the carpets. She didn't want the sex she could have, she wanted the unfamiliar, unrealised sex of her dream.

Pete was happier now they were having sex. He stayed out less and began to help out more round the house. Rachel hardly noticed. She looked out of the window at the terraces opposite and saw the pyramids of Egypt, the ziggurats of ancient Babylon and the great carved mountain temples of the Incas. She stopped going to Marion's out of fear of seeing Col unexpectedly, so one day was no different from another. When she got up she worked out the hours and minutes till she could go to bed again. She put Roy in his bouncer in front of the telly and marked off time in her mind. After a coffee, sipped slowly, she would do some ironing. She could spin that out till about ten, then she would wash up and maybe have another coffee. She would feed Roy and change him and take him to the shops. She didn't want anything but she could look round them all, slowly. In the afternoon she would sweep some leaves from the yard, watch the afternoon soap and think about tea. It was hard to make the list of things in her mind spin out to take up the full nine and a half hours Pete was away. Sometimes she miscalculated the length of time it would take her to do something and was left with several minutes in which she had nothing to do. All the time she felt as if she were waiting, waiting for Roy to finish his breakfast, waiting for the shops to open, a television programme to start, waiting for Pete to come home so that finally she could go to bed. Roy was seven and a half months old, she told herself. When he was two and a half he could go to playgroup, when he was four years, seven and a half months old he would go to school. That was the way she lived her life, spinning out the jobs she had to do, marking intervals of time in her mind. Sometimes she felt as if that was all she did: mark time.

*

150

Julie caught up with her near the shops. I thought you'd moved, she said. Rachel murmured something about Roy not being well.

Why? said Julie. What's wrong?

It was difficult to think, to break through the frozen, unreal quality of her day. She told Julie about the clinic: they had finally called Roy in for his six-month assessment and the new doctor had gone mad. Roy couldn't sit up, reach for things, focus or smile.

That child should have been in hospital months ago, he said. He would arrange it immediately. Rachel was still waiting for the card to tell them to go, but he had said immediately.

O well then, Julie said. It's bound to be some time before he's twenty-one. Then unexpectedly she linked Rachel.

Don't worry, she said. They'll sort him out.

Rachel couldn't explain that she didn't feel worried any more, none of it seemed to matter.

Anyway, Julie said, if you are worried that's all the more reason for you to come round. There's nothing worse than staying in on your own, brooding.

Rachel didn't ask if Col was back.

Julie said, Why don't you come round now? Rachel said she couldn't, she had to get back.

What for? said Julie, and Rachel, improvising, said her mother was coming round.

Come tomorrow then, Julie said, and Rachel said she'd try. They walked together and Julie told Rachel she'd finished with Luke, he was driving her daft, but she had met a new bloke in the pub where she went sometimes on the nights when they had a band. He was called Keith, he was older than Julie, thirty-four, and he had two kids of his own, only they didn't live with him.

He keeps asking me out, Julie said. Rachel nodded and

smiled. At the Junction Inn where the road forked Julie took one road and Rachel another.

See you tomorrow, Julie said. At Marion's. I'll expect to see you.

At home Rachel stood at the window holding Roy against her shoulder. She stroked his back gently to bring up the wind. He struggled and strained less these days, he'd gone almost limp. She looked out at the hazy day and the narrow street, thinking about places she would never see. She wandered over to another window and looked out at her back yard, remembering what Marion he said about the days when she used to wander from one window of her flat to another with Saffron. But she didn't want to see Col, she thought. Then she thought, what did it matter, whether she saw Col or not? Nothing would happen. Nothing ever happened in Rachel's life.

Hello stranger, Marion said, and Rachel manoeuvred the push-chair through the door. Julie said she'd seen you.

Rachel felt awkward now she was here, there was the feeling like fear at the back of her neck. The trolley tangled with the draught excluder on the way into the lounge. He probably wasn't even there, she told herself.

Hello stranger, Julie said. You've come at the right time. Col was just telling us about sex magic.

Rachel wouldn't look at Col. She bent to unfasten the straps on Roy's trolley.

He's thinking of doing a book. Aren't you Col? Julie said. Ceremonial sex for beginners, with an introduction for wankers only.

Col looked amused. He never seemed to get riled by Julie's remarks.

What's this? Rachel said, looking at Julie and sitting down with Roy on her knee.

152

I was just explaining, Col said, the role of sex in magic ritual. And the way it gets misinterpreted, he said, aiming a kick at Julie's foot. Julie tolerated this quite well, as if they had been getting on better in Rachel's absence.

Well go on then, Marion said from the doorway. Tell us.

Col told them that the purpose of sexual magic was to incarnate the god within. It could only happen when there was a perfect blend of male and female energies.

So what happens when you've incubated the god, Marion said.

Incarnated, Julie said. It's not like hatching an egg, is it Col?

Incarnated then, Marion said, and Col said, When you'd done that, if you ever managed it – it was a lifetime's work – but if you did it you achieved knowledge of your true self.

So you have to spend a lifetime bonking, Marion said.

Julie said, What if you're gay?

What is it like then, your true self? said Marion.

Col said it didn't matter if you were gay, the male and female energies were inside. And he didn't know what his true self was like because he hadn't got there yet. But he did know it was godlike.

We're all of us gods, he said. And goddesses.

Well I know I am, Marion said. But I didn't think you were, she said to Julie.

Col said they all were, and when the male and the female came together, and were really together, they produced a divine energy.

O so you've both got to come at the same time, Julie said, and Rachel laughed in an embarrassed kind of way.

No, Col said. In fact, most of the time you're not supposed to come at all.

O well then, Marion said. I think I've managed it already.

You have to channel your energy, Col said. You had to reach

heights of ecstasy without losing control, then at the moment of release the god could be born.

Some people were at it for days, he said.

Well it sounds more fun than Sunday school, Julie said, and Col said that was definitely true. But that had been one of the main aims of Christianity, to suppress sex and make it a sin. The old church leaders knew its real potential but they wanted to keep people slaves.

If everyone practised sex this way, Col said, it would be a society of masters and equals.

A society of people with sore bits, Marion said. At it for days, but Col ignored her.

It's true, isn't it? he said. If you're a Christian you're not supposed to be equal to God, not even after death. The angels who said they were got kicked out of heaven, didn't they? It's a sin to go after your real potential, so no one ever does. Which one of you thinks you've got to your real potential, eh?

He looked at them all and Rachel looked at Julie. She was fending off Dermot who wouldn't play with his toys. He played for about a minute then ran to Julie, drumming his boots against her shins and, when she sat him on her knee, tugging at her hair. Don't, Dermot, she kept saying to him and, to them all, He's in a right mood today.

Dermot was twenty months old, in a few months' time he could go to playgroup, then Julie would be free for a couple of hours, three mornings a week. And probably, Rachel thought, she would carry on doing exactly the same things, coming round to Marion's for coffee then collecting Dermot and touring round the shops. Because what else was there to do? Things had been different before, she used to travel about and fight political causes, but now she was a mother. She had the same worn-down, resigned look of all mothers, the look of patience you had because you spent your life waiting, waiting for your kids to stop crying, to go to sleep, to grow up. It changed you for good, Julie would never go back to the way she used to be. Probably in the end she would have another child, that was what people did when they couldn't think of anything else to do, like Marion. Rachel thought of Marion, with her magazines and gadgets, hair dyes and diets, different from the old Marion who ran away from home and travelled and left a child, but probably not much happier in the end. Then there was Rachel of course, but Rachel didn't even want to start thinking about herself. She went back to listening to Col.

Not only are you supposed to find your true potential, he was saying, you're not even supposed to know about it. When man ate of the tree of knowledge that was it – wham bam thank you mam – chucked out of Eden into the eternal fall. So knowledge is a sin and sex is a sin and we're all slaves. It's freedom people are really scared of, Col said.

Marion said she didn't think sex was a sin any more, it was on telly all the time, but Col said that was just the same thing: because people thought sex was dirty it sold – books, films, magazines, anything, and the papers were all full of scandal. That wasn't what witches meant by sex. To them sex had a higher purpose, even than reproduction, which was what Christians said it was for. Christians couldn't handle the idea of anyone having sex for any other reason, so whenever they talked about witches, right through the ages, they talked orgies and pornography.

And now it's child abuse, he said. Whatever's the worst crime of the moment . . .

There was a pause because no one wanted to remember what it said in the newspaper, then Julie said,

So what do you do at these ceremonies then?

Col said it was only at special ceremonies, not all of them, and you always worked with one partner, either privately or in front of the coven.

You mean everyone watches, Marion said, and Julie said, Sounds kinky to me.

Col said that most were private, but at the Great Sabbat, the union of the High Priest and Priestess was essential for the celebration of all life. The coven made a circle round them and the High Priest took the robe off the Priestess and anointed her breasts with oil. He said some more, about kissing the points of power on the Priestess's body, and Julie and Marion made loud noises of appreciation, but Rachel was absolutely quiet.

Yes, Col was saying. You're taking the piss because you can't handle it, but it's not like that. Everyone's naked and it's very formal. There's nothing sexy about a group of naked people you know.

Rachel cut across him.

So who chooses the High Priestess then?

Julie and Marion laughed.

Why, are you thinking about applying for the job? Julie said, but Col said she was usually someone who had been through all the grades of apprenticeship, it took years.

They don't ever choose anyone outside the coven, then? Rachel said.

Col said that happened very rarely, the High Priest might choose someone from outside if he thought she was specially receptive, or his true partner, someone he needed to work with.

Suppose she didn't want to work with him? Rachel said. She was aware of herself sounding hostile and sharp, but she had to know.

Col said the Great Rite couldn't be performed without the consent of both partners, of course it couldn't, but it could be done inwardly, on the level of the soul.

Might you dream about it then? Rachel said. She was looking at him very hard and Col looked back.

Possibly, he said.

What I want to know is – Marion began, but Rachel interrupted her.

What does that mean then? she said.

What? said Col.

What does it mean if someone chooses someone else and does the ceremony with them and they're not even there?

Col said again that it couldn't be done without the person's permission, there was always consent on the level of the soul.

But what does it mean? Rachel said. She was aware of Julie and Marion looking at them both but she wasn't going to give up now.

Col looked at Rachel, then he looked at Julie and Marion, turning the pressure down.

If you're chosen to be a Priestess, he said to all of them, you're bound for life. All other ties gradually become unimportant.

Rachel sank back on the chair. It was hard to take in what he was telling her. She felt as if he had told her too much and not enough.

Col was saying that though you could do ceremonies on the inner level of the soul, it was always better to use the body, that way you earthed the energies. Christians thought that the body was inferior to the soul but in witchcraft it was just as important. The spiritual had to be balanced with the physical, that was the important thing.

I have to go, Rachel said.

What, now? said Marion.

Pete's home early, Rachel said. I have to get his dinner. She was already pulling the trolley out of the rooms. Col got up.

I'll see myself out, she said. Col followed her anyway.

Look, he said. I hope I didn't upset you with any of that.

Rachel said nothing, but struggled with the lock on the door, which was stiff. Col took her arm but she shook him off.

What've you been playing at, she said.

Nothing, Col said. I'm not playing at anything. I just had a dream about you, that's all.

Rachel stared at him.

I could tell you knew what I was talking about in there, he said. Did you dream about it too?

Rachel wouldn't talk to him. She turned away again and tugged the door open.

Sometimes it happens like that, Col said. Look, you're worried about it now, because you don't understand. Why don't you come round sometime and we can talk it over?

Rachel felt as if she didn't want to know any more. Then she felt that if something was messing with her head she ought to know more about it.

I don't know, she said, lowering the trolley down the step.

Come next Friday, Col said. I'm baby-sitting. Marion and Jim'll be out. You can bring Roy.

Why do you want me to bring Roy? Rachel said, facing him. Col rolled his eyes.

Well don't bring him then, he said. I just thought it'd be easier for you, that's all.

Rachel turned again and pushed the trolley towards the gate.

Look, Col said, whatever you decide, it's up to you. I don't want to put pressure on you either way. It's your choice.

That's right, Rachel said, and she pushed the trolley out of the gate, on to the pavement and across the road.

So how long has your little boy been like this? said the consultant.

Rachel sat next to Roy's cot in the cubicle set apart from the rest of the ward and remembered the interview she wanted to forget.

I don't know really, she'd said, and the consultant tried not to look scandalised. She couldn't explain to him that she'd wanted

158

to stop comparing Roy to other children, she'd long ago stopped reading the charts that told you what babies were supposed to do and when. She wanted to accept him as he was.

The consultant thought she was stupid, she could tell.

I have to tell you, he said, that his condition is very serious. And in Rachel's stomach all the old, sick fear returned.

Through the windows of the cubicle she could see Val, mother of Robert. Robert had cystic fibrosis. Val sat by his bed all day, moving his limbs and massaging them, propping him up when his breathing was bad, marking down on a chart when there was blood in his shit. She had done this every day, for most of his ten years.

Rachel had been in hospital nearly two weeks. Time had taken on an unreal quality, it felt as if she had always been there. She stayed in the room set aside for mothers: it had nine beds with pink flowery duvets, a shower room and a tiny kitchen leading off. The kitchen had a fridge, a cupboard and a kettle. Rachel had stopped eating canteen food, it cost too much. She bought in supplies from the shop near the hospital – bread and apples and spread cheese, margarine and biscuits and tea. Sometimes she went to the canteen with other mothers and ate her food there. Once or twice she'd noticed another woman, foreign-looking, who sat on her own.

That's Sonia, Ellie said. Her little girl's in intensive care.

After a few days Rachel didn't see her any more and eventually she asked Ellie, who seemed to know everything. Ellie told her that Sonia's little girl had died in the night, they had known it would happen, Sonia had sat up all night with the nurses, waiting.

Rachel absorbed the horror of these things, the details of illness and suffering silently, like a sponge. She could never let them go, but it was as though they remained in a compartment of her mind without affecting the rest of her, which went on waiting, waiting all the time to be set free. Yet sometimes, like now, as she watched Val wiping the vomit and phlegm from Robert's face, the horror surged violently as it had when the consultant spoke.

She said nothing as he told her what he thought was wrong, and she left his room quietly, but in her mind she was shouting, No, and running, just running in any direction at all. She didn't go back to the ward. She went to stand by the double doors marked Exit while she brought her breathing under control, and gazed out at the car-park and the field beyond, the trees. She stood and watched people come and go and told herself that she would leave too, she would just walk out and leave, then she hurried all the way back to the ward.

People live in chains, Col said, because they're afraid to be free.

Rachel sat in Roy's cubicle and stared at his crumpled body in the cot, the tubes to help him breathe. All the old, dry, pounding terror had returned. She couldn't remember the name of the illness Roy's consultant thought he had. It wasn't cystic fibrosis, like Robert, and it wasn't spina bifida, they tested you for that when you were pregnant. He didn't have the same problem as Ellie's little girl, Matilda, who'd had fourteen operations on her bowel. Ellie always managed to look cheerful, but Rachel couldn't stand it, she just couldn't cope. Now they had given it a name she felt as if a sentence had been pronounced. But she couldn't remember what the name was, or what it meant, except that it was some kind of disease of the nervous system, rare in babies, and the chances of survival were uncertain.

Rachel clutched at the bars of Roy's cot and sobbed once, twice, dry harsh sobs. She didn't know what it all meant but she did know her life was being swallowed by her baby's illness, like Val's had been, and it wasn't fair. That was what the fear was, that there would be nothing of Rachel left. And she remembered what Julie had said about babies: they were little vampires who sucked you hollow.

160

Rachel pressed her head against the bars of the cot and looked at Roy. She watched the movements of the fingers which were never still, even when he slept. She'd always thought he had beautiful hands. In the back of her mind she'd always held on to the thought that one day Roy would be all right, he would grow out of whatever he had, it was just a phase. One day he would be just like any other child, he'd go to playgroup, then school. It was impossible to make sense of her life without this thought. And she reminded herself that the consultant didn't really know yet, they hadn't done the final tests because they'd run out of serum and something else, they couldn't be sure for at least another week. So she didn't have to believe it and she didn't have to tell anyone anything because nothing was certain. She didn't have to tell Pete.

Slowly Rachel began to feel better. She raised her head from the bars of the cot and looked at Thomas, the other little boy in the cubicle. He had some kind of brain damage and had to be fed through a tube into his stomach. No one visited him at all. This bothered Rachel a lot at first, then she saw how the nurses took care of him. He was in the special care of two of them, they washed him down and fed the food through the tube, they stretched plastic toys across his cot, played the musical mobiles for him and talked to him whenever they could. One nurse came over from another ward just to see him, she held him and sang him songs. To Rachel he didn't seem to respond to any of this but they did it anyway. Sometimes when she watched them she thought that it would be all right to leave Roy, just leave and never come back, because someone would be there to love him.

Other babies came and went. Max, who was only four months old, had gallstones and was in five days. Trudi had a fractured skull, but was only in three. Before they left their mothers brought in pizzas and lager and everyone sat up in the mothers' room till late, laughing and joking and wishing one another well. There were these diversions, and Roy had visitors – Pete most nights, Rachel's mother once or twice a week, her sister once, bringing her three kids and a toy clock that played tunes, Marion twice and Julie once – but nothing seemed to break into the numbing routine. Tea trolleys and medicine trolleys came and went, beds were made. It was hard to sleep with all the noise and hard to stay awake in the hot, dull air. Rachel jiggled Roy's rattle for him and wound up the musical clock. She wandered up and down the ward with him, looking at the murals. Mostly however she sat by his cot and stared out of the window.

Rachel remembered what Marion had said, about motherhood being the loneliest job in the world. Julie had said that once you were a mother you knew you were never in control. She closed her eyes and made her fingers relax round the bars of the cot. It's all right, she told herself. As long as you didn't think too much, or give things names, everything would be all right. And she could go home tonight, the consultant had told her. There was no point waiting round for tests they couldn't do yet. Roy had to stay in one more night because of his medication, but Rachel could go. So just for one night she could live her life normally, as if nothing had happened. She didn't have to tell Pete or anyone else. They would take Roy home tomorrow, but for this one night Rachel could go home alone.

They sat outside, on the grass square behind Marion's house. Marion had brought some cans of lager from the fridge. It was a hot evening for late September and the air was full of tiny, flimsy insects. Marion swatted at them with a paper napkin, to no effect. Col was around, Rachel could hear his movements in the kitchen. With part of her mind she was following him intently, but with another she was staring up into the whitening sky, wondering why it was so hot. She hadn't told Marion about Roy, only that he had to go in for more tests. Marion poured lager into a glass.

Jim's putting the kids to bed, she said. Here's to marriage.

Rachel smiled, still looking at the sky.

I don't think I'll drink to that one, she said. As soon as she said it she was sorry, she didn't really want to talk. Marion put her glass down.

Now why not? she said. Rachel smiled but didn't answer.

You know, you never talk about Pete, Marion said. I don't know much about him.

Rachel laughed. There's not much to say, she said.

Behind them Col was running water from the kitchen tap. She wondered if he would come out.

No go on, Marion said. Tell me.

Rachel sighed, then laughed again and shook her head.

What do you want to know?

Well, Marion said. How old he is and where you met.

Pete was a year older than Marion, twenty-four now. They met when she was sixteen and working in the same place he worked, stacking crates. They'd gone out together a long time before getting married, over four years. It would be their wedding anniversary next week.

Which one? Marion said, and when Rachel told her it would be two years a week on Saturday she said,

So you didn't have to get married then.

No, Rachel said. People had thought that before but she didn't know why, they had wanted to get married.

Why do you say that? she said.

Well you don't seem that keen on him, Marion said. I just wondered, you know, if you'd had to get married.

Rachel shook her head and went on looking at the sky. It was the dead white of old, dead skin now, but the heat was smothering.

Well go on then, Marion said. Tell us what he's like.

Rachel searched around in her mind but she couldn't think of anything to say. He's all right, she said, and they laughed.

Well you must have liked him once, Marion said. Rachel sighed. She kept sighing and laughing, maybe it stopped her crying.

She had liked Pete at one time. She used to hang round the pubs where he went and sit at a table where she could see him in the staff canteen. She watched him when she thought he wasn't looking and giggled with the other girls when he was. It had taken him a long time, though, to ask her out.

Col brought some dirty water out and washed it down the outside drain.

You see, I've got all these men trained, Marion said.

Col was barefoot and stripped to the waist. He waved at them before going back inside. His tan was deeper, Rachel thought.

So you don't like him at all now then, Marion said. Rachel looked at her.

Who? she said. Marion rolled her eyes and flicked her napkin at a fly.

O Pete, Rachel said. Then she said, He drinks too much.

Does he? Marion said.

Then without meaning to Rachel told Marion about the rows they had over Pete's drinking, and about Roy.

Pete's never liked Roy, she said. Not really. He was never that keen on the idea of kids in the first place. And when he visited Roy in hospital he only stayed as long as he had to, not the full hour, just long enough to read his newspaper.

Marion sat and listened, then she said, Two years isn't that long for a marriage, you know.

She said it as though she'd read Rachel's mind. Rachel stared at her, then she looked away and said,

It feels like it's over.

There it was. She had never put it into words before, but as she said it she remembered Pete's face one time after the health visitor had been and said the usual worrying things. Pete had looked down at Roy as he lay sleeping.

He's not normal, is he, he'd said, and in his face there was a mixture of fear and disgust. Maybe it had been over then, Rachel thought. All those months ago. And she remembered that Pete had really started to drink around that time.

Marion touched her arm.

It's not over, she said. You're still together, aren't you?

Only on the outside, Rachel said. She felt hollow with the truth.

Look, Marion said. It's your anniversary soon, right?

Rachel nodded.

Have you got anything planned?

Rachel shook her head. She doubted they would be celebrating this year.

Well why not? Marion said. That's the trouble with you two, you've had a hard time, too much to cope with and not enough fun. That's all you need, a bit of a lift.

Rachel shook her head.

Yes, Marion said. Take it from me. You can't live on bills and housework you know. Sometimes you need to enjoy yourself, get out and have a good time. When was the last time you went out together?

Rachel couldn't remember.

Well then, no wonder you feel like it's over. Pete can drive, can't he?

Rachel said yes, but they didn't have a car.

I'll get Jim to leave you the van.

No don't, said Rachel, but Marion said yes, it was only an old van. Jim had dozens at work. They could have it for the day on their anniversary.

Get Pete to take you out, she said. Rachel was doubtful, but Marion insisted, it was what they needed, she said. She wouldn't drop the subject until Rachel had promised to ask Pete, at least.

Col came out, wiping his hands.

Hi, he said.

Have a drink, Marion said, but he didn't want one.

He said to Rachel, Are you in a hurry?

Why? she said.

I wanted to show you something, Col said. In my room.

Marion laughed.

Probably his etchings, she said. I wouldn't go if I were you.

What is it, Rachel said, and Col smiled.

Well if you come up to my room, he said, you'll find out.

Rachel looked at Marion, as if she had to ask permission.

Go on then, Marion said. But if you're not down in half an hour I'm calling the police.

Half an hour should be long enough, Col said, for what I've got in mind, and Marion called him a cheeky git.

The attic wasn't properly kitted out as a bedroom: there wasn't a light or a wardrobe or a proper bed, just a skylight in the sloping roof, a mattress on the floor and a low table. Col helped Rachel through the hatch. It was dark, Col was lighting candles. The table was draped with a beautiful thick cloth and behind it there was a wall hanging, a picture of a woman with several arms. She sat watching a lotus flower on water.

Kali, Col said. The Hindu goddess.

Have you gone Hindu now then? Rachel said, but Col said no, all representations of the goddess were equal, you chose which one appealed to you or which was right for a particular ceremony.

On the table there were candles and an incense burner. There were herbs growing in an earthenware pot and big shells filled with water. To the left there were two or three small skulls.

This is my altar, Col said. There was something on it for each element: candles for fire, shells for water, crystals in a tray full of soil for earth and incense for air. Skulls and a little dish of salt represented death, and the green herbs life. He had made it all, he said, including the pot and the incense burner. He had searched the moors for skulls and grown the herbs himself. He had even put the altar cloth together from material he'd found in an Age Concern shop.

Col lit and flame beneath the incense. That was the point of it, he explained. All the materials a witch used had to be made with his or her own hands, and you could only have natural things, nothing artificial.

Things have to have value, he said. They have to mean something to you.

To witches life was a celebration, not a burden like it was in Christianity, so everything you used had to have value.

Don't tell me you made the wall hanging as well, Rachel said, and Col said no, he had picked it up cheap at a market.

But it is handmade, he said. He looked at her with his light eyes and said, Do you like it? And Rachel, who had been meaning to say something sarcastic, said,

It's beautiful. Because it was. The colours of the shells and crystals and silk were luminous. There was the smell of herbs and incense.

Col took Rachel's hand and sat down on the mattress so that she had to sit down too.

I'm glad you like it, he said, and he stroked her hand.

Rachel thought about leaving, she would have to go, but Col said,

I'm looking for a partner, you see, to do some work with.

Rachel could feel her face burning up, she knew what kind of work he meant.

Col said, I had a dream about you and I know we could work together.

Rachel couldn't quite believe it was happening. Col said he didn't want to put pressure on her but he wanted her to think about it. If they did the Great Rite together they would be bound

167

for life: no matter where they were, if one of them wanted to perform it again they would have to meet up.

How am I supposed to do that? Rachel said. I can't just leave my family when I feel like it.

Col said he realised that, it would be better if she left now. Rachel pulled her hand away.

Don't be daft, she said. But Col was very serious. He wasn't asking her to decide there and then, just to think about it. What was there for her here, he said. She was doing nothing with her life. If she went with him they would travel all over the world, they would perform rites and ceremonies with different covens and worship the goddess together.

You don't have to spend your life in chains, he said.

All of this had the familiarity of a dream. It echoed strangely in Rachel's head and it was a while before she realised these were her own thoughts coming back to her. She didn't know what to say or do, there was a kind of sickness building up in her stomach.

I can't leave Roy, she said.

Col's face hardly changed but Rachel could tell what he was thinking.

It's up to you, he said. You have to decide what you leave behind.

He wasn't saying that she couldn't take Roy. For a moment she could see it clearly, long sunny days, the three of them travelling all over the world in a kind of gypsy caravan, then she said,

I don't think so, but there was hesitation in her voice.

Don't tell me now, Col said. Just think about it.

Thoughts clamoured in Rachel's head. She moved away from Col.

I'll have to go, she said.

Just think about it, said Col.

Rachel crouched down and began lowering herself through the hatch.

Don't give up on yourself, Col said. You could do a lot with your life. Look, he said, crouching down over the hatch. Come and see me Thursday night – I'm baby-sitting then, we could talk it over.

Rachel shook her head, it was all too much. Now it was actually happening to her she couldn't handle it. She wouldn't commit herself either way. As she left by the back door she realised her heart was thumping uncomfortably. It was as though she was being threatened, as though Col, by trying to pin her down, was threatening the perfection of her dream.

All week things went on as if nothing had happened. Rachel went with Pete to bring Roy home from hospital, she told him nothing. So Pete went to work and Rachel stayed at home, washing, feeding and changing Roy, trying not to notice the floppiness of his little body. Sometimes she thought he was looking at her, trying to tell her the things he couldn't say. She turned to housework, emptying cupboards and clearing stuff out in an attempt not to notice the silence of the house.

On Tuesday she met Julie coming back from the shops. Julie was in a bad mood. She was wrestling with Dermot who had somehow learned to climb out of both his safety harness and his trolley. He had done it in the co-op and almost the entire queue of people had walked past Julie to the till.

You're lucky, you, she said, nodding towards Roy as she tightened the harness into a stranglehold. He hardly moves, does he?

Rachel added this to the list of things she wouldn't notice.

How's Keith? she said.

Fine, said Julie. She was seeing him later on. The trouble was they spent most of the time trying to get Dermot into bed. She was going to cook for them both tonight, that was why she'd been to the shops.

But if you ask for garlic round here you're talking exotic, she said. Anyway, how's things with you?

Fine, Rachel said. She told Julie that Roy had to go back into hospital, just for tests. They pushed the trolleys uphill in single file because the pavements kept disappearing, so it was hard to talk, but Rachel said,

What do you think you'd do if you didn't have Dermot?

Christ, Julie said. I've forgotten what it's like, not having Dermot. It's like asking what I'd do if I was someone else. Why, what would you do?

I don't know, Rachel said. Then she said, I'd like to travel.

Yeah, said Julie. See the world. She tugged the trolley over a large crack in the pavement and the shopping tray fell off. But at least you've seen Marley, eh? she said, cocking a large grin at Rachel as she reattached it. See Marley and die. It's all right for a bloke like Col, she went on, no responsibilities, no ties –

What do you think of Col? Rachel said. The pavement had reappeared now and she could walk by Julie's side.

He's all right, Julie said. I didn't like him at first, but now I think he's all right. King of the goddess worshippers, she said.

Rachel wanted to confide to Julie but she didn't know how. She said, What do you think about that sex magic stuff? Julie laughed.

Well it's one way of getting your end away, she said. Why?

Rachel told her. He asked me, she said.

You're having me on, Julie said. What did he say?

He wants me to perform the Great Rite with him, she said. Julie fell about.

Not that old come-up-and-see-me-and-we'll-perform-the-Great-Rite-together line? Roll over lie down and let the goddess in.

They laughed about it all the way home.

What will Marion think, Julie said, when the goddess arrives in

170

her attic? Maybe that's the real reason they built the extension.

So you don't think I should take him up on his offer then, Rachel said, and they laughed again.

Well I didn't say that, Julie said. It's up to you. He's not a bad-looking bloke, our Col.

Rachel noticed she didn't say anything about Pete.

I hope you'll keep me informed, she said as Rachel turned off. Let me know what happens.

Rachel waved. I might have the goddess with me next time, she said.

That's right, Julie said. Bring her round for a cup of tea, and she wheeled Dermot round the corner and disappeared.

Pete came home early, in a good mood. He'd met Jim on the way home and Jim had told him about the van.

It's a great idea, isn't it? he said to Rachel. Where shall we go?

Rachel hadn't mentioned it to Pete, she'd forgotten all about it.

Wherever you like, she said, stooping over Roy.

We could go to that pub on the moors, Pete said. The one we went to when our Dave got married. You said you liked it.

If you like, Rachel said. She felt tired.

We could take Roy's kite, he said. You'd like that, wouldn't you, Boy Roy, and he chucked Roy under his lolling chin. Rachel felt a stab of hatred. He only called Roy that when he was pretending to like him, to win favour. He'd been doing it a lot recently, in response to her remoteness.

He wouldn't know if you took the kite or not, she said.

Yes he would, wouldn't you, Roy the boy? Pete said. He went on about the other things they could do. They could take a picnic if it was fine, and a bottle of wine, or they could eat in the pub. Rachel listened restlessly. She wished Marion had never mentioned the van. As soon as she could she carried Roy into the living room and switched on the TV. It was a gardening programme. She always watched them, though they didn't have a garden. Pete followed her.

Don't you want to go? he said. Rachel shrugged.

I thought it'd be nice, he said. There was a silence, then he said, I'm doing my best, Rachel.

Rachel felt bad because she knew it was true, then she hated him for feeling sorry for himself. When she still didn't answer he went upstairs.

Thursday morning they had the card from the hospital: Roy had to go in the following week. Rachel thought about Col. She didn't think about sex with him exactly, she thought about him touching her face, and her breasts. She could have sex any time with Pete, she didn't want it. Her dream hovered on the brink of sex with Col, postponing it indefinitely. So much dreaming made her restless, she prowled around the house dropping things, leaving them half done. She was less and less aware of what surrounded her, she felt as if she was shutting up inside her dream.

By evening she was white and tense. She made tea but could hardly eat it. Pete washed up, then he came into the front room where she sat perched on the edge of the sofa. He sat down next to her.

What's up? he said.

Nothing, said Rachel. She was too drawn in even to snap.

Pete put his arm around her, she drew away.

Is it the hospital? he said. Rachel stared at the wall.

He's been in before, said Pete. It wasn't that bad. Anyway, he said, whatever it is we'll manage. We've managed so far.

Rachel got up and walked away.

Yes we'll always manage, she said, bitterly. We've always had to. She had other things to say but she bit them off in her mind.

Well how bad can it be, eh? Pete said. He had picked Roy up

172

now and was jiggling him gently. Roy used to hate that and strain away, but now he just lay still and limp. When Rachel didn't answer Pete said,

Look, why don't you go out tonight, take your mind off things?

Col, Rachel thought. She sank back on the sofa and let her breath out in a shuddering sigh. She didn't answer Pete for a moment, then she said,

I thought you'd be going out with your mates. She tried, but couldn't entirely keep the hatred from her voice.

Not tonight, Pete said. I can look after Roy if you like. Why don't you go and see Marion.

He was telling her to go. Rachel stared at the carpet. Marion isn't in tonight, she thought. She must tell him that. After a moment she said,

I might just see if she's in, and she took her cagoule from the back of the settee and left, without looking back.

Rachel was in Col's room. He wanted her to wear a ceremonial robe but she wouldn't. She felt daft, she said. Now she was here she was still restless, as if she still wanted to be somewhere else. She let him take her cagoule off and kiss her hair. Then he unbuttoned her shirt. He took a phial of oil from his altar and massaged some into her breasts, she felt nothing. Between them they tugged off her jeans and pants. Col kissed her on the forehead, the mouth, the breasts and womb, then he laid her down on the bed. When he entered her he muttered some words under his breath. Rachel felt strange, as though she wasn't there at all. Somewhere inside she began to shake, then the shaking spread outwards to her limbs. It had never happened before.

Col didn't seem to mind. He stopped what he was doing and stroked her hair.

There's no hurry, he said. Then he began to talk, to tell her about the places and the people they would see, the things they would do. He had finally made a contact on the Faroes, he said. they would go that way, via his friends on Orkney, then on to Iceland. Rachel clung to him and listened. She noticed he didn't talk as if Roy would be with them. Even in her own mind she couldn't imagine the three of them living together, but she still felt she had to say something. She said,

What about Roy?

Col shifted a little and in the darkness she couldn't see his face.

Yeah, he said. Like I said, it's up to you. Then he didn't say anything else and Rachel couldn't think of anything to say either. She rolled away from him and got up.

I have to go, she said.

Col held on to her hand.

Look, he said. I really want you to come with me but I can't wait much longer. I have to go. Next week.

Rachel stared at him.

Next week, she said. Col said he had to visit friends who were going to put him in touch with the bloke on the Faroes, and they would be leaving themselves soon. Rachel pulled her clothes on slowly.

I don't know, she said.

You don't have to decide right now, said Col. Just think about it, eh, and let me know. Rachel didn't look at Col. She stood partly turned away from him.

I'll think about it, she said. But now it was here, the decision almost upon her, she didn't want to think about it at all.

Out on the moor the wind rose to a shrill whine. Even so Pete couldn't get the kite to stay in the air. Rachel watched him tugging the string this way and that, the kite landing in a clump of trees, then catching on a barbed wire fence. Pete was getting angry but he wouldn't give up. Roy sucked his fingers and stared at the sky.

Over the crest of the hill Rachel could see the top of a stone circle. Col had told her about it before. It was smaller than the ones at Stonehenge or Glastonbury, but of the same kind, made thousands of years ago for the same mysterious reasons. It's like looking straight into the past, he'd said. Rachel had asked Pete to stop the van when she saw the stone circle but she didn't say why. She didn't want to bring the world of Col too dangerously near her own world. Now she looked at it while Pete struggled with the kite. Col got all kinds of weird sensations from them but Rachel couldn't feel anything. Except that it was getting cold. She picked up Roy and the bag she'd brought for him, and the camera. A little while before Pete had asked a passing couple to take a photo of the three of them, they hardly had any. It was an instant camera and the picture had turned out well, with Roy squinting at the white sun as if he was taking notice. Rachel gathered together their scattered things, tucked Roy under one arm and called to Pete that she was taking him to the van. From the passenger seat she watched him trying to untangle the kite from the barbed wire. She felt a sudden savage pity, because nothing he did turned out right, but she had made her decision. She was leaving.

Rachel laid Roy across her knee and changed him, wiping him down with tissues. It was harder changing him like this these days because he had grown, though at nearly nine months he was still very small. She propped him up with one hand to wind him, it was an automatic action and funny to think she wouldn't be doing it much longer. Then she heard Pete shouting and when she looked the kite was finally aloft, twisting and bobbing in the wind. Pete waved frantically with one hand and tried to steer with the other. It fell, of course. Pete ravelled up the string any old how and came running, like a big kid, she thought.

Did you see that? he said. He clambered into the driver's seat, then suddenly he cupped her face in his hands and kissed her, a big kiss, she wasn't expecting it. He said,

I love you Rachie, you know that, don't you?

Rachel didn't say anything, but as they drove away she felt like crying. She was furious with herself. They'd had one nice day, it didn't change anything. She had to leave; she owed it to herself to find some happiness while she was still young. People had a duty to themselves as well as others, Col said. If she wasn't happy she wasn't likely to be able to make anyone else happy either. People were afraid of freedom, Col said.

On Monday she went to Marion's as usual. She had stopped going to Mums and Tots, she felt that the other mothers were talking about Roy, making comparisons. Julie was already at Marion's and Col was there, but he didn't join them. She could see him through the window in the kitchen extension, all the time they were talking she could feel his eyes watching her. She hadn't told him yet she had decided to go with him, it was easier to think about it somehow when he wasn't there.

Julie said Keith was already talking about her moving in with him, he lived in a nice part of Marley, towards Clough Bottom. Marion thought it was really romantic, but Julie said he'd probably got sick of doing his own cooking. And cleaning and ironing, she added.

O you know, you're a real cynic, Marion said, but Rachel thought she was right. But she also thought there was something in people that was afraid of change, you clung to what you knew no matter how bad it was.

You're quiet today, Marion said, but Rachel didn't want to be made to talk. She said she was going to the loo.

Col caught her hand as she reached the top of the stairs. He appeared out of the shadows, making her jump.

Have you thought about it yet? he said. Have you decided?

Rachel pulled her hand away. She didn't want to answer him, to be pinned down.

Only I'm leaving, he said. Early Wednesday morning.

It was the day before they had to take Roy into hospital. Rachel was filled with dread. She whispered,

Where will I meet you?

By the park, Col whispered back. His eyes were strangely luminous in the shadows. We'll get the first bus outside the park, ten to six.

She would have to leave before Pete got up. Without looking at Col Rachel nodded. She felt as if everything was being arranged around her, as if it had all been settled long ago. She didn't want to look at Col or talk to him any more, not even to discuss the details, how much money would they need, what about tickets for the ferry . . . She went into the bathroom and shut the door.

The next day seemed stretched out, as if it would never end. Rachel put clothes in the washing-machine and ironed the ones that were dry. She went shopping and made the tea. When she shopped she thought, I won't be eating this food; it didn't seem real. When she changed and fed Roy she thought, I won't be doing this tomorrow, and that seemed even less real, as if she had somehow wandered into her own dream. At the same time part of her was working out the practical details. She cashed a month's family allowance and hid it in the inside pocket of her coat. She drew out the twenty-odd pounds she had in the building society and saved two or three pounds from the shopping. It wasn't much but it was hers, she wouldn't have to ask Col for everything. She packed the lightest load possible in her rucksack and left it behind a stack of things in the shed. She tried not to think about how Pete and Roy would manage once she was gone. Roy would be in hospital, that would give Pete some time to sort himself out. Over and over again she planned what she would say in the note to Pete. None of it seemed right, and in the end she decided she wouldn't leave a note, it couldn't explain anything. It was better just to go.

Rachel dreaded Pete coming home, but when he did it was all right. They never talked much anyway, so she didn't have to put on an act. She made tea, then they watched telly. He didn't go out, as she'd been hoping, but later he went to the shop for some cans of beer and she had a drink with him. He put Roy to bed for once, she could hear him talking to him in the back bedroom.

You're going into hospital, aren't you? he said. We'll soon get you put right.

When he came back he slipped his arm round her. She knew what he wanted but she couldn't do that. She got up hastily, collecting cans and glasses and took them into the kitchen. When they went to bed she pretended to fall asleep right away.

Of course she didn't sleep, she was afraid of not waking up at the right time. She lay listening to Pete's rough breathing and to the whimpering noises Roy still made in the back room. She lay and thought about what she was going to do, none of it seemed possible. It didn't seem possible either to stay or go. Finally she got up, though it was only just past four, and slipped downstairs to the kitchen. She would have a cup of coffee before she left.

Rachel wasn't afraid of waking Pete, it was hard to wake him even with the alarm. Even so, she didn't want to put the kitchen light on. She crept around the kitchen in the vague light wondering if she would kiss Roy before she left, she didn't want to wake him. She replaced everything she used, coffee, sugar, teaspoon, as though she were removing all traces of herself, then she sat at the table with her mug of coffee.

The table was littered with sheets of newspaper, Pete never read his papers tidily. There were two bills, and under one of them was the photo taken that day on the moors. Pete had talked about getting it framed, but now it just lay about the kitchen along with everything else. Rachel picked it up. Roy was looking at the sky, his face creased against the brightness so he looked as if he was smiling, but he had never smiled. Rachel looked at the picture and was stricken with loss. He didn't deserve it, she thought. He didn't deserve his illness and he didn't deserve being left. He wasn't even nine months old.

Rachel sat in the little room with its moving lights and shadows. She didn't have to go. She could just go back to bed and no one would ever know. Col would leave, she would carry on meeting Julie and Marion as if nothing had happened. Then she thought about the hospital and moaned in a low, desperate way. She couldn't face it. But she couldn't take Roy with her, it was no life for a baby, and he needed medical care. For a moment Rachel sat very still with her eyes closed, wondering if she would always have to live like this, pulled apart. Then she opened her eyes on to the flickering light of the outside lamp. She rinsed her mug and left it to drain. She went out to the shed for her rucksack.

All the time as she sorted and checked her things, Rachel watched the movements of her hands. She watched them as they opened the shed door and closed it again, she watched them unfastening the straps on her rucksack, then doing them up. They were small, precise hands. She had left her hairbrush in the front room, now she watched her hands packing it. They adjusted the straps of the rucksack on her shoulders. After she crept passed the stairs, hearing the vague moans from the back room, her hands unfastened the locks on the door. It was early, but she didn't want to wait any longer. She would go and wait in the park.

Rachel left quietly by the back door, lifting the latch on the yard gate. Out of habit she pocketed the key though she wouldn't need it again. The air was damp and clinging, it wasn't cold. Rachel walked along one street then another, her eyes shone with the reflected gleam of lamps. She looked up at the halo of the moon. I'm free now, she thought. Then suddenly she was running, back the way she'd come, as fast as she could go. The rucksack bumped and scraped against her spine. She was going back for Roy.

I thought I'd bring him after all, Rachel said. She stooped low over the trolley so she wouldn't have to see Col's face. She held Roy under one arm and struggled to close the trolley with her other hand and her foot. The rucksack was bulging now with extra clothes for Roy, nappies and baby food, but she didn't feel she could ask Col for help. The trolley wouldn't close and Rachel struggled with it. Wordlessly Col took it off her, clicked it into its folded position and carried it into the shelter. Rachel followed, carrying Roy. She felt stupid now, and pathetic. How far would they get with a baby, especially a sick one. She wondered if Col would talk to her at all.

Col stared down the road. Rachel chanced a quick look at his face, but it gave nothing away. She told herself that she couldn't go back, Pete would be up by now, she would have all that explaining to do. She wanted to feel the sense of mystery and adventure she had felt when sitting at home thinking about leaving, but all she felt was a clinging sense of fear.

When the bus came Col didn't speak, but he did help her on. Then he paid for their tickets, he wouldn't let her pay. They were the only two passengers. Rachel held on to Roy and looked around. She read the signs and notices, then the adverts. Finally she said to Col,

So where are we off to then?

Col didn't answer for a minute, then he told her they were going to stay with some friends of his in south Manchester, then they would head south towards Birmingham and the M5.

I thought we were going to Orkney? Rachel said. And the Faroes?

Not at this time of year, Col said. He said it as if she should have known. Rachel didn't know what to think and she didn't want to speak to him again. She clutched Roy tightly and listened to the jogging rattle of the bus. Eventually, in spite of the fear, her head nodded forwards and she slept.

Is that it? Rachel said of the tent. It was certainly small. Col walked round it, securing pegs. He looked up at her briefly.

I'm going to try to light a fire, he said.

Rachel wanted to ask how he thought he was going to do that, in the mud and the rain, but she didn't. She crept inside the tent as he wandered off. They'd hitched a couple of hundred miles and they were both dog tired. Roy's whimpering was getting Col down, but Rachel was past caring. He hadn't liked it either when people had assumed he was Roy's father. You shouldn't bring your baby out hitching, the last lorry driver had said to him. Yet it was mainly because of Roy they were getting the lifts.

It's a good job I brought him after all, Rachel said at one point, but Col didn't respond. And she was pissed off with him as well, she stopped even trying to talk. And now they were here, the middle of nowhere, in the rain.

Col wanted to stay with more friends somewhere in the Forest of Dean, but it didn't look as if they would find them tonight. Rachel only hoped they were better than the last lot in Manchester, she hadn't liked them at all. The woman especially had only been interested in Col. She was tall and thin with long black hair and dressed all in black. Rachel called her Morticia to herself, but her real name was Ann. She lived with Les and a number of other people who seemed to come and go. They talked to Col about Hallowe'en, but Col said he wanted to be in Cornwall by then. He wanted to spend the winter there and on Guernsey, then head up north in the spring. It was the first Rachel had heard about it, but she was glad there seemed to be a plan. She sat a little way from them in the kitchen and helped herself to the stew which seemed to be available to everyone. Les picked Roy up once and tickled him and tried to get a response and Morticia said,

What's wrong with him?

That baby doesn't know he's not perfect, Marion's voice said, and Rachel took Roy back from Les and said,

Nothing.

She turned away from them and tried to feed Roy some of the stew. She spooned it in, it trickled out again. She missed Julie and Marion powerfully.

Occasionally, though no one spoke to her directly, she overheard bits of conversation, words like cartomancy, chalcomancy, and the Mystic Cross; it was like listening to another language. When she changed Roy he seemed more limp than usual and he didn't want any food, but she didn't feel as if she could ask for help. Col had held Roy at Marion's and been good with him, now he was ignoring them both. That night he found a spare sleeping bag and slept a little way from them on the floor. He made no move towards her and this made her feel bad, she'd thought that was why he'd brought her. But she told herself it would be better when they were on their own. And now here they were, in the mud and rain.

Roy slept and Rachel held him, listening to the drops of rain spattering against the canvas. They're all nutters in the Forest of Dean, Marion had said once, but she wouldn't think about that now. At the back of the tent was the parcel Morticia had given Col. He was to take it to the Faroes; for some reason it couldn't be posted. It was a peculiar shape and there were symbols scrawled all over it, Rachel didn't want to know what it was. She sat and looked out at the big, mysterious trees. I'll never sleep here, she thought, and wondered how long Col would be. She thought about people of long ago, living in the woods, there would be camp-fires and songs, then she thought of herself and Col singing in the damp tent, it didn't seem likely.

Through a gap in the trees Rachel could make out where the road was. That was comforting, though there was no traffic at this time. Her head drooped forwards and she dozed, then started awake thinking, he should be back by now. She listened hard, but could only hear Roy's uneven breathing and the steady drip, drip, drip of the rain.

Rachel wrapped Roy in the blanket she had brought, laid him down, then crawled stiffly out of the tent. She walked round it but could see nothing.

The bigness and quietness of the dark trees frightened her. Even the drip of rain was unnerving in the stillness. Rachel wandered a little way down a rough track.

Col, she called. Col?

When there was no answer she returned, shivering. She crouched into the tent and panic crept up on her. What did she know about Col? She must be mad. Anything could happen to her here, she thought, and nightmare images flitted through her mind. She sat, unable to think what to do, when the crunch of a twig outside made her freeze. She couldn't make her mouth say Col, she stayed where she was, bowed, flesh shrinking from the contact to come. She thought of being jumped on as she crawled out of the tent, hit from behind and falling without a sound. She thought of their bodies being found, but not for months, half rotted away. Worst of all she thought of Col's face, hideously changed, appearing suddenly in the opening to the tent.

Nothing happened.

Rachel picked Roy up and put him down again. Then quickly so she couldn't think, she scrambled out of the tent and stood, peering every way into the darkness. She could see nothing. Perhaps whatever it was had got Col.

That was daft, she wouldn't think like that. Rachel pressed her fingers to her face, unable to think properly at all. She wanted to cry loudly, like a child, but she was afraid of the noise she would make. After a moment she crouched down again and picked up her rucksack, then Roy. The road, she thought. She had to get to the road.

She went slowly, because once she tripped over the root of a tree, and another time slipped on the stony track. The road was further than she thought and she had to push her way through bracken. A faint light seeped through the trees, it was almost morning. The light grew steadily and she was in a deep green world, even though it was autumn, with the different greens massed together, blue-green and yellow-green and cabbage-green leaves. There were pale points of clover in the grass, long feathery ferns and thick brambles. Rachel pushed her way on steadily as the light grew. Everything would be all right, she thought. She would find Col. He would come looking for them and they would travel together, first to Cornwall, then Orkney. Maybe they would settle for a while on Orkney, she had heard it was cheap. They would live there in a cottage and one day Roy would go to school. Rachel's mind wandered on. Her arms and legs and back ached from carrying Roy and the rucksack. Then suddenly she stumbled on the road.

It was empty. Rachel stood with Roy half tucked into her coat, his legs dangling down. She looked along it both ways. On either side there were bushes and bracken and the bare, still trees. The road itself curved into nowhere. Far ahead there was a dull orange glow in the sky, that was the city.

Rachel thought about getting back to Marley, then she remembered the time when she had talked to Julie and thought, you could never go back. Once the time had passed you could never return. She stood a long time, holding her baby, the bag on her back, there wasn't anything else she could do. She felt as if she were trapped inside her own dreams. The world turned and the sun rose on a misty day. Rachel stayed where she was, looking down the long road in the mysterious autumn light.

4
Lower than Angels

Night blurred the boundaries. There was only the shaggy rolling moor, with the greater darkness of hills printed against the night sky, like silence itself taking shape. And in her side there was the catch of cold breath, and in the back of her legs the tightening pull of muscles. At this point in the night her legs felt heavy, her steps were less measured, and she stumbled frequently on the uneven loosening ground.

Don't you get scared, Dora said. Janice wished she could say no.

Out here there was an infinity of things she couldn't name, insects beneath a stone, the skull of an unknown animal. In the darkness she couldn't identify the different mosses and lichens she had once studied for her degree, the thirty or forty different types of grass. When she listened the moor wasn't silent, but she couldn't distinguish the different voices of the night. At this stage, after so much walking, she had stopped looking and listening, there was only the long, upward slope of the hill. Earlier that day, in the library, she had pinned up an exhibition of children's drawings under the heading, My Local Area, pictures of houses, shops, streets and, usually in the background, a hill, a smooth green hump attached to nothing beneath a band of blue sky. You would think they'd never seen a hill.

She hauled herself to the summit. Below was the glittering spread of Oldham, behind the more patchy lights of villages curving away. For the first time Janice realised how far she'd walked, how far she had to go back. She wanted to feel a sense of achievement, but she only felt tired. And as she turned away from the lights towards the darkness which seemed thicker now she also felt fear. All the time on her night-time walks she was warding off not only fatigue, but fear.

Mad, said Dora's voice as Janice stumbled back down the path. You'll never meet anyone that way you know. Why don't you join a walking club?

Gwen, more anxious about psychopaths and gangs of bikers roaming the moors, said she wished Janice would be more careful and take a friend.

No one's mad enough, said Janice.

You said it, Dora said.

She wasn't afraid of marauding bikers, or lonely psychopaths, nor of anything the human voices told her to fear, but of the non-human voices: the skid of a stone, a snapped twig, or an overhead, invisible screech. The non-human voices telling her things she couldn't hear took shape in her mind as the cries of murdered children, whose bodies had never been fully recovered, or as nightmare images springing from some primitive place, ridiculous in the light of day, but at home here, on the wild, unsocial moor. Here fear always drove her the same way, back to the road, towards lights, cars, pubs, houses. But always after she had made her descent in a kind of smothered terror towards the orange lights of the road she felt the same pangs of failure and loss.

The committee for grass borders met every Tuesday evening in the room at the back of the library. Actually they called themselves the Committee for Civic Improvement, but since their main campaign each election time, when they harassed councillors from all parties, seemed to be for better-kept grass borders and a proper park, they had come to be known as the committee for grass borders. While local businesses closed down almost as soon as they opened and mills stood idle and boarded up, and the nightly transportation of nuclear waste went on unimpeded through the village, the committee for grass borders gained daily in strength and fellowship, having the support of three of the local churches for whom they fund-raised regularly. They had been meeting for years now in the room at the back of the library reserved for meetings. Their leader, Florence Owen, a thickset woman with straight grey hair parted in the middle, would stand for no nonsense from any councillor.

I knew him when he was in short trousers, she would say, as if that ended all arguments. Marley was that kind of place.

Its real name was Marle Lea – Marl after a type of earth found both locally and (according to Milton) in hell, and Lea meaning field – but most people ran the two syllables together into Marley, as in ghost. It was divided by the river into Upper and Lower Marley. To the outside eye it looked like one long village, picturesque stone cottages clustered either side of the meandering Lym, as it said in the brochure from the Tourist Board. To insiders the division was absolute. People from Upper Marley had little or nothing to do with people from Lower Marley and even claimed to be of different stock. The river, they said, marked the dividing line between that part of England which had been conquered and settled, first by Romans and then Vikings, and that part which had not. Camps may have been made north of the river, but it had never been fully taken over. Occasionally a representative from Lower Marley would turn up at the committee for grass borders and furious arguments would ensue; about allotment rents (higher in Upper than in Lower Marley) or the site of the latest council dump (provisionally planned for

Lower Marley) or the travellers (wanted by neither end of the village). The one issue about which there was complete agreement was that the council estate, promiscuously straddling both sides of the river, should never have been built. It had brought house prices down and lowered the tone.

Apart from this meeting, little happened in the library on Tuesdays. It was half-day closing for the shops, which meant that no one went out much, not even to change their books. Janice watched the drizzle through the big windows and thought that nowhere looked quite so deserted as the main street of Marley on half-day closing, even before the shops shut. Behind her Dora sat filing her nails; Gwen was in the stock room drawing up lists for the next library sale.

The trouble with Janice was that she was too intelligent for the job she did. At least that was what her mother said. She'd been to university, and might have made something of herself, but somewhere along the line she'd lost her drive and given in, throwing away a career in science for a tuppence-ha'penny job as a library assistant. Whenever the opportunity for promotion had cropped up Janice had wilfully refused to apply. And what did she do in the library that was so good she could turn her nose up at other careers? She stamped dates on books.

There were days, like this one, when Janice was inclined to agree with her mother. Brownish-grey light filtered through the windows and the silence and stillness seemed to soak into everything. From time to time someone spoke, but each brief conversation was punctuated with silence. You could hear the short rasp of Dora's nail file as you checked through the list of overdue books. They were going to run another amnesty soon. Dora yawned and stretched.

I can't think what to make for Dave's tea, she said, too loudly. Isn't it difficult? He only ever wants chips.

There was a brief pause and the rasp-rasp-rasp of the nail file.

I think I'll do chips and mince, she said.

This Tuesday, unlike most, was not going to be totally empty. They were expecting a party from Greenfriars, the school for disabled children. Janice had set out a display unit of books about children with disabilities and Dora was going to read them a story.

But you don't like children, Janice had said.

O I don't mind disabled ones, said Dora.

Janice wheeled the display unit to the space at the far side of the library where Dora was going to read, and went to look for a chair. As she passed the great windows she could see the hills out of the corner of her eye. She could tell how cold it was from the sheep, packed tightly into one another in a brownish rosette, heads tucked into the centre. On fine days they stood dotted about the fields in no particular formation and their coats seemed brighter. On windy days they ran from one side of a field to another as if in one body, pausing to reassemble, then, at some unseen signal, racing back again. On unsettled days of rain and snow they stood apart, facing the brunt of the weather with lowered, bony foreheads.

Janice nudged the edge of a bookshelf and a book fell off, a minor explosion in the silence of the library, she could hear Dora exclaiming in alarm. She bent down to pick it up. *Garden Pests and How to Deal with Them*; one of their more popular volumes, the date sheet was thickly stamped. Janice looked at the book without seeing it. Her mother was right, she thought, she was wasting her life. She should push ahead, motivate herself, get on. But even as she thought this she felt resistance. It was a television urge she felt, it came from magazine ads: you had to be more beautiful, richer, and more ambitious. Because God help you if you just got satisfied.

The town hall clock struck eleven and there was the roar of an engine outside. Gwen and Dora hurried to open the double doors. Janice could see the back of the van open like an ambulance, part of it extending into a ramp for the wheelchairs. The next moment the children were all in the library, noisy like the kids from any school, most of them ignoring offers of help, hobbling down the steps or clambering sideways like starfish. Once in they became noisier and more excited so that their teacher had to keep telling them to be quiet. She tried unsuccessfully to round them all into the corner where the display unit and the chair stood next to each other, waiting. Janice stayed where she was, partially hidden behind a section called People in Other Countries. She had other things to do, other display units to organise; Science Today, The Environment, and How We Lived Then. As soon as the children seemed settled she picked up some books and strode quickly to the far side of the library, feeling a sensation of pressure in her chest, wanting it all to go away. She found another display unit and began stacking books briskly, efficiently, aware without wanting to be of the children spread in a crescent on the floor around Dora's chair, and Dora sitting in her elevated position, with her blonde curls spread about her shoulders.

Mr Norton, Chief Librarian, liked women to look good, by which he meant smart, well-groomed. The three of them must be a sad disappointment to him, Janice often thought. Gwen had started off smart, by Mr Norton's standards, in tailored suits and twin sets, but had become progressively more unconventional. Now almost sixty, she wore her silver hair cropped close to her head, multi-coloured leggings and a variety of thick knitted jackets down to her knees. Janice herself wore men's trousers and baggy sweatshirts with, often as not, some kind of food stain down the front. And Dora went for pretty rather than smart, short, flouncy skirts, skin-tight tops. When she reached up to the higher shelves, as she was doing now, you could see the lacy edge of her knicker leg which came down on to her thighs, Bo-Peep style. Mr Norton could see it too. He kept glancing over, in his thin-nosed way. Janice's eyes met Gwen's over his shoulder and they smiled. In spite of her progressive new image Gwen didn't look well. Her eyes and the smile were tired. She had left her husband, a Maths professor, six years ago when their two sons had finally left home, but he had been unable to cope. He'd taken to drink, lost his job, and his health had gone downhill. Most days he could be seen lingering outside the library or on the other side of the street. Even Janice felt sorry for him. Gwen did not give in to the pressure to go back. But now she divided her time between her own small flat and the big house they had once shared, cleaning, shopping, cooking for him most days as if she'd never left. Between her husband and work her time was pretty much taken up, but she also had a dream. She had joined a campaign for a women's centre which was to be set up in a large abandoned house in the next town; a place where women could meet in the day with their kids and talk while the children played or leave them for a while to go shopping. There would be tea and coffee, and literature on benefits or healthcare or opportunities for women. There might even be a bed or two for women who needed to stay the night. This was Gwen's dream and she had tried unsuccessfully once or twice to involve Janice. Janice, noting how it consumed Gwen's life, resisted. For in no time it seemed Gwen went from being just a member of the campaigning group to its secretary, once she told them she could type. Now she spent whatever free time she had typing leaflets and newsletters, distributing them, and attending council meetings. She was developing a thin, stretched-out look.

There was a time when Gwen and Janice could have been friends, they liked each other. Gwen had once cooked Janice a meal in her new flat, they had been to the cinema together twice. That was before Gwen's time had been so entirely taken up, and before Janice's resistance to the campaign. She couldn't believe that in an area where cut-backs were so severe that anyone could think they would get money for a women's centre. These days Janice and Gwen were on separate paths, going different ways. Janice couldn't live like Gwen, having no time, ever, just for herself, but she had noticed before that some people couldn't live any other way.

People won't put the hours in these days, said Ernest Broadbent, thrusting his book at Janice.

I'm sorry?

You people here, in libraries. You don't stay open half the hours you used to. When I were a lad I worked longer hours and I could always call in on library on way home and read if I'd a mind. But now you can't be bothered. You're all too busy wanting your tea, and he winked at Gwen as he spoke. Gwen smiled. Janice waited for her to say something about government cuts, but she just went back to Mr Norton and his list. Janice herself could hardly be bothered wasting her breath on Ernest Broadbent, who probably preferred, in any case, to think the way he did, blaming early closing hours on librarians, lazy librarians who wanted to get home early for tea. She didn't explain anything, not a damn thing. She handed him his books back without smiling and he left, shaking his head. Why should she care, Janice thought.

Mr Norton presented Janice with her list of books and things-to-do on the day of the library sale. She stood near him as he read them out, aware that he didn't like this. She was aware of his awareness of her size. Next to her he seemed fragile and diminished. In fact they were about the same height, but her relative mass was greater. Standing so close she could see herself through his eyes, ugly and elephantine. She lowered her eyes meekly as he gave his final instructions and said Goodbye Mr Norton, as he left. It was the least she could do.

Now that the children had gone Dora was back behind the

counter, engaged in the kind of conversation that always set Janice's teeth on edge.

I'll be eighty-two in the spring, said Iris Platt.

Eighty-two, said Dora, you're never eighty-two, not in a million years. You don't look a day over seventy, does she Janice?

Janice grunted and stamped the book so hard she almost punched a hole in the date sheet.

Eighty-two, Dora said again, and Iris Platt smiled a smile of quavery delight.

Janice couldn't do it, she just couldn't do it. But she didn't know why. It wasn't such a big deal, God knows they weren't asking for much. Maybe that was it, she couldn't stand the thought of them asking for so little. Or maybe it was the vision of her own old age, the isolation, the lack of self-esteem, driving her to stand in public places telling her age to complete strangers, her day made if they looked surprised. It wasn't out of the question. Even now she knew so few people that by the time she was eighty there would be no one around to slit her throat before anything so appalling could happen.

Dora couldn't see her point of view at all.

You're daft you, she said, where's the harm in it? And she went on, flirting with the old men, discussing recipes and *Home and Away* with the old women, effortlessly making their day. And what was wrong with that? People came in just to talk to Dora. It was nice in a way, Janice had never been able to say precisely where the harm was, except that listening to it made her want to grind her teeth to a powder and gaze out towards the hill, with the kind of hunger that she had once read Vikings had for the sea.

Out of the back window the bowl of the moor seemed to contain light. A soft fan of light spread across it through a chink in the clouds. Janice took the list for the amnesty through to the stock-room. She wondered, not for the first time, what it must be like to be Dora, so pretty and fashionable, effortlessly able to say the right thing at the right time, and therefore popular. Her father had called her Dora, she had once told Janice, because when he looked at her just after she was born he'd thought she was a-dora-ble, get it? Well after three boys he was bound to really; even after all these years she was still her daddy's little girl.

Sometimes Janice looked at Dora and thought that the gap between them could not be more immense, more impassable. And the worst thing was she had never quite killed the longing to pass it, to starve off four stones and dye her hair blonde and go round saying the expected thing. The part of her that didn't want to be Dora despised this bit with all its heart, but it wouldn't go away. How could it, when being even a little bit more like Dora would make her life infinitely easier and more pleasant?

Yet there were times, Janice had noticed, when Dora's face looked positively thin-lipped in repose, as if some bitterness were eating away at her after all; as if somewhere along the line she had been led to expect more than this, seven years of marriage, nine at the library, four years at the same holiday resort. And Janice had noticed that lately Dora had taken to making plans that never came off; plans to vary her going away routine, plans to start an independent nightlife with her girlfriend Angie, or to visit the gym three times a week and take up Spanish; even plans, made with Mavis Willshaw, to exchange videos of *Home and Away*. She made each plan with equal enthusiasm and in great detail, and was never apparently disturbed by the fact that none of them came off, as if just making them was enough to somehow siphon off the vital energy making her restless, so she could carry on her life the way it was. And in this, Janice thought, Dora resembled Gwen, though in other ways they couldn't be more different. But neither of them could bear to live through the next few minutes of their lives alone, with nothing but the space to sit and think, so they had to consume their time somehow. Janice was not like that.

*

198

Ken was a driver on the little bus, the only one that ran to the outlying areas of the village. It went on a complicated route and was mainly used by the elderly. They all knew Ken.

Not you again, Agnes Weaver always said.

'Fraid so, said Ken.

Haven't they sacked you yet, said Bob.

Doesn't look like it, Ken said.

I don't know, what's world coming to, drivers like you on the road.

You can say that again, said Ken.

They never let up the whole length of the journey, for Ken was a great favourite with them. Mavis Willshaw always said he was a lovely lad, and could come home with her any time, and Ken always shook his head.

I don't know about that, he would say. Not with your Ted there, I'm a bit feared of your Ted. And Ted would grin foolishly while Mavis called out,

He won't mind, it's a big bed.

Ken never started these conversations, he let his passengers have the upper hand. He didn't reply to some of the cheekier comments, almost as if he were shy. And he dropped them off anywhere they wanted and always gave them plenty of time to get on and off the bus.

He's a good lad, they always said, whenever he seemed shy.

He wasn't much of a lad, balding with a saggy face. And he wasn't shy either. Whenever Janice got on he looked at her very directly from under long lashes and smiled a big, slow smile as he gave her her change. And each time Janice felt hot and cold and stupid. Then comments would be directed at her.

'Ere, you'll have to watch him, he fancies you, you know.

Have you got a boyfriend love, because Ken's available if you are?

'Ere Ken, shall I get her address?

And Janice would stumble to her seat feeling like a twelve-year-old in pig-tails and ankle socks, wishing she had walked, and blushing, not prettily, but an awkward, blotchy red. She felt that he knew everything about her, with his big, knowing smile: that she'd never had a boyfriend, that at twenty-eight she'd never even been kissed.

Leave her alone, someone would say eventually, laughing heartily.

I've not touched her, Ken would say, you started it.

And Janice would stare out of the window, feeling the awkward, apprehensive feeling she'd had repeatedly at twelve, that she'd just stumbled into something she didn't understand, but which was probably hostile. All the journey long she concentrated on the view, determined to avoid catching Ken's eye in the driving mirror.

That was almost ten years ago.

Dora was listening to the radio.

Can't you turn that thing off? Janice said.

I'm listening, said Dora.

The voice on the radio said that there were crowds outside the court where the Sandman was being tried, shouting and chanting. Janice dragged a chair noisily across the floor.

Librarians are supposed to be quiet, she said. Dora looked round.

There's no one in, she said. Janice thumped a stack of newspapers down on the counter. Whenever she could she avoided the news. It wasn't easy. While she could read she couldn't help taking in print off the page, on the newsagent's counter, or in the paper of the woman sitting next to her on the bus, or in the ones she stacked herself each day in the library. Then, more often than not, someone would say to her,

Did you hear about that woman up Mossbrook, and she would say,

Don't tell me, I don't want to know, and they would say,

O I know, terrible isn't it, pregnant and took the two little ones with her.

Don't you find you're getting out of touch? Dora said. Janice stuffed a sheaf of papers into the rack.

Not as much as I'd like, she said.

It was true, you couldn't avoid it. Janice didn't want to know, as she tapped into her early morning egg, that some pensioner's skull had been smashed in with a hammer, or some baby had died of abuse, but try though she did, she was still aware of Events. Sometimes she felt she had stumbled on to a secret, that there was actually no way in the world you could get out of touch, even if you burned all the papers and turned off all the receivers, the air itself would be alive with transmission, entering your body like a massive intravenous drip that could no longer be turned off, though your veins and arteries were bursting with it.

Well I like to know what's going in, Dora said. Don't you, Gwen? Janice shuffled more papers into a neat heap. TRAIL OF BLOOD, one said.

Look, she said. I'll tell you what's going on. There's a war somewhere, and a famine somewhere else. More people are dying of AIDS and the hole in the ozone layer's getting bigger. One serial killer's on trial, another'll be starting somewhere soon. And there's a spate of break-ins in local shops. There. I haven't even listened to the news, but the stories are always the same. It beats me why they call it news, she said, and shuffled off into the stock-room.

Well I think it's important, she heard Dora say.

Don't you, Gwen? It's important to know what's going on.

Well, yes, Gwen said.

Janice shut the door of the stock-room. She almost felt like locking it, but that would be over-reacting. You do over-react, Janice, her mother said. It was true. She over-reacted and she

201

didn't want to know about the world around her. She would probably end up in a home for the terminally out of touch. She sighed and began marking off books on her list.

Then later she was left on her own. Gwen left an hour early, zipping up a brightly coloured jacket and picking up two bags of shopping for her husband from behind the counter.

Going anywhere exciting? Janice asked with some irony, since she already knew the answer.

O you know, just round to Bill's for a while, then I might call in at the Centre.

They paused and looked at one another, and for a moment Janice considered telling Gwen how tired she looked, and that she was stretching herself in too many different directions, but she didn't. People didn't welcome it in the end, she thought, just as she didn't welcome the many comments on her appearance made by her mother or Dora. In the end she just said,

Don't do anything I wouldn't do, and they both grinned, acknowledging the irony of it, the narrowness of their lives.

The large room of the library with its background of purple and tawny hills seemed more spacious in dimming light. Janice sat at the VDU. She had to update the microfiche file before she left.

Before Dora left she had talked about getting Dave to take her somewhere different for a change, on a different night, like tonight.

I just feel like getting dolled up and going out, she said. There's a new nightclub opened in town.

All day the road outside the library had been up and roadworkers had been in and out of the library on their breaks just to watch Dora stack shelves and to ask her out. None of them wanted to borrow books. Dora treated them all with equal amounts of disdain, but they kept coming back. Janice couldn't imagine it, that kind of experience, what it must do for you. She didn't even think Dora was that pretty. Beneath the long sleeve of her dress her arm was bone thin and the curve from cheek to chin was rather sharp, but she'd come to accept the idea of Dora's prettiness, just from watching the reactions of other people. And it was obvious what it had done for Dora – the unstinted admiration of men from her father onwards – it affected everything about her, the way she carried herself, what she expected from life. Yet when she talked about getting Dave to go somewhere different there was a real wistfulness in her voice, as if she too wanted more from life but didn't know what. Maybe that was true of everyone, beautiful or not, an ongoing condition of chronic wistfulness. Still, it was some comfort to Janice to know that even the beautiful felt cheated.

Well she was cheerful tonight, Janice thought, pushing herself away from the desk with sudden energy. She'd noticed it before, a condition of isolation, the natural downward tendency of her thoughts, she couldn't help it. It had been a day like this, not long ago, the first time she'd felt she would always be alone. She'd been alone in the library, working on the VDU, thinking about Ken. It came to her then, suddenly, that she would never meet anyone else. And part of her said that was ridiculous, she was still only in her thirties, people met other people at all times in their lives. If you watched telly or read the magazines you might be excused for thinking that was all people ever did. Yet deeper than logic she felt it keenly, she would always be alone.

Janice carried the left-over books on the counter back to the shelves. Why should she worry about loneliness, she thought. Most of the time she actually preferred being alone, other people had the peculiar effect of emphasising her loneliness. Sometimes though she would like physical contact, it didn't have to be sex.

Who needs sex anyway, said Becca's voice. The only times I ever tried it gave me thrush or lockjaw.

Janice caught sight of herself in the glass of a print which showed the original library building; rounded shoulders, thick glasses, and, faint but unmistakable as she leaned closer, the brownish wisp of a moustache.

You could be done for wilful ugliness, said Becca.

But you didn't have to be beautiful, Janice thought, just thin, and young. More and more she felt the loss of her youth as the loss of some indefinable attractiveness she'd never even known she had. But now she noticed it all the time in others, anyone at all young, they didn't even have to be pretty.

I look at myself as a kind of social therapy, Becca said. When people look at me they feel good about themselves.

Becca wasn't ugly, just fat. That was the crucial factor however, fat made you featureless. Becca was smaller than Janice, more round, but to the rest of the world they were just two fat women. And people felt an obligation to interfere, as if they were breaking some unstated rule.

You shouldn't be having that sugar, Mavis Willshaw said as Becca stirred two spoonfuls into her coffee. Becca stared at her then ladled another one in.

I've been on a diet all my life, she said before Mavis Willshaw could speak. I've lost a total of about seven hundred pounds. I should be the size of an amoeba. But hey, she said, addressing everyone. I'm half way there. I'm the right shape.

That was the first time Janice thought she might like Becca, in spite of the relentless jolliness that clawed on her nerves. For Becca was always making jokes, she always had a funny story to tell, and the story always had to be funnier than everyone else's. Most people didn't mind, they liked it in fact, but Janice thought Becca was trapped inside the Fat Woman's act, compulsorily jolly. She drew attention to her fat all the time, as if no one would notice otherwise, and talked all the time, as if keeping a barrier between herself and the rest of the world. When she first came to the library she wore the kind of flowery tent dresses with Peter Pan collars that were available at the time in outsize shops. She drew a mocking attention to these too, as if she always had to be more vigilant than everyone else. Janice thought it was a kind of trap and felt scornful of Becca for falling into it. She spent the first few weeks avoiding Becca as best she could in the small library. At the same time she admired her ear-rings – great bunches of purple grapes, or curving moons – so different from the clothes she wore they were like a mute protest.

Grandmother, what big thighs you have! Becca said, wobbling the flesh on her upper legs. All the better for churning people's stomachs with . . .

Janice turned away from her reflection. She wore thick glasses and a thick jumper. Men were not attracted to her.

Well if you will go round looking like a road accident, Becca said, and Dora said,

If you'd just make more of yourself.

Hey, said Becca. How much more of me do you want?

They used to laugh at the way they looked. Of course they both had their good points. Janice's eyes were light and clear, Becca had abundant dark hair. But neither of these features counted against the overwhelming presence of fat.

A sudden spattering of stones against the large window shook Janice out of her thoughts. She looked round sharply. There were kids massing around between the roadworks and the iron railings outside, throwing small stones at different targets. As she crossed to the window another shower hit at the level of her face.

Cut that out, she shouted. Clear off.

The kids paused momentarily.

You can't make us, the one with the shaved head shouted back. Janice returned to her shelves. This, she felt, was certainly true.

Out here the moor was scrofulous, haggard. The wind-dry grass had flaked away in patches exposing pinkish-grey shale and dark slabs of slate. It was as though the surface of the moor were peeling. Janice sank her head further into her padded jacket. Days like this it was easy to forget what drove her on to the moor, the aggravating urge that wouldn't leave her alone until she shut the door of her house behind her. The moor, which from a distance looked so colourful and rich, was like this up close, barren and eaten away. From where she stood it was the next part of the moor that beckoned and was beautiful. Janice stood still, sweating a little because of her sense of nakedness beneath the sky, knowing her condition to be chronic. One day she'd be unable to stop. She would press on further and further, looking for the patch of moor that finally fulfilled its promise. She would disappear entirely, like a character in a folk tale.

As far as she could see in any direction a broad sweep of moor stretched as if humanity had never happened, black and purple, pinkish-brown and patches of a light, sage green. It had a name of course, each part of it was named: Hollin Brown Knoll, Swinsey Dike, Boggart Stones, Shiny Brook Clough; odd, inexplicable names whose origins were lost. Janice wasn't interested in names, but they were hard to lose. She couldn't lose her training in botany which told her that the slippery tufts of grass beneath her feet were mat grass, almost uniformly, except for a scatterings of horse-tail and sorrel, which Janice chewed like the sheep to keep her mouth watering. Naming things didn't grant you power in the old magical way. It didn't help her to feel a part of her surroundings. Out here even the sky was angled differently, poised like a kestrel. There was nothing for her here in his heavy, sombre sea of sky and stones and moss. She plunged her hands more deeply into her pockets and, hunching her shoulders, turned to go.

The house Janice finally bought was on the edge of a croft, overlooking the far end of the valley. At the bottom of the valley was a disused power station, its corrugated roof and cables obscuring the lower part of the view. On the other side of the valley was a flat-topped hill. There were no houses on this hill except for a single farmhouse, high up, whose lights Janice often watched in the evenings. The farmer owned the sheep which were dotted about the hillside, and the dogs which chased the sheep. You could tell there was a road because of the lorries crawling up it to the quarry on the other side. But apart from this there were only the changing colours of the hillside, sliced off neatly where they met the changing colours of the sky.

Janice's house was so run down she'd had difficulty getting a mortgage. Her mother had warned her against taking it. It'll be nothing but trouble, she'd said. Janice could have had a perfectly good house with the housing association. But this house had appealed to her, its loneliness, the flat, uncultivated croft on one side and the small, tangled garden in front. It was one of a row of equally tumbledown two-up-two-down houses, but it was the end of a row and all the neighbours were elderly. They'd lived there a long time, no one else wanted to live in that abandoned end of the village, so far away from the shops. Beyond the garden there was a dirt track with a tree and a lamp-post at one end, and beyond that nothing, just the downward slope of the hill. No one ever went along the dirt track unless they had to, to deliver milk or post.

Janice had some help with the house from her brother Peter, who was a builder, but he was too busy to come often. Then a neighbour, Mr Harding, started helping out. He was nearly eighty, but had taught himself to do all kinds of jobs over the years: plumbing and plastering and minor electrical work. With his help Janice tackled several jobs herself, once Peter had built a new roof and put in a damp-proof course. She'd fitted new gutters, plastered the kitchen and repaired the drystone wall bordering the garden. She took floorboards up, clearing the rot beneath, and replaced two window frames. But the fireplace was

207

her great achievement. The old man who'd lived in the house before had had a cheap gas fire installed over the original fireplace. Janice got the gas board to take it away and set about restoring the original fire. She had to unblock the chimney, then she tiled the surround herself, prising bricks out with a chisel, plastering then covering the plaster with dark-blue tiles with yellow lilies which her mother said didn't go with the overall colour scheme.

There wasn't a colour scheme as such. The carpet was a dark red square with blue and brown patterning, there was a pale-green *chaise-longue* with a woven blanket draped over it which was the cat's favourite seat, and a flowered rocking chair which was Janice's. There was an ancient sideboard, books in the alcove and a black and white television left by Ken. Above the fire was one of her mother's tapestries, not the usual kind – thatched cottage with hollyhocks – but a swan on a lake, reflections of trees and sky. Her mother had given it to her when she was ready to move in, to show she didn't bear grudges. There was also a deep window-sill with a cushion so Janice could sit watching her garden and the valley as the sun set, unafraid of being overlooked.

In the garden, though the soil was bad, Janice was growing flowers in old containers: a metal bucket, a tin bath, the drum of her last washing-machine. She had induced a trailing buttercup to grow in the crevices of her stone wall. In early summer poppies seeded themselves generously and there was a froth of something orange she'd not identified yet near the gate.

That was the extent of her success with the house so far. In the kitchen the old misshapen cupboards were still on the walls, paint peeling, and there was a stain of something indefinable but smelly seeping through the tiles. Janice had picked up a solid table at an auction for next to nothing, but it needed stripping and sanding down, and the washing-machine wasn't working.

Upstairs things had hardly changed since the old man had died, and all these things served as constant reminders of neglect.

Today, coming in from the moor, Janice could take no pleasure in her garden or front room, or in the cat, who was winding himself around her legs. She could feel only the blind compulsion to eat. Before going out she'd prepared a big stew with tinned tomatoes and pasta and vegetables, and all the way home she'd thought of nothing else. Now she fried sausages and emptied a tin of tuna into the bubbling tomatoes. She made a sauce from cream and peas, parmesan cheese and butter. All the time she was preparing the food she was eating: scooping out large chunks of butter with bread, stirring syrup into powdered-milk and eating it from a spoon. When the sausages were almost black she tipped them into the pan and poured the parmesan sauce over the top. Then she carried the pan into the lounge.

She sat with her back to the window and the pan on a tray on her knee, scooping up stew with the bread, then, as it cooled, with her fingers. It was very important to her to be able to eat like this, exactly what she wanted in the exact way she wanted to eat it. While she could eat like this, with the tomato running down her chin and wrists and sleeves, she could forget herself, forget everything except the urge to cram one fistful after another into her mouth. She wasn't aware of the room around her nor of the fading light outside, eventually even her mother's voice disappeared in a way which never otherwise happened, even on the hills.

The bursting pain in her stomach became bad, but she wouldn't give in until the panful of food had gone. She ate with the kind of concentrated, absorbed energy she couldn't give to anything else, and when there was a small noise outside it caused her to shudder violently, dropping the pan on the floor.

Janice scurried to the other side of the room, frightened by the beating of her heart. She felt as though she was clinging to a cliff-

209

face with the light of a thousand torches suddenly switched upon her. When the beating of her heart became manageable she was able to see that it was only her next-door neighbour, Mrs Briggs, sweeping the path outside.

Slowly Janice returned to the window. She stood to one side where she couldn't be seen and for the first time noticed the evening light. The sun had stained the valley until it seemed to be suspended in a clear, peachy-orange gel. In the diffuse light even the cables and corrugated roof of the power station were beautiful.

Janice remained by the window, suspended in light. It illuminated the clear green of her eyes and the dullness of her hair. It illuminated also the red stain of tomatoes on her cheeks and round her mouth, down her chin and the front of her sweatshirt, discolouring her hands. She looked as though she had been drinking blood.

Janice's mother, Evelyn, ate sandwiches cut into tiny triangles with a scrape of margarine and fish paste or potted beef and cucumber for filling. She made a lot of them for church fêtes and coffee mornings, bringing home the leftovers.

Janice knocked at the door, clutching the bunch of carnations she had bought on some impulse she could not now remember. Her mother stood in the doorway, blinking at the flowers.

O it's you, she said. Come in.

Janice lowered her face to the flowers and followed her mother along the hall. Maybe she hadn't held them out far enough.

You know Janice don't you Iris, her mother said, and Iris Platt (eighty-two), a wispy woman with a red felt hat and dark grey fizzy hair, said she'd seen her before at the library. Janice laid the carnations down on the edge of the sink and scanned the frosted glass of the cupboards for sign of a vase.

Sit down Janice, her mother said. You're making the place look untidy.

The kitchen was tiny, too small for the three of them, but Janice's mother went on with her thrashing and pounding of dough as if it made no difference to her, moving expertly between the litter of baking tins, whipped cream, greaseproof paper and plastic containers. Janice used to live on a different part of the same estate, in an identical housing association flat. When a chance came to buy a house on the same estate by some scheme which meant you only paid part of the mortgage at first, Janice's mother had felt strongly that she should take it. They had viewed it together. It was a modern house, set down lower than the road, with steps leading down the sloping garden to the front door, and enormous windows.

It's a quiet cul-de-sac, her mother said.

Everyone can see in, said Janice.

When Janice took the house on the croft her mother reacted as though it was yet another of the blows she'd come to expect over the years, in the same category as Janice failing to pursue her degree, or a proper career, or get married. Her erect body became a little stiffer, but no more was said.

I'm not one to interfere, she said, frequently. You make your own bed.

Janice's mother made pastry the way some people might slaughter animals, pounding and carving ruthlessly, making incisions. Everything about her said it was a bad job, but the best had to be made of it. She applied this philosophy to the whole of her domestic routine, which was relentless and had never varied over the years. When Janice was a child the air had been stiff with her mother's burdens as she drove the vacuum cleaner over the carpets and scrubbed the kitchen floor. Though she didn't enjoy it she ran her life around it, it had apparently become her reason for living. At least it took up her time, so she

211

had no time for anything else, and maybe that was what she wanted.

Iris has just come to collect my contribution to refreshments for the church roof committee's day, her mother said. I'm afraid I'm not going. I haven't time.

It was difficult to imagine her mother being afraid, even of time, Janice thought, watching her ignore Iris, who was talking in her wispy way about Mr Tetlow's pace-maker, and the Hollingworths who were getting divorced after all this time, twenty-six years and the children all grown up.

Make yourself a cup of tea, Janice's mother said, cutting right across Iris. The kettle's just boiled. Iris has just had one, haven't you Iris, she said, forestalling Iris's request for another one. She'll be going soon.

Iris wavered a moment, then said there'd been a row at the Mothers' Union about who'd take charge of the brasses. Everyone wanted to do the flowers.

Janice found herself a mug and a tea bag and was about to pour water into the mug when her mother prodded the teapot.

Warm the pot, she said.

Janice warmed the pot, though she considered it to be yet another of the useless rituals around which her mother's life revolved. She poured the tea, edging away from her mother, who removed cakes from the oven on to cooling trays and from cooling trays into empty margarine tubs and Tupperware containers. Neither she nor Iris offered to help, they both knew her mother too well.

Iris talked about the Greenwoods, who hadn't made a go of the off-licence, even with Barry's redundancy money, and now it was up for sale.

Barry Greenwood never did have the sense he was born with, Janice's mother said. He couldn't run a bath.

Nothing to do with the recession, Janice thought, reaching

behind her mother for a large jug in the cupboard, it wasn't a vase but it would have to do.

It used to be nice when Joan Hepworth ran it, Iris said. She always had nice bacon. I like a nice bit of bacon.

That was before the war, Janice's mother said, rolling her eyes at Janice. Janice began sorting through the carnations. The jug wasn't tall enough for the tall stems.

O are those for me? her mother said as if she'd only just noticed them. You might have known I don't have any big vases. Janice said nothing, but continued arranging the flowers in the jug in which they didn't fit, then she sat on a stool in a corner of the kitchen and looked down at her tea.

At times like this she sometimes reconstructed a memory she had, building one detail on to another. She was walking along the pavement of a main road, holding her younger brother Peter by the hand, as her mother had told her. Her mother was carrying heavy bags, even so they were lagging behind and she had to keep turning to speak to them sharply. It was a bright, watery day. The sun's diluted gleam shone on the metal bumpers of cars and the water streaming in the gutters. Janice's older brother, David, had met his best friend Gary and they were running ahead towards the next main road, stamping in all the puddles. Janice's mother cried out, then everything in Janice's memory seemed to slow down, and yet blur, as if it were actually speeding up. She remembered the screech of brakes from the lorry, which, as it slid through a long puddle, sent up a flare of water. She remembered her mother's spilled bags, the tin of carrots tumbling over her foot, and the acute sense of shame as her mother screamed and screamed, in a deep rough voice like a man's.

Though the kitchen surfaces were so small her mother's energetic movements announced her control of their spatial organisation. Iris's talk drifted on like smoke. This time Janice cut across her, leaning forwards.

I saw Peter yesterday, she said. He said he might call round. She monitored her mother's reactions, the way her face relaxed and softened like it never did for Janice. Still she went on.

Jamie and Laura are well, she said. Jamie's making you a card himself for your birthday.

Her mother smiled.

Janice watched herself doing it, arriving vicariously at the response she wanted for herself, cutting a little deeper into her own wounds.

I've made them both jumpers you know, her mother said. I'll be taking them round Sunday.

That was the end of another conversation. As if she'd never been interrupted Iris told them about Mavis Kenworthy's mastectomy. Janice closed her eyes, letting the soft stream of talk drift by. Then another memory returned, sharp, her mother clinging to Peter at the funeral and sobbing as Janice stood by.

Father James is going to Torremolinos, Iris said, but it's church business.

Father James wasn't Catholic, but High Church. Janice's mother disapproved of High Church and had given the vicar short shrift when he called round to see why she no longer attended. She still belonged to various committees and the tapestry circle, but attended even these irregularly, preferring to do the work at home and send in a contribution.

Janice's mother pressed the last lid firmly down on to the last Tupperware container.

There, she said.

Iris showed no signs of leaving. She mentioned that Robert, the vicar's son, was doing well at school, and that Mrs Jacques had dropped out of the Lady's Day committee just because they hadn't asked her to run a stall.

Janice observed, as Iris didn't, her mother becoming increasingly irritated by Iris's talk. Despite the many circles she

214

was attached to she wasn't really interested in gossip. In any case she already seemed to know everything, perhaps because she'd lived in Marley all her life, and people told her things.

O I forgot to say, said Iris. Did you know Linda Brooke's having triplets? They're having to build an extension.

Janice's mother packed the last Tupperware container into a plastic bag and stood by the door holding them out to Iris.

She's wondering what to call them all, Iris said to Janice. She was saying she'd like to give them all names beginning with the same letter, you know, with them being triplets.

Janice's mother opened the door.

She could call them Milly, Molly and Mandy and have done with it, she said. I'll just show you out, she added, when Iris failed to move.

Janice glanced downwards at her tea as Iris left. There were times, it had to be said, when she almost liked her mother.

Janice stood in front of the mirror, running her hands down from her face over her clothes. Her body sloped outwards, small breasts for a fat woman, a thick waist, massive hips and thighs. It was hardly a female shape at all. When she walked the hills in her shorts and boots with her cropped, brownish hair, she looked more like an overgrown boy scout than anything else.

Well you never know, your basic walrus shape might be in next year, said Becca's voice.

Even her face was boyish, round and smooth, but when you looked closely, covered with fine lines from so much country walking.

You're old before your time, said her mother, and Becca quoted at her,

Nothing ages a woman like living in the country.

Janice thought of her mother's immaculate appearance, the white coiffure like a stiffly-whipped meringue, a brooch always pinned to the front of her blouse. She never looked disordered, even when baking.

You're letting yourself go, Janice, she often said. In her mother's eyes this was the ultimate offence. She used to say to Janice that even a plain woman could look well if she was properly turned out and had some consideration for the people who had to look at her. Janice used to hate her for that, in the way that you had to hate people who were supposed to love you but who didn't find you beautiful. She didn't want to play the game, spend the money, kowtow to what people expected to see. She continued exposing, even promoting the ugliness she had. And mainly these days people left her alone. Even Dora had stopped cutting out magazine articles on diet and making the most of yourself, and buying her make-up for her birthdays. They left her alone, to herself, to the self she found so hideous and inescapable.

Janice went into the kitchen and prised open the large Tupperware container her mother had insisted on giving her as she had left, soon after Iris. It was full of the remains of her baking, the bits of it she didn't think perfect enough to display: mince pies, jam tarts, apple tarts, fruit loaf and most of a collapsed chocolate cake. Her mother's insistence on feeding Janice was matched only by her many warnings about Janice's weight.

She pushed the first mince pie into her mouth and crammed in a jam tart before she had time to swallow. Then she poked in the first chunk of chocolate cake, scarcely stopping to gag.

It sometimes occurred to Janice that the aggression with which her mother baked the food was equalled only by the savagery with which Janice ate it.

She choked on a piece of pastry but continued to push it down, four pieces of fruit loaf, another slab of chocolate cake. She retched for the first time but went on with a terrible patience.

Becca reckoned she could eat up to twenty-six thousand calories a day, providing she threw up enough. Her record was forty times. The throwing up didn't work, she still expanded steadily all the time she worked at the library, and afterwards. Eventually she began to suffer from gallstones, and no longer needed to make herself throw up. Janice remembered one day when she'd asked Becca a question and Becca didn't reply. She'd turned to see her hanging on to the counter with white knuckles.

Becca, Janice said, then Gwen, Dora.

Between them they manoeuvred her on to a chair and Dora ran to get her a glass of water. Becca's face was swollen and congested. The veins at her temples swelled until Janice thought they would weep blood. She gripped Janice's hands hard and made no sound. That was terrible to Janice, the formidable control.

When she recovered enough to speak she wouldn't have the doctor, but allowed Gwen to drive her home.

Janice wiped her fingers round the Tupperware container, licking up the last smears of chocolate before starting on the fruit pie.

Why was she thinking so much about Becca today?

It was Dora's fault, she'd started it. They'd all been sitting together at lunchtime, since it was pouring down outside and the library was empty. Dora had a yoghurt, two sticks of celery and some cottage cheese, which was all she ever ate. She didn't eat breakfast and rarely had much for tea. Gwen had been to the bakery for herself and Janice, they had wholemeal rolls with cheese and salad. Gwen also had a flapjack, but Janice had refused, eating, as she always did in company, with great restraint.

They ate in silence as the rain beat hard against the windows. The quality of light made the strip lighting inside the library lurid. Janice was wondering if the rain would stop before her next walk, when Dora said,

I wonder what Becca's doing now.

Gwen smiled and looked downwards, Janice looked away. She

didn't like Dora making any kind of reference to Becca since Dora had benefited from what happened to her. If Becca hadn't slid so far downhill Dora would still only have a part-time job.

So no one responded to Dora's question but Dora didn't seem to mind. She packed away one stick of celery and half the cheese to save for later and hummed a little, staring into the distance.

Janice too stared into the distance, trying to remember that it wasn't Dora's fault, even if she had leapt straight into Becca's place. It wasn't Dora's fault that Mr Norton had disliked Becca so much he could hardly bear to look at her. He could hardly bear to look at Janice either, but Janice had been there longer than either Becca or Mr Norton, or maybe it was simpler than that, the simple fact that she was bigger. At any rate, his dislike didn't have the same devastating effect on her. But Becca changed when he was around, she became foolish, and incompetent. He only had to be in the same room for her to start making mistakes. It was a painful thing to watch, the way he would stand just near enough to her for her to start dropping books and smudging the ink from the stamp.

It's good to see your work is up to its usual standard, he would say, so that anyone in the library could hear. He gave her all the worst jobs and Becca, forceful at any other time, just accepted it, leaning further over her work with a red and bursting face. It was as though she had no resistance to him at all, as if he brought to the surface of her mind everything she despised about herself, and she became everything he thought she was: slovenly, inadequate, stupid. The mystery of it was it didn't work on Janice, he couldn't take Janice's direct stare, what Becca called her meat-cleaving stare, but with Becca it was like watching a child being bullied at school. Whenever she saw him Janice could sense her despair. Her attacks of illness became more frequent.

Mr Norton couldn't sack Becca, he didn't have the the direct power. But he talked all the time about government cuts and the necessity of cutting back on staff. She took days off. He issued warnings about absenteeism, she stayed off work. It was as though they were locked into a synchronised dance.

One day he called her into the office. After a while he left and she didn't come out. Janice went to find her. Becca was sitting quite still, staring at the surface of the desk. When she saw Janice she jumped up and began to fumble for her bag, just as if Janice were Mr Norton. Janice remembered the trembling, unco-ordinated movements.

Becca, Janice said.

Becca wouldn't look at Janice.

I forgot my shoes, she said, scurrying around one side of the desk for the spare pair she always kept. She went on talking in a breathless kind of way.

Have I got everything, I don't feel as though I have – you know the feeling – when you're about to leave the house but you're sure you've left the gas on?

It was a polite, distant, hurried kind of talking, as if Janice were a stranger.

Becca, Janice said again.

Or when you've packed to go on holiday, Becca said, but you're sure you've left something behind? She picked up some papers, shaking them into a pile, then stuffing them into her handbag, spilling them as she pushed them down. Janice bent down to pick them up, and glancing upwards managed to catch Becca's eye for the first time.

Becca, I'm sorry, she said.

O don't be, Becca said quickly. Don't be that.

Janice said nothing. She felt foolish. It wasn't what she'd meant to say, she didn't even know why she was apologising. She'd meant to ask what had happened, to express support and encourage resistance, but she felt herself caught up in the helplessness of the moment. She looked down at the papers.

These aren't yours, are they? she said. But Becca was hurrying round the table again, fluttering and fussing like a large hen.

Did I bring my umbrella? she said. I don't think I did . . . Where did I put my coat?

Silently Janice held out Becca's coat. She could feel her face burning up like Becca's. Becca fumbled with the coat but when Janice made a move to help her Becca jumped violently and they stared at one another in a profound kind of helplessness.

I don't feel as if I've got everything, Becca said.

Janice looked away. When she looked back Becca was leaving in a flurry of plastic bags, coat flapping, through the side door so she wouldn't have to walk past Dora or Gwen.

Janice watched her go. She did nothing.

These two facts haunted her to this day yet she still didn't know what she could have done. She couldn't have interested the union since they had never been less active. Besides it wasn't something you did any longer. You sat tight in your job, thanking God you'd got one. Janice did nothing, Gwen did nothing and Dora got the full-time job. Janice didn't say a word about this either, to Mr Norton, or Dora (whose fault it wasn't) and after a time her dislike faded into the general uselessness of disliking anything, outside yourself.

Janice could feel nothing but the bursting pain of her stomach; not shame, nor guilt nor hatred, just a fugitive pleasure at the thought that she might be sick.

After a while she began to want to move, though it felt like too much effort. She closed her eyes and could see herself moving but it was a while before she could grope her way from the kitchen into the lounge. She switched on the small TV and sank back heavily into the flowered rocking-chair.

A man was talking about his sex life. Janice didn't want to

watch this any more than she wanted to watch anything else, but she wanted the flickering images of the screen to distract her.

The man was saying that he had a need to be punished. On his days off his girlfriend kept him trussed up like a chicken and suspended from a hook in the ceiling. She made him walk in the park on a lead, dressed as a dog. There was a shot of them both in the park, the man on all fours and dressed in a shaggy outfit. Janice hoped for his sake he didn't actually think he looked like a dog.

It was amazing to Janice that he could say that on television. Didn't he have to go to work the next day? Maybe that was all part of the humiliation, or maybe you could get to a point of being so cut off from people it felt more natural to be talking to a screen, like the one you always carried round inside your head.

Becca used to be an expert on day-time television. During her long periods of unemployment she had watched it all, *Pebble Mill*, *Good Morning Britain*, Anne and Nick. The real danger, she said, was that you did actually get to enjoy it. She could take them all off, the guest celebrities, the interviews with people who had peculiar problems to talk about, or startling gynaecological experience, like giving birth to quins at sixty-five.

Today we'll be talking to Mrs Tomkins, she said, who has managed to incubate an entire emu in her colostomy bag.

More and more people, it seemed were exposing their whole lives to the glass screen, living under it, acting out their own lives.

The thought made Janice feel bad enough to lean forwards and switch off the set, despite the groaning pain in her stomach. She sank back, wiping the sweat off her upper lip, feeling the lumbering weight of her body, gross and shapeless in the chair. She felt she would rather die than eat so much again, but she knew that tomorrow or the next day she would eat, and she didn't know if she would stop.

Janice sat very still in her chair, trying to contain the sensations of pain in her stomach. She made herself open her eyes and watch the window, with its views of sky. There was a fly crawling up the pane, sliding a little then crawling back up towards the frame. When it reached the frame it stopped, then instead of crawling on to the wood it turned, and followed the path of the frame horizontally along the glass, as if it too didn't want to lose its view of sky. Maybe that way it could convince itself it was outside. But it could never get out, unless Janice opened the window. Janice didn't move, but watched the fly crawling up and down and along the pane of glass. She thought of all the people living mainly lonely, hidden lives – the man telling his fantasies to the screen. Everyone had fantasies, about the way they were, and the lives they led. Maybe it was the same for everyone; you were, all of you, crawling around inside your fantasies like the fly inside its pane of glass, convincing itself it was on the outside.

One day, soon after she had left her mother's flat to move into one of her own, there was a knock on the door. Janice jumped violently, she wasn't used to visitors. When she opened the door it was Ken.

She was completely thrown. For days she'd avoided getting the bus because she felt so shown up whenever he talked to her. The weather had been fine, she'd made sure that she got up early enough to walk. Her flat was near the end of the bus route. On her days off she could just see him sitting in the bus at the terminus, eating his sandwiches. Today she hadn't bothered to look. But now here he was.

Ken asked if he could trouble her for some hot water for his flask. She hardly heard him, suddenly conscious as she was of her old trousers and shirt with paint stains, her unwashed hair. Then she grabbed the flask off him and hurried inside without asking him in.

Nice place you've got here, he said, following her.

Janice ignored him. She filled the kettle, plugged it in, and hastily swept some crumbs off the work surface. All the time she was telling herself to calm down. Why should she be thrown into a nervous panic because a balding man with a sagging face had called round for some hot water?

Ken seated himself at the table and leaned back, watching her with half-closed eyes. When she filled his flask he didn't seem in a hurry to move.

Thank you, he said, with the smile that seemed too big for his face. He unscrewed the lid and poured himself a drink.

Want one? he said. Janice stood on the other side of the table.

Won't you be late getting back? she said. Ken smiled.

Not me, he said. I'm finished for the day. I've just got to take the bus back. When I'm ready. And he raised his eyebrows and looked at her very directly. His eyes were hazel with yellow flecks. Janice said nothing. Tension hung between them like a thin bright cord and she couldn't look away. Then Ken released her from his gaze and looked round the kitchen.

I've often wondered where you lived, he said, and Janice heard herself say,

I've only lived here a few weeks.

And before that you lived with your mother, right? Ken said. Janice stared at him, disconcerted by his assumption of knowledge. He didn't seem at all shy now, the way he sometimes seemed on the bus. He took out a packet of cigarettes and offered her one. Janice wanted to tell him to leave her flat. Instead she said,

I'll get you an ashtray, and almost ran into the lounge. She stood for a moment pressing her hand to her face, wanting not to feel so peculiarly disturbed.

On the coffee-table was the Chocolate Orange she'd been eating before Ken knocked on the door. She took it and quickly began to cram the remaining segments into her mouth until a movement behind her made her freeze.

My aunt has a flat like this, said Ken.

Janice kept her back to him, chewing frantically. She spotted the ashtray and went towards it. When she held it out to him without turning he took it, then caught her hand and began to play with her fingers. There were chocolate stains on them, Janice snatched them away. Her stomach was burning, she would have terrible indigestion. Even without turning she could still feel his movements and his eyes. He stood between her and the door. Any minute now she would turn round and order him out of her flat. But even as she was thinking this he was right behind her, putting his hands on her shoulders, turning her around.

You'll have to go, she said, not looking at him. Ken pressed her chin up with his fingers and kissed her. His face was very bristly.

Just calm down, he said. Relax.

These days she was relieved to leave work. It wasn't the work itself, though they were undoubtedly being asked to do more. Bit by bit their normal duties were being increased, it was difficult to keep track. Sometimes they were told it was temporary, but the situation never seemed to revert to normal. Ideas of normal had gone. At first you didn't notice so much except for an extra feeling of tiredness which you put down to feeling under the weather. And because the goal posts were shifting, and everything had been renamed, you sometimes wondered if anyone else knew what you were talking about. Dora would deny it, for instance. Things had changed, but they hadn't got worse, there was all this new equipment; and Gwen, working mechanically on throughout the day, her mind on other things, wouldn't notice, but it irked Janice because the job she'd applied for bore so little resemblance to the one she was doing. And her pay, relative to inflation, had gone down. Still she knew she was lucky to have a job. If Gwen hadn't been so near retirement she knew one of them would have been asked to leave and she suspected it wouldn't be Dora. So it was better to forget, and not to analyse the changes too closely. It didn't improve her state of mind, it just made her furious, and tired. Maybe that was why she needed to eat so much, just to keep going.

She was eating now; a pork pie and a vanilla slice she'd picked up from the baker's near the library. As she walked she ate, breaking them apart with her fingers and stuffing them into her mouth. She saw nothing of the silvery light around her, the saturated green of the hills. The persistent part of her that kept remembering wouldn't let her forget that things were changing, things had changed radically in the fifteen years she'd been at the library, and the atmosphere was tense with the expectation of worse things to come. And if she didn't remember she might start blaming herself, she was always tired, she wasn't up to it. She certainly wasn't like the happy, fulfilled go-getters on telly or in magazines. And the effort to forget pressed her on from one thing to another so she never got to look at anything too closely. Even now as she was eating she couldn't taste the food. As soon as it was in her mouth she was pushing the next mouthful down. When she got to work she couldn't wait to finish, but home was just a transitional space between work. When she switched on the telly she was impatient for the end of each programme, even now she was pressing ahead to the end of her walk home.

Janice paused, realising she was near the paper shop. She craved chocolate, not with a physical hunger but with a kind of mental clawing. There was a queue so she would have to wait, when really she wanted to get on. For a moment she hovered, poised between conflicting desires. Then she went in.

Towards the front of the queue a fight broke out between schoolchildren.

You pinched it.

I never.

Give it us back.

Then a scuffle broke out so that the man behind the counter had to throw them out. Janice jiggled her foot in exasperation then forced herself to look round.

Glossy cover girls beamed over such headings as, *I lost all my children in a fire*, or *Impotence and You*. *My husband let all his friends rape me*, said the cover of one magazine. *Knit this marvellous matinee jacket*.

Something for everyone, Becca's voice said. Sexual perverts and knitters.

The cover girls were all different, but none of them was memorable. You would walk out of the shop and be unable to remember the face on the front of *She* or *Ms* magazine, but the composite image stayed; full lips, high cheekbones, large or slightly slanting eyes. The same headings recurred like items of news; on women's magazines they were mainly about men, attracting them, curing them of impotence and premature ejaculation, or the failure to commit. Men's magazines, not the ones on the top shelf, had famous men on the covers, and had features like, *Ten Top Businessmen – How They Made Their First Million* and *Could You Be a Super Stud?* They expressed no curiosity about women at all.

Further along the shelves were magazines dedicated to the lives of the rich and famous: movie stars, aristocracy. And even Janice, who wasn't interested and worked hard at avoiding it all, knew things she didn't want to know – the faces at a film festival, or a Hollywood party. She could roughly pair up the ones who were married and knew that one couple had just had a baby. It was mysterious to her how she knew these things, and a kind of violation. What happened to all the famous faces in your mind? Did they just stay there, lodged permanently, like food you couldn't digest in your gut?

Below the fleshy section on the top shelf, where women pressed buttocks and breasts towards the camera until their nipples were the size of tennis balls, were the slimming and beauty magazines. Gina had had her jaws wired and her stomach stapled. Five months later the staples burst and you could read her incredible story inside. There was an article on liposuction and how it might work for you. Janice hesitated a moment, then put it back. She didn't want to know. Or rather, and more problematically, she did want to know. She couldn't say that, in moments of despair, she had never thought of offering herself up to the butchery of knives. Becca thought about it all the time, though she did say once that her grandmother used to stuff a cushion up her skirt to look fatter. Fat had been in then, in England, though now it was definitely out. And try though you might, you couldn't prefer it yourself.

Once in the library Dora and Gwen had been talking about AIDS and Dora read aloud from an article that one of the symptoms was a dramatic weight loss, up to a stone a week.

O well then, Becca had said. I could do with it for about a month.

Janice glanced round the shop again at cadaverous models, the frozen, immobile faces of movie stars with their bared teeth, and felt herself chill slowly, as if she was surrounded by images of death.

It was a relief to get to the counter, to push the slimming magazines back on to the shelf and buy the biggest slab of chocolate she could find.

Outside she ripped the paper off the chocolate and began eating it quickly. The pressure to be somewhere else had taken over again, and she set off again, towards home.

Away from the centre of the village more and more buildings were boarded up: houses, businesses, mills. In the next village, Clough Bottom, attempts had been made to turn the old mills into craft centres, originally with the idea of keeping an interest in local crafts alive. Now, however, since there hadn't been any interest, the different units inside the mills all sold the same things: pot pourri, enamel ear-rings, scented candles and greetings cards. Janice despised the tourist trade of the next village even more than she resented the decay of her own. She finished the chocolate, screwed up the paper and tossed it through the broken window of an empty shop.

Round the corner of the shop a pair of geese waddled on to the road, followed by six chicks. Taken by surprise Janice watched as a car slowed down to let them pass. The driver smiled tolerantly at Janice.

It was a good area after all, she thought, where sheep and ducks and geese could wander on to the roads and hold up the traffic. She shouldn't ignore its good points. A little further on she stopped on the outskirts of the small park. Though April had been wet and cold the blossom was beautiful this year. One hawthorn was so laden it looked like a huge sheep hunched over in the grass. The horse chestnuts were thick with white candles.

On the other side of the park there was a bench overlooking the valley. Janice thought that she should sit on it for a moment, take a moment out of her life to sit on that bench and look round. Ignoring its damp surface she sat down.

Whoever had planted the park had done it with inspiration. There were rhododendron bushes with their heavy burning colour, purples and pinks. In the middle of the park there was a white one with big white blossoms piled floppily all over it in a kind of mad bouffant. The seasons seemed to have shifted slightly this year, all the blossom was early, even the elderflower was out in thin sprays. Everywhere wet petals clung to the streets, people slipped on them and complained.

Janice sat back and tried to take it all in, the moist untidy blossoms on the bushes and at her feet, the bus tickets and shopping receipts scattered amongst them, the smell of rain and flowers. How could she have forgotten to look? She wanted to be like this permanently, permanently alive to the beauty around her, but even as she sat her mind wandered, straying through the jumbled up fragments of her life: Gwen and Dora and the magazines, Becca, her mother, Mr Norton, the washing-machine and the need to diet. She tried again to focus on the blossom. Then she remembered that her mother hadn't liked the flowers she'd brought her and was suddenly struck with bitterness. Resolutely she closed her eyes.

At the crunch of gravel she opened them again. A man sat down on the opposite end of the bench. Janice felt the intrusion deeply. Worse still, he was talking to her.

I often come here for a sit-down, it's one of best views in the village.

Janice closed her eyes again to show she would not be intruded upon, but she could only be aware of him, and an image of him remained imprinted against her eyelids. She was surprised by how much she could see of him with her eyes closed. He was a tall man in late middle age wearing a shabby raincoat. His prominent eyes ranged over the valley without resting on anything, as if he too were held by his own inner track. Long tobacco-stained fingers, you hardly ever saw fingers that burnt yellow colour these days, and a red, slightly scaly neck. Shabby, obnoxious, and worst of all, still talking to her.

It's a fine old place, Marley.

Janice couldn't really claim to have been on the brink of self-transcendence, but now he was spoiling everything. She considered moving but felt stubborn about it. She'd been there first.

The man drifted on, apparently not noticing her lack of response . . . memories of Marley. Janice let him, sitting slightly turned away. Gradually, without her wanting them to, other images began to superimpose themselves over the ones she already had in her mind, images of him looking at her sidelong and Janice looking back. Then him getting up without looking at

229

her again and walking off, she after a pause following, to one of the derelict houses she'd just passed. No words, he pushes her down on to boards and begins binding her down; arms stretched wide, then the legs. She can hear the clink of instruments, but between her legs his fingers are light and delicate, touching her until there is a feeling of congestion there. Her body is in pain, bruised and stretched into an unnatural position, but her cunt begins to open and flower, swelling with an energy of its own.

Janice's desire welled with a simultaneous hollowness. She felt keenly the contrast between her surroundings and what she was imagining in the depths of her mind. And when she realised where she was getting her fantasy from she felt a seeping shame. She fought to bring her desire under control. She felt she'd become transparent, that he could surely see everything she was thinking. At the same time she felt there was nothing she could do to prevent this strange, savage leaking of desire. The man was silent now, and after a while he said Goodbye, and left. Shame flooded Janice, she was sure that he knew. How had sex become such a sickness with her? Perhaps it was putrefying inside her, she thought, like a wound.

She remembered Becca saying that she was never in her own fantasies, she couldn't stand the thought of herself naked. Her fantasies were peopled by beautiful, anonymous young women with pert breasts, and men she couldn't even see clearly. Janice was usually in her own fantasies but she was never unclothed. On the rare occasions when it wasn't her it was Dora in the central scene, not Gwen, nor Becca, but Dora. And what that was supposed to mean she didn't know.

In no time at all, it seemed, Ken had moved his spare telly, a portable black and white one, into Janice's bedroom. When Janice objected he said he always watched the lunchtime news. They made love in an increasingly perfunctory way before the news, Janice wasn't even enjoying it. Of course she had nothing from her own life to compare it to, but it did seem to her that the kind of jerky, unsynchronised humping she'd experienced so far was unlikely to lead to the multiple orgasms she'd read about, or to anything other than a bruised groin.

All the glossies at the time seemed to be running features on the orgasm: the existence or non-existence of the G-spot, the controversy about vaginal orgasm and the different kinds of orgasm women could experience, the multiple, slow, ecstatic kind, or the fast and powerful, almost too intense kind, which read to Janice like an epileptic fit. The problem pages, on the other hand, were full of complaints from women who felt they weren't experiencing either of these, or who felt they were almost achieving one but not quite getting there.

Dear Marian, said L. from Ipswich, I have always enjoyed sex with my husband, but I am not sure if I have ever achieved an orgasm. How can I tell?

Dear L., said Marian. You would undoubtedly know if you had experienced orgasm, so I can only assume you have not. Perhaps you should . . . and here followed a list of recommendations, from learning to relax more to doing it in unusual places.

But Janice's problem wasn't that she didn't know what an orgasm was, she'd worked that one out for herself years ago, but how she was ever going to experience one with Ken. Their couplings were spasmodic and inept. No sooner had he got into her than he was falling out again and had to push his way back in with a determination that left her clenching her jaw in pain.

Kay, from St Swithun's, wanted to know if there was any way a man could definitely tell if a woman had had an orgasm or not, to which Cathy replied that there was no sure way really, except that a woman's nipples were always erect afterwards, but if she was at all aroused by her lover they'd be erect anyway. She was sure, however, that it would be wiser to talk things over, either

231

with her boyfriend or with a trained counsellor, rather than faking the experience.

This wasn't Janice's problem either, since Ken didn't seem to require her to have orgasms, faked or otherwise, unless, that is, he mistook the occasional outcry of pain and protest for ecstasy. To be fair he rarely seemed to have one himself, and never inside her. He occasionally rolled off her and began pumping himself vigorously, while she lay lamely by, but otherwise didn't seem to bother.

To Janice this was worse than her own lack of satisfaction. She lay there gamely while he tried different methods of attack, but in the end he seemed to get as little out of it as she did. And he always finished in time for the news, and the lunchtime soap which followed. She watched him as he pulled on his socks and trousers and sat engrossed on the edge of the bed. She took to making him a sandwich while he watched. The first time he was pleased, but it soon became part of their regular routine.

Meanwhile, worse than the women's magazines, there was Dora.

Dave's so romantic, she said. We went out last night and he turned up this morning with a dozen red roses. He said he couldn't go a full day without seeing me again.

or,

Guess what, Dave's bought tickets for a surprise weekend away – we're going tonight. Can I leave a bit early to pack?

and,

Dave just can't seem to stop spending money on me – I don't know where he gets it all from. And I don't like to ask – he doesn't like me talking about money.

Meanwhile Dave's rival, Tim, was also pursuing her with enthusiasm.

He was outside my window again last night, she said. When I got back from seeing Dave. He must have been stood in the garden all night. I heard this noise and when I looked out of the window, there he was with his tape deck playing, I Love You Babe, Show Me the Way, dead loud. All the lights went on next door, I felt really shown up.

Once Tim managed to get Dora to go with him down south by buying tickets for her favourite band. The complications and subterfuge at this time reached epic proportions, since of course it all had to be kept from Dave, who seemed to have a sixth sense about these things and took to turning up unexpectedly after work. This unnerved Dora horribly since that was also the time Tim used to hang around. Janice and Gwen got daily bulletins about the conspiracy, the times she had nearly given herself away, or when she thought her mother was going to spill the beans, and the one awful time when her father let Dave in the front door as she let Tim in the back. Then after the concert they got daily bulletins about Dora's guilt. She had slept with Tim without meaning to in the back of his van.

I think it's Dave I want really, she told Janice. But Tim's just so *nice*.

When Tony, the married man at the club, also began chatting Dora up whenever she was in with Angie, the convolutions became too great for Janice to follow, yet she couldn't help giving the whole affair her reluctant, resentful attention.

Ken continued to turn up between shifts at work. There was no spoken arrangement and Janice thought this suited her fine, but on the days when she was off and he failed to turn up, her whole day was dominated by his absence. It preyed on her mind, whether or not to go out, the peculiar emptiness descending sometimes into a savage depression by evening. So she was trapped by it, when the whole point was (or seemed to be – they had never discussed this either) that they make no demands on each other. And since that was exactly what she thought she wanted she couldn't understand it. She was trapped, exactly as if she were in love.

233

Does your Ken . . . buy you things . . . you know, Dora said. Dave had just bought her a gold locket with the initials D and D entwined upon it.

Janice was sorry she'd ever mentioned Ken. It had been a moment of foolishness when Dora had looked at her coyly as Mrs Webb mentioned that Christine Mercer was getting married after all these years.

It'll be Janice's turn next, Dora said, and Irene Webb said,

Now there's a thought, and both of them looked at her enquiringly. Janice ignored them and Dora said,

O Janice'll never settle down, she's a bit of a Don Juan you know, a love'em and leave'em type – a bit like you, Irene. And Irene said,

Chance'd be a fine thing, and then she said,

Go on Janice, you can tell us – isn't there anyone a bit special like, on the horizon? And Dora looked at her in an amused kind of way and Janice said,

There might be.

Both Dora and Irene made noises like they wanted to know more, but Janice wouldn't be drawn. After that Dora had probed, dropping comments and hints and when these didn't work, asking direct questions. She'd finally dragged Ken's name out of Janice, and what he did for a living, and the fact that he was quite a bit older than Janice, but after that Janice clammed up. Then Dora tried a different tack, inviting them both out to make a foursome. Ken's job came in handy there, he was always on shifts. Janice never thought of actually inviting him, it just wasn't that kind of relationship. Eventually Dora stopped inviting them out, but then she started making references to Janice's mystery man, Ken the Black Shadow, as if she didn't quite believe in him. And sometimes Janice didn't mind, it would be easier for her if no one really believed Ken existed, but other times she minded a lot. And on one of these times she said, in response to Dora's question,

Not really, I think he takes me a bit for granted.

That was it. She had let Dora in and Dora, immensely gratified, began giving her advice.

O you don't want to do that, she said. Don't be too nice to them or they'll treat you like a doormat. That's what my mum always says and it's true.

It stayed with Janice though she didn't want it to, the idea that Ken might be using her. She began to wonder why they never went out, though it suited her just as well to stay in. She didn't like pubs and hated eating out. But it began to torment her somehow, the whole thing, what she was getting out of it, how it looked to other people.

Is Ken taking you anywhere special tonight? Dora asked, and Janice shrugged. She couldn't say aloud that he never took her anywhere and that it suited her that way, that he never bought her presents and didn't even know her birthday.

Dora was doing a quiz entitled *Does He Really Love You*.

Here you are Janice, here's one for you, she said.

When he comes in unexpectedly from work does he

a. Suggest you eat out
b. Put his arms round you for a kiss and a cuddle before telling you to brew up
c. Send out for an eat-in meal for two
d. Make something himself
e. Sit in front of the telly without saying a word – he knows you'll make him something to eat

What shall I tick? said Dora, and Janice said,

Well normally he'd cover me with yoghurt before licking it all off.

Lucky you, said Dora, and returned to the magazine. *So he's wooed you with flowers and whisked you off to Paris*, said the cover, *but where do you go from here?*

One day Ken came to Janice with a kind of light in his eye and held out a bag to her and her heart jumped, though she didn't know why, but when she looked it was full of old clothes.

I was wondering if you'd put these in the wash for me, he said.

And later, stuffing them into the machine, she thought, what was she doing? Why was she putting up with this? Was she out of her mind, or was she really that scared of being alone?

It seemed ridiculous to be scared of being alone, she'd been alone all her adult life. And it wasn't as though she loved Ken, she was quite clear about that. And surely she'd got over the idea that one day she might meet her ideal man, that someone like Ken might metamorphose into him given time, but maybe she hadn't. Maybe in the deepest recesses of her mind she was more stupid than she'd ever dreamed.

That afternoon she lay beneath him, stubborn as wood, but by the next day she'd made a plan. Before making him something to eat she said,

The kitchen tap keeps dripping, could you have a look at it while I get you something? And Ken looked surprised but he did it. Then the next time she wanted her overflow fixing and the time after that the lock on her front door. These were all jobs she could do herself but she kept them for Ken. Each time he complied grudgingly, but as if he'd half expected it all along. She got him to put up shelves for her and to bring litter for the cat in the little bus, and he did these things as if not knowing exactly how to resist. They were locked into a new game now, and he didn't know the rules or how far she would go. He began to retaliate, bringing ironing, buttons for sewing on, socks for darning, and the more he brought her the more she found for him to do. They were behaving like a married couple. Then one day she asked him to decorate. She asked him while they were still in bed and he rebelled.

You're always asking me to do things, he said.

What about you? said Janice. Bringing your ironing and your

236

socks. What have you ever done for me other than rolling on and off me and expecting me to be grateful?

Ken was angry, his face congested with rage. She expected him to leave and she felt the wired contraction of fear she'd felt at other times when she'd thought it was over. Then he leaned over and shoved her backwards, hard. He pressed down on her and was hurting her, holding her arms down, pushing in hard. When she cried out in surprise and pain she knew that was what he wanted her to do.

She lay still as he held her legs apart with his knees and pushed into her, harder than before. She knew he wanted her to respond. And soon the terrible, forbidden thing happened. She was responding, at first with anger and outrage then with a congestion of feeling between her legs, as though her cunt was distending and the least touch would trigger something violent, uncontrollable. She arched her back and let it happen. And after a few moments Ken shut his eyes and let out a shuddering gasp.

She pushed him off. She got up and walked unsteadily to the bathroom. She saw her face in the mirror as she mopped her thighs. It had a shining, unholy glow she couldn't will away. She felt peculiarly disturbed, as if she had been touched by angels.

When she went back Ken was already watching television. She ignored him and began to dress. When she was dressed she went into the kitchen to make him a sandwich. Nothing was said, but she thought he looked at her with a new kind of triumph in his eyes.

That day marked a new phase in their relationship. Janice stopped asking Ken to do things for her, she didn't always make him lunch. They went to bed immediately and sometimes didn't finish until at least part way through the news. And it always started the same way, Ken pushing her on to the bed and holding her arms down, then prising her legs apart with his knees. Then leaning his body against one of her arms to release his hand he slipped his fingers inside her, moving them gently before easing himself in. All the time he was inside her he held her down, watching her face with a tender, almost paternal concern. And always Janice felt the same initial protest dissolving into the formlessness of desire.

The trouble was she never came to accept the way she felt or to understand it, to tie it in with what she believed about herself, that she was tough and intractable, she needed no one. As weeks went by she felt she was being moved into areas of her personality she didn't understand and couldn't control. When Ken wasn't there she spent her time waiting with a compulsive aggravation that wouldn't leave her alone. She couldn't imagine being with Ken for ever, marrying him or even living with him, but she couldn't give him up. What they did together existed in a sealed off compartment of her life, without affecting the rest of it, but it was as if more and more of her personality were becoming sealed inside it. Then too things changed and there was no longer an agreed level of force. One time as she had her orgasm he slapped her face hard, and the fear sparked and flared in Janice that she might let him do anything to her, anything at all.

One day at the library Dora came in with a huge sparkly ring.

Dave bought it me, she said. Everyone who came into the library had to see the ring and discuss plans for the wedding. It was two years to the day that she'd started going out with Dave, he'd remembered their anniversary.

I was beginning to think it wasn't going anywhere, she said.

Of course that was the point of a relationship, it had to go somewhere, all the magazines said so. If it wasn't going anywhere they usually suggested you should end it. But Janice and Ken weren't going anywhere, that was the single most obvious thing about them. After nearly three years they still didn't even go out. No one saw them as a couple and their relationship didn't progress along the accepted lines: dating, gradually seeing one another more often, a few quarrels perhaps, maybe even a break when they saw other people, but which only served to strengthen their commitment to one another, then finally engagement and marriage. None of this would ever happen. Janice could no longer imagine their life without what they did together, yet she wasn't sure she even liked Ken. One day she looked at his feet as he lay watching television and thought how ugly they were; bunched up toes, the big toe making an angle with the rest of the foot. She could never love a man with feet like that. Still she went on, torn by conflicting arguments. She felt she was turning into someone she didn't know.

Then one day after she'd waited in all afternoon and Ken failed to turn up, Janice made up her mind.

The next time he knocked on her door she didn't answer. She held on to a clump of bread, shredding it and stuffing the pieces into her mouth. He knocked again.

Janice, he called. Jan?

Janice stood behind the door, pressing the bread and her fingers into her mouth.

Come on Janice, Ken shouted. I know you're in there.

He'll make me pay for this, she thought, and felt an obscure weakening, the desire to open the door. Then Ken banged hard on the door, making her jump.

I said come on! he yelled. Janice flung open the door.

Go away Ken, she said. Tufts of bread fell from her hands, but she felt suddenly tall again. Go home.

You what? said Ken, and stared at her, but in his eyes there was a light of fear. She had never thought before that he might also be dependent on her. It made her strong.

I said go home, she said. I don't want to see you again.

Well, said Ken. That's nice isn't it – after all I've done.

Janice could read the fear in his eyes, but also a kind of relief, as if he too needed to be released.

Just go, she said. Ken began to bluster.

Is there someone else? he said. Is that it, eh?

Janice shut the door. She waited for him to bang on it again, feeling less sure of herself now she couldn't see him, but he didn't. He stood there a while then she heard him say something and leave, she heard his footsteps going away from her door. She propped herself up against the wall, weak with relief.

In the following weeks however she felt less good. Triumph faded and was replaced by nothing. At times she felt she could return to the Janice she'd always believed herself to be, at other times she felt nothing would ever be the same. It was a bad feeling and for weeks, even months, after finishing with Ken she did feel bad, though she didn't know why. She got up in the mornings feeling rough, with a bad taste in her mouth and whenever she was in she couldn't stop expecting him to turn up, at least for the telly which he'd left in her bedroom, and which she eventually took with her when she moved. She walked to work and if she caught sight of the little bus she hurried away. She felt a kind of terror at the thought of meeting Ken by chance. Some days, and this was what she couldn't get over, she felt actually ill. On these days she didn't dress but lay propped up on pillows in her towelling robe, eating and watching the news. She went over and over the details of the relationship; she'd been twenty-eight when she met him, he was forty-six. That was a little more than three years ago, now it was over. It wouldn't happen again. How often did someone actually come knocking on your door? Sometimes when she got tired of thinking like this she thought instead about what they did together in bed, but she couldn't say that these things, the eating and the fantasising, began at this time, because of Ken. They neither began with him, nor finished when he left, but this didn't comfort her or help her to understand why she felt so bad. Finally she came to the conclusion that she was grieving, grieving for something she hadn't wanted and could hardly in the end say she'd had. It was as though her body were grieving without her permission, remembering the imprint of Ken's body, trying to adjust itself once more to the absence of touch. Her body was grieving and there was nothing she could do about it, except to drag it around with her like a carcass and try to comfort it with food.

All the way home Janice thought about chips, soaked to just the right degree in lard. Though she'd eaten the pork pie, vanilla slice and large size Dairy Milk, as she neared her house the thought of chips grew in her like a mushroom cloud. By the time she reached home she was almost running. She didn't understand the power of food to make her its prey, she didn't try. For the moment her only problem was how to get through the length of time it would take her to cook the chips. As she fumbled for her key she could see herself peeling the potatoes, heating the fat, she couldn't imagine how she could wait that long.

She started on the bread, scooping up thick wads of butter with the crust. It meant she took twice as long with the potatoes and ate three times as much. When she'd prepared a pan full of chips and eaten three quarters of a small loaf she turned to the lard. It was gone. All this time she'd forgotten that she'd used up the lard. She hunted through her cupboards, all the ones with food and those without, but could only find a little vegetable oil. She only liked chips done with lard.

Janice felt despair. She went through all the cupboards again, stuffing everything she could find into her mouth: cheese, liver pâté, marmalade, pickles, she poured milk over Weetabix and jam. In a kind of revenge on herself for not having the lard she began to eat the raw chips. Only when the bursting pain became too terrible did she stop, resting her forehead on the cupboard door and moaning. She could feel sweat on her upper lip but she wasn't satisfied. Because she hadn't found the lard.

Becca once told Janice a story about lard, the first time Janice visited her. She'd been invited many times but had always made some excuse. Finally she'd given in, bought wine on the way home from work and stood on the doorstep, feeling already that she'd changed her mind and wanted to go home.

Becca's flat was in the basement of a big house. When she opened the door Janice was surprised to see how exotic she looked in a green and gold kaftan with big ear-rings like orange blossoms. The flat was exotic too, with rugs and wall hangings and African masks.

At first they were stiff and polite. Becca opened the wine and set some crackers and cheese on a tray. They ate daintily and then with more enthusiasm as the conversation warmed. Soon all the crackers were gone and they paused and looked at the empty plates. They both knew they were thinking of food.

Cake? Becca said. Janice hesitated.

O you shouldn't, Becca said. You really mustn't. You're so full you couldn't eat another thing. Appetite like a bird, you don't know where the weight comes from. You only have to look at food and it goes straight to your hips.

Janice laughed and Becca said,

Well what the hell, what have we got to lose? Apart from this of course, and she shook the roll of fat around her midriff. This time they both laughed and there was conspiracy in their laughter. Two fat women eating together, maybe they would even binge. It was unheard of, a shared binge.

They didn't binge, though they did finish the cake. And they laughed together about the way they looked. Janice complained about breasts.

A fat woman with no bust, she said.

Well mine never did me any good, Becca said. You've got to have little upstanding ones really, and mine always grew down. You had to admire them for it really. I did all the exercises and strapped them into the best harnesses money could buy, but they just had a mind of their own.

Janice said she thought men liked women with a bust even if it hung round their knees, but Becca said,

Don't you believe it, my chest never got me anywhere. There was a lad at school I fancied something rotten, dead rough but kind of cute, you know. I was for ever shoving my chest his way, over the desk, in the canteen, but it did me no good. He went off with a girl called Karen in the end, built like an ironing board. They're married now, they've got three kids and she's still built like an ironing board.

They sighed at the injustice of it all, then began to talk about food, the inescapability of it, everywhere you looked, on the telly, on big posters in the street, loving couples dining out, bone thin models eating only the crumbliest, flakiest chocolate. They talked about the ridiculous things they'd done in the name of food. Janice had once been asked to pick up a cake for her nephew's birthday party. The shop was only open in the morning and the party wasn't until the afternoon. She'd tried to refuse, knowing she couldn't be trusted with an entire cake alone, but it was no use. Then she'd said she would take it straight over to Peter's, but they wanted her to keep it for them until the party.

All the way home the thought of that cake gnawed on Janice. She bought and ate an entire trifle in an effort to distract herself; she ate toast and jam and crackers. But just before noon she started on the cake and by quarter past twelve it was finished. She had to run round three bakeries before she found one vaguely similar. She got them to ice it for her and turned up at the party late, lying strenuously to stop people ringing up the shop to complain. And all afternoon she felt her mother's hardest gaze nudging her when she wasn't looking.

The last party Becca had been to was at New Year. There had been magnificent food prepared by caterers, and publicly she'd abstained all evening, discussing her new diet with anyone who cared to listen. Whenever she could she slipped food into the capacious handbag she'd brought for the purpose. Then, part way through a conversation about orchids with the hostess, Cynthia, someone had joined them and she'd taken her chance and headed towards the bathroom.

Cynthia called out something about the plumbing, but by this time Becca was in a hurry. She pushed the bolt to on the door then, because she still didn't feel hidden enough, climbed into the shower and drew the curtain. There she found out what Myra had meant about the plumbing. Half-way through an immense slab of black forest gâteau she nudged the cold tap and water shot forth with a fury that made her lungs stick together – she was completely unable to breathe. Worse, she couldn't turn the tap off and couldn't get out without dripping water and runny gateau all over the floor. In the end, though, that was exactly what she had to do. She left the party looking like an accident in a chocolate factory. Somewhere else she could never go back.

They went on laughing, telling horror stories about how much they ate in secret, sharing the thrill of conspiracy and flaunted authority. Janice felt completely relaxed in the orange-red glow of the room, completely herself. She didn't mind that Becca's stories had to cap hers; she lay propped up on orange and gold embroidered cushions, replete, beaming indulgently at Becca. But at some point Becca started telling her about the tub of lard.

There was nothing else in the house and she'd run out of money so she'd eaten it, spooning it slowly out of its tub and trying not to gag. It sickened her and soon the pain to the right of her stomach had started and worsened into one of her attacks. She described it as starting off like a twisting of the gut, with lots of small surrounding pains like little knives. Then it was like a single blade driven inwards, then the whole of her gut was in the kind of spasm a runner sometimes gets in his leg, when all he can do is fall

244

down and roll on the floor. Which was what Becca did. At some point in the intense pain she seemed to lose consciousness, at any rate she remembered coming to, covered in the watery bile from her gut. There was fat in the watery shit down her legs and on the carpet, but the pain was fading and she was able to clamber back on to the chair. She hung over the table for a few moments, retching a little, eyes closed. When she opened them she could see the lard, and the spoon. Slowly she put it back into her mouth.

By the end of the story Janice wasn't laughing any more. She felt revulsion, mixed with a powerful sadness for all the fat women of the world, putting themselves through the kind of torture only a psychopath could inflict on someone else. Becca wasn't laughing either now and there was a silence in which Janice tried and failed to think of something to say. Eventually she said,

I'll help you clear up, and they began in a mechanical way to carry the plates and glasses through to the kitchen, not looking at one another and hardly speaking. Janice offered to wash up and Becca refused to let her. Before she left though they were laughing again, about Mr Norton and Dora.

Janice ran her finger round the remains of food in the mixing-bowl. It occurred to her that she'd become the ultimate consumer. If you put a dustbinful of old food down in front of her she would probably manage to eat it. Nothing was bad enough for her. They were all the same – Gwen, Dora, Janice – each locked into their little cocoons, consuming themselves endlessly in their different ways.

Janice ran water slowly into the mixing-bowl. She remembered the last time she'd seen Becca, though the memory was tinged with the quality of myth, or nightmare, larger than life and slightly unreal, like Becca's stories. She remembered the darkness and the debris, the soft snuffling noise. It had been some months since Becca had left the library and Janice had been meaning to visit all the time but had kept putting it off. Now, driven by guilt and fear, she stepped over food and broken crockery, calling Becca's name. She wasn't out in the back, hanging up washing, she wasn't in the bedroom. In the lounge wall-hangings hung off walls, the African masks lay amongst the litter on the floor. The darkness, the debris and the smell began to oppress Janice into claustrophobia, she felt she had to get out, yet she could hear, almost beyond reach of hearing, a snuffling, shuffling noise she couldn't locate. Janice called out, Becca, once more then told herself she could go, she'd tried hard enough. She turned into the hall to leave. Then, moved by an unaccountable impulse, she glanced back. There was Becca, blinking in the light from the part-opened doorway. She was holding a bowl of something in her hand.

Becca, Janice said.

Becca's small, black eyes settled nowhere and everywhere like flies.

I didn't know, she whispered. I wasn't expecting . . .

That's all right, Janice said quickly. I just called by on impulse really, to see how you were getting on.

Becca looked down at the bowl she was carrying and her hands trembled.

It's all right Becca, Janice said gently. We're old friends, aren't we? You don't have to worry about me.

Becca said nothing but she lowered the bowl on to the telephone table and wiped her hands on the front of her dress. Janice felt nervous in sympathy.

I can't stay, she said, but Becca ignored her, walking towards the lounge with her face lowered so she wouldn't have to catch Janice's eye. Janice felt most strongly the desire to leave, but she felt obliged to follow. She cleared some papers and plates and perched on the edge of the settee. Becca lowered herself tenderly into the armchair. No one spoke.

246

As she became used to the dim light Janice could see that Becca was massively fatter. Folds of flesh hung over her ankles and wrists and her face seemed to have slid into her neck. Even sitting still she had difficulty breathing, that was the snuffling noise Janice had heard. Becca's hair was matted and the ear-rings had gone. She wore a skirt Janice remembered from the library, it was pinned at the waist with a big pin.

Though she had nothing to say Janice began to talk as well as she could about the house she was buying and the mortgage and the long walks she'd started to take over the moors.

You'll have to come with me some time, she said. Even as she spoke she felt a pang of fear at the thought that Becca might take her up on this, then she knew she never would. In the silence that followed she wondered if Becca had even heard, but just as she was going to say something else Becca said,

Maybe, I don't know, we'll see.

Janice didn't know what to say any more. She asked about her breathing, but all Becca would say was that she was seeing a doctor. She expressed no curiosity about Janice, or Gwen or Dora. She seemed to be waiting for Janice to leave.

Janice knew she would have to go. She could hardly think in the dim, stuffy atmosphere. She felt appalled about Becca, and a heavy sense of guilt as if somehow it was all her fault, but overriding both these emotions were the mixed sensations of fear and disgust. No one should let themselves slide so far downhill, she said to herself in her mother's voice, then felt bad for thinking it. All at once she stood up gracelessly and said she would have to go. Becca's eyes didn't even flicker, but as Janice reached the door she could hear Becca's footsteps padding behind her. She half turned, then, to prove that she wasn't repelled, put an arm swiftly round Becca's shoulders and kissed her lightly, on the matted hair. Becca didn't jump or pull away as Janice expected, but all her flesh seemed to shrink beneath Janice's touch. Of course she'd probably not been touched by anyone for a long time, and the absence of touch seemed to create its own powerful atmosphere, almost a smell. Janice didn't know what it was, but it made her stumble over her words as she promised to call back again some time, and fumble with the lock on the door.

Of course Janice never did go back, and now she'd be too afraid. But as she washed and stacked the last dishes she felt she'd never be free of Becca. Becca's image lurked at the back of her mind and each time she was jolted into awareness of it she was wrung with pity and fear.

Janice left the kitchen and went to the window seat in the lounge to watch the valley in the milky evening light. As soon as she sat down Alf leapt on to her knee and began treading the fabric of her trousers. Janice stroked him absently, thinking about those golden people she read about in the magazines – stars, their spartan, athletic beauty. They ate only orange juice in the mornings and a mixed green salad at night, after many hours working out in the gym. They were all at the top of their professions. She didn't want to think about them but somehow after thinking about Becca she always did. She didn't even really believe they existed, but it didn't matter. The urge to be like them never quite went away. They were always so much in control.

Janice sat on the sill, stroking the cat. Above the hill there were ripples in the sky like crumpled silk. She thought about Becca, and herself. Well, she thought, at least I've got the cat. And the view.

The sheep grazed peacefully as the hill evolved its own darkness, wrapping itself in shade. Janice stroked Alf more consciously now and his purring swelled to fill the dim room. She rumpled his silky, orange fur and he rolled ecstatically on her knee. They sat together as the light ebbed from hill and room, woman and cat transported by the mysterious alchemy of touch.

*

The doorbell rang and Janice looked up sharply, her teeth sunk into a hot buttered roll. Then there was a sharp rap on the door. Janice scuttled to one side of the table then the other, overtaken by a sudden helplessness. The room was covered with the debris of food.

Whoever it was knocked again. Janice grabbed bowls and dishes from the table and dumped them in the sink. She pushed muffins and butter into the bread bin and swept scattered crumbs on to the floor.

It occurred to her that she was behaving like Becca.

A louder knock made her jump violently and she ran to the door, then stopped in front of it.

It couldn't be Ken.

Janice, called the voice.

It was Peter.

Dusting her hands against her sweater she drew back the lock and opened the door.

She stood still, blinking stupidly in the light.

I thought you were in, said Peter.

I had the radio on, Janice said.

Can I come in, Peter said. Janice went red.

Of course, she said.

I've just come to have a look at the washer, Peter said. Mam said it wasn't working.

Janice followed him into the kitchen, aware that she was acting strangely, feeling like she was slipping out of a dream.

Peter put some tools down on a worktop. Janice could see him ignoring the mess in the kitchen.

I was baking, she said, hastily thrusting a cereal packet and a jam jar into a cupboard. It's very good of you, she added.

O don't mention it, Peter said, grinning at the formality. He turned to the washer. Janice swept the dirty cutlery on top of it into the sink and reached for the washing-up bowl, whilst explaining rapidly that the washer was leaking and the door kept jamming. Mr Harding had tried to fix it and couldn't, one repair man had been, got it working perfectly while he was there, but the problem had started again the next time she used it. Over the weeks it had just been neglected, she'd almost got used to using the launderette. Peter levered it out of its place and tilted it forwards.

I think I'll need a wrench, he said and disappeared back to his van. In his absence Janice washed up furiously and wiped down surfaces.

Do you want a cup of tea? she said when he returned. Coffee? She was coming back to normal now, thinking more clearly as she filled the kettle with water.

I hope you haven't come all this way just for my washer, she said.

O well, Peter said. I thought I'd look in on mam. I haven't seen either of you for a while.

Janice caught herself smiling as she made coffee for them both. She didn't see Peter often though he lived only a few miles away, in a bigger town, with Ann and the kids.

Peter was a builder. Even as a little boy he'd loved taking things apart to see how they worked. He'd taught himself everything in the building trade, there was no job he wouldn't tackle. Now he worked over a team of men and together they had constructed whole estates, residential, industrial. Janice was repeatedly amazed at the size and scale of the construction work that came from her little brother. For he was little, and fragile looking, a different build altogether from Janice. Janice had looked like David, she could remember that much, and both of them like their mother, but Peter looked like no one in the family. Janice used to call him the changeling. He looked elfin, with pale, pointed features and green eyes, a different green from Janice's. He never minded being teased, and used to say himself that his father must have had a bike. This was funny to both Peter and Janice, knowing their mother as they did. That was family, Janice thought. You laughed at things no one else found funny. When she wasn't with Peter she frequently resented him because he could do no wrong in their mother's eyes, though he'd made mistakes like anyone else. He'd married at nineteen and divorced at twenty-two, they had never seen his first wife nor their baby son since. Janice's mother never referred to this. She'd never liked his first wife anyway. And now he had a nice wife, and two lovely children, and was doing so well at work. When Janice thought like this the burning sore place she'd come to identify with over the years surfaced again and she thought black thoughts about Peter and her mother. But now that he was actually there, with her in the kitchen, it all faded. She felt only pleasure, because he had called round specially to see her.

They couldn't talk much over the whirring of the machine. But afterwards, when Peter had soldered something, and connected something else, and fitted a new hinge to the door, they sat together drinking more coffee and laughing at the jumpers their mother had knitted for Jamie and Laura.

She just won't accept that she can't knit, Janice said.

I know, said Peter. And the kids won't wear them. If it's not got Adidas stamped all over the front of it they don't want to know.

Then he stood up.

I'll have to be going, he said. Janice hesitated then reached for her purse. She handed him two crumpled notes.

You don't have to pay me, Peter said.

No, said Janice. It's for the kids. Get them some decent jumpers.

Unexpectedly Peter leaned forwards and kissed her. Janice didn't shrink away, but she couldn't respond. It wasn't the kind of thing they did.

Well, I'll be seeing you, he said, imitating an old neighbour of theirs, Mrs Cox, but not yet awhiles.

Janice went with him to the door. She stood watching him walk away. At the end of the path he waved before getting into his van, then Janice went inside.

The lounge was almost dark, but in the pale light of the window the twigs of forsythia she'd broken off earlier glowed a pale, translucent yellow. Beside them was the deeper gold of Alf. Janice picked him up and perched on the window-sill, watching the pastel shapes of sheep on the dark hillside. For a short season just at this time of year her garden was beautiful, with a wild, derelict beauty. There was broom, and the orange flower near the gate, a tangle of climbing buttercup and wild geranium, the first poppies. Janice looked up and great pewter coloured clouds were drifting over the hill. In between, here and there, were splashes of intense light, whitest of all round the rim of the hill, in the intimate interplay of hill and sky Janice had noticed before. She sat quietly with the cat on her knee, thinking about her mother.

She felt prongs of guilt at having undercut her mother's present to Jamie and Laura. But why shouldn't she buy them a present as well? As usual when she thought about her mother she felt caught between resentment and shame, but now as she sat getting angry, a memory returned. It was something their neighbour, Mrs Cox, once told her about her mother, but Janice had built in the detail herself, lovingly, until it was as real to her as her own memory. It was Whit Sunday, a long time ago. Everyone was out in the park that no longer existed, wearing their best clothes. There was a band in the bandstand. Janice's mother was wearing a white dress with lilac flowers, and delicate lace gloves stretched over her broad, mannish hands. Mr and Mrs Cox had drifted away from them in the crowds, walking round the outskirts of the park. They heard noises coming from behind a hedge. Mrs Cox worried that it might be a courting couple, but Mr Cox said it sounded more like someone in pain, and before Mrs Cox could stop him he'd gone to look. There was Evelyn, with the front of her nice new lilac dress all stained with blood, clutching her stomach with one hand and her mouth with the other, as if trying to stop the brute noises coming from her.

Evelyn, said Mr Cox, and Janice's mother's eyes, which had gone vague and glassy with terror, gradually focused. She lowered her hand from her mouth.

Please could you get me an ambulance, she said, her diction at its most precise.

That was the miscarriage, quite a late one apparently, when Janice was about five years old.

Janice's mother had never loved Janice, but by the time she was forty she had lost one child, miscarried another and been widowed. How much pain did Janice want her to have?

Then it occurred to her that she didn't want to see her mother hurt so much as out of control, to shake that invincible control. And she saw suddenly that all her mother had wasn't control, but her illusions of control, that was all anyone had, illusions, propping them up. Janice let Alf slip from her knee and thought, if her mother wasn't in control of the way she was, Janice was obliged to forgive her.

Overhead an aircraft winked its slow way across the sky. The lamp at the end of the path filled the tree with orange light. Janice wished to be free of all the bitter guilty thoughts that kept her wrapped so tightly in her own cocoon, and all the fantasies that propped it up. She wished she were out on the hills, in relationship to nothing but the beauty and terror of the land. She thought of Becca, and Gwen and Dora and thought maybe that was what they all needed, a sudden shift of perspective broadening a narrow view, a chink of sky through curtains. She turned to find her jacket and her boots.

5
Living with Vampires

It was on the little bus which ran between Marley and Clough Bottom that Lizzie Baker first experienced the fear of death. Nothing changed, the shadowy yellow day of early winter remained the same, mist rising from the valley below as the bus made its steep ascent between the two villages, so that the earth itself appeared to be smoking. Almost at the crest of the hill Agnes Weaver made a forward movement, shifting her immense bulk towards the edge of the seat.

Next stop driver, please, she said, and lurched forwards again without quite managing to get up, and the driver, a balding, middle-aged man, rolled a little way past the stop to the gate of Mrs Weaver's garden terrace, and then got up to help her with her many bags.

Eee that's grand, said someone at the back. A little help's worth a lot of pity, eh Agnes, and Agnes, hauled to her feet, beamed all the way around the bus and laughed her rusty laugh; whether from good nature or embarrassment Lizzie couldn't tell.

Clumps of tissue fell from the sleeves of her coat as Agnes and her bags were finally manoeuvred off the bus. The driver sat down again to a chorus of approval.

He's a grand lad, someone said, and Lily Ashworth said,

Heart of gold. Eh, maybe we should put his name down with that Esther Rantzen?

Lizzie looked round at the purple and beige and brown felt hats, the flat caps and trilbys all nodding in laughter and approval. She couldn't understand why she should feel herself to be singled out by death. There was Agnes Weaver, in her seventies, fat, asthmatic, apparently without a thought of it. Immediately in front of Lizzie, Ernest Broadbent, eighty if he was a day, deep in conversation with Wilfred Higham about bowls, neither of them appearing to be haunted by death, yet there was Lizzie, in her early thirties, clammy with the certainty of it. She would surely die. And all the small symptoms she'd been experiencing recently, a bad stomach, a chesty cough that wouldn't clear up, gathered like shadows in her brain into the big shadow of conclusive evidence. She sat very still, staring at the people around her and at the messages on the sides of the bus, *To seat 16 + 5 standing, smoking not allowed on any part of this vehicle.* Everything became strange as if the angles of her vision were changing, drawing things into new, incomprehensible relationships.

Part of her knew all the time that nothing was happening, everything was going on as usual, the lurch and sway of the little bus rocking its passengers as they laughed and talked. Only Lizzie sat still and silent and glassy, on the surface at least, but with the fear flapping inside her like the wings of many birds.

Logically she knew that it was far more likely that the brakes on the little bus would fail as they teetered on the edge of yet another precipice, and they would all plummet to their deaths together. Few things were more likely, as the engine wheezed and gasped like Agnes Weaver, and the gears ground as they slid forwards. None of the passengers seemed to fear that prospect either, perhaps they were all too old to care, but she, Lizzie, was young and afraid to die. Already she could feel life draining out of her, sucked by some nameless disease, and it wasn't fair, she told herself, it wasn't fair. She sat still for two more stops until the walls of the bus pressed in on her too far, then she got up suddenly as it jolted to a halt and blundered past the other passengers just in time. It wasn't the stop she wanted, but once off she held on to it and sagged forwards so that someone asked her if she was all right, and she nodded, then shook her head, then ran, further down the hill towards Clough Bottom, the cold air catching at her side.

Each day Lizzie dressed herself with care, whatever her mother said. Though the end result was one of studied carelessness it took time to achieve. And now that she could no longer afford to buy many clothes she had to be creative with the ones she had, adding a chiffon ruffle here, altering a collar there and staining her white satin pumps with tea. She added beads on to denim waistcoats and sewed multicoloured scarves round the necklines of men's shirts. She never went out without applying a bright layer of lipstick to her wide, slightly crooked mouth and fluffing her hair more over one side of her face than the other, the way she'd worn it ever since she was scarred. Now it was winter she wore a long woolly coat in purple and gold that wasn't practical because it didn't fasten, and needed dry-cleaning, or ideally replacing, and a cherry- red beret which had appealed to her sense of herself as an artist the moment she saw it. These days most of her artistic talent seemed to go into her appearance.

Presentation was important, she knew that now, after years of opting for the merely scruffy. Only the very young could afford to be truly scruffy, in anyone else it suggested a loss of hope, which she couldn't afford. In any case, as her Aunt Edie used to say, you never knew when you might bump into your Prince Charming. Only this time, she always added, she hoped he wouldn't look quite so much like a frog. This was a dig at Eric, one of Lizzie's boyfriends Aunt Edie had particularly disliked. Eric had been no oil painting it was true, but he'd had something that had made Lizzie forget his body at least for a time, stumpy, flabby and bandy even though it was. It had been a while since she'd felt like that about anyone, some days she wondered if she ever would again. Those were her bleaker days, when she thought she'd lost it, that quality, whatever it was, that used to attract men to her. A kind of charm, or maybe just confidence; something at any rate you couldn't put down to looks. Lizzie didn't consider herself to be a beauty, though she had nice hair. Like Eric she was short and stumpy, though thankfully not bandy, nor overly flabby. Since art school she'd been surrounded by images of beauty which were enough to give any girl a complex, but the study of art had also taught her to recognise beauty where it wasn't normally seen, in the wrinkles of an older woman, or in a dark, crooked smile.

Even on her worst days she didn't think the problem was her age, she'd known women of all ages attract men. It was something more substantial, as inexplicable as losing your touch, or as insidious as the slow seeping of confidence through the cracks in your self-esteem. It was something that, once started, you couldn't seem to stop, and it affected everything. Lizzie stared at herself in the mirror, half-way through applying her lipstick, and told herself not to be daft. One bad experience or even two didn't add up to a lifetime's celibacy.

You old drunk, he'd called her, but she wouldn't think about that. She finished applying her lipstick, set her hat at an angle and left her flat, tucking her sketch pad under one arm.

It had been a while, though, since she'd even had the nerve to try. And the last time she had tried, still smarting from the way Robo had finished things, she'd made a complete fool of herself. She had been invited to give a workshop at a local college – it hardly ever happened these days – and to talk about her own work afterwards. Julian was a little older than the other students, he'd asked a lot of questions and stayed behind to talk. Then, because he'd kept her, he offered her a lift to the station so she wouldn't miss her train, and when she missed it anyway insisted on driving her all the way home. Lizzie was sure he was interested, as sure as you can be; they'd talked and laughed all the way. It was a dark, misty evening; Julian had driven slowly, which had given them time to talk. He had given up law to study art. His family were well off but they weren't pleased about his decision. They had been paying for the law degree but he was having to work his way through the art course himself. He said this with a touch of pride, but Lizzie thought he must have some kind of private income to be running a car as well. Then he asked her about herself and as she filled in a few facts she could see herself through his eyes: bold and independent, surviving off the dole in order to avoid compromising her artistic integrity, supplement-ing her money occasionally by selling a sketch or giving a workshop or even (though this was going a long way back) doing street art on the pavements. She knew that none of this was strictly true, though she wasn't exactly lying. It was truthful enough for the kind of conversation they were having, she thought, it wouldn't be appropriate right now to say more. So she let herself carry on making an impression and she could see the result for herself. He really admired her, she could tell.

Towards the end of the journey, as they approached the row of shops Lizzie lived above, she began to think about inviting him in, choosing the right moment to ask. As he pulled up she thanked him, then on impulse leaned over and kissed him, sliding her hand quickly over his knee.

He could hardly have jumped back further if she'd pulled a gun. She had misjudged everything, the atmosphere, his feelings, then she went on to make it all much worse by inviting him in anyway. Finally, seeing the full extent of the mistake she'd made, she opted for flippancy.

Don't look so worried, she said. I'm only after your body.

Even as she said the words she could hear how clumsy they sounded, how appalling. Julian *was* appalled, and crimson, looking at her now as if she'd not only drawn a gun but shot a small defenceless rabbit with it. There was nothing for it but to back out of the situation with what grace she had left.

O look, she said, clambering sideways out of the car, I'm sorry. Let's forget I ever said anything, OK? Just don't worry about it. And thanks again for the lift.

Julian muttered goodbye with an averted face, and then roared away almost before she was properly out of the car.

More than a little appalled herself Lizzie let herself in, running up the stairs to her flat. She filled the kettle, wondering how she'd managed to get it quite that wrong. She had frightened him properly, but maybe he was scared of sex in general, or of women making the first move, a lot of men were. Maybe he was gay, you couldn't discount that. But then again, she thought, pouring hot water on to the tea bag in her mug, maybe he just thought she was a desperate old dog. It was hard to tell.

Lizzie hadn't had an exhibition for nearly two years. And even then she hadn't sold a picture, these days there wasn't the interest. The last piece of work she'd done was for the landlord of a local pub, an impression of the building as it might have looked in the eighteenth century, when it was built. She had drawn it surrounded by fields and, because it was called the Hare and Hounds, with a faint suggestion of the hunt in the background.

The landlord had been pleased, he'd given her twenty pounds and stood her a pint, and the sketch hung framed behind the bar. Lizzie should have been pleased, at the time she had been. It was a good thing, she told herself, to be able to get money for doing what she wanted to do, even if it wasn't exactly great art. But part of her said if she wasn't painting the way she wanted to paint she might as well be doing any other kind of work she didn't want, like the kinds of work she'd done in the past, cleaning or washing up in a school canteen. It wasn't practical to think like that since she hadn't sold a painting for years, but she knew that while she would happily admit to cleaning or factory work – and had mentioned both to Julian in fact, she would never tell anyone that these days her art work consisted of drawing sketches of local pubs.

Lizzie's last big exhibition had been four years ago. It had been memorable for three reasons, the first of which was the sale of the big painting, the kind people were always advising her not to do because they wouldn't sell, they wouldn't go in people's living rooms. She remembered the woman who bought it, a well-dressed woman in her late forties who had returned many times to look at the same picture, a huge oil painting done entirely in shades of orange, burnt ochre and burnt umber. The subject was a wood in winter. Lizzie was particularly pleased with the haunted quality of the rain-soaked trees. And beneath each tree was a body, the bodies of men women and children cocooned in the dark earth. She had called it The Shortest Day, but had come to see it as her vision of death. Now she thought that even four or five years ago that painting had prefigured the way she would come to feel, haunted by the prospect of death.

She had watched the smartly dressed woman with some cynicism, waiting for her to say that she liked it but it wouldn't go with the paper in her lounge. The woman half smiled in her direction once or twice and finally walked over. After hesitating a bit she said,

I think it's very fine, that picture – well – all of them really, and Lizzie thanked her, wishing she didn't feel so stiff and sullen when people talked about her work. She was desperate for feedback, then embarrassed when she got it.

What I find interesting, the woman said, is the way the bodies aren't feeding the organic life around them, they're entirely cut off by those cocoons. And Lizzie, who hadn't thought about it much before, agreed that it was very interesting. Then they got into a discussion about death and the transcendence of the ego; it turned out that years ago the woman had trekked across India in search of the Dalai Lama, and had finally had a private audience with him. Lizzie was sorry for her arrogance, looking at people the way she did, dismissing them. She herself would love to trek across India and talk to the Dalai Lama, except that he wasn't there any more. Then she thought, as the woman (whose name was Frances) talked, that she was becoming more and more cut off from people and that was why she looked at them the way she did, with a kind of quizzical contempt.

Frances told Lizzie what the painting meant to her. She thought the cocoons were like egos, enclosing people, cutting them off, and because death was no longer accepted as a natural part of life, but resisted and shut away, the ego was never transcended. People remained in their little cocoons and never felt themselves to be part of the organic whole, even in death.

Lizzie wished she'd thought of this. She hoped she would remember it if she were ever interviewed by the local press or radio as they were always promising. Whenever she had been interviewed she sounded terrible, stumbling or twee, whereas with Frances she sounded wise and enigmatic, coming out with a wisdom she never knew she had.

They talked about travel, about art and death and spiritual discipline, then out of the blue Frances asked her how much she wanted for the painting. Lizzie never could make the transition from art to business, reckoning the work in terms of money. She left it to the gallery to print a leaflet with the prices on, but still people asked Lizzie. It aggravated her, as though she were being put on the spot, especially when she told them and they looked shocked. Her first impulse was always to apologise then to excuse herself by explaining how much effort went into a painting, how long she'd worked on it, how much the oils and canvas and framing cost. At the same time she felt she must resist this impulse, it wasn't dignified. Teachers and bus drivers and dustbinmen didn't have to go around justifying their incomes, or have to cope with shocked looks, the interest sliding away in a glance, and listen to the apologies and excuses people made, just as if Lizzie were putting them on the spot: things had been tight recently, so many bills, they'd love to buy something but it was a toss-up between a picture and a dishwasher. It was embarrassing, Lizzie and the customer apologising at one another, Lizzie feeling as if she should reduce the price. For the nth time she decided she wasn't going to haggle, anyway, Frances didn't look poor. So she looked hard at Frances and told her the price on the leaflet and Frances didn't even blink.

Is that all? she said, and Lizzie immediately wished she'd asked for double. But Frances didn't say any more and nor did Lizzie. Mentioning money had killed the conversation. She watched as Frances wandered casually around the other pictures, called goodbye and left.

That's the last I'll see of you, Lizzie thought, and in fact she was right. But a week later she heard from the gallery – she'd made the sale. Lizzie remembered that just making the sale had sparked off a spate of painting, but that was then, this is now, she thought, and tucking her sketch pad more firmly under her arm she walked the canal, looking for the exact spot that would trigger in her the desire to draw.

Light from a storming sky reflected greenly on the surface of the canal. A family of ducks bobbed about, indifferent to the oily blobs of rain spattering through the leaves. The weather was too bad to sit and draw, Lizzie thought. It had been fine that morning, but the light changed so much in the course of a day. Only that morning Lizzie had been struck by the quality of light: grey, but with the yellow tinge of dispersed sun. She had clambered out of bed to have a proper look.

Lizzie had taken the flat, above Kumar Bros. Off-Licence and General Groceries, for the open view. On the other side, where the shop entrance was, there was only a council playground and flats, but her windows looked out over a road, then fields. Now as she looked she couldn't see the sun at all, just the yellow light infusing itself steadily through the grey; unusual, even given the fact that light changed all the time. And in the field on the other side of the road the cows were so still, their breath rising in smoky columns. Lizzie stood still a moment, then, moved by a familiar excitement, she ran for her sketch book and pencils. First though she grabbed a jumper and some socks and fingerless gloves to ward off the frigid air of her flat. But quality of light was such a shifting, elusive thing that by the time she got back to the window it was gone, faded to a simple grey, the cows merely stumpy and sullen. Without the light she couldn't feel what had made her want to capture the scene. That was the thing with art, you had to be immediately there, open; she was hardly ever in the right frame of mind these days. Yet sensitivity to light had been one of the the few things she was ever praised for in art school, mainly the tutors hadn't liked her work.

After a bad start she'd finally got dressed properly and decided to go out. On impulse she took with her the old sketch pad and pencils. But now she felt more than anything a resistance to being still, to just sitting down and contemplating the canal until she was taken over by the kind of quiet absorption she needed for her painting. Anyway, she thought, why should she bother? Who these days would care that somewhere in a remote village, along the banks of a muddy canal, an unemployed artist was trying to improve her technical grasp of the shifting lights of water?

But if she were a real artist, she reminded herself, she wouldn't care. She should be able to transcend what people thought.

Of course you can't, said Nigel's voice, that's nonsense. We're all inescapably embedded in the values of the society we live in. We can't transcend them, we live them out.

Given the fact of society's profound ambivalence towards art, its decreasing status, Nigel wasn't at all surprised that Lizzie should experience the same conflicts and irresolutions, the same degenerating sense of status, the same *paralysis* in the end. Nigel was half-inclined to change the subject of his thesis to study exactly this phenomenon – the effects of a shifting social and economic climate upon the artist.

So did that mean she was doomed, then? That when society changed, shutting its doors on her work, she also had to change, shutting doors inside herself? Maybe she should start painting pots for the craft units in the newly converted mills, an outlet she had thought of before, and she walked on through the aquatic light, smoking now, though she rarely smoked these days, and wondering why, after all this time, Nigel still had the power to frighten her.

Smoking gave her another reason not to sit down and start drawing; she would just finish this cigarette, then another. And on she walked, passed the allotments in Lower Marley, on towards Mossbrook, knowing that really anywhere would do, she could sit down anywhere and start to draw. Still she kept on walking, looking for and failing to find the exact spot that would make her pause long enough to start the work she had told herself to do.

Sometimes Lizzie dreamed she was pregnant. She dreamed that she lay in the bath with her swollen stomach, her heavy breasts falling to either side. When she moved she could feel the sway of fluids in her breasts and belly, there was a thin trickle from her nipples into the surrounding water. Yet though she could feel the liquids shifting inside her she could feel no baby, somehow she knew there was no baby in her womb.

There were times when Lizzie longed for a child, a little boy; she would call him Joel, or maybe Tobias. He would go everywhere with her, to art workshops and galleries, to the pub in the afternoons. Everywhere they went he would be a talking point, a point of contact with the rest of the world. She would dress him unconventionally as she dressed herself, in patched dungarees with a small cloth cap and a coloured scarf like a tie round his neck. He would be precocious, even cheeky, and artistic like Lizzie herself. She could see them both working in the room she used for painting, Lizzie with oils and a canvas, Joel with paper and watercolours on the floor. Sometimes they quarrelled as he got older, they were so alike. But when you had a child you were never entirely alone. She could imagine lifting his small damp body from the cot, cleaning and drying him and tucking him into her own bed. There would always be someone to hold when you were lonely yourself.

Lizzie knew there was more to having a baby than this. Both her brothers had children, she had looked after all three nieces at different times. She knew it was hard work, so hard it defeated some people, broke them up inside. She could remember the night her brother Richard's wife turned up at Lizzie's mother's house. Angie had battered her fists against the door and when Lizzie's mother opened it, cried hysterically. She pushed Stacey into Lizzie's mother's arms, she hadn't slept for weeks, she said. The doctor said nothing was wrong but Stacey never stopped crying. And Richard had run out on them both, just slammed the door and left, he'd said he was never coming back and he'd driven off like a madman, Angie was sure he'd kill himself. And she wasn't being left alone with Stacey because she just couldn't stand it.

Angie looked terrible, with the mascara running all over her face. She cried in a high-pitched kind of way with great gasps of breath. She pushed nappies and a baby bag at Lizzie and ran into the night, leaving Stacey to bawl in Lizzie's mother's arms. Lizzie felt obliged to stay with her mother, so they were both up all night, rocking and feeding and pacing up and down with the unappeasable Stacey, who at four months old seemed beyond all comfort.

Richard was just the same, Lizzie's mother said.

God, said Lizzie, and you had another one.

You were just as bad, said her mother.

Christ, Lizzie said, jiggling the apoplectic Stacey up and down. I don't know how you coped.

Why do you think we stopped after you? her mother said.

So Lizzie knew about babies. Her oldest brother Tom had one daughter, Lynne. Then Angie and Richard had got back together and the passing of time had either clouded their memories or addled their brains long enough for them to go through it all again. They had another little girl, Sophie, when Stacey was nearly six. Admittedly she was a lot less trouble than Stacey, still it made you wonder what had possessed them to repeat the experience. It flew in the face of reason, economics, even sanity, but it was as though they were all seduced by a fantasy of parenthood, including Lizzie herself. At different times she'd looked after all three nieces, read them stories, sang them to sleep, fed and changed them and dragged them round super-markets while they kicked and screamed and flung themselves on the floor. She'd seen her oldest niece, Lynne, grow into adolescence and turn against her father and her father's wife, building barriers of ice between the three of them. She knew all this and she knew that of all people she was hardly best placed to look after a child, but it made no difference. She hungered for a child of her own, someone to hold on to in the night, to shape her life and give it meaning – a little boy. Her parents would love a little grandson . . . perhaps Sebastian, or Zachary.

This daydream alternated with the moments of blank terror in which she thought she might actually be pregnant; the many trips to the toilet in search of bloodstains, the long, long days before she could do a test. When she and Rob finished, her period didn't come at all and she was swallowed up by horror at the prospect before her. She even prayed once, propped up against the tiled walls of Marley's public loo.

Please God, she prayed. Please God, please God, please. But when she opened her eyes there was no answer, only the scrawl of graffiti on the wooden door: *Joanne is a fridged cow*, it said. But she couldn't have a baby, she had no money, no one to help her, single parents weren't even a priority any more on the housing lists. Three days later, when her period finally came she was euphoric, out in the wind and the cold, the sky above her bursting with colour. Hours later she was doubled up on her bed weeping, for the loss of the child she would never have.

The second reason Lizzie's big exhibition was memorable was that she met Nigel. Nigel was doing a PhD in art history.

The textures are so suggestive, he said. Such juxtapositions. It subverts its own mythology, he said of Lizzie's painting of the grieving Demeter. It was a kind of introspective *jouissance*.

Nigel was very thin. He had a small goatee beard and John Lennon glasses. Right away Lizzie felt a kind of attraction for him that was part repulsion, and this never changed. He followed her around the exhibition asking questions she didn't know how to answer.

Is the ideological framework of your paintings deliberately neo-classical? he said.

When Lizzie asked him if he always talked like this, he blinked and said,

Like what?

Then, sensing that she was getting tired of his questions he changed the subject and went on to enthuse about a landscape.

270

The effect of light on the moor was Turneresque, he said. She'd made the moor reflect the light of the sky and charged even the stones with energy.

Though she got tired of him talking at least it didn't throw her into a stiff silence. This was partly because it was so impersonal, he never mentioned the effect the paintings had on him. Even so it was unusual to meet a man so interested in her work, usually they ignored it or made suggestions about how she could change it for the better, so it would sell. In all the time she knew him Nigel never suggested she should change her style. In fact he supplied her with more reasons than she'd ever thought of as to why it should stay the way it was. It subverted the discourses of race and class and gender, he said. It formed a discourse of its own. Lizzie couldn't help feeling gratified, though she was cynical at the same time, put off and attracted by his ability to put things into words. He came nearly every day to talk and Lizzie let him, fascinated by the way he approached her paintings as if they were disembodied things, hardly connected to Lizzie at all.

One day he asked her what the response of other people had been. Lizzie shrugged a little, and Nigel waited. She hoped she would say something clever. Finally she said,

I always get the feeling that people don't know how to respond to paintings, not just mine, any paintings. Nigel nodded enthusiastically.

It's just that – they expect everything to be put in words, she said, encouraged. If it hasn't got a written explanation with it they don't know what to do. They have to come to everything through words.

Nigel looked surprised, though it didn't seem to Lizzie to be a very genuine surprise.

Of course, he said. We come to everything through words.

Lizzie argued with him though she was no longer sure of her ground.

An artist shouldn't have to explain art in words, she said. They don't ask novelists to dance. But Nigel was ahead of her there.

Yes, he said, but you can't make sense of the world without language. Art is a language, everything is, and you have to be educated through language into responding to art.

Lizzie resisted being shifted on to his ground.

I want people to have a gut response to my work, she said. Not to stand around trying to work out what they think. Or, she added pointedly, to have to take courses to find out.

Nigel laughed, then shook his head in a smiling kind of way.

There's no such thing, he said, as an unlearned response.

Aunt Edie used to lay out the dead in her street, washing them down, closing the stubborn eyes. She always laid them out nicely; in her own way Aunt Edie was an artist too. When they were all ready people used to take their children to see. That was thought to be dreadfully morbid these days, Lizzie used to think so too, but now she wasn't sure. Because what else was there to prepare you for it, the final experience you all had to face sometime, alone? People passed on their experience of childbirth and marriage, though in the end of course you were on your own there too. But nothing at all helped you face death. Lizzie had heard of rituals of death, where you went underground and eventually emerged into the light, or even ate bits of the corpse, but now there was only this insistent denial, people fighting off old age and mortality, sealing away their dead. Only recently she'd read about a place where an abattoir had been built too close to a supermarket so the customers, buying their neat squares of frozen meat, were made too aware of what went into them, the squealing and blood. There had been an outcry, of course, no one wanted to face what was really happening. But maybe now that you no longer had to face the animal you wanted to eat it was all distanced and unreal, civilised. And harder all the time to keep in touch with what was really happening.

Lizzie said all this to Michael the mortician when she saw him in the pub. He agreed with her that death was the biggest taboo. It had been a long time, he said, since he'd told anyone what he did for a living and they'd said, Ooo lovely, tell me more. Lizzie laughed and said it was just the same being an artist, people never knew what to say to that either. And then she said that she thought it was because they both dealt with death in one way or another.

Well yes, Michael said. Didn't those old painters all used to learn their anatomy and that from corpses?

That was true, though it wasn't exactly what Lizzie meant. She didn't know exactly what she did mean, and for a fleeting moment she wished Nigel were there. He never had trouble putting thoughts into words, his own thoughts or anyone else's. No one respected you unless you were good with words, she thought, her mind beginning to wander in the stuffy room. What would Nigel have said?

She told Michael about Aunt Edie and about how you never got to see a corpse these days.

You could always come and have a look round the mortuary, Michael said, joking.

Yes, said Lizzie. Yes I think I'd like that, and Michael seemed surprised and pleased, like someone who has always wanted to show off the scar from his operation.

Well that's easy enough arranged, he said. Let me get you another drink, and Lizzie settled back with the one she had while Michael went to the bar, thinking what a nice bloke he was and wishing she could fancy him, he seemed keen enough on her. This was the third drink he'd bought her. But his cheeks were very red and he had too many teeth, she couldn't fancy him. Then she thought about the trip to the mortuary, and felt excited, not everyone got to see one. It could make a big difference to her art, she thought, all the difference in the world. If people lived with the consciousness of death it might bring meaning back to life. Perhaps that was what she was meant to do, it was what she wanted to do with her painting.

Michael came back and said,

What about next Thursday, then? I'll be in on my own in the afternoon. So it was arranged, and Lizzie was excited all week, but when the day came she felt reluctant to go. She had dreamed about Aunt Edie who'd died in that very hospital and would have been laid out in the same mortuary. Now she felt gripped by her ghost.

She had visited her at first of course, taking flowers, holding her hand and telling her all the things Aunt Edie always liked to know: who Lizzie was seeing at the moment, what he was like, who was pregnant, getting divorced and so on. She'd done this even when Aunt Edie stopped recognising her and was unable to reply. Then Lizzie had to face the sight of her shrivelled body stippled with tubes, loose skin over bones, so little substance that the whole of her seemed to inflate and collapse with each breath. The hospital did its best to keep her alive; it churned Lizzie's stomach in the end, all those tubes and drips sustaining a life so minimal it barely registered on the machine. Long after all the organs gave up they kept pumping fluids into the veins, sending the sluggish heart into spasm, and Lizzie was gripped by the nightmarish fear that they would never let her die at all. So she stopped visiting, taking flowers; it was easy to miss one visit, then another. There was no point, she told herself, but secretly she was haunted by the thought that somewhere inside the little carcass there was a flickering consciousness that knew it had been abandoned, that was frightened of dying alone. But Lizzie told herself she wanted to remember her aunt the way she was, bright and brave and energetic, not as a shrivelled up sack.

Then when Aunt Edie finally died, Lizzie hadn't gone to visit the body. Her parents had gone, to the little chapel inside the mortuary, but Lizzie wouldn't go. And she felt bad about this. She wasn't next of kin, since aunt Edie was really her father's aunt, but she had been closer to her than anyone else. She'd practically lived with her in her teens, when the rows at home, about boyfriends and staying out late, or about wanting to do art, had got so bad she could hardly walk through the door without causing a scene. But Aunt Edie had been comfortable about whatever Lizzie wanted to do.

It'll all be the same when we're dead, she said, in response to any crisis, and,

Leave the child alone.

So she'd always stood by Lizzie and supported her, but Lizzie had abandoned Aunt Edie, running away like everyone else from the presence of death. Then when the funeral came she felt nothing, nothing at all.

Now she stood outside the mortuary. She'd made herself get dressed and come out, but she couldn't make herself go in. For the first time she realised that what she was doing was a kind of atonement, nothing to do with art at all. And now she was there she didn't want to go through with it, she would go home, she thought. But just as she thought this Michael poked his head round the door and grinned, frightening her.

Coming in? he said, and Lizzie nodded, failed to smile, and allowed him to take her arm.

Before she went she'd had a kind of vision of how it would be. She imagined a long, low room, white tiled and brightly lit, with windows from floor to ceiling looking out on to green fields. She could imagine the smell, of disinfectant and formaldehyde, and the long cupboards like filing cabinets where the dead were kept in drawers, like the ones she'd seen on American TV. She imagined being left alone as the light seeped out of the room, making some sketches, perhaps even touching a corpse to feel for herself the waxy texture of the flesh – she'd read somewhere it was waxy – quietly coming to terms with the consciousness of death.

It wasn't like that. For one thing there were no windows. Of course there wouldn't be, no one wanted to walk past a *post mortem* by accident. She was taken into a small room, maybe it looked smaller because it was crammed with equipment and dimly lit with fluorescent strips. Lizzie supposed they could turn the lighting up if they needed to.

It was metallic, reminding Lizzie of nothing so much as a dairy. There were metal slabs where the corpses were laid out for dissection, hoses to wash out the blood, a great array of cutting tools and metal scales to weigh the bits and pieces. There were blackboards like children's blackboards, with the weights and measurements of various organs chalked on, and above each slab there was a VDU screen. There were metal filing cabinets, but they didn't look big enough for the corpses.

Michael talked as they went round, explaining what everything was for, but Lizzie found it hard to take things in; she asked none of the questions she'd meant to ask. At least she'd been right about the smell, or half right, it was disinfectant, not formaldehyde, that was the biology lab at school. Then Michael took her into another room and Lizzie was almost knocked back by a different kind of smell, the carnal smell of decay. Somehow she'd expected only the hospital smell. Here this time there were the white tiles, and a whirring noise from great fridges. The corpses were kept in fridges, not filing cabinets.

It's not like American TV here, Michael said, and he opened a door to show her. They were all on trays, wrapped in white. He asked if she wanted to see one and Lizzie nodded, not wanting to breathe in more of the smell which was worse now the door was open. Michael pulled a tray out and unwrapped the head: an elderly woman with wispy hair and no teeth, like Aunt Edie, Lizzie thought, flinching a little as the head lolled. Michael was jocular.

You've no need to worry, he said. I know you hear all kinds of things about corpses – about them breathing out, passing wind, even sitting up. The blokes that worked here used to really wind me up when I started, but this lot are all past that stage now, and he patted the unwrapped head with a familiarity Lizzie found unpleasant.

Come a bit closer, he said. Take a proper look.

Lizzie took a few steps forwards and looked at the yellowing skin, not papery with wrinkles but pulled into a rigid smoothness like the smoothness of plastic surgery.

We do our best for them, you know, Michael said. After we've finished we always do them up nicely. We sew the scalp back on and you can hardly see the join, and he pulled the hair back to show her, then he rubbed the poor head until Lizzie wanted to tell him to stop.

She wanted to go now, though she felt she should have asked more questions, but Michael wanted to take her into one more room. He shoved the tray back unceremoniously and locked the door.

This is where we put them on show after, he said, for family and friends, and he led her through to the chapel: yet another windowless room, this time with fake wood panelling and a metal crucifix at one end. There were flowers on the little altar and the air was thick with freshener, presumably to offset the other smell. In spite of this, somehow the overall effect was even more deadened and enclosed than in the other rooms.

Lizzie blinked once or twice, trying to come to terms with the peculiarly horrible colour scheme: lilac wallpaper where the fake wood ended, and a mustard carpet. No artist could have chosen that, she thought, and then she thought, and no woman either, though death used to be the business of women, women like Aunt Edie.

The corpse itself was the least intrusive thing about the place, lying in its coffin in front of doors in the panelling. It was a middle-aged woman this time, with dyed black hair. A coral-pink coating of lipstick disguised the uniform marbled colour of lips and flesh.

When Lizzie thought about it later, the overwhelming presence of the place itself, its metallic power and closure, seemed to obscure that of the corpses, making them almost unimportant. And any sense she might have had of their presence had been ruined because she'd been chaperoned the whole time, she'd seen everything through Michael's eyes.

Lizzie was so quiet by the time they finished Michael thought she might be feeling faint. She suspected that he wanted her to feel faint so he could exercise even more fully his protective authority. He insisted on taking her for a cup of coffee, but as they approached the canteen she shook her arm away and said she'd rather be alone. Michael looked hurt.

Are you sure? he said, and Lizzie felt she'd been a bit hostile. She pulled her face into a smile and thanked him, but said what she really wanted was some fresh air, and not to worry about her, she'd be fine.

Michael still looked concerned as she pulled away, then he looked as if he wanted to say something. Lizzie felt a pang of fear that he might be going to ask her out.

Goodbye, she said. Thanks very much – I'll see you in the pub some time.

In fact she stopped going to the pub after that, she didn't want to see him any more though she didn't precisely know why, and when she thought about it she felt a stab of guilt. But whenever she saw him in the street afterwards she hurried away.

Now she hurried into the wan day outside, towards a bench

surrounded by wet grass and flowers, for the mortuary didn't overlook fields but a small enclosed garden. Lizzie breathed deeply and she could smell the flowers, but behind them was the greater smell of corpses, lodged somewhere in the space between the bridge of her nose and her brain. It was days before she could get rid of it, weeks before she could bring herself to eat meat; she thought she would smell them for ever. Now she looked up at the whitish sunlight and suddenly her eyes were wet for Aunt Edie, though she'd never cried for her before. Aunt Edie had washed and dressed her corpses with care, but she herself had been left alone in that place, to be carved up and hosed down and stored like so much meat, all by strangers. I'm sorry, Lizzie thought, I'm sorry, then she rubbed her eyes hard because it was too late now, and anyway it wasn't her fault, it was the law. Still she could have visited, she thought, she could have visited, and inside her she felt a great mourning breaking loose.

This wasn't what she wanted to feel at all, it wasn't what she'd come for, and she rubbed her eyes again and pinched the bridge of her nose where the smell was, and tried to focus more calmly on what she'd seen. In the back of her mind she was already going over the colours and textures she'd need, the yellows and greys, the waxy finish, but she didn't get very far. At the front of her mind there was a jumble of facts and impressions with Michael's voice presiding over them all, his proprietorial air. We don't have windows, he had said, out of decency, and he'd hinted darkly at improper goings-on. Lizzie had heard of such things before, but what could it mean, people lusting after dead flesh? She would never understand it. And then there was the overwhelming sense of enclosure, the whole structure kept away from the public, access strictly controlled. Michael called it decency, but didn't it also erase the dead, deprive them of all power except perhaps the power to smell, to linger in the nostrils of the living? They hadn't managed to defeat that with their disinfectants and air fresheners.

She shook her head a little, still pinching the bridge of her nose. She knew she shouldn't resent the smell, which was the final power left to the dead. It was inside her now, a whispering smell. Remember us, it said, remember us. Lizzie rose and shook the damp from her coat, but she couldn't shake the whispering smell. Remember us, it said, remember us.

On the telly happy black men sang a song in praise of their white boss. A cowboy forced his girl to kiss him, she resisted at first then gave in, overwhelmed. Then there were the adverts, housewives in ecstasies about their floorshine, famous models going ape-shit over aftershave. Later in the evening there were feature films, a psychopathic killer stalked a lonely female, Michael Douglas shafted Glenn Close in a lift. In everything there was passion, trauma, ecstasy, yet the effect of watching it for so many hours was draining, she felt drained into a slow, dull deadness inside. Sometimes she watched serious television out of a sense of duty – documentaries and news – but that was worse: disappearing species in Africa, another oil slick, drugs and pornography amongst Aborigines and the discovery of more bodies killed by the Sandman. It filled her with a bleak horror. The world was a terrible place and there was too much of it to cope with. She sat in a state of dull absorption as light leaked from the sky; it was like and yet unlike the state she got into when she was painting; it was like the complete absence of passion. If she sat long enough she felt she was becoming frozen inside. If she sat longer still, she thought, she would never need to die. She could stay for ever in her frozen, indeterminate state.

Nigel was never big on passion, not even at first. Their first night together had been disastrous, she couldn't understand why she hadn't given him the push right away.

Towards the end of her exhibition he'd turned up every day,

she'd come to expect it. He always had something new to say about her painting and sometimes the things he said were illuminating. On the last day he helped her pack away her canvases, then he took both her hands in his and said,

I can't believe I won't be seeing you again.

What could she do but invite him back? He seemed genuinely pleased and helped her carry the smaller stuff back on the bus. He talked enthusiastically all the way, about the prospects of art in general and Lizzie's in particular. He talked about her getting an agent, and marketing her work abroad, exhibitions in Amsterdam. He seemed very knowledgeable. Lizzie found her hopes rising in a general way, there were new possibilities round every corner if you only knew where to look. He made her believe in herself; by the time she got home she was more attracted to him than ever before.

Nigel helped her store her paints and papers in the smaller room where she kept all her artwork. He talked so much that eventually she felt she had to stop him somehow. She leaned over and took his hand. He patted her hand absently.

It's late, she told him. The last bus has gone.

Nigel blinked in the disconcerted way which was one of the few things about him Lizzie ever found endearing. It contrasted oddly with his usual opaque assurance.

I'm sorry? he said.

He didn't seem to realise that he might make a move at this point. Wondering how much encouragement he needed, Lizzie said,

It's getting late, you can stay if you want to.

When Nigel still didn't say anything she said,

Unless you'd like to call a taxi. Nigel seemed almost shy.

I forgot about the time, he said, as if coming round slowly.

I could call you a taxi if you like, Lizzie said. But it'll cost you a fortune at this time.

I don't have any money, Nigel said. He looked really embarrassed now, and Lizzie felt a further spark of attraction.

You're welcome to stay the night, she said, feeling more confident by the minute.

Well that's very kind, Nigel said, retreating into formality. I'll sleep in the chair.

Lizzie felt quite sorry for him.

You may as well sleep in the bed, she said, looking at him very directly.

O no, I couldn't, he said. Where would you sleep?

Lizzie could see that this wasn't going to be easy. She turned to walk down the passage to the bathroom.

We can both sleep in the bed, she said over her shoulder. There's room for two. And I won't eat you, she added, disappearing.

When she got back from the bathroom he was perched on the end of the bed in his boxer shorts, T-shirt and socks, looking very thin. Lizzie was wearing the long T-shirt she normally wore in bed.

Are you sure about this, he said. I don't want you to feel pressured in any way.

Lizzie sat down on the opposite side of the bed.

Do you feel pressured? she said.

No, said Nigel quickly.

Then don't worry about me, she said. I can look after myself. She was aware that she sounded a bit hard, he brought it out in her. Before getting into bed she stripped the T-shirt off. He wouldn't look at her naked. She lay waiting for him, feeling the slight movements of the bed as he edged into it and lay as far away from her as possible. She was cross now, and dejected. She'd made a mistake. But he'd been so interested in her and her work, he'd wanted to know everything about her.

In the old days you knew where you were with a man, Aunt Edie said.

Lizzie didn't know, she didn't have a clue what to do next. She could either lie there in an annoyed kind of way while he slept – men always slept first – or she could tell him to get the taxi after all, since he'd failed to perform (though she felt this was a little crude), or she could roll on top of him and insist on having her way.

None of these options seemed ideal. The annoyance and dejection she'd been feeling deepened into a kind of pain. She wanted him to touch her. It felt bad, worse than she'd expected, that he wouldn't when they were lying in the same bed. He didn't even want to touch her hair, most men liked to touch her hair, which was thick and tangled.

So what do I do now? she asked herself the darkness.

As if in answer there came a stifled sound from Nigel's side of the bed. Lizzie propped herself up. Surely to God he wasn't crying, she thought. Could things get any worse?

Nigel, she whispered. Are you all right?

Silence.

Is anything wrong? she said. After a moment Nigel said,

No, I'm all right. I'm just very cold. I can't seem to get warm.

Lizzie could hear his teeth chattering. She stroked his arm and shoulder and said, It's all right, to him as he lay stiffly.

Can I get you a drink, she said, but he shook his head. Then she said,

Look, turn round to me, and obediently he turned; she could feel his bony knees digging into her thighs. She hugged him and he clung to her. Eventually, by stroking his body, she managed to produce a wavering erection which she took into her mouth. It rose then withered again, and he made no attempt to touch her, he appeared to be clutching the sheets. After a while she stopped and asked him what was wrong. He didn't answer at first, then he said,

I don't want to rape you.

Lizzie almost laughed.

Rape me! she said. She had all but raped him. But he was earnest. He'd thought about it a lot, he said. There was more than one kind of rape. Women were under a lot of pressure all the time as far as sex was concerned, it was a form of coercion. You couldn't avoid it altogether, the best you could do was to put the woman under minimal pressure. Nigel was on his own ground now, gaining confidence. He had come to the conclusion, he said, that every sexual act was an act of rape unless the woman made the moves all the way.

For a moment Lizzie didn't know what to say, then she said, But what about passion?

Nigel was dismissive of passion. Any number of atrocities had been committed upon women in the name of passion, he said. Unwanted pregnancies, abortions, syphilis and AIDS, the horrendous unfairness of rape laws which assumed that a woman was responsible for what a man did –

Yes all right, Lizzie said. It wasn't precisely what she'd meant, but she didn't want to get into an argument. What do you want me to do now? For though she'd virtually lost all traces of passion herself the stubborn part of her wouldn't give up.

Nigel was tentative again. But eventually he suggested that if she held his arms down when she kissed him he wouldn't feel that he was taking advantage in any way.

Lizzie was willing to try almost anything by now. She straddled his wispy body with her sturdy one and pressed down hard on his arms, even biting his lips a little, as much out of resentment as anything else, but he seemed finally able to respond. On different occasions she tied him down, struck him, pulled his hair back hard, made him dress again and leave after he'd undressed and even dug her nails into his balls. Even so it never drove him to extremes of passion. At most he closed his eyes and changed his breathing pattern a bit, except when she

284

dug her nails in, which made him cry out, but he never made any attempt to retaliate.

None of this was really Lizzie's scene, though she couldn't deny she got a kick out of some of it. But none of it generated the intensity she wanted in either of them, the crucial abandonment of control. The first night Lizzie worked hard, but became more and more abstracted, preparing a comic description of it all for Aunt Edie's benefit in her mind. Eventually, by unspoken agreement they gave up and lay side by side, without acrimony. Perhaps the only place you can have real passion these days is on the screen, Lizzie thought.

In my day we just got on with sex, Aunt Edie said. There's never been so much fuss, despite the fact you're all supposed to be at it like rabbits all the time.

Lizzie lay in the dark, thinking that it was a lot easier discussing sex than having it, at least in this particular case, though Nigel lay next to her companionably enough, and beneath the sheets his hand searched for hers.

Lizzie's T-shirt clung to her as she fought her way out of the bedclothes. Then she still couldn't breathe, so she struggled out of bed and fell into the armchair opposite. Rob sat up and peered at her.

What's up? he said.

She knew the vampire was there, he'd drawn her blood.

She couldn't say this to Rob. She said,

I can't sleep.

Come back to bed, said Rob. He hated being woken up. In the darkness Lizzie shook her head. She couldn't speak. She'd felt the shadow of death.

Are you coming to bed, or what? said Rob.

She wanted him to stop looking at her, sure he could see already the wasted flesh between her breastbones, beneath her eyes.

Come to bed, he said again.

Lizzie tried and managed to speak, in a sore, cracked voice.

I can't, she said. I'm scared. Tears rose in her eyes at the acknowledgement of her fear.

Scared? Rob said. Scared of what?

Lizzie's voice disappeared into a whisper. She was caught between the primitive urge not to name her fear, and the knowledge of how ridicuous it would sound anyway, spoken aloud.

She said, I think I'm going to die.

You what? said Rob. She couldn't tell if he was laughing or angry.

I'm going to die, she said again, and her breath came in a shuddering gasp. Even as she said it she could feel the cold points of teeth on her neck.

What are you going on about? said Rob. You're not going to die, you're not even ill. How old are you, thirty-three?

Four, whispered Lizzie.

Jesus, Rob said. He flung himself back down and rolled himself up in the bedclothes. Just get back in bed, will you.

Lizzie wanted to beg him not to leave her alone in the dark. She wanted to get back to him in the bed, she was afraid to stay where she was, but she couldn't move. Please, she whispered, but Rob was no longer speaking to her. He was only a few steps away from her, in a different universe, where there was no fear. If she just took a few steps she could press her cold body up against his warm back, but she seemed to be trapped, and moments elongated themselves unbearably. Finally she managed to push herself out of the chair, stepping into the abyss between it and the bed. Lured by the sound of Rob's breathing, by her need for his warm-blooded flesh, she groped her way towards him.

Do you do this kind of thing often? he had said.

Now and then, Lizzie said. What about you? He squeezed her waist.

As often as I can, he said.

A fire-engine shrieked past the window, there was another burst of laughter from the noisy table, but Lizzie sat very still, smoking and sipping mechanically at the tea she could no longer taste.

Outside the light was so bright everything seemed shadowy and unreal. People walked with their heads bowed, bent beneath the burden of light. Lizzie made herself look round the café at the different people, though already she felt the familiar sensation of being cut off from them, as though sealed in a polythene bag.

At the far table four lads and a girl sat dressed in the leather gear of bikers. Lizzie watched the girl most; she was attractive – in a tarty kind of way, Aunt Edie would have said – tall with dyed blonde hair and thick eyeliner. She was having a good time, not obviously the centre of attention, she sat and listened and laughed at all the jokes, but in some way the group revolved around her. Whatever they did, cracking jokes, making farting noises, having mock fights, they did for her, so she could reflect them back to themselves. And she seemed entirely at ease with this, laughing when it was required of her, smoking a cigarette.

Lizzie envied the girl her poise, her slovenly good looks, the way she seemed to feel herself to be part of things. She imagined her life; she must be eighteen or nineteen years old and probably called Debbie. She would live at home because neither she nor her boyfriend would have a job. There would be screaming rows at home because of the number of times she went out and stayed out late, and about her boyfriend, who would have long, lank hair. She would tell her problems to her friend, who was probably called Tracey, but she would forget all about them when she went out. She had that ability to live it up with other bikers, forgetting the crushing routine of life. She would never question things too much, not like Lizzie, who wore herself out with questions. She would just go out and get drunk with her boyfriend, who would batter anyone who made a move on her. Debbie of course would batter anyone who made a move on him, that was the way it was done, no questions asked, nothing civilised about it. It was ridiculous to envy her, Lizzie knew. In two or three years' time she would be pushing a pram up the hills of Marley looking dowdy and grim while the boyfriend she used to go out with now went out alone.

Still, it was a different world, Lizzie thought, a different world from her own, and she often wished she could climb inside other people's worlds. She knew it was dangerous, the way she looked at people, it was like putting them under glass; she didn't really know anything about the girl in the café, yet she was fixed now for ever in Lizzie's fantasy.

Aunt Edie always said there were different worlds to live in, all the people they knew lived in different worlds. Even within the working class of Marley there were different layers that rarely overlapped except in a hostile kind of way. Only the other day, looking over someone's shoulder on the bus, Lizzie had read about a local girl attacked and raped by a gang of both girls and boys. In the grocer's she heard people talking about it, everyone was shocked, they felt the same sick incomprehension Lizzie felt. Yet, she supposed, if there was a war on tomorrow, a real war on the streets of Marley and Clough Bottom, not just on the telly, people would be out committing atrocities they never dreamed of in daily life. That was the way it must be in that gang, Lizzie thought, a world of its own, perpetually at war.

Lizzie's gaze wandered away from the group in the corner, and away from the other two customers in the café, a man with tattoos and an old woman in a woolly hat, with many bags. She looked out of the window, into the blaze of light.

A group of schoolgirls were walking down the hill together,

skiving off school in their lunch hour, Lizzie thought. As they came closer she recognised one of them as her niece, Lynne. She was at the centre of the group, dressed like all the others, but so fashionably it hardly looked like a school uniform: short tight skirts, ankle boots and stripey blazers. Lizzie used to go to the same school, as far as she knew they'd never had stripey blazers. The hair, too, was distinctive, taken up in a kind of stalk from the crown of the head, then falling forwards in a floppy frizz, or all pulled over to one side. Lynne wore hers that way, in a pony-tail which dangled from the middle of her head to the left.

She's a leader, that one, Lizzie's mother often said. She's got a mind of her own. Yet apart from the fact that Lynne had black hair and three of the others were blonde you could hardly tell the difference.

This was the set of girls Lizzie had heard about, the ones with money. Lizzie's brother, Tom, had made a lot of money plumbing, even in these days of recession, and went about in a Porsche. Lynne got whatever she wanted. Even so, as the group drew nearer, Lizzie thought Lynne hadn't improved since she'd seen her last. She was thinner, anorexically thin, and the painted face was sharp and unappeased. Lizzie used to think Lynne was beautiful. She used to take her for walks in the park and play round-and-round-the-garden, like-a-teddy-bear, tickling her fat palms. Then she'd been rosy and chubby, happy in her acceptance of the world. Now, despite the clothes and make-up, she looked, not as if she felt herself to be beautiful but as if she felt keenly the complete absence of beauty in her life. She didn't look pleasant, though Lizzie couldn't put her finger on the exact change. She thought of letting on to her as the group passed the window, then changed her mind. She was sure Lynne wouldn't want to let on to her shabby aunt in the run-down café. Even Tom rarely let on to her these days. She sometimes saw him swanning past in the Porsche with his young(ish) wife Cynthia, who ran a dancing school. Tom's first wife, Joan, had died of cancer when Lynne was eight, but he'd been knocking around with Cynthia well before then and they'd finally married five or six years ago. Now they lived in a big house in Upper Marley, and both Cynthia and Lynne went about done up to the nines. Every New Year's Eve Tom and Cynthia threw a party to which everyone was invited for miles around, except Lizzie. It wasn't quite true to say she wouldn't have gone anyway, she never liked to miss a good spread, and they hired caterers specially, but she knew it wouldn't be her scene. She used to like Joan a lot, even when Tom first went out with her she'd seemed middle-aged and motherly, but she couldn't take to Cynthia at all. Neither could Lynne. She ignored her father and had no time for Cynthia. Fortunately the big house was big enough for the three of them to lead separate lives, while the money lasted.

Family gatherings were best avoided in any case, Lizzie had found. Grouped together they always seemed to take a united stand against her. She was the youngest and they couldn't stop treating her that way, as if she'd never grown up and was never going to stop doing foolish things, like painting. Her mother could never refrain from mentioning Cynthia's housekeeping, for which she was famous. Lizzie knew what they thought, and that there was a core of bitterness to it; she of all of them had escaped responsibility: no work, no family, kept by the State. She failed to live in the real world as they knew it. The trouble was when she was with them she tended to see herself through their eyes. In their company she could feel herself becoming more immature, saying wild or eccentric things just to shock them, or maybe to live up to what they thought. They didn't know where she got it from, they would say, shaking a collective head. There were no artists in the Baker family as far back as anyone could remember. The sooner she settled down the better. So it was bad news being round her family, in case she started thinking the same way, and now she let Lynne and her friends pass by without waving. She watched them disappear into the intense light and went back to staring at her cup of tea, which had gone cold. There were grainy droplets on the surface. She'd come here to escape the silence of her flat, all those blank canvases, really she was just frittering away her time. She was foolish to think that by stepping out of her flat she was stepping into the world; she was as perfectly cut off from the world as if sealed in a polythene bag, or a shroud. Lizzie stretched out trembling fingers on the table to see that they were real.

You've done this kind of thing before, he said, and Lizzie looked up at him and smiled.

Now and then, she said.

The third reason Lizzie's big exhibition had been memorable was because of Frank and Mavis West, parents of Caroline. Lizzie had noticed an elderly couple returning several times to look at a series of pictures she'd done, taking the human face through various stages from the embryo to extreme old age. It wasn't her best work, she'd thought twice about putting it in, but this couple certainly seemed interested, though they didn't seem to want to buy. Lizzie watched them from the corner of her eye as they conferred. Finally when they did approach it was the woman who spoke.

It turned out they'd had a daughter called Caroline, who'd disappeared when she was fifteen years old, just disappeared, no body had ever been found. Lizzie had heard of such things before but she never thought she'd meet anyone it had happened to. Caroline was their only child, they had never stopped looking for her though everyone else had lost interest. It was over twenty-seven years ago.

As the woman talked Lizzie became conscious of the overpowering loneliness of their lives: friends, relatives, neighbours, the police losing interest as the years passed, unable to cope with a grief that didn't mend with time. They went out less and less, talked to fewer and fewer people. In the front room of their terraced house they designed handbills and leaflets which they handed out on the streets of different towns or left in libraries: Have you seen this girl? They sought out the homeless on city streets, they visited bodies in police morgues. They were mousy, ordinary-looking people. They would never give up.

We can't give up, the father said. Not while they haven't found the body.

She went out that morning happy as a lark, Caroline's mother said. The police tried to make out she wasn't, that there was something wrong at home, but it wasn't like that. She went out on her bike, it was a sunny day. She said, Tara Mam, Dad, I'll see you later, just like that.

They found the bike, her father said. Down by canal. But they dredged canal and then never found a body.

The mother looked as if she wanted to say something else, and tried once or twice but stopped. Finally she produced a photograph.

Caroline, she said.

Lizzie looked at the smile of a young girl in school uniform. She wasn't particularly pretty. She had a long, slightly horsey face, pale prominent eyes and braces on her teeth. She looked like her father. Lizzie didn't know what to say about the picture but the mother said,

She always had lovely hair, right down her back. It doesn't do her justice that picture, but it was the one taken nearest the time when she – went away. The hair was whitish-blonde and shiny, in the picture it was scraped tightly back and plaited.

Lizzie could see it all through their eyes, the moment on a sunny day when a young girl kicked off from the doorstep on

292

her bike, white-blonde hair whipped by the breeze, braces flashing in a final smile.

Tara Mam, Dad, she'd said. See you later. And she could see also how their lives had frozen round that single moment, and had become increasingly cut off from the world around them, which went on as if nothing had happened.

We don't think she's dead, you see, Caroline's father said, and they both looked at her defensively. Lizzie could see that, and she could see clearly the effects of trauma on their lives, breaking up their old world, drawing them together into a world of their own. That was trauma, Lizzie thought. A kind of paralysis.

So what do you want from me? she said.

They wanted Lizzie to paint a likeness from the photograph, not of the fifteen-year-old girl Caroline was then, but of the forty-two-year-old woman she would be now. Lizzie balked at the idea. Faces could change in any number of ways, she said. People got fat or thin, or scarred, or dyed their hair. The paintings on the wall were just her impression of the ageing process, she couldn't guarantee any kind of accuracy –

We know that, Caroline's father said. But we just want some idea. We keep thinking about her, you see, the way she was –

We might walk past her on the street, her mother said, and not be any wiser. She might not know us at all, and her voice trembled.

Lizzie felt sorry for them. She knew she was going to agree to do it, though there was something about it all she didn't like. Part of her said it should be piss-easy, she could draw anything and no one would know. God knew, she needed the money. The rest of her hung back, but because she couldn't explain her own reluctance to herself she finally accepted.

That's grand, Caroline's father said, and he pressed Lizzie's hand in both of his.

How much will it cost? her mother said. Lizzie breathed in.

Don't worry about the money, she said. I'll do the work and you see what you think. She hated herself for saying it. When would she ever get business-like about her art? But Caroline's parents both looked very pleased and a bit emotional.

So I'll be in touch then, she said. Mr and Mrs – ?

West, said Caroline's father, then he added, Frank and –

Mavis, said her mother.

But I can't promise anything, she said again, still feeling as though somehow she was cheating them when they looked so pleased.

Lizzie wanted to get rid of Nigel. She couldn't and this bothered her. It was almost as if she were afraid of him, though she didn't know why. She mocked him out of a need to feel that he wasn't a threat. Why should he be a threat, when he only wanted the best for her and her art? He didn't want her to change her style in any way, he wanted only to help her improve on it, to help her bring out the potential he could sense.

There's something about this quality of light here . . . he said.

But I don't want it to be a natural light, Lizzie said.

No no, of course not, said Nigel. But is it unnatural enough? How about a little more green?

or,

It's wonderful of course, but there's something not quite . . . not quite the right contrast, I think, here, and here.

Sometimes Lizzie shouted at him, telling him to get the fuck out of her life and her art, but he wouldn't go. She was being unreasonable, he said. What would happen if she got rid of everyone who disagreed with her when they were only trying to help? What would happen to her art? Didn't she think she needed feedback?

At these times he became almost as impassioned as Lizzie, such was his commitment to seeing reason prevail. And he had the advantage of becoming more articulate when he was angry, whereas often Lizzie could hardly speak at all. So sometimes she threw things at him instead, and screamed that it was over, she never wanted to see him again. Then he would try unsuccessfully to catch her flailing arms and tell her she was wrong, it would never be over between them. What they both needed was commitment, they'd said it months ago. They were both tired of drifting, of having nothing in their lives, because without commitment there was nothing, nothing at all. They had their differences, of course they did, but that was what commitment was all about, working through differences so that something real could emerge, something that was neither more of one of them than the other, but a blend of both – surely that was the ideal. If they weren't prepared to do that they would never have commitment, they would never have anything. She would carry on drifting through life, packing people off whenever they disagreed with her or things got rough; what would she have left but loneliness? Wasn't that what she'd said about her life, that she'd always been alone?

Many of these were Lizzie's own words coming back to her in a torrent. She listened in despair, but his fear was catching. He had her paralysed with words. She kept trying to argue with him on his terms, as if she only needed to find the right argument and he would see what she meant and go, but there was no way through the barricade of his reasoning, and time after time she caved in. But she was frightened for her art. Once he compared her work to the paintings of Bosch; she didn't see it and they argued, but after he explained it to her she kept seeing the similarities. She felt that he had somehow managed to crawl inside her skull and she could only look at her work through his eyes. Secretly she took to reworking her paintings on the basis of what he said.

Aunt Edie's death resolved all that. That was the thing about death, Lizzie thought, some time after her visit to the mortuary. It changed your life in unexpected ways. She hadn't visited Aunt Edie in hospital, she'd felt nothing at the funeral, yet scarcely a week later she could look at Nigel as he sat eating soup in her kitchen and experience a moment of absolute clarity. She wasn't going to have him in her life any more. She waited for him to finish his soup then told him so. Then she waited calmly for all the arguments. They didn't come. Nigel looked at her as if for the first time he believed her, but couldn't take it in. Then he said,

Don't you love me, then?

It wasn't what Lizzie had expected him to say. She half-turned to look out of the window.

No, she said. It had never occurred to her before. She waited for him to tell her she was wrong, she did love him, she just didn't know what she wanted, but he didn't say anthing. When she looked back at him his face was loosening with grief. He looked as if he were going to speak but stopped. Then he said,

You're breaking my heart.

It was the kind of thing he never said. Perhaps for that reason it stayed with her for years, returning to reproach her long after it became hard to remember their rows, his incessant preaching.

She didn't speak to him after that. When he asked if she wanted him to move all his stuff right away she shrugged and turned back towards the window. Then she listened as he moved around her flat gathering his things. She wasn't throwing him out of a home, she told herself, he didn't live with her. It was just that he'd stayed with her so often over the past two years that his stuff had accumulated in her flat. She would have more room now, she told herself.

Lizzie stayed where she was, watching the first lamps lighting on the main road, and the dim outline of cows in the field beyond. She felt nothing, as she'd felt nothing at the funeral, but the clarity was fading. There was a pause in Nigel's movements, then he said,

If there's anything else, perhaps you could post it on. He was being civilised again, but for once it didn't drive her wild. She still said nothing because she could think of nothing to say. She heard Nigel come up behind her, then he put out a hand and for the first time touched her hair. Then he left.

Just at the moment of his leaving, as the door clicked to, Lizzie felt the urge to call him back. She felt suddenly and keenly the loss of two people who'd been close, who had loved her in their way, Aunt Edie and Nigel, it was too much. But as suddenly as the impulse came it left again. Her new serenity returned like water filling a hole.

Lizzie sat alone in the crowded club. It was dark and smoky, the basement of a hotel in the city centre. At the back of her mind she had an image of how disapproving Nigel would be if he knew.

Since finishing with Nigel she'd decided to go out alone, no one else had asked her. She had started going in the evenings to the pubs she normally went to at lunchtimes. She attracted one or two stares, nothing too hostile. Once or twice men approached her, she ignored them and they went away. It was no good though, when she got back she still couldn't sleep, she lay awake in the shadows of her room. Then one night she picked a pub further away from home, with a disco. She drank a bit, watched the people on the dance floor for a while, then danced herself, alone. If she closed her eyes she didn't feel she was being watched. She danced to one or two tunes then left in time for the last bus. A few days later she did the same thing in a different pub, she didn't want to get known in any one place. She didn't mind too much feeling out of place, she'd almost forgotten what it was like not to feel that way. Each time before she went out she dressed up as though she were going on a date, it made her feel good. Then sometimes when men talked to her she talked back, though she rarely felt attracted. But you had to be open-minded, she thought. Just because things hadn't worked out with Nigel didn't mean she should give up. So once or twice she took men home with her, preferring to be on her own ground rather than theirs; but mainly these were sad encounters and the worst part was getting rid of them in the morning. It seemed there were a lot of people with nowhere in particular to go. Sometimes when they'd finally gone she promised herself she'd never do it again, then days later she'd prowl restlessly round her flat, the need to go out pressing in on her.

She was transcending her limitations, she told herself, doing something about the rut she was in. When she bathed and sprayed perfume on herself and polished her nails she felt alive. Fortunately the bank didn't know as yet that she was un-employed, so she had her cash card and overdraft.

So here she was, further from home than she'd ever been, drinking in an all-night club in the heart of the city, and trying not to think about the cost of the taxi home. She'd started the evening in a pub close to home, but it was deadly quiet except for two old men playing darts. After a while she'd felt nearly as enclosed there as in her flat, and had left, heading for the nearest cash card machine and a bus into town. Already it was too late to catch one back. She sat on a tall stool near the bar, with the darkness and the flashing lights around her, looking at herself sidelong in the mirrors that were everywhere, behind the bar and on pillars all round the dance floor. She'd looked too dressed up for the pub, but wasn't out of place here, wearing a short stretchy skirt and an off-the-shoulder glittery top. The bouncers had looked at her as she'd gone in alone but she'd ignored them and headed straight for the bar. When she'd had another drink she promised herself she'd go on to the dance floor.

Lizzie was a good dancer, she closed her eyes and just moved. Once or twice men came up to her, attracted by the way she danced and by the fact that she was alone, but she turned away.

She was just beginning to dance the way she liked to paint, wholly absorbed, when another man began to dance close by, but not close enough for her to be able to decide whether or not he was trying to dance with her. She watched him through half-closed eyes. He had thick, dark hair and looked foreign, Lizzie thought. He was a good dancer and good-looking too, tall and athletic. Even so, she didn't want to be picked up, she knew what he was probably thinking. When the record ended she went back to the bar. Of course he followed her and sat a little way off. Lizzie wouldn't look his way, but she was interested. For one thing she could see by the light of the bar that he was even better looking than she'd thought. He had big, dark blue eyes, not a watery blue like Lizzie's, but the kind usually described as violet in romantic novels. Lizzie had never thought eyes could really be that colour. For another thing he wasn't too pushy. It was a while before he offered her a drink and then he was hesitant. Lizzie accepted, but she was cool and distant, neither of them had much to say. By now though she was willing him to make another move, and when he didn't she got up to dance again.

At first she thought he wasn't following, then she noticed him coming her way. When she danced he partnered her more obviously this time. Lizzie felt a bit flattered, he was certainly the best-looking man in the room. He had the kind of face she thought she might like to paint. Portraits weren't really her thing, but she'd met people before who made her want to paint them. When a slow record came on he danced closer, then he took hold of her and drew her up against him. That was it then, she'd made some kind of assent. She felt a little wary but not frightened, and as the record went on she relaxed and leaned against him. They danced together well, soon Lizzie began to think about taking him home, of having someone in her flat again, in her bed. Beneath his shirt she could feel the outline of his body.

Back at the bar again she got him to talk. His name was

Andreas, his father was Greek and his mother Welsh, which was where he got the eyes from. He worked in his father's business, looking after sales. That was what he was doing in the hotel, booked into the most expensive suite; he always travelled in style, it was one of the few perks of being the boss's son.

Andreas smiled a lot as he talked, Lizzie began to feel better than she had in weeks. The club wasn't really his scene, he said, he was just having trouble sleeping so he came down. They had something in common then, and Lizzie told him so. Then he wanted to know all about her; he was really interested, Lizzie could tell, especially in her art. When she talked she felt as though she were teaching him something. Of course she was a lot older than him, she guessed he was about twenty-five. As they talked he kept leaning closer, it was hard to hear with all the music. Once or twice he touched her arm, but she decided not to notice this. When she talked his large, luminous eyes never left her face. Soon they were dancing together again, holding on to one another though it wasn't a slow record this time. In between records he leaned very close and said,

What's your sign?

Aquarius, Lizzie said, smiling. What's yours?

Pisces, said Andreas. Then he said, Are Aquarians any good in bed?

It was the first off-colour remark he'd made, and for a moment Lizzie didn't know what to say, then she smiled her crooked smile and said,

As good as Pisceans I should think, and they both laughed.

Andreas made no more remarks like that, but from then on the conversation shifted, becoming more jokey. Lizzie flirted in earnest now, she'd made up her mind. She would take him home with her, why not? It might even be more than a one-night stand, maybe she was ready again to try for a real relationship. Then after they danced again, laughing a lot this time and doing a version of the hokey-cokey on the dance floor, he took her hand and asked her if she'd like to see his suite upstairs.

Lizzie hesitated. She did prefer being on her own ground, but he had to start work early the next morning, he needed to stay in the city centre. Lizzie thought about going home alone to an empty flat, and the cost of the taxi, and the fact that she'd never seen an expensive hotel suite before, and she asked him to wait a bit while she freshened up.

In the toilets she splashed herself with cold water, brushed her hair and re-applied her lipstick. In the mirrors her face looked dark, flushed and shiny. She wished she had a mint for her breath. Still she looked good, she thought, better than she had for months. It was the prospect of romantic excitement, she supposed, taking years off her, making her feel alive.

They went up two floors in the lift, which had oak panels and mother of pearl insets, and a full-length mirror. Lizzie couldn't stop looking at them both in the mirror as if she couldn't quite believe it, his arm around her, his tall, powerful build. She kept checking herself to see that her mascara hadn't smudged, she hadn't spilt anything on her clothes. She leaned against him and her face was shiny with anticipation. She wondered if she seemed too obvious, too keen, but in the mirror his face smiled down at her. They looked good together, she thought.

They walked down the corridor, his arm still around her, she didn't want him to take it away, though once or twice she stumbled and they laughed. Even in her state of heightened anticipation Lizzie took in the William Morris wallpaper, the plush carpet. As they approached the room Lizzie said,

Do we get to book room-service for the morning, you know, fruit salad, coffee with cream, kedgeree? Andreas smiled down at her.

You've done this before, he said.

Once or twice, Lizzie said, airily. What about you?

Andreas squeezed her waist then slipped his key into the lock. Whenever I can, he said.

Now Lizzie was left alone with her art, or what was left of it. She spent long moments hovering over a canvas with her brush, trying to get the things Nigel had said out of her head. Finally she produced a sketch which was a flat imitation of Bosch and then decided that what she needed was a long walk.

She caught a bus to the nearest town with a precinct and wandered around shops and market stalls. Not being able to paint wouldn't be too bad, she thought, it might even be a relief, if she could only stop observing things, eyeing them up as possible material. The world was all material, but none of it came together in her mind.

The precinct was full of advertisements, and people hurrying or ambling by. Someone was shouting, Dishcloths, five for a pound, five dishcloths for a pound. Closing down sale, said a sign in a shop window, Everything must go. And, 15% discount off all main lines, said another. These days sales were a permanent feature, people hardly took any notice. They just showed up the unreality of prices as they moved up and down. Posters advertised everything from last-minute Christmas stock and stocking fillers to cheap winter breaks and videos telling you how to make love. Nothing in all this captured Lizzie's attention except in a general kind of way. That couple on the bench though, unmoving among the crowds, they were worth a second look – an Asian girl asleep in the arms of a white boy, his face with the bad skin and dull stare, everything about them suggested nowhere to go. Then the man with no legs at the entry to Woolworth's, resting on a kind of hand-made cart with wheels, the kind you hardly ever saw these days, and prising scratchy tunes from a worn harmonica. He had parked himself next to a fat plastic Santa which intoned, A Merry Christmas, in a nasal kind of way at regular intervals. And all the people went by without seeming to notice any of this, or one another.

I should be able to get some of this, Lizzie thought. Put these things together on paper, make them speak.

She would gather them together beneath great fat angels of money and glamour, dancing boisterously and unregarding above the crowds, their tawdry glitter, the dull rain. And she hurried on now, her mind racing, wanting to get home for the first time in a while. But as she walked things complicated themselves in her mind. She thought of the models on the posters, their tanned athletic beauty, the unloveliness of the people who walked by. Then she saw it all as a kind of machine, producing money, driven by fantasy, all the people caught up in it, running as fast as they could to keep the wheels turning . . .

By the time she got home the complications were multiplying, the images had lost their urgency, she'd lost faith in them. They were trite and over-used, they didn't work. She let herself in and sat down in the dimming light; all the jumbled-up figures of her vision danced and jiggled before her like a series of grotesque cartoons.

He half-tilted her inside the room and they kissed. He cupped her face in his hands and kicked the door to behind them. It was a mannered gesture, reminding Lizzie of something she'd once seen in a film. She pulled away and made a move towards the drinks cabinet, but he held her hand.

Where do you think you're going? he said. Lizzie laughed at the change in his voice.

Let's have a night-cap, she said. His grip on her hand tightened.

You've had enough, he said.

You what? said Lizzie, laughing, but he didn't smile.

I want a drink, she said. He was lifting her arm up and twisting her fingers in his.

You old drunk, he said. Lizzie tried to pull her hand away.

What are you talking about, she said, let go.

What are you talking about, he said. Let go.

Lizzie pulled her arm back and when he wouldn't let go slapped his face. Instantly she was yanked up close to him, her arm jerked up behind her back.

I said no more drink, he breathed into her ear.

Get off me, Lizzie shouted. Let go.

The fingers of his other hand pressed down over her face, silencing her.

You're not going anywhere, you cunt, he said, and he lifted her arm still higher behind her back. Then he moved his hand from her face and in a sudden movement rammed the heel of it down hard into her elbow. Lizzie heard the cracking noise before she felt the pain. Her arm had snapped easily, like the wing of a bird.

Time and again Lizzie told herself that it hardly mattered what she drew, she could still take the money, but in the end she worked harder at the portrait of Caroline than at anything she'd ever done. She went through all her old books on the art of portraiture, and looked up an article on a new technique for ageing photographs of children. She studied archaeological magazines for reconstructing impressions of the human face from a skull.

Sometimes she knew that all this was just another way of putting off the moment when she would have to lift her brush and press it to the canvas. She wanted to give up, but felt driven by the eroded hope in the eyes of Caroline's parents. The fact that they would never know whether what she produced was accurate or not should have been liberating, but it wasn't. She needed some kind of vision to direct her, to tell her what to do.

All the time their suffering haunted her, it became the suffering of all parents. She felt it in herself, for the children she'd never had, or when she listened to reports on the news saying that another naked, pathetic body had been found, stretched out cross-wise on planks of wood. The sick pain she felt then came nearer than anything to convincing her she should never have children, no parent could suffer so much and live. And she followed anxiously the reports on the parents which were featured in the newspapers from time to time. One had lost her job and been admitted on to a psychiatric ward but was out now, though heavily sedated. Another had actually died less than a year after his daughter had been found. He'd suffered from a number of illnesses since that day, though doctors couldn't diagnose a precise condition. And it wasn't suicide, they said, though he was taking a large number of tablets. Not suicide, just a complete withdrawal from the world when life became too difficult to sustain. Lizzie was haunted by this, the thought that there were some kinds of suffering you could not recover from, that altered you for ever, as though Frank and Mavis had been altered. She made herself miserable with such thoughts, and all the time Caroline's bright smile in the school photo, and in the other photos Mavis sent, mocked her inability to even start the work. She lost sleep over it and took to smoking more. Then she took to staying out of her flat for long periods, preferring the muddy paths of the canal, or the impersonal rooms of the university library, to staying in with the blank canvas.

All this time Frank and Mavis never bothered her or tried to contact her at all after asking her to do the work. She'd told them not to, she would phone them, she'd said, when she'd finished; it might take a while. Even so she felt worse and worse about it until one day she woke up with the pressure bursting inside her and when straight to the canvas without thinking about it. She picked up her brush and the miracle happened, Caroline's ageing face revealed itself to her, feature by feature, as if appearing out of the canvas itself. Lizzie was excited and moved by the revelation, the whitish-blonde hair that didn't grey easily, the long bony face with its prominent teeth were all the same, only the flesh was a little sunken and creepy, the eyes haunted. In the photograph Caroline was smiling, in the portrait she was wary, disturbed. Lizzie worked all day not knowing where it was coming from, just grateful as hell that it was coming. She moved the canvas into her living-room so she wouldn't have to leave it; within four days she'd finished. She sank back on her bed in an exhausted triumph. Then she slept.

She dreamed she was painting on the canvas when there was a flapping noise at her window and she was shaken by dread. It was the vampire, she knew. Even so she went towards the window to open it, unable not to. It was a woman with wild, whitish hair, her face distorted with rage. She was mouthing words Lizzie couldn't understand, she knew she would have to let her in. And the woman wouldn't be still, she kept bumping up against the window like a great moth, or bat. Then suddenly the message was clear. With her face and hands pressed up against the pane, her mouth moving like the mouth of a fish, the woman said,

Don't look for me.

Then she was gone. Lizzie was left staring at the black pane with its criss-crossed droplets of rain.

She woke up, sweating from the effort to wake, and switched on all the lights. She tuned into a local radio station and put the kettle on. Slowly she began to feel more calm. Outside the road was quiet, the village clock struck two. She thought about going to see Frank and Mavis the next day, and giving them the portrait. Her pleasure in the thought had gone. Then she thought about Caroline, driven by suffering as her parents were driven by their suffering. Who could say which of them was right? Only one thing emerged clearly from the jumble of Lizzie's thoughts. She was no longer worried about how accurate the picture was. She believed in her portrait of Caroline.

*

Once or twice he let her get almost all the way to the door before dragging her back, by the hair, or the ankles, over the thick blue carpet. It was a kind of game.

Go on, he said, giving her a little push. You can go now. Get out.

Lizzie didn't move.

You don't believe me, do you? he said, and Lizzie said, No. It was difficult to speak with the swelling of her jaw.

I said, get out! he said, shoving harder, and very slowly, trying to control the chattering of her teeth, the urge to be sick, she picked up what clothes she could with one arm, waiting all the time for him to pounce.

Get on with it, he said.

Almost crying, because she remembered this game from school, Lizzie took steps towards the door. She glanced sideways once or twice, but his face gave nothing away. Then, as she put her hand out towards the door he was always there before her, laughing or angry.

You think I'm stupid, you stupid fucking cunt, he said. Then it all began again; tied, untied, fucked in the backside and then the mouth, his hand pressing down hard on her nose until she knew she would choke. Then from behind, butting her face into the scalding radiator, saying he would kill her if she made a noise. He burnt her hair away with his lighter, then the hair on different parts of her body. He was very careful, and nothing he did drew blood.

At times she cried aloud and then he comforted her. She made great gasping noises, snorting and gasping as a child who has lost all sense of what to do; he rocked her and patted her and stroked what was left of her hair. Then he told her again it was all over now, she could go, and knowing he would stop her she dragged herself towards the door, allowing him to drag her back, to knock her head into the wall and stub his cigarette out on her breast.

At one point in the night she could feel herself giving in; she knew it would never be over and she began to weep silently. At the same time she knew she would never question anything he did. If he told her to crawl like a dog she crawled, if he'd opened the window and told her to fly she would have climbed up and leapt off the sill. And with this knowledge she felt an absolute, shining peace. But the moment passed and there was the pain again, and her resistance to it, the struggle.

Then, in a moment of deep exhaustion, deeper than she'd ever known, she knew she would never leave that room. This was followed by a powerful image, so powerful she lost consciousness of where she was. She was in the back of a van, being driven somewhere, she didn't know where. She was covered in some kind of plastic sheeting, she slid about as the van moved. She knew who was driving it, he was taking her somewhere to bury her. Already she could feel the clods of wet earth, the shower of small stones against her skin.

In fact it wasn't like that. Dawn leaked through a crack in the curtains, he told her yet again she could go. When she didn't move he pushed her so she fell off the bed and still she didn't move, knowing she could never leave him. Then he kicked her and she began to crawl across the carpet. She forgot about her clothes until he threw them after her, then she gathered them up as well as she could and rose with difficulty to her feet. She opened the door and stepped out naked into the corridor, blinking in the yellow light and waiting all the time for the sudden grip on her hair, around her throat. It didn't come.

She took a few steps then began to stumble, faster and faster down the corridor, struggling into her clothes. She'd left her underwear and stockings, the blouse and the little hat, but at least she had her shoes and jacket, her skirt and bag. She felt that she was on a kind of extending leash, at any moment he would haul her back in, but the further she got from the room the more her fear changed into a painful hope. She missed the turning to the lift, and by the time she reached the stairs she was blinded by panic. He would be there, she knew, round every corner she expected to run straight into him, and the stairs were endless and no one was around. By the time she passed the first floor her breath was coming in sobbing gasps, then suddenly the fear shifted, she wasn't afraid. She felt clearly the unreality of it all, she herself was unreal and her eyes became glassy as she took in the unreality of things around her. As she reached the ground floor the sensation intensified. She was calm, very calm as she walked past the porters, their dull stare of surprise. Through the revolving doors she walked into the greying, dirty air, across the main road as the traffic thickened, towards the bus station where she waited alone for the first bus of the day. She was shivering with cold, wrapping her jacket tightly around her, at the same time she didn't believe in the sensations of cold in her body. She stood in the glass shelter, feeling the steel rail press into the small of her back, looking in disbelief at the whitish rivulets of sky, the pigeons and sparrows and gulls, crying and wheeling and settling on to the city roofs.

For weeks after that night she only wanted to sleep. She kept her doors and windows locked and bolted and used up her tins of soup and a large tin of drinking chocolate her mother had given her. But the important thing was to sleep. If she could only sleep enough she knew she would heal. She had good dreams, about being a child again, and woke in the middle of the night happy enough until her memory returned and she was sick with fear. He was there in the room with her, that was what had woken her up. She lay beneath the covers until the pressure of her bladder forced her to get up. Then she went round and round the flat, checking the doors and windows, sometimes she clung to the door and cried with fear, knowing he was already inside. Then in daylight these fears shifted into a profound indifference. She turned on the small TV and lay in bed, watching Delia Smith do appalling things to geese.

For the first few days pain kept her in touch with the reality of her body. She went to the toilet constantly, she was pissing blood. Fear returned, she was infected, she was pregnant, but it alternated with wretchedness, she didn't care. And she couldn't stand the thought of doctors or police. She felt she'd been exposed in all her ugliness, she couldn't bear exposing herself again. Then gradually the pain went and the wretchedness remained. But in her moods of indifference she took care of herself in a mechanical kind of way, rubbing ointment into the burns on her body and the side of her face, cutting her hair into a shape that was roughly equal on both sides, leaving her arm to set as well as it could. While these moods lasted she was able to slip downstairs to Kumar Bros. to pick up supplies of cheese and crackers and soup, which she ate dully in bed. There were days when she couldn't stop eating like this, it stopped her thinking. Mostly, however, she wanted to sleep, though this became harder, because before she slept she had to check everything in her flat again.

From time to time she had to go out, to sign on and to cash her cheque. On these days she wrapped herself in layers of baggy clothing, and combed what was left of her hair over the scarred side of her face, then pulled back the bolts on her door, suppressing sensations of nausea as she stepped outside. When she got back she went through the same ritual each time: checking her rooms, the doors, the windows, the wardrobe, under the bed. She knew it was ridiculous but she couldn't rest until she'd done it two or three times. Then she climbed into bed in her clothes, pulling the telly up close. If she watched it long enough, all the drama and trauma and excitement, she fell into that profound listlessness in which nothing mattered. This was the new Lizzie. She didn't paint, or even think about painting, she didn't talk to anyone. But sometimes she lay awake thinking about him. She tried not to, but powerful images returned. She remembered crawling about on the floor, gazing up at him, she would have done anything for him then, and the thought of it made all the nausea return. She cried, stuffing her fingers into her mouth so he wouldn't hear. She thought of him walking out of the hotel room as if nothing had happened, going to his business meeting, laughing and joking, the other women he would pick up, and she stopped crying. She stared into the darkness and her hatred seemed to burn her hollow.

Meanwhile her body healed. Her arm set, though imperfectly, her hair grew and the scars whitened, though they would never entirely fade, and there was something wrong with her hip, as if a muscle, deep inside where she couldn't reach, was in permanent cramp. She waited for the evidence of some terrible disease, but after a few days of cystitis nothing happened, and in less than a week her period came. She was grateful for these things, in a distanced, unbelieving way, but she still went on living minimally. She didn't believe enough in the reality of her life to live it.

In this way almost three months passed. Then one day she woke up to the sound of drills and hammers. When she looked out of the window there was scaffolding all over the front of the building. No one had told her. Outraged she drew all the curtains, but she couldn't shut the noise out, there was no chance of sleep. And it was the day she had to go out, to the post office at the end of the row of shops. Shaken, she made a cup of tea and turned the telly up to drown the noise of radios outside, but eventually she could put it off no longer. She had to go out.

As she left the building there was an immediate uproar, catcalls and a piercing whistle. Lizzie flinched. She kept her head down and hurried to the post office and back, but the same shouts followed her as she let herself in. When she got inside she remembered that she needed a bottle of milk, but she wouldn't go out again, she would do without.

Over the next few days it happened whenever she went out. It was an irritant, like someone sandpapering raw skin. All day long radios blared, she could hear the hammers, chisels and drills. Now she could no longer sleep in the day she was lonely and bored. She took to watching the builders through a chink in the curtains. The one who most often whistled was called Rob, he was long and lean and had brown hair tied back in a pony-tail. She watched him most closely, and one day when he whistled at her she stared up at him and said,

Can you only whistle or do you have other talents as well?

That was the old Lizzie speaking, she didn't know where it came from. Rob's mates stamped and clapped and cheered. Rob himself looked shown up, but he grinned a wide grin. Lizzie hurried inside, sure she'd only made things worse for herself. But the next time Rob saw her he grinned and waved. Lizzie smiled, a quick, uncertain smile, and hurried on. Then that afternoon she heard singing beneath the window, *Love is in the air, everywhere you look around*. When she opened the curtains there was Rob, trowelling putty beneath the sill.

I thought I'd show off some of my other talents, he said.

Don't give up the day job, Lizzie said, and shut the curtains on him again. Still, she wasn't shaken by his apparent lack of interest in her, she even felt a spark in return when she'd thought she could never feel interest in a man again. The part of her that wanted to be well wanted to be interested, she was bored with the way she was living her life. She caught herself wondering what it would be like to touch him, undressed.

Even so, all the next day she stayed in with the curtains closed. She dug out some old art books and looked at them, no longer

312

minding the radios so much or even the drill, the noise reminded her that she wasn't alone. But by the end of the day she'd fallen into a mood. She moved restlessly around her flat, her skin crawling with her need to get out, but she didn't know where to go. She jumped violently at the knock on her door. It was Rob, carrying wine. He leaned against the frame of the door and said,

I thought we could discuss my other talents. Since you didn't like the singing.

Lizzie smiled incredulously, resting her head against the door. There was a pause as Rob waited to be asked in.

I brought some wine, he said. And these, and he produced a slightly squashed box of chocolates.

Lizzie let him in, wondering even while she was doing it what she was doing. When he was inside the flat she felt nervous. She picked up some things that were scattered around and rubbed her hands against her jeans. After a moment she said,

Have you had anything to eat?

No, said Rob. I thought you might do that bit.

Something about the way he said things, not funny in themselves, made her laugh. She didn't have much food in, though Rob said she shopped enough. But Lizzie wasn't big on shopping, or cooking either. She found some bacon and eggs, so in the end that's what they had: bacon, eggs, wine and chocolates. Lizzie grilled the bacon and Rob fried the eggs. He told her he lived a few miles away, in the big town, and he worked for a bloke called Peter. He liked coming out here to work, where you could see the hills. He was quite a lot younger than Lizzie, twenty-six. A few months ago he'd been going to get married to a girl called Trish, but it hadn't worked out. She'd hated all his mates and been suspicious whenever he wasn't with her. It did his head in, Rob said.

Lizzie found it easy to talk to him, or rather listen. She just had to listen and he talked on, about football and about going in for a darts competition with his mates. He didn't ask her anything and she was relieved by this, it was a relief to sit back and make hardly any effort. She wasn't even worried about the way she looked, and he didn't seem to mind. He seemed at home in her flat, so much so that after they washed up he said he'd miss Coronation Street if he left now, did she mind if he watched it there, and Lizzie said, No. So they sat on the bed together since there was only one chair, and Lizzie didn't mind that either. Rob kicked off his shoes and slipped an arm round her, gradually she began to lean against him. They watched Coronation Street, and the film after whilst finishing off the chocolates. After the film Rob leaned over and turned the telly off. Then he kissed her swiftly, unexpectedly.

I could go now if you like, he said. Or I could stay.

Lizzie didn't know. She pushed him away.

I don't know, she said.

Rob didn't seem offended. He waited for her to say something else but she couldn't think. She leaned forwards so that her head was in her hands.

God, she said. Rob pushed himself to the edge of the bed beside her.

Hey, he said. It's all right. I'll go.

Lizzie got up and took two or three steps away from him.

No, you can stay, she said. She said it with her back to him and was unprepared when he caught her hand and pulled her back on to the bed. She fell against him a little clumsily, but he caught her and kissed her hard. Lizzie felt nothing from the kiss, as though her whole face was numb. She felt she had to go to the bathroom. She pushed him away again.

I'll be back in a bit, she said.

As she walked along the hallway she felt bad. She couldn't do this, she told herself, she couldn't go through with it. She fumbled at the bathroom door until it was locked. He would have to leave after all, she would go right back and tell him he would have to go. But then, suppose he didn't?

Lizzie couldn't think straight. All the time she was acting as if she intended to sleep with him, pulling off her clothes, washing beneath her arms, between her legs, splashing cold water on her face. When she stopped to think about what she was doing she couldn't do it any more, she couldn't think what she had to do next. Then her teeth began chattering and she gripped the edge of the sink. God she was a wreck. He would ask about the scars on her body. She grabbed her towelling robe and wrapped it tightly around her. She had to leave the bathroom. She had to go back to the room where he was waiting for her.

Rob was standing by the window, looking out. She was glad he wasn't looking her way.

Nice view you've got here, he said, without looking round. I know it's a main road and that, but the fields on the other side, and the hills – nice, and he turned round.

Lizzie had dropped the robe while he wasn't looking and slipped into bed, wrapping herself tightly in bedclothes. She was beginning to feel unreal again. Rob undressed near the chair with no self-consciousness at all, dropping his clothes over it. Lizzie watched in a hostile kind of way.

I don't suppose this is all some kind of stunt, she said. To impress your mates. Rob paused before getting into bed.

No, he said. That was all he said, but Lizzie believed him.

I bet, she said. Rob ignored her, kissing the side of her unresponsive face. She could go through with it, she told herself. She could go through all the motions of sex and it wouldn't matter. In the morning he would go and she'd never have to see him again. He kissed her again, pressing her down against the pillow.

Then when he was inside her and she still felt nothing she fell into a kind of despair. She would never feel anything again, she might as well be dead, and silently she began to cry. Tears ran from the corners of her eyes to her ears. Rob didn't notice. She didn't want him to notice, but part of her felt that he should have. When he'd finished he fell asleep. Lizzie looked at the shape of him beneath the bedclothes. It was all over, she thought, and was cold and hard again. But part of her kept saying, time, she must give herself time. And thinking this she fell asleep.

Then later she woke up with his lips against her flesh, he was kissing her, she him. She stroked the small curve of his belly and the harder curve of hip and cupped his balls in her hand. He was beautiful, she realised, and she kissed him gratefully; it was a long time since she'd found anything beautiful. His flesh was smooth and warm where she kissed it, she could understand why men loved one another. She felt that he was good, she could sense goodness in him, as if to know his flesh was to know him in some special, intimate way. And she didn't want anything from him, not even orgasm, though of course he thought she did and kept trying. She just wanted the sense of being warm and real. Then later she wanted him to cry out, which he did.

Afterwards they got up and watched the lightening sky. There were bars of light over the hills, the sky was a deep, dull blue. Traffic was increasing, pouring slowly towards the city like glue. As Lizzie made coffee there was a commotion outside, a honking of horns and geese, the WA-wa wa-wa of ducks. Rob and Lizzie watched as the ducks and geese from the pond at the bottom of the field waddled in formation on to the road, passing the surprised cows. There were maybe thirty birds, strutting down the middle of the road as if they owned it, holding up traffic. Drivers pressed their horns and shouted, and even got out to run at the geese, who flapped their wings, extended their necks and hissed. Lizzie and Rob stood together and laughed at the geese marching with outstretched necks, the ducks waddling behind, and behind them the cars, allowed out of the village at a slow trickle.

Rob pointed to a big white house, high on the hillside.

Who lives there? he said.

I don't know, said Lizzie, though she remembered something about a tragedy, a girl in Lynne's class. I know I'd like to, she added. She'd often thought about it, how many rooms it would have, the log fires and oak beams inside, the wide stretch of land around it for growing food.

Yeah, Rob said, and he told her he planned to live in a place like that one day, but he wanted to build his own house. He told her what it would be like over coffee and the rest of the bacon. Yellow stone of course, with four bedrooms and one long room running the length of the upper storey for the kids – he wanted two or three kids. And he would have two bathrooms, one leading off the master bedroom, and an extra toilet downstairs as well. And then in the basement of the house, what he really wanted was a swimming-pool. He would build all this high up where he could see the moors.

O yes, Lizzie said. She could see herself living in a place like that, with a room all to herself for painting. It would have windows on three sides through which she could see the tremendous skies. Of course she'd never planned on having as many as three children, but for the moment it was enough to dream about the house.

What about the kitchen? she said, glancing round at her own, which consisted of a sink, a cupboard and a cooker. They planned the kitchen together as they washed up, it was the star piece of the house, huge, with windows on three sides again, overlooking the different valleys. It would have a halogen cooker and carousel units.

Then Lizzie said, How much is all this going to cost, and when

Rob told her she choked on her coffee, and said, Well you'd better ask your boss for that rise then, and Rob flicked at her with the tea towel and they ran around the room. Then, because it was so cold, they went back to bed.

At Lower Marley Vi got on the little bus.

Hi, she said to Lizzie.

The driver waited as she tapped her way with her stick to Lizzie's side and sat down. Lizzie knew Vi from the library at Upper Marley, she saw her there regularly.

Off to the library? Vi said. Lizzie shook her head.

I'm making a meal tonight, she said, and I'm completely out of soya sauce. They've never heard of it in Clough Bottom.

Sounds special, Vi said enquiringly, but Lizzie only grinned.

John Hutton, the man known as the Sandman, has today been sentenced to life imprisonment, the radio said, and in front of Lizzie Mavis Willshaw snorted.

Life imprisonment, what's that? she said to Irene Webster. A comfortable cell, everything paid for, no worries –

Home from home, said Irene Webster. He'll be doing a degree next.

Soon all the bus was talking.

They ought to bring back hanging, said Lily Ashworth.

I heard he was pleading insanity, said Iris Platt.

Insanity, my eye, said Mavis Willshaw. He wants hanging.

Lizzie looked at Vi, who smiled. She thought of all the disappearing girls, like Caroline, their broken bodies. She said,

You have to wonder what makes them do it, though, and Vi said she'd heard he'd said he was glad to be caught, glad that he could stop at last.

It must be terrible to live like that, she said.

She said it quietly, to Lizzie, but Mavis Willshaw turned and said,

So put him out of his misery then, and everyone agreed.

AIDS, Lizzie thought, he'd given her AIDS.

She sat in the chair, watching the shape of Rob in the bedclothes.

By now he would have slept with other women. And she'd slept with Rob. It was like the kiss of the vampire. She would never be able to leave, she thought. Even now she was with him in the van, waiting for the spatter of stones on her upturned face. She wondered when she'd feel the first symptoms, the rush of sweat, the constricted breathing. She had never really been able to believe since then in her own life, her own ability to live.

Rob was easy to be with. He talked all the time and never asked questions, about her family, or what she did. Once or twice he touched the scars on her body, but he didn't ask about them either. When Lizzie showed him her paintings he said, They're big, and that was all. It was a relief, after Nigel, not to have to explain herself in any way. Then, just sometimes, she resented him for not being interested. Most of the time though she was happy to be with him, especially in bed. He laughed at her night fears and was indifferent to the worst of them, she loved him for that. He accepted life, like an animal, she thought, and she was reassured by this. At first she thought that when the builders moved on she wouldn't see him again, but he came round the next night as usual, bringing beer. Lizzie tried not to show how glad she was. She was careful not to seem too demanding, always remembering his last girlfriend, Trish. She made food for him, but nothing special, cheese and garlic sausage on toast, or just beans on toast, or egg fried rice. On the nights when he couldn't make it she never asked where he was going and he offered no explanations. But most nights he turned up regularly, some time after the six o'clock news. They ate together, watched telly, made love and slept. It suited Lizzie fine, she didn't want him to take her out, she wanted him to stay in with her.

After a while she began to feel that he was a bit distracted in bed with her, and she made extra efforts, but to no effect. When she asked him what was wrong he said,

Nothing, why? and once they argued about it but he wouldn't be drawn. Then one evening he turned up with a stack of magazines. They could have a look through them later if she liked, he said. Lizzie glanced at the covers. They were all pictures of women with no clothes on.

Why would I want to look at them? she said. Rob shrugged.

Suit yourself, he said. But he always used to get them when he was with Trish, they used to read them together. Lizzie was torn between the desire to lecture him about the exploitation of women, though she knew it would run off him as water ran off a duck, and the desire to share with him whatever Trish had shared. So after tea they sat on the bed together leafing through the magazines, and Lizzie sat stiffly, prepared to make her most caustic comments. But most of them were just naked women, like something out of life class, except that the poses and the lighting were more artificial so you couldn't see the real texture of the skin, mottled or creepy and patterned with veins, hairs and stretchmarks, moles and scars. All the texture was smoothed into a uniform golden gleam, like wax. Then there were one or two pictures of models with their legs open, fingering themselves, and others where they were being spanked. The camera showed red marks on naked behinds, hair, and the pink slit beneath. As she looked at the pictures Rob began to touch her hair and breasts and to kiss her neck, then he pressed her down on to the bed. Lizzie responded to the renewed passion in him, and to something else, flickering images in her mind, in which she was at once behind the camera and over Rob's knee.

After that Rob seemed to take it for granted that he could

bring the magazines over. He had a wide range. He got them from a bloke at work called Joe, who got them from someone else. Some of them were worse than others: bondage, rape, women with dogs or pigs. Lizzie objected to these violently, but Rob said they all came in the same batch, he didn't check through them all first. Then he asked her what she was getting so worked up about, it was all art, just art, like any other kind of art. Lizzie knew he was trying to wind her up, but she got mad anyway.

Well, go on then, Rob said. Tell us, what's the difference between you drawing blokes with no clothes on and men taking pictures of women with no clothes on?

It depends why you're doing it, Lizzie said, and she dragged a box of posters in from the other room. Look, she said. There were her prints, nudes by Rubens, Titian, Picasso. It was the best explanation she had.

There you are, said Rob. It's all the same.

Lizzie wanted to hit him.

You can't seriously say, she said, that these turn you on.

No, Rob said, but someone might have been, then.

For Christ's sake, said Lizzie.

No I mean it, said Rob. You don't know these blokes weren't wanking themselves off all the time. They didn't have cameras then.

Lizzie was so angry she ran out of words. She pointed to a picture of a woman with her legs spread.

What's lovely or lyrical about that, she said.

Hey, said Rob. You have your idea of art, I have mine.

To be fair he didn't seem to be particularly moved by pictures of women tied up, or with animals.

It's just a laugh, he said. He only seemed really interested in the pictures of naked women, preferably with their legs open. Rob thought this was straightforward enough and needed no explanation. That was the way he thought of himself, Lizzie knew,

321

as an uncomplicated working bloke with simple pleasures. She'd thought so too, after Nigel. He didn't ask questions to complicate things and he hated it when she started to argue.

We can't all be educated, he always said. It annoyed the hell out of Lizzie, because he wasn't stupid, and he was more complicated than he liked to appear. It was as though he'd fallen for all the stereotypes of the working bloke, just as Lizzie had, temporarily. His views were right because they were uncomplicated and downright, cutting through the crap. He only thought and said and did what other people wanted to. It was natural for a man to look at pictures of naked women, and further than that he wouldn't think – not because he couldn't, Lizzie soon found that in arguments he was capable of leading her round in circles – but because he didn't want to. He wasn't shocked or put off by any of the pictures they looked at, except for one in which a little boy was being masturbated by an older man. He ripped this one up.

Bastards, he said with some energy. Lizzie looked at him in surprise.

Well, she said. What's so different about that one?

Rob stared at her.

It's a little boy, he said. Lizzie stared back.

Yes, she said.

It's kids, Rob said. Lizzie raised an eyebrow.

What, kids in general? she said. Or just little boys?

Rob waved a hand impatiently. Kids of any kind, he said. It's wrong to use kids.

Lizzie wanted to know where he drew the line, some of the girls in the pictures looked pretty young to her.

Rob wasn't going to get drawn into this one. He knew the difference, he didn't need to think about it. It's tits and that, he said.

Lizzie rolled her eyes. Some girls get tits and that pretty young, she said. Like ten.

322

Rob turned away. Yeah well, he said. They're probably ready for it then.

The problem was they always seemed to be arguing on shifting ground, the difference between art and pornography, or between sexual and emotional maturity. Lizzie knew what she meant, she'd always taken it for granted that other people would see it the same way, but with Rob, before she knew where she was, she didn't know what she was talking about any more. Rob didn't like talking about it at all, he wanted her to accept it as he did, but Lizzie couldn't. She couldn't accept the way some of the images stayed with her, recurring unexpectedly, like when they were making love. Sometimes they were the same images that had sickened her when she first saw them. Maybe that was the way it worked, she thought.

Rob didn't know and he wasn't bothered. Lizzie's need to know was driving them apart, just as Nigel's endless analysis had driven her daft in the end. Why couldn't she be like Rob, accepting whatever turned her on, instead of fighting it so hard? It would kill the relationship, she knew. And solve nothing, she would never understand anything that way. She decided she needed to stop passing judgement for a while and just watch, the pictures and Rob's reactions to them. She would monitor his reactions, it was easier than trying to monitor her own.

She did notice that pornography made sex easy. Its characters, so far as you could call them that, didn't spend hours agonising over their relationships, or worrying about their bodies. It was a given fact that they were going to be turned on, at least in the pictures Lizzie saw. Once in the act there was no trace of anxiety that someone was going to say or do the wrong thing, have bad breath or lose an erection. When there was a power struggle it was simplified: one person had the power, the other didn't. It left the way clear for the powerful, uncomplicated sexual response. That was what people thought they were going to get from children or animals, Lizzie thought, the pure, primitive response, no ambivalence, no doubt. She could see the attraction.

But she also noticed what whatever they looked at it wasn't enough. Rob got tired of the magazines and brought his own video one day, wiring it up to Lizzie's television. He had an assortment of films with plain covers, all from Joe. They sat and watched a strip sequence, then a strange little film about a vacuum cleaner salesman and a housewife – he tried all the parts on her while she moaned and gasped on the carpet. Then there was a film about a woman being assaulted on a train – two men unbuttoned her blouse and put their hands up her skirt, they spread her legs wide and masturbated her. Finally there was a film about college boys in a car, picking up a hitchhiker, having sex with her in turn, then throwing her out on the motorway.

In all of these films the woman was initially frightened or reluctant, then she gave in, abandoning control, and at this moment experienced ecstasy, the camera focused on her face, loosening with desire. And there were no consequences, no complications. But also it wasn't satisfying, you wanted more. When they watched the films Rob always wanted to touch Lizzie, to slip his hands inside her shirt or into her jeans. Sometimes she pushed him off, feeling that it wasn't her he wanted to make love to, and sometimes she was eager for it as he was, she couldn't say that she wasn't turned on.

Once when they were watching a film called *Gang Bang at Little River Creek*, Lizzie sat very still with her stomach churning; she said to Rob,

Have you ever done anything like that? and he wouldn't answer, he wanted to watch the film. Lizzie knew he had. After the film she mithered him until he told her. There was a girl called Sandra, he said, who used to work at the club where he went with his mates. She was a slag and would go with anyone. Anyway, one night they all got drunk together, Sandra and Rob and Rob's

324

mates. They stayed after closing hours and Sandra and Lennie got up on one of the tables and started doing a strip. Then when they'd finished it had just sort of happened, Lennie and Rob and Rob's mates all giving her one, she was too far gone to even notice. Then they'd left, leaving her there; they'd gone home feeling good, singing songs.

But it wasn't rape, he said to Lizzie, forestalling her. She'd have gone with any of us anyway.

Lizzie felt sick when she looked at him.

And what about her? she said.

Who? said Rob.

The girl, Lizzie said. Sandra. Rob shrugged, but he had the kind of look on his face that meant he was winding her up.

Anything could have happened, Lizzie said. She could have been pregnant. Rob turned the video off and put the film back in its case.

She wouldn't have known whose it was, though, he said.

Lizzie could see it all clearly from the girl's point of view. She was there with the girl in the club, waking up to the cold morning, sore and cold, with the terrible taste of beer and smoke and come in her mouth, not knowing what had happened. And then the days that followed, thrush or cystitis, worrying about worse infections, and pregnancy. Lizzie tried to shake these images off, she couldn't really know what the girl had been through, but they stayed printed on her mind. But another part of her mind could see it from Rob's point of view: sex without emotion, without complications or consequences, the girl was fair game.

It bothered her that she could see both ways so clearly, as though having double vision, but she couldn't stop it, it asserted itself whether she wanted it to or not, most powerfully when she was in bed with Rob. They came together in a kind of blindness, making love not to each other but to the running track of images in their minds.

*

It was the winter solstice. Once again Lizzie was faced with the choice of whether or not to visit her parents over Christmas, and what she could buy them if she went. The prospect wasn't inviting: endless variety shows, tapes of Foster and Allen's Christmas songs, sugared fruits which made Lizzie feel sick after the turkey, but which she ate anyway because she got so bored. On the other hand Christmas alone didn't seem that inviting either: an ordinary day, tinned soup and tea, unless she could force herself to make the effort to cook.

Or she could go out walking, like this. She'd walked out for the first time in months to an area outside the village called the Clough. It was a dip in the hills, part of a country park with a lake and trees. The valley wardens conducted walks there regularly for nature enthusiasts, but just now there was no one around.

The whole of the Clough was caught in a low bowl of light which had a fine, transparent quality. Lizzie always loved the lights of winter, low and clear and fine. The sky was a shade of blue softer than the intense blue of summer, but very deep. Over in the west clouds flamed to a tender pink. Looking at the sky Lizzie suffered pangs of loss. If she'd kept up with her art she might have been able to capture it, that luminous pastel quality; now she could no longer be sure. She sat by the lake surrounded by the moist, mysterious trees, feeling her impotence keenly. It was part of the reason she'd stopped going out, the same way she'd stopped reading art magazines to find out who was doing what, she couldn't stand it any more. Other people's successes hurt, and that was the worst thing, she'd lost her capacity to be generous, she was becoming small and mean and shrivelled.

But if she could just sit still and look at things, she thought, she might save herself, it was wrong to seal yourself off from beauty. She hadn't been out for months – long before splitting up with Rob – she was losing her relationship with the world. Now she was finally outside she was reluctant to move, though she could feel the cold eating into her fingers and face.

On clear frosty days like this the smell of car fumes seemed to cling to her more persistently than usual. Sitting on the bench surrounded by so much beauty Lizzie could smell herself, unclean, her skin felt tight with a film of soil. As she sat different voices and fragments filtered to the surface of her mind.

When I was a girl, Aunt Edie said, a car was an event. We all used to run out on our street when one went past.

Now you had to go a long way to get away from them and still their dirt clung to you like a shroud.

You must remember this, went the song in Lizzie's head. *A kiss is still a kiss.*

You've given us back our daughter, said Mavis, and she clung to the picture with tears in her eyes.

The gaps between the times when Rob turned up grew longer. Lizzie still didn't ask what he was doing and Rob still didn't tell her, except that he was tired from all the extra work they were doing. This seemed to be true. Sometimes he came round, ate, watched telly and fell asleep. Lizzie lay by him like a wife. She couldn't understand why she put up with it, why she didn't just throw him out. She seemed to be on some kind of track that she had to follow right to the end, though it seemed to be heading straight for a trough.

One day, when she'd been waiting for over a week, she decided to make him a special meal, his favourite, steak and mushrooms and red wine, and invite him over. It almost wiped out her money for the week, especially when she bought cheesecake for afters, but while she was preparing the food, the salad and baked potatoes, she was able to forget that she hadn't invited him yet. When she'd seasoned the steaks and put them in the oven she slipped out to phone him from across the road. As she dialled the number her heart beat thickly, she couldn't remember what she had to say. It would be his mother or father, she knew, they would ask her to wait a minute, then come back to the phone to say he wasn't in.

But it was Rob who answered the phone. Lizzie made her voice bright, she said,

Hi Rob, it's Liz. There was a pause.

O hi, he said.

I'm at a bit of a loose end tonight, Lizzie said, hearing her own voice carry on as if everything was normal. So I thought, what's a nice girl like me doing alone. Why don't I cook something up and invite some sexy hunk to share it with me?

I'm a bit tired tonight, Rob said.

Well I wasn't going to ask you, said Lizzie, but Rob didn't laugh. She said, We could just relax if you like. Watch a film.

Not tonight, Rob said. I'm knackered. Some other time, eh?

Lizzie sensed she was losing ground.

Well OK, she said. But I got some nice stuff in, steak and mushrooms, your favourite.

Rob laughed in an embarrassed kind of way.

You shouldn't have done that, he said.

Why not? said Lizzie. Got to pull out the stops some time. There's a limit to how much beans on toast the mortal frame can stand. Anyway, she added in teasing tones, I'm cooking it already. So you've got to come.

Rob laughed a bit and said nothing. Lizzie said nothing either, then she said,

You're not coming, are you? and Rob said,

I don't think so. Not tonight.

Lizzie knew she needed to back out of this one gracefully.

O well then, she said. I'll just have to call Mel Gibson instead.

You do that, said Rob, still sounding embarrassed, but willing to share the joke.

Or get my list out, said Lizzie. In my little black book. Now where were you on the list – what did you say your name was again? and Rob laughed.

Lizzie could hear her voice going on. *Get off the phone*, she told herself, but she couldn't seem to stop. Rob helped her.

Look, he said. I'll call you sometime, all right?

Fine, Lizzie said. You do that, and she hung up, not wanting to say more.

She ran across the road and up the stairs to her flat. She could save the salad and the baked potatoes for tomorrow, she thought. And the cheesecake would keep. But the steaks were nearly done, she should try to eat them. She sorted out dishes and cutlery, lifting trays from the oven. She looked at the two steaks and the heap of mushrooms. Christ, she thought. All this food. She must have been mad.

She wasn't very hungry, but she was damned if she was going to throw it all away. She set the table properly and poured some wine, took a long gulp of it, then burst into tears. She cried noisily for a long time, surprised by the violence of her grief, then she blew her nose on kitchen roll and was quiet. She served the steaks with the mushrooms and a bit of salad, and put a dab of mustard on the side of the plate. Then she sat down and caught sight of her face in the mirror, still pinkish from crying. She raised her glass to herself and smiled her crooked smile.

Cheers, she said.

Now sitting on the bench Lizzie felt ashamed of the way she'd behaved with Rob, clutching on to him as though she were drowning and he were driftwood floating past. She had changed, she was no longer the Lizzie she thought she knew.

Shadows striped the yellow fields and the bars of pink in the sky massed together. Lizzie stared at the sky but she was thinking about her relationships, how they'd all ended badly, Nigel, Rob, Aunt Edie, even Eric. She'd stopped writing to Eric when she moved to a different college. She'd got one of the girls in the flat she shared to answer the phone and if it was Eric to say she wasn't in. She'd been a real bitch to Nigel. And clearly as she sat by the water she heard his voice.

I'm sorry, he said. It always takes me a long time to come. Lizzie's arm ached.

It's all right, she said. You usually manage it before I count to a thousand.

Christ, what a bitch, she thought, and heard a wicked cackle inside her head. Then she heard him say, You're breaking my heart, and she sobered up. She'd hurt him badly. No one had the right to inflict so much pain.

As she sat feeling small and humiliated Lizzie got angry. If she really believed what she always pretended to believe, that people were driven by forces beyond their control, why did she feel so much guilt? But she couldn't talk herself out of feeling bad. She felt a sham, as though all her life she'd been pretending to be an artist. No real artist would let men take over her life, the way Nigel had, and then Rob.

The last time she'd seen Rob he'd brought a film as usual. Lizzie thought the girl on the screen looked about twelve, but Rob said she was older. She had little fatty breasts and almost no hair between her legs. She sat blindfolded between two men who were taking her school uniform off. Lizzie sat on the bed, trapped between sickness and desire. Turn it off, she told herself, turn it off, turn it off . . . Instead she kept interrupting it, disturbing Rob.

So why is this different, she said, from raping little boys? Then she said,

God, it's pitiful – they're old enough to be her grandfathers – they're just two old grandfathers who can't get it up.

Finally Rob told her to shut up. Lizzie leapt off the bed and ripped the video out of the machine. Rob yelled at her, she'd ruin the video and the machine.

Good, Lizzie shouted back. I ought to burn it.

What's up with you? Rob said. He was very angry. Lizzie was angry too.

I'm sick of having this shit in my flat, she said.

As she said it she knew two things, that she should have said it months ago, and that she was losing Rob, it was the end of their relationship. He knew it too. For a moment he looked angry enough to hit her, then he went cold and methodical. He put the film back in its box then began detaching the video from her television.

What are you doing? Lizzie said, then, Where are you going?

Out, said Rob.

Lizzie wanted to think of something to make him stay, but all she could think of was,

Will you be coming back? Rob shut the flap of the cardboard box down over the video and tucked it in.

Not tonight, he said.

Any time, then? she said, hating herself. Rob didn't look up.

Maybe, he said.

He left then, walking towards the door without saying anything. Lizzie felt clammy with fear. She said,

I'll see you then. Rob didn't turn round.

'Bye, he said, and was gone. She could hear his footsteps along the hall, down the stairs. When she couldn't hear him any more she sank into her chair. He would be back, she told herself. It was just a quarrel, everyone had quarrels, she would see him again. Then she thought, why was she so afraid of being alone?

When she thought back to that day she remembered the feeling, like a balloon when the string has been cut, released into nothing. She felt as though she had no remaining connection to the world.

This troubled her, but what disturbed her more was the desire she'd had that day to watch the film through to the end, to see the little girl being raped.

On the far side of the lake a swan ventured on to its glassy surface. Over to the left its mate waited. Lizzie watched, expecting him to slide somehow over the ice. Instead he broke into it, not using his beak, but the sharp blades of his breastbones. Lizzie watched fascinated, the swan's partially unfurled wings and arched neck, the protruding bones of his breast. He was breaking a path to his mate, making faint swishing and splintering noises as the thin ice gave way. Soon they'd be able to eat, or to perform their strange mating ritual, looping their necks together and dipping their beaks alternately into the water. Apart from the faint noise of the ice everything was profoundly still. The swan concentrated on the ice, his mate watched him and Lizzie watched them both. It was the kind of absorption she needed to paint. Lizzie found she was remembering things she thought she'd forgotten about swans: how they rarely leave their mates or their place of birth, the long, long months it takes them to learn to fly, the number of deaths in early flights. Sometimes in winter they slept in the middle of roads, which were warm from the traffic. After deaths in flight a common and more drawn-out kind of death was from lead poisoning.

Lizzie thought about the swan, living without guilt, unable to avoid the kind of deaths which for humans would be avoidable. But maybe you spent so much time avoiding death, she thought, your life was consumed by the struggle.

The swans were together now, unfurling their wings slowly and folding them again. The light faded but still Lizzie was reluctant to move. Maybe you turned away from death, she thought, because it proved to you there was no such thing as control; that was why you needed fantasy, to put you back in control. But then when you couldn't live like that, permanently in

332

control, you felt guilty, and then you needed more fantasy, it was all a big cycle.

The swans drifted off together, out of sight. Lizzie was glad she'd seen them, she had seen them for herself instead of watching something like it on television. Nigel had driven her mad with the telly. He only ever watched serious programmes, the documentaries and news, whereas Lizzie preferred something she didn't have to think about. They'd rowed about it once. Lizzie said watching the news manipulated her ideas about the world, Nigel said it was important to be in touch with what was going on. Lizzie said he was mad, how could a machine keep you in touch, what was real about watching a war in your living-room and then turning it off? Nigel took her seriously for once, he thought about it then he said, maybe reality today *is* the reality of the camera.

Lizzie rubbed her cold hands against her jeans and chafed her face, aware of the gathering darkness; she would have to leave. Then suddenly she was blind to everything around her, to the lake and trees and fading light. She was back in the hotel room, with the man whose name was probably not Andreas.

You old drunk, he'd called her, and Lizzie began to tremble. She wouldn't think about it, she told herself, she would think about the swans. But she couldn't get rid of his face. Then in a moment she saw it all, the whole cycle of trauma and guilt and fantasy, the need for control. He was locked into it too, she saw, he would never be free. And she thought of other people like him, like the Sandman, producing trauma in other people's lives, part of the big cycle, along with all the power structures and hierarchies there were in the world. For a moment she held it complete in her mind, together with the fear of death. Nosferatu, she thought. He could neither live nor die. And wasn't that the way she'd been living her own life, locked into her own cycle of trauma and fantasy like the rest of the world, like the Sandman?

Lizzie gazed at the empty lake. She felt the glimmering of an image in her mind, together with the urge to capture it before it faded. She got up stiffly, then began to hurry through the cold dusk. She wanted to get home, to capture the images swimming in her mind.

Rembrandt said that blue was the most difficult colour to use in painting. Picasso of course used it with tremendous, unrepeatable power.

So what? Lizzie kept saying to herself. So what, so what? And she pressed her charcoal down hard on her sketch pad, snapping it. Because she'd decided to do her picture entirely in blue, to capture the haunted light of winter, but part of her was already trying to talk the rest of her out of it.

What's the use? it kept saying. *No one will ever see it. What's the point, everyone today will be famous for fifteen minutes, no one will be memorable?*

Lizzie moved the small electric fire into the room where her canvases were, she fitted a bulb into the overhead light so she could work in the evening. She stretched and prepared her canvas, but she still felt the pressure to work; she wasn't wasting it all on preparation.

Days passed in the little room. Lizzie couldn't afford to keep the fire on all the time and got very cold. She caught cold and seemed to be endlessly chafing the end of her nose with tissues and rags, but she kept on working out of a terrible fear of giving up.

Christmas came and went, there were no visitors. Lizzie heard only the hum and roar of traffic, silenced on Christmas morning. The voices in her head told her it was a ridiculous way to spend Christmas, she should be with her family if she hadn't any friends. But for the most part she wasn't lonely.

Sometimes she worked with a furious energy, hardly able to see what she was doing, and sometimes she worked in a halting, stumbling way, unable to give herself up to it. And sometimes she sat and smoked and tried to look at it, but she couldn't, for all the critical, comparing voices in her head. She'd always wanted something pure and transcendent to come out of her work, but now she knew it wouldn't, art wasn't like that, she heard herself saying in Nigel's voice. And often when she sat smoking she felt the creeping lethargy which threatened to stop her altogether. Then she was gripped by a feverish impatience to finish that drove her back to the canvas, but the picture wouldn't be rushed, and she felt despair, it would never be finished. Just sometimes, she felt her consciousness widen into the present moment and she was able to work without inner comment, and she knew that was the reason for her work.

Finally it was finished, though she still didn't know if it was any good. She stood it in the middle of her room, a blue, wasted landscape, vast and shadowy, with a cliff face to the foreground on either side. In the crevices of these cliffs were women, surrounded by the artefacts of their daily lives, consumer goods, food. A young woman gazed at the glittering blue idols of the screen, and another woman stretched herself out in a porno-graphic pose, her bluish skin given the waxy texture of a corpse. In the bottom corner on the left lay Aunt Edie, as lovingly drawn as an icon, her shrivelled body with its tubes, sustained, but unalive, incapable of death.

Then in the centre of the canvas was the figure of the vampire. Blue light streamed from behind him, he was wrapped in a dark-blue cape. She'd been frightened of drawing him, of recognising his face, but he was no one she knew. It was an ordinary face, vulnerable, hurt, the lines of blood from his teeth looked like wounds. And all around him the land was wrapped in a blue, haunted silence.

Lizzie didn't know precisely what he was, some massive draining power, money, or the power of fantasy itself, maybe just fear. She didn't know if she'd succeeded in what she wanted to do but she did know it was finished. She felt as though she'd shed a skin. And despite all her fears of not finishing, she'd actually finished very quickly, in less than nine days.

She was very cold and a little dispirited as she packed away. There was no one to tell her how good or bad it was, she didn't know if she'd ever start anything again. She went into the main room, kicked off her pumps, switched on the electric heater and massaged her feet in an attempt to warm them. Her flesh was waxy-yellow with cold. Lizzie sat in the quiet room, without turning the telly on, trying to work out what day it was. Gradually she began to feel a faint glow of warmth inside. She'd done it, she thought. She'd done what she'd set out to do.

It was Near Year's Eve, blue and misty, as Lizzie set off to her parents', carrying a bottle of brandy from the shop below in atonement. They would want to know where she'd been over Christmas.

The air was damp and clammy but Lizzie was glad of the wet roads and shiny lights. She felt prepared for anything, even her parents. Besides she knew they were going out later, to her brother's party, so she wouldn't have to stay too long.

For the first time in weeks she'd made a real effort with her appearance. Beneath the purple and gold coat she wore the short velour skirt that used to be her favourite, she hadn't worn it since the night in the hotel. Now she wore it with a tight pink top with long sleeves and a short, chiffon blouse knotted at the front. She had her black ankle boots on and black woolly tights. In spite of all this she still didn't feel she looked her best. The cold had left its mark and the flesh under her nose was chafed raw, her lips cracked and peeling beneath an extra layer of lipstick, but she felt festive enough to cope with her parents. They would be able to tell she'd had a cold, it should let her off the hook about

Christmas. They might even feel guilty for not trying to find out why she hadn't been around. Didn't you feel well enough to phone? her mother would say, and Lizzie would say no regretfully, and with just a touch of pathos. Then her mother would make her sit down and drink some of the brandy she'd brought . . .

Lizzie swung her bag a little as she walked. She had the feeling that she was starting a whole new phase of life. Though on the surface nothing had changed, she could feel new life waiting for her with the new year, more paintings, more exhibitions. She even felt there might be another kind of life waiting to grow inside her. Why not, though she was single and almost thirty-five, you didn't have to be in a relationship to have a child, people always managed somehow. As she turned off the main road of Marley to the estate where her parents lived she could almost feel the new life growing already, a little boy. She would take him everywhere with her and dress him in her own, unconventional style. She would call him Tobin, she thought, or Joss.